DARKWORLD

DARKLIGHT 3

BELLA FORREST

Publication place Cyprus 2019

ISBN 978-9925-7621-7-0

CHAPTER ONE

I ran hard. The slick path wound before me like an abandoned snakeskin, speckled in brown and gray, studded with rocks. I leapt a trickling stream, the smell of the fresh water and damp turf catching in my nostrils.

It was early afternoon in the Scottish Highlands, an overcast August day filled with misting rain. A few thin streaks of light broke through the haze of clouds weaving through the peaks that surrounded me. I sucked in a breath of cool air and pushed my bangs, wet from rain and sweat, from my forehead. Beneath my pale blue athletic jacket, sweat pooled as my body fought to keep up with the punishing pace I had set for today's solitary run. After hiding in caves and living off scraps for over two weeks while on the run from the Occult Bureau, I was out of shape.

At a sharp bend in the path that jutted out into an outcropping, I paused for a moment to tighten my laces and look out over the landscape. It was a patchwork quilt of gray granite and the hardy green of tough grasses, slightly taller green-brown splashes of heather, and dabs of yellow gorse. The mountains thrust their way up from the landscape—bold, jagged sentinels of ancient stone. Why would Bryce ever leave such a beautiful place?

I restarted my run, continuing up into the steep foothills of one of the mountains not far from Glencoe. Getting to see such beauty every day made me even more grateful that I was finally getting back into a proper training regimen.

It was my first time in Scotland. Just over three weeks ago, I'd stood on a rooftop at the Chicago HQ of the Occult Bureau, an organization sworn to protect the public from supernatural threats, staring down at the man I had once called uncle. Alan Sloane, director of the Chicago HQ, had been hunting me, my team of human dissenters, and the group of vampires we'd saved from extermination at his hand. In the process of taking down Director Sloane and his equally genocidal fellow board members, my team and I had revealed the existence of vampires to the world and were now receiving asylum in Scotland while various agencies in the US investigated the Occult Bureau and discussed how to proceed.

I currently lived with the rest of the rebels in a secret ex-military facility nestled in the mountainous Highlands. Our accommodations had been arranged by our current handler Major Morag Bryce, older sister of my former Bureau captain Nicholas Bryce. We were now on a mission to figure out our next move forward. Some of our group had been here longer than I had. I'd been delayed by the congressional meetings I needed to attend for the Bureau investigation.

I pumped my arms harder, pushing for the burn in my muscles. My limbs felt loose and powerful. I bounded up the path like a sure-footed young deer, wishing the future might be as easy as running along a hiking trail.

My runs were an excellent time to think, and that's what I needed to do. Thinking meant planning. While my feet struck the damp trail, I turned Dorian's plan for saving the vampire species over in my mind. We had to consider the international political uproar *and* whatever secrets the Bureau still kept from us about their connection to the Immortal Plane. The heavy media attention only added to our concerns. I had stopped listening to the morning news, realizing the reporters were cycling around the same issues over and over. Vampire this, vampire that. Most of it was misinformation or scaremongering.

I increased my speed for a moment to make it up a switchback in the trail, enjoying the burn in my lungs. The harsh but impressive landscape passed me in a blur—a pleasant reward for my efforts. I liked the solitude of this ancient land.

I slowed my pace as the slick path became even steeper, skirting around a hole I had a habit of tripping on if I didn't look out for it. The first day I'd done this route, I'd returned with bloodied elbows and a scratch on my face from a gorse bush, much to the amusement of various humans and vampires. The path eventually led to a summit of the small mountain I'd claimed for my exercise the past few days. I jumped over the patch of sodden peat that soaked my shoes yesterday. My favorite part of the ascent was the determined tree growing directly out of a large boulder on the mountainside. I felt a connection to that tree. *I don't give up, either.*

A mile in, I stopped for a break. Panting for breath, I shook my head free of water droplets, and a feeling of victory surged through me. I grinned at the downslope of the mountain. From my vantage point, I could see our humble accommodations. Major Bryce had explained that the modest stone buildings and surrounding area had once been a croft, one of the many tiny farms that littered the Highlands. The military had bought the land in the eighties, planning to use the farm as a base for soldiers to do survival training in the wilderness.

The army barracks were newer, featuring low buildings that looked industrial and square amid the less deliberate lines and shapes of nature. The military had painted the concrete structures black in the past, but time had rusted patches of the roof, and the paint was being worn away by the extreme weather.

Its current iteration looked thrown together... because it had been. The Scottish military had quickly renovated it for my team of merry dissenters and our vampire allies. On the roof of the original stone cottage sat an impressive collection of satellite dishes and signal boosters. Several more were affixed to the top of a gray-and-blue portable trailer. Together, they formed our command base, communications hub, and formal meeting room. A few other trailers were spaced around the site, and several green Land Rovers covered in mud sat parked near the gate. Yes, we had a gate.

A fifteen-foot chain link fence topped with coils of barbed razor wire stretched around the perimeter, except for one entrance gate that always had two guards. Major Morag had assured us it wasn't meant to keep the vampires in, but to keep anyone hostile out. Our location had not been made public knowledge, but hikers roamed the landscape, and if the news had shown me anything, it was that some people weren't happy in the slightest at the idea of vampires. Although these vampires lived far from civilization and the temptation of dark humans, more extreme groups of humans had gone on the offensive in mobs of "vampire hunters."

Sitting on a lichen-covered rock, I pulled my brown hair, now falling nearly to the middle of my back, into a fresh ponytail. I rubbed my hands together for warmth and considered how foreboding the compound looked. Blissfully, it also felt temporary, and despite the gloom, I got to be near Dorian every day, which was a definite bonus.

Dorian and I spent a lot of time together. We went on walks and talked strategies. Yesterday, a sudden downpour forced us underneath a canopy of trees during our march around the perimeter. I huddled next to him, suffering only mild heartburn as he held his cloak above us like a makeshift tent. I could still smell his natural scent of cedar and feel the warmth of him next to me. I smiled to myself.

When we came back, Morag spotted us, dripping all over the clean floor in the barrack entrance.

"If you want alone time, you can do it in a dry room as long as you don't pass out," she said with a raised eyebrow, but I'd learned not to take offense to her blunt way of talking. She did a lot for us.

Morag had caused quite a stir when she publicly announced an offer of asylum for vampires and defectors in Scotland without really checking it with anyone first. She had pushed the decision through by sheer force of personality. Since the nation had obtained its independence nearly a decade ago, its English neighbors didn't have much of a say in the matter. Scottish officials made Morag director over the entire vampire situation, seemingly as a punishment for stirring up trouble, but she'd taken it in stride with her usual level of delightful, no-nonsense determination.

At her suggestion, the official name for the current operation was the Vampire Asylum Military Program of Scotland, or VAMPS. When I first heard it, I thought it was a joke, but I had to admit it was easy to remember. VAMPS currently acted as the human liaison between the US, Scotland, and, to some extent, the rest of the countries that were interested in seeing how the situation unfolded internationally. And who was Morag's second-in-command? None other than her own brother. The arrangement was equal parts amusing and infuriating for them, and they butted heads as often as they got along. I tried to imagine a situation in which Zach was above or below me in a vitally important international dispute. *Hard to put siblings into roles like that.*

Thinking of Zach and the rest of my human team, I wondered what they were all doing in the barracks right now. With the vampires who had joined us—over forty at my last count—and some Scottish researchers Morag had brought in to work with the vampires, the camp could be quite a hub of activity some days. It had been a hard but necessary sell to our vampire allies when they'd caught wind of the scientists being brought in. Could anyone blame their hesitation, after first-hand experience or tales of Bureau torture? Not me. But Morag had to appease the international community demanding information. The researchers wanted to do preliminary vampire studies to verify the Bureau's files. The scientists wanted to study dark matter. At least they were personable and seemed more awed than disgusted by the vampires. The absence of hostility impressed me, but that was honestly a pretty low bar.

I rolled my neck, stretching a sore muscle. The sun broke through the clouds, briefly warming me in my spot atop the peak. Tilting my head to let the sun warm the side of my face, I spotted a flock of small, dark shapes in the far distance. After a minute or two, they were close enough for me to recognize their silhouettes. Redbills. Three of them.

The Scottish military had been wonderful about allowing the redbills to fly freely. It was forbidden to fly a drone near an airport, but our supernatural birds were free to move over Scotland. The redbills flapped their wings in a flurry. My fingers tingled as I stared at the approaching birds, a feeling of unease stealing over me. A vampire feeding party had been dispatched to the Immortal Plane this morning, but they'd said they likely wouldn't return until evening or even tomorrow if they had to travel far to find food. Had they forgotten something? No, they were flying in too fast for that. Had something happened?

Shaking the stiffness from my legs, I started down the path that would lead me back to the camp. The wet trail was treacherous, and I had to take my time until I reached the foothills that stretched for about a mile across relatively flat ground.

Let's see if I can break my mile record.

If it ended up being nothing, at least I would get a sprint in. My body groaned at the increased pace, but I leaned into the strain, keeping my breathing as deep as I could as I raced across the open moor. Just under ten minutes later, I trotted up to the gate, gasping for breath.

"No tumbles today, Sloane?" one of the guards, a rosy-cheeked blond guy, asked as I flashed my ID badge.

"Not today, MacGregor," I replied, still panting, splattered with mud and water. "Did three redbills just come in?"

"A minute ago, aye," he replied, raising his eyebrows as he waved me in. Maybe he saw the beat of panic in my frown.

The redbills were gathered near the barracks as I raced up the path toward the compound. Maybe it was nothing. I hoped so. Inside the fence, the world seemed much smaller, the wildness outside feeling just out of reach.

On the other side of the barracks, the Scottish military had converted an old structure into a "stable" to house the six redbills we'd brought over to Scotland via military cargo plane. The redbills had been furious. I never again wanted to share a flight with an epically pissed off supernatural bird made of rage and razor-sharp talons.

I caught sight of a tall and sinewy frame in the distance.

"Kane," I called, jogging closer. "You're back early." The rest of my words died as I realized Kane was shouting orders. Two other vampires stood beside him, crowded around a tense, hissing redbill. One, named Neo, was tall with the sides of his head shaved down to skin, the black hair on top left long. The other, whose name I couldn't remember, was a burly fellow wearing a worried scowl. Harlowe hovered near one of their redbills, her long platinum-blonde hair draping over her shoulder in a braid. Without warning, the redbill shrieked and beat its wings, nearly rising into the air before the vampires called it back to the ground. Something was strapped over the redbill's back. My stomach twisted with unease. I ran up and, catching sight of Castral's long green-toned blue hair in its usual braid, realized it was the final member of the party that had gone to the Immortal Plane to hunt.

I needed to help. The redbill would have to calm down so we could move the injured vampire off its back. If we jostled him too much, it could further injure him before we reached a medic. Were the medics in the trailer? I could run and check. The redbill carrying him jerked to the side as Kane attempted to step closer.

"Calm the redbill down. We won't be able to move him with feathers flying all over the place," Kane ordered. Harlowe held the redbill's head close to her chest, rubbing its forehead and murmuring under her breath. The redbill emitted a disgruntled squawk but settled down. What happened to make it so upset? It had to be something they encountered in the Immortal Plane. I'd seen reactions like that before when the redbills tangled with immortal creatures. The injured vampire groaned.

"Is he safe to move?" I asked, immediately snapping into crisis management mode. "Where's the injury?"

"His leg. Get a medic!" Kane shouted. "Castral's been wounded. Badly. We're going to try to get him off this redbill."

Castral, strapped to the redbill, moaned. I didn't know him well, but he was part of the vampire cohort Kane brought back from the Immortal Plane. Castral only stood out in my mind because instead of the long cloaks that most of the vampires wore, he sported a rust-colored leather jacket he'd won in a card game with some compound guards on his first night here.

Before I turned to run toward the medical trailer near the barracks, I saw the blood oozing from deep punctures in Castral's thigh. The skin around his leg and his arm appeared blistered and burned, the flesh raw. Something more powerful than a regular knife had stabbed him. His jacket was ruined on one side.

But it was the blood that hypnotized me.

I'd never had the chance to study large quantities of vampire blood before. Injuries like this hadn't occurred during our Bureau battles. It was red, but shadows shivered through the color. Even when the vampires had fed on Dorian after he'd been hit by the Bureau's dark energy weapons for the first time, I hadn't seen blood. God, the Immortal Plane was far more dangerous than the human world.

I tore myself from the sight and sprinted to the large trailer that served as the medical center. Yanking open the door, I yelled inside.

"Medic! We've got a vampire down. He's bleeding out!"

There was a flurry of movement as several medics tumbled from the trailer and ran toward the gathered vampires, who were carefully lifting Castral off the redbill. From the corner of my eye, I saw Neo returning with a vampire I'd seen working with the medical team before, sharing treatments and information on how to treat vampires. Another human medic ran past me, and I followed. My body ached from my run, but I pushed past the pain. The group descended on Castral. Harlowe held the redbill more tightly as it chirped irritably, upset at all the noise and fuss.

"We need to get him stabilized. Can you carry him without jostling his leg?" the first medic, an earnest brown-haired man with blue eyes, asked the vampires. He looked too young to be serving on a military mission, but we had started young in the Bureau too.

"Definitely," the vampire medic replied. With the help of Neo, he carried Castral, darting across the yard to the trailer. The human medics rushed behind them. The door shut with a slam.

I stared at the medical station, unsure what to do. My body felt sore in all the wrong places, but adrenaline rushed through me. I wanted to do something, anything. Two weeks ago, I would have had to do everything myself along with our ragtag team of survivors, but now... it was out of my hands.

Kane stood a little way off, his face for a moment displaying how equally helpless he felt. I couldn't help with medicine, but I could help Kane clean up the spilled blood marking the tarmac and grass around him.

"Want a hand cleaning up?" I asked. "The redbills might calm faster without the smell of vampire blood surrounding them."

I almost expected a snide question about when I'd become such an expert on redbills, but instead he just nodded. Harlowe gave me a worried frown. Some blood was smeared across her cheekbone, and the edges of her cloak were singed.

A shiver of worry passed down my spine as I headed back to the stable to gather buckets, water, and mops.

What had they run into over in the Immortal Plane?

CHAPTER TWO

Vampire blood had a distinctly more metallic scent than human blood, I discovered. I scrubbed myself in the women's communal showers for a half hour after helping Kane, watching the swirling red disappear down the drain. On my way to the mess hall for dinner, I smelled my hands. The pine soap had replaced the grisly aroma of Castral's blood. Good.

A strange habit had developed among our group. My human teammates and our vampire friends had taken to gathering around the TV in the mess hall before dinner. I could smell some delicious, hearty Scottish food being made in the kitchen, but I focused my attention on my crew.

Last night's gathering in the mess hall had been light and airy. Tonight, I felt like I could swim through the lingering questions in the air. We had already lost so much; how would we keep moving forward? My limbs felt heavy as I moved toward the table. Each new loss hit us harder than the last. Could we afford another?

Zach, Gina, and Louise sat on one side of a mess hall table. Louise braided her shoulder-length, strawberry-blonde hair absent-mindedly as Sike watched, amused at her instinctive habit, his dark brown eyes following every movement of her fingers. Louise suddenly flinched, losing her hold on the braid. Zach said something to Gina, and she nodded in response. Her birthday had been a few days earlier, and the number twenty-four was still faintly visible on her forehead where Zach had written it in marker as a prank. In retaliation, she'd wrestled him to the ground and drawn a mustache on him.

The barrack's dining area was like most military buildings, something akin to a high school cafeteria. Everything was in plain, muted colors like beige and faded greens and blues. Most of the color in the room was provided by its inhabitants and the large TV playing on the far wall. Roxy and Bravi sat on the other side of the table. Roxy had let her red hair down from its usual tight French braid, so the soft waves draped across her shoulders. The female vampire was the closest to the TV, her bright green eyes narrowed in concentration. She furrowed her brow.

"Why do humans constantly advertise food?" she wondered aloud. "Don't you have enough of it in your bright warehouses?"

"You mean the grocery store?" Zach asked. He jerked his thumb at the TV. "That's different. This is an ad for some fast food place. They advertise it because humans love to look at delicious pictures of food, and it makes us want to buy some. We're easily manipulated."

Dorian was nowhere in sight. Arlonne sat with Gavril at another nearby table—this one slightly farther from the TV—puzzling over a game of checkers. Roxy gnawed her thumbnail, her eyes looking past the TV. A tense cloud hung over the group. Gina gave a half-hearted wave as I walked up. *Looks like I'm not the only one who's worried.*

"Any news from the scouting trip?" I asked, breaking through their small talk.

"Not yet," Roxy replied. "Med bay is too busy to give updates."

They were still holed up in the medical trailer with Castral? His rust-colored leather jacket sprang to mind. The color seemed plain in comparison to the vampire blood and how it danced with shadows.

I sank into a seat beside Roxy, who said nothing but scooted over an inch to give me more room. Louise had nearly finished her second attempt at a braid, her nervous hands looking for something to occupy their time.

"Back to our report on VampCon," the TV announcer recounted cheerfully. "Although the event's official title is the World Summit for Vampire-Human Relations, social media users have decried this title as too long and gave it a cheeky nickname. Tonight, we go to our panel of psychological experts to discuss the possible impact the integration of vampires could have on the human psyche."

I blocked out the sound of the TV. The organizers had invited our group to this summit, but we'd put off the decision. Some, like Bravi, thought it would help, or at least it couldn't hurt. But most of the vampires had no desire to undergo another round of invasive questions and abuse from the media and general population. More media scrutiny wouldn't help our cause—we could barely navigate it as it was. Truthfully, I'd been a little naïve about how the public would react to the supernatural. While Louise's livestream of the Bureau's admission of guilt had been excellent in the moment to gain us support, it might not have been the best way to break such news to the international public. But we'd been desperate and exhausted, and the Bureau had forced our hand. All we could do now was find a way to move the situation forward.

While we recovered here at the VAMPS camp, the outside world continued to churn with anxiety and speculation. It felt like a new expert or pundit came out of the shadows every hour to give their (almost always incorrect) opinion.

The Bureau had been slightly wrong in their prediction that the public would respond to the idea of the supernatural with nothing but hostility and chaos. The chaos was there, but the hostility was... complicated. Older generations generally polled at higher levels of fear and distrust of vampires, while younger generations had started fan clubs and pledged their support to vampires, sometimes in uncomfortably... ardent ways.

Others firmly clung to denial and decried it as a giant hoax or an elaborate art project. Fanatics claimed this officially signaled the apocalypse. Vampire hunting groups reportedly began organizing all over the globe, though not all of them meant to kill vampires. Some wanted to find a vampire and request to be "turned," which was impossible.

On the screen, the news now showed a group of people gathered outside the summit, waiting to go inside. One teenage boy dive-bombed the camera with a poster. In all caps, it read: READY FOR MY VAMPIRE LOVE.

Bravi shook her head with a snort of laughter.

I was so glad I'd left hormone-fueled puberty behind. But then again, who was I to talk when I had my own vampire romance going on? That kid had no idea what he was asking for.

I glanced at the main door of the mess hall, hoping Dorian would join us soon. He could be resting, but I wanted to ask him what he'd heard about Castral. Maybe he would know what could have caused that kind of damage. The Bureau had never managed to land a serious blow on the vampires, so what the hell did? Even the X-75s couldn't do that. My feet felt restless, and I considered going to search for him.

The cook—a tall, broad woman with a thick braid of dark hair—stuck her head out of the kitchen and pounded a frying pan with a mallet. "Food's done!" she bellowed.

The vampires winced at the explosion of sound, but it had the desired effect. Humans and vampires began appearing through the main doorway to congregate in the mess hall. They couldn't eat with us, but the vampires had taken to gathering for discussions among themselves. Dorian said vampires could be quite social. I pressed a hand against my stomach, my hunger a pleasant reminder of my run.

I grabbed a clean metal tray and inhaled the homey, simple scent of bread and stew, with an undercurrent of something fruity. Maybe they'd made crumble again. After our time on the run, it felt like such a luxury to be somewhere with a designated cooking staff. The servers, all volunteers or junior guards on kitchen duty for the day, stood on the other side of a buffet line, serving food.

"Thanks, Eskra," I said to the female vampire who had been part of our fugitive group not so long ago. She'd taken up cooking duties as a way to give back to the group, citing the time we saved her and her child. She gave me a healthy portion of hot, rich stew, a jumble of roasted potatoes and turnips known locally as "tatties and neeps," and a hunk of warm brown bread. *Much nicer than starving in a cave.*

"How's Oten?" I asked as she returned the plate, referring to her toddler.

"He's doing fine," she replied with a sweet smile, a wisp of her long, deep blue hair escaping the hairnet required for all food staff. "Sleeping now, but he's been playing outside all day with Ayless and Kren. I know those girls are a little older, but he loves running around after them. They don't seem to mind."

I smiled. "I'm glad to hear it." I grabbed a cup of water. "Please tell Corporal Fraser her food looks delicious."

Eskra saluted me playfully and went on to serve Louise.

Roxy nudged me when we sat back down and pointed toward the entrance. I looked over to see Kane and Harlowe coming in through the set of doors closest to the medical trailer. Kane walked with a swagger in his step but a scowl on his face. The light caught the scar running along the edge of his eye socket. Both looked healthy from their recent feed, their pale skin dancing with deep shadows, but the tightness around Harlowe's gray eyes told me she was stressed.

"Castral is finally stable, and his wounds are being taken care of," Kane announced as he threw himself down beside Louise. He had a little trouble working his long legs under the low cafeteria table. Louise scooted up the bench a few inches to avoid his elbows. He glanced at me with a look of pointed expectation. "Ready for my horrible tales from the Immortal Plane?"

He read me like a book. I leaned forward, unable to help myself. "Please." I didn't mind that I was giving Kane exactly what he wanted by giving him the spotlight. For the most part, I'd stopped caring about his cocky attitude after he saved our asses on the roof of the Chicago HQ.

"Well, there we were. We flew to the stone circle Harlowe found when we first arrived."

I nodded along with the others. Dorian had explained it to us a little. The vampires were the only creatures who could cross the barrier between planes without going through the tear. But they couldn't do it on a whim; they required a place where the barrier was thin enough to slip through without getting lost inside forever. They flew there on redbills and left the birds in the Mortal Plane while the vampires jumped through to the Immortal side. Dorian had shown me the stone circle area once when we were surveying the camp and surrounding mountains from the back of a redbill. It was a circle of standing stones on the other side of the peaks that surrounded us, long forgotten in a small valley about half an hour away.

"It's always been funny to me"—Harlowe's voice sounded less than amused—"how humans spent millennia protecting vampire gateways without even knowing what they were. They sensed the spot was important somehow, that it was a place where things traveled and changed, yet had no concept of what existed on the other side." She rested her head against her hand, as though exhausted. "It's strange every time I see it from this side, unguarded. Maybe it's just because that used to be my job in the Immortal Plane before the breach."

Her job? I remembered Dorian had once said that Laini had trained as an architect, so maybe most vampires used to have positions besides purifying souls. Mentally, I made a note to ask one of the other vampires later.

"Strange or not," Kane broke in, apparently uninterested in Harlowe's musings, "we passed through to the Immortal Plane on foot, keeping stealthy. But as soon as we came through, *they* were waiting." Anger crossed his face in a pulse of shadow.

"They?" Zach echoed, egging him on. Kane knew how to tell a story.

"The immortal rulers. Our enemies. A group of their hunters found the circle on the other side and set up an ambush," Kane relayed bitterly. "Well, tried to. We sensed them immediately. We slipped in so quickly and quietly that they didn't notice while they set up their ambush. Luckily, we caught them in the middle of final preparations. We darted to a hiding spot and fanned out in the opposite direction to look for something to feed on. There was nothing close, and going farther into the Immortal Plane to feed would risk alerting the patrol, which would make it even harder to escape. We didn't have a lot of options. And... we needed to feed. So we decided to chance ambushing the ambush."

Harlowe's mouth twitched restlessly. "In hindsight, not an amazing plan, but we didn't have any other options. The vampires back here needed to feed."

"Also, the irony was too strong a temptation to resist," Kane added, blunt as always.

I imagined the immortal enemies as something close to vampires, but scarier. The vampires were reluctant to talk about them but not about the monsters we'd fought a few weeks ago: the soul-scourger, a burning black mist, and the shrieking decay, an acid-spewing lizard that Dorian and I had killed. The immortal rulers had to be worse than these creatures for the vampires to fear and hate them so much, but when I'd pressed for details, Dorian told me that rulers looked more like humans than anything else. Their magic was the deadly part.

"We took down three, at most, before they noticed us feeding," Kane continued, sounding bitter. "The ambush party was more heavily armed than we expected. One of the soul-bound beasts got Castral before we could retreat back to the Mortal Plane."

"They didn't let it kill him," Harlowe interrupted in a speculative tone. "They had the opportunity, but it seemed like they wanted to take him away. Castral pretended to be unconscious after the beast got its teeth into him, so it dropped him. Then, before they could get any restraints on him, he surprised them and dove for the circle so we could come in for a quick rescue."

"Harlowe, Neo, Drinn, and I still fed on plenty of dark energy. We have enough to pass around to the other vampires in the compound after that fiasco. After that ambush, though…" He shrugged, but I could sense his frustration. "We need to find a new spot to send our feeding parties through. They'll double down on watches at that stone circle."

Harlowe nodded. "It's a death trap now." Her eyes softened. "I don't want anyone else to go through the same thing as Castral."

Understandable. I didn't want that either.

Kane smacked his hand on the table with a groan and pointed a wagging finger toward Zach's face, the noise and movement catching the attention of the rest of the mess hall. "You tell me something, Mr. Public Relations. Why can't we just feed in the Mortal Plane? Going to the Immortal Plane is annoying and dangerous, and I'm tired of it."

I could sympathize with Kane; the vampires were risking their necks, going back and forth through the dangers of the Immortal Plane. But we'd had this conversation before. We couldn't have hungry vampires running around and feeding on the very citizens offering us asylum. Even if someone ended up being a murderer, Scotland and the international community would have a fit.

Zach drew himself up straighter, temporarily ignoring his dinner. Over the last few weeks, while finally recovering from the bullet wound in his right leg, my brother had grown into the role of public relations expert for our group. He worked closely alongside the Bryce siblings, monitoring both public and international opinion.

"The Mortal Plane may be less dangerous in terms of monsters, but you still have enemies and threats here," he said firmly. "Feeding in the Mortal Plane could derail our Scottish asylum *and* the Bureau investigation in America. Everything is tenuous. Right now, we're building a house of cards and praying it doesn't fall," he explained gently.

I picked at my food but didn't eat. My mind churned. Zach was right. Our current state was anything but stable. Until the international community decided how to deal with or integrate vampires into human society, the vampires couldn't hunt humans. A month ago, I would've found that perfectly reasonable from a not-super-down-with-murder perspective... but now I grew more and more concerned about my vampire friends having to brave the Immortal Plane. I bit into my food, appreciating the ease with which we humans could eat right now, enjoying the full taste of it.

"I understand," Harlowe muttered. She tucked a strand of her hair behind her ear.

Kane simmered next to her, visibly chafing at Zach's reasoning. His scowl told me he grew impatient. If the situation with the Immortal Plane continued to worsen at this rate, the vampires might have to starve again or space out their feedings to near starvation.

"Tomorrow we'll look for another stone circle or some other doorway," Kane said gruffly. He slouched, eyes on the tabletop, and didn't say any more.

Still, I appreciated that he was at least trying to be optimistic in his own way. He was stubborn, and that wouldn't change, but I found him easier to deal with now. Dorian certainly seemed to appreciate having Kane back.

"Sounds like it's all bad news today," Louise said mournfully. Harlowe shook her head.

"Not quite," she countered. "Although Castral's injury was bad, he told us everything after the medics stabilized him. He got captured, but it meant he got close enough to hear the hunters talking when he pretended to be unconscious. They thought he was one of the vampires they'd seen near Siron, a huge lake in the mountains."

Kane grinned wildly. "*More* vampires."

The corner of Harlowe's mouth lifted slightly, but her eyes stayed serious. "The Immortals sounded angry that they had known of the group's alleged existence for some time but hadn't caught them yet. They wanted to *persuade* Castral to talk when he woke up, hoping to connect our group with those at Lake Siron, but he managed to get away, and we dragged him through the portal in time."

"You know what that means?" Kane asked with a gloating smile. "If the vampire community still stuck in the Immortal Plane is strong enough, we won't have to hide in the Mortal Plane anymore at all. We could reclaim the area."

The vampires might have allies waiting for them in the Immortal Plane. I leaned back in my chair, trying to imagine what that might look like. They could have hidden in caves like the vampires did here in the Mortal Plane. They must've found some way to evade the Immortals.

"Too bad we rescued Castral so soon," Kane lamented after a pause. "Maybe we could've learned more."

Harlowe cast a sidelong look at him. "Maybe. That's assuming he *lived* long enough to tell us."

Gina fidgeted with her napkin. Roxy put her chin in her hand, her glare made even fiercer by the scar that sliced through her eyebrow. Zach looked thoughtful, obviously processing the new information. Were they wondering what type of immortal ghouls these creatures were? The Immortals certainly seemed intelligent enough to threaten our vampire allies. Could they match vampires' strength and speed, both of which were far superior to our human abilities?

I needed to ask Dorian more about the Immortals, but it was like pulling teeth. The vampires were trying to keep the existence of the Immortals a secret from the government, not wanting a repeat of humans contacting Immortals and working together to kill the vampires. And there was little time for questions that weren't imme- diately relevant; our recent conversations had been focused on educating me about the finer points of vampire existence, to help me in any government hearings I might be called to. We weaved our talks in through stolen moments away from strategy discussions. It was odd to be able to spend more time with each other, and I enjoyed it despite the constant low buzz of pain in my chest.

"Could we help more vampire survivors if we found that group?" Roxy wondered aloud. "We could bust in and grab them before the immortal creeps notice we're there."

Bravi ran a hand over her face, humming with thought. "It's

unlikely. Lake Siron is a day or more on foot from any entry point that I know of. If we went via redbill, we'd have to go through the tear, which, even if you were allowed back into America, is even farther away from the lake."

"Even if we could get in, staying beyond the reach of Immortals' eyes is difficult and dangerous," Harlowe added. "I'm reluctant to even consider the idea."

"Hard not to be, after watching Castral get chewed on," Neo piped up from his place next to Arlonne and Gavril at another table.

I was surprised he had joined us this evening. The newer vampires from Kane's group didn't always come to dinner. It wasn't like they could eat with us, and not all of them were interested in the social aspect.

He moved to sit by us, his movements quiet and deliberate. "What I will say is that before we followed Kane through the tear, we heard similar rumors. There's supposedly an underground vampire group that established a safe colony in the Immortal Plane. They send scouts to fill up on dark energy that they bring back to feed the rest of the colony."

An underground fugitive group that strategically ferried back dark energy to feed its members? Sounded familiar. It must be necessary, since the immortal enemies knew the group was there. I wondered if their hideout was as precarious as some of ours had been. Near Lake Siron, Kane had said. What kind of place was that? Probably a crater full of bubbling black water, hiding creatures with long, oozing tentacles that would snatch anyone walking by. It seemed like when it came to the Immortal Plane, all I could imagine were terrible, strange creatures with malicious intent. To be fair, my experience so far had demonstrated this to be the norm.

"It seems far too convenient," Arlonne pointed out, breaking through my thoughts, "that our enemies would discuss a surviving group of vampires in front of a prisoner, apparently unconscious or not. The hunters aren't foolish enough to talk idly and let important information slip out."

She had a point. The various nodding vampire heads around the table indicated that many agreed with her. If the rulers were as bad as everyone said, it seemed very possible that they would purposely let us know about the other group in order to set up a trap.

"I don't know," Bravi countered. "I've met some really stupid Immortals in my time. Regardless, going to find such a group would be a dangerous task." Her serious gaze found mine. She'd guessed I would talk to Dorian soon. Since Bravi's confession on the Chicago rooftop, I noticed she was more distant from Dorian. Still fiercely loyal, but she appeared happier to leave some Dorian business up to me. It was like having the world's strangest blessing, but since it was Bravi, I felt honored.

I quickly finished my meal while the conversation drifted to the latest happenings at VampCon. I then excused myself, pausing to drop off my dirty dishes in one of the tubs left by the kitchen. It surprised nobody to see me leave. It was no secret that I sought out Dorian every evening, though some newer vampires seemed mildly amused or slightly unsettled by our relationship. Dorian sometimes skipped the dinner socializing hour due to late check-in meetings with Morag or Bryce. At least we'd received no open harassment from any of the vampires, beyond the scalding looks that Halla gave us whenever she saw the two of us together. Unfortunately for her, we'd been spending quite a lot of time in each other's company.

We had grown increasingly close in the past few weeks, finally free to interact without the threat of the Bureau lurking over us. When we weren't stealing kisses despite the low heartburn, much of our time was spent researching the Bureau archives, access kindly granted by our friend on the current board, Martin Fenton. The pickings were slim, with most of the archives locked behind fire-walls and clearance that Louise couldn't break through, even though it would look very good on her record as part of the investigation into the Bureau. So, Dorian took some time to tell me bits and stories of vampire lore and culture. Between the arrival of the new vampires and the fact that I was now publicly considered somewhat of a vampire expert, I figured I should know as much as possible if I expected to help our cause. Knowledge was power in an interdimensional conflict.

Right now, however, all I wanted to know was where Dorian had tucked himself away instead of coming to the mess hall. I'd seen him in the library just before my run this afternoon, enraptured by a book of Scottish history. If he wasn't in the mess hall or library, then Dorian would be in his quarters. As the bedrooms were closer, I headed there first, planning to drop by the room I shared with Louise to pick up a hoodie. There was a chill in the evening air, and my well-exercised muscles were starting to tighten uncomfortably from the cold.

After retrieving the blue fleece-lined hoodie from my bed, I padded quietly down the hall toward the room Dorian shared with Sike. Peeking through the half-open door, I saw that Dorian was indeed there. He sat at his desk, staring out the window at the moor. The sunset behind the gray clouds made it dark outside, but his vision was better than mine. His strong shoulders looked broader than usual from behind. As I snuck up behind him, the weak shadows beneath the skin of his bare arms prompted a pang of worry within me. There would be dark circles under his eyes, too.

I hugged him from behind, resting my chin on the top of his head as I gave him a gentle squeeze.

Dorian jerked upward with an exaggerated gasp. "You scared me!"

I couldn't help but laugh at him. At least I'd never have to worry about him lying to me. He was terrible at it.

The weakness of the burn in my chest at our proximity reinforced my concern that he hadn't fed enough recently. He tipped his head back to see me, and a burst of pain pounded in my chest as he gave me a slight smile. The sensations rushed through me. I'd grown used to them by now, and in fact, the burst of pain reassured me that maybe he wasn't as weak as I thought.

We'd never officially decided that Dorian's starvation was worth it for us to be able to touch. He argued that it was easier for him to go hungry for long stretches of time, rather than risk me falling into a coma when we were close to one another. I'd told him it was intensely unhealthy for him to regularly starve himself for long periods. The bones of his face grew sharper, the muscles of his arms thinning, as the shadows beneath his skin faded by the day. The thought of him suffering like that made my heart hurt almost as much as the heartburn.

Our working agreement, partially unspoken, was that he would feed lightly when necessary. After his weakness in Chicago turned out to be a liability, he'd realized he couldn't forgo it entirely and fed sparingly off the vampires who brought energy back from the Immortal Plane. He hadn't gone himself, instead remaining at the camp to oversee the day-to-day operations, liaise with the researchers and Major Morag, and keep track of the international state of affairs regarding his people. Kane was in charge of the Immortal Plane missions, and that worked well for both of them.

Our compromise seemed to be working for now. He was definitely hungry, but not debilitated. My pain stayed at a bearable level. I could touch him. Our system was manageable when we weren't in combat.

"I don't know why you still try to surprise me. I recognized your footsteps at the other end of the hallway," he confessed, taking one of my hands to press a kiss to the back of it.

I enjoyed the soft rumble of his voice through his chest, so I kept my arms around him. "Well, aren't you perceptive?" I teased. "Are you saying I have a heavy step?"

He smirked. "Not heavy. Just your own," he assured me, pulling me around into his lap to kiss me.

I gasped with pleasure and surprise, but as soon as it started, it was over, leaving a pleasant tingle on my lips. I wanted to close my eyes and savor it for the night... but there were more pressing matters.

"Have you heard about the Immortal Plane feeding party?" I asked, settling more comfortably into his lap.

He nodded slowly, a stitch of worry in his brow as he absent-mindedly ran his thumb back and forth on my thigh. "From the start, we knew that this feeding arrangement wasn't sustainable in the long term, especially not when we were using the same circle every time to travel between the planes. I'm trying to brainstorm other ways to get enough dark energy without damaging our chance for asylum. We've come too far to lose protection because of hunger."

I stood, leaning against his desk to look out at the moor. The last scraps of light fading from the yellowish sky gave the world outside the fence an eerie, otherworldly presence. As if something were out in the mountains, watching us.

I turned my back on the tableau, refreshing myself as I took in Dorian's glacial eyes, the soft tumble of his black hair. "And the rumors about the other survivors?"

"Could be promising," he said, a note of hope in his voice. "Very promising. If there are other vampires out there in the Immortal Plane gathering together like we have here, we could form a resistance with them. Together, we would have more hope of being able to fight against the Immortals."

"But we would need to find them first." Plans were forming in my mind. "It doesn't sound as if they want to be found. I get the sense that they've evaded rather than tried to fight the Immortals."

"I don't blame them. We would need to figure out where they are, but an expedition to find them and bring them back would be perilous. If the Immortals are hunting the group..." He paused. "It feels terrible to say it, especially when we were so recently on the run, but if the Immortals have caught wind of a vampire group, they'll almost certainly find them before we do. Or worse, we could lead the hunters right to the survivors' door and die with them."

He, unlike Arlonne, thought the group existed but was still a danger. Interesting. Good to know he was excited but cautious. I gave him a closer look, appreciating how handsome he was when frustrated. It really brought out the line of his jaw...

"Remember we've got our fun mission tomorrow," I reminded him, to key up his frustration even more. "You need to be at the top of your game." He scowled. *Just the reaction I expected.* And it was beautiful.

"I'm sick of all these publicity stunts just to try to convince people that we're not going to randomly murder them," he said, shaking his head. "All I keep hearing in the coverage is how difficult it would be to integrate us into human society. Most of us don't even want that, and it's distracting us all from the real problem. The tear between planes and the Immortals waging war against vampires are far more pressing issues. Why won't the humans listen to us when we tell them that these things are just as dangerous to you as they are to us?" His genuine anger made me feel bad about teasing him.

"I know, but we need to be level-headed," I said. "We're still waiting on the international consensus on the supernatural. We can't rush them any more than we already have. The US has yet to legalize any kind of vampire immigration. There are government officials chomping at the bit to detain or kill any vampires on sight, even with the reformed Bureau." Fenton's face flashed in my mind. "The new board is spending all its time on the Bureau investigation and monitoring the tear in the Canyonlands. They can't let us help them fight the creatures coming through with our entire nation watching them like hawks."

"They had no problem throwing their manpower at us," Dorian muttered.

"When they had corrupt officials and no morals, they could do anything," I agreed with a shrug. "We wanted the Bureau and the old board to be held accountable, and we made it happen. Now we have to wait for that process to finish, even when it doesn't benefit us."

"This isn't something that can wait." Dorian lifted his chin with determination. "I will not wait for the Bureau to give me permission to fight a war they helped start. At the end of the day, it affects vampires the most. It has already affected us more than most of them can understand." He crossed his arms tightly across his chest and stared out the window. I could see the gears in his mind turning. He wanted to put plans into action.

So do I. But before we could, we had to let the ones we'd already set up run their course. Dorian always wanted to forge ahead in whatever way he thought was best, but we needed to be cautious. His single-mindedness had accomplished a lot and was especially endearing when directed at making me happy, but it wasn't the most helpful right now.

"All this commotion isn't great for the actual danger at hand," I said in agreement. "I'm also itching to investigate the connection between the Bureau and these immortal enemies of yours. But Scotland won't approve a mission without the American government's permission, and we need access to the tear to take the redbills with us. If we tried to sneak into the US and got caught, we'd cause an even greater political mess, and you would lose any chance at asylum in Scotland. Or anywhere, in fact."

His anger seeped away, and his shoulders dropped. I wanted to hug him again. "You're right. It would be useful to have the Bureau's backing to bless our operation with resources and permission. We need a way to get back to the tear and get supplies for it. I saw what they could do in their fight against us. Their pockets and determination run deep when they have a vested interest in a fight."

Money and international opinion. It was a far cry from the usual strategies I preferred to utilize in battle, but it was a necessary part of our lives now. Congress had temporarily frozen our financial accounts for an audit to make sure there was nothing shady going on. Not that it mattered, since our combined human savings weren't likely to be enough to charter a plane and supplies. Even if we had money, we needed clearance to enter the country. We had to play the political game, whether we wanted to or not. Dorian definitely didn't… but at least he could see the reason we had to keep playing.

"We'll press the issue soon," I promised. "We need to put more pressure on international bodies to investigate the Immortal Plane."

"Any ideas on how?" he asked, drumming his nails on his desk. His glacial eyes swept over me.

The memory of Castral's blood came to mind, and I looked down at my hands. They were perfectly clean, but I could still feel the slick red with shadows across my fingers. The Immortal Plane promised danger. I thought about what would convince *me* to let the vampires have their way.

"Make humans see how much more dangerous the Immortals are, compared even to vampires," I said. "Whatever these things are, they scare vampires. The governments and the public need to be scared too. We can use that fear to our advantage."

I compulsively rubbed my hands together and went to tuck them into my hoodie pocket, but he stopped me. He gently grabbed my fingers and squeezed them. The heartburn flared, but the pleasure of his touch swallowed the pain. I closed my eyes for a moment, savoring our closeness. It was hard to steal these intimate moments together from our busy lives. As much as I wanted to touch him, sometimes the guilt of the never-ending work hung in the back of my mind. I could push it away at certain moments.

"We'll figure it out," he said. "Together."

I nodded slowly. We would. I would refuse to stop working until we fixed this.

I dropped my gaze to his hand on mine and smiled playfully. "You can let go now."

His eyes lit with mischief, and a smirk flashed to life on his elegant lips. "What if I don't?"

I laughed, not resisting as he pulled me close. My nose brushed his. Excited butterflies stirred in my stomach. It was nice to step away from my professional role with him for a few moments out of the day. He pressed feather-light kisses across my cheeks and eyelids, slipping down to my jaw, my neck...

Pain pulsed behind my eyes, and I blinked black spots from my vision.

When I first arrived at the compound, the medical staff argued until I agreed to let them evaluate me every few days for heart trouble. They'd warned me not to push past my limits, and Dorian had ganged up on me with them. My body yearned to touch Dorian as much as possible, but my brain knew it was time to stop.

"I should get some sleep," I croaked, halfheartedly pulling away. The anticipation faded, replaced by a deep disappointment.

"Are you sure you don't want to stay with me tonight?" he asked with exaggerated longing.

I chuckled at his dramatic tone. Part of it was serious, but we both knew it was impossible.

"We can't banish Sike to the couch in the rec room," I reminded him and took a step back. The two camp beds per room were close together. It was all the Scottish military could manage for us at the moment.

He squeezed my hand one last time, admitting defeat. "Goodnight, Lyra."

I could tell he didn't want to let go. Neither did I.

I reluctantly backed out of the room, forcing myself to return to my quarters. I wanted a few minutes alone before Louise came to bed.

One thing hadn't changed from being on the run. None of us had much privacy.

CHAPTER THREE

I checked my watch as I made my way out of the mess hall. Seven thirty a.m. exactly. We were supposed to leave for the press conference in half an hour. Since I'd already done my morning run, hit the showers, and had a full stomach, I figured I could gather everyone. We couldn't be late for our press conference.

Hopefully my teammates would miss the dark circles under my eyes. I'd slept fitfully last night. Waterfalls of red blood with flitting shadows filled my dreams. I'd abandoned sleep at just after five and headed out to run several laps around the camp, letting the sweat wash away my restlessness. Louise had said nothing when I passed her in the showers an hour later, so I was pretty sure I hadn't called out in my sleep, at least.

Small blessings.

The barracks extended farther than one might think when looking at them from the outside. I headed to the rec room, knowing I was likely to find people there. The camp operated on an "early to rise, early to bed" type of schedule, so it wasn't uncommon for everyone to be up and already busy at this time. As the humans and vampires grew closer, more and more time was spent hanging out in shared spaces. *We can't help but be around each other now.* Which was convenient when you needed to gather everyone for a mission.

"The picture on the screen looks different today," I heard Sike remark as I entered the rec room. He and Louise hovered in what I called our technology junkyard—a U-shaped formation of three tables with various deconstructed computers and gadgets. Louise spent her downtime piecing enough parts together to create her own, one-of-a-kind personal computer thanks to donations from the Scottish military, which was happy to unload its scrap on someone. Louise, with Sike helping to pass her tools and parts, had done everything herself from memory. Her technological prowess both impressed and frightened me.

"I changed the monitor's display size," Louise explained. She clicked something, and Sike leaned toward the screen, watching with great interest. "Now, let's pick up where we left off yesterday. We're going to open up a new internet window and search for some information."

"And the internet is a computer program?" he asked, narrowing his eyes and tapping a finger to his chin.

"The internet isn't, but the browser is," Louise explained gently. "The browser is a software application that lets us look at the internet. Literally, *browse.* The internet itself is a complex network. The US originally commissioned research on it, but it was a global endeavor."

Combat was my specialty. Computers? Not so much. Sike would no doubt have a better grasp of these things than I did before long. A teenage vampire with long, intricately braided red hair, whose name I was pretty sure was Fynn, hovered behind Louise and Sike in their swivel chairs. I was glad to know Louise was a good teacher for our ongoing pursuit of vampire-human relations.

"Louise. Sike. Don't forget we have to move out in twenty minutes," I called to them from the door.

Sike barely reacted.

"Sure thing," Louise replied easily, her eyes glued to the screen. *Let's make sure we don't give the vampires a bad case of internet addiction.*

My next stop was the gym at the other end of the same building. The mess hall separated the two. Between my former Bureau comrades, the soldiers at the camp, and all the vampires, it was a popular haunt. In a time when everything was unfamiliar and it was sometimes a daily struggle to connect with the experiences of those around us, there was a simplicity in the controlled violence of training. As I pushed through the swinging doors out of the mess hall, I could already hear the sounds of exertion and fists hitting pads before I arrived at the gym. Most of the space was covered in mats to create a large area for sparring, with the rest of the room taken up by a fairly extensive weights section.

Right now, only one person—a grizzled older woman from the Scottish military group—was using the weights, bench-pressing an impressive amount with only the occasional grunt. Her spotter hovered nearby, waiting to switch roles. Everyone else was paired up for sparring. Bravi, stripped down to a tank top, military shorts, and bare feet, swiped at Zach with a quick punch, her movements sharp and precise as she bounced back and forth on the balls of her feet. He dodged and then came back up to hold his padded hands in front of him. Bravi punched the pads fiercely, finishing with a yell and a solid kick before letting Bryce, who hovered nearby, cycle in for striking practice. Bryce gave me a friendly wave before landing a vicious uppercut on Zach's left pad that made my brother wince. Our ex-captain burned with new energy on Scottish soil, and his accent had definitely thickened.

It must be nice to be home.

Beside them, a much livelier and less structured exercise was taking place. I raised an interested brow as I watched Roxy lunge for Kane.

"Come here, fang face," she barked, a taunting smile on her face. "I don't want to hurt you. I just want to rearrange your bones."

"In your dreams," Kane snapped, but there was something odd about his tone. He dodged another blow from Roxy and went to kick her, but she successfully spun away. "Must be hard to be so weak, when you're among a superior species constantly reminding you of your inferiority."

Roxy let out a peal of laughter. "Superior? You've hit me twice, toothless." They lunged for each other at the same time in a flurry of movement. Roxy grabbed Kane in a headlock, trying to use his height against him by levering him down and off balance, but he grit his teeth, straightened his unfathomably long legs, and lifted her off the ground with a grunt. Using a powerful motion, he threw her over his head. She landed flat on her back with an explosive grunt on the mat as the air was slammed from her lungs, but she scrambled back up.

"That all you've got, blood breath?"

"Come and say that to my face, weakling."

I crossed my arms and studied them. Kane usually took offense easily, but he seemed to respond far more positively to Roxy's direct insults than the genuine politeness of most people he interacted with. He brushed off the ribbing and slung it back without anger. Likewise, Roxy fired insults and retorts right back at him. In another life, I might've mistaken them for siblings. I could never have predicted this outcome.

"Hate to interrupt the fun," I yelled, and I genuinely did. This was *fascinating*. "But everyone going to the press conference needs to shower and get ready, ASAP. Remember to throw some deodorant on, too." It stank to high heaven inside the gym, relieved only slightly by the mountain air filtering in through the open windows to cool down the room. Personal hygiene wasn't much of a priority for most missions, but today it would be vital.

I reluctantly peeled myself away. I'd spent a lot of time trying to keep my most fractious team members away from each other over the last few weeks, and I now resented that effort. I could have had this entertainment weeks ago.

I found Colin in the shooting range, a designated field just outside the gate. A few weeks ago, I'd been doing my best to dodge bullets. It was a pleasant return to normalcy to have a target for practice again instead of *being* the target.

"You want to keep your gaze steady on your target," Colin explained to a group of gathered vampires, his short-cropped black hair covered by a tweed flat peak cap that he'd adopted as part of his look for some reason. I stared at the paper target tacked to a dummy down at the end of the range. "Your eyes may be more powerful and more accurate than humans', but there's a lot more that goes into hitting a target than just looking at it. Wind speed. How you hold your weapon. Your breath. How quickly the target is moving. Accuracy all comes down to practice."

Teaching the vampires to shoot had been Morag's idea. "There's no such thing as being too prepared," she argued when pitching the idea to the vampires. "Even if you are faster and stronger than humans, you can still be wounded or otherwise compromised. Those X-75s, the nasty dark energy guns the Bureau developed, can take you guys out in, what, five shots?"

"That seems to be the minimum," one of the researchers confirmed. "In the tests we've been able to conduct so far, it seems one shot creates dizziness, nausea, and an energy spike similar to an adrenaline rush. Two shots intensify these symptoms and begin to overload the senses, increasing the heart rate to an uncomfortable level. Three shots remove most of the vision and make the subject incredibly sensitive to sound in addition to all other symptoms. The fourth shot activates a deeply primal mode in which the subject is incapable of rational thought and communication."

"If you guys know how to use a weapon of your own," Morag continued, "if you get hit once or twice or end up having your fangs restrained or something, you can back out of the range of the X-75s and still be able to fight. If you know how to handle a weapon, you will know how to disarm someone without endangering yourselves. I know a few of you are still recovering from bullet wounds." She looked at Sike, Gavril, and a few others. "Gunshot wounds may not hurt you for as long as they hurt us, but they still bloody hurt. So"—she held up a pistol—"if you want to learn how to shoot this and other firearms properly, drop by the range."

Most of the vampires, even Kane, had started taking lessons after that. Sike was an impressively good shot. Apparently, he found the practice meditative, although he said he didn't like the idea of killing with guns. "The death is wasted," he'd said. That was something many of the vampires struggled with—to kill a human with a bullet left the soul unclean. But it was better than dying themselves, as Dorian had pointed out.

I caught Colin's eye and tapped my watch. He nodded and began to wrap up the lesson.

My last stop was the library. It was a smaller room, permeated by the yeasty smell of decaying books, which had once been someone's office. Local people and Scottish organizations had donated the books to our group for our stay in Scotland, with more arriving each day from charities and pro-vampire groups. Some of the vampires burned through them quickly, eager to learn more about this world they found themselves in. I poked my head in the door to see Laini and Gina sitting on the desk, reading. Arlonne sat in the chair with a book open before her, but she was looking at a second book with Kren, one of Eskra's adopted daughters. The tween vampire read from the page as Laini clapped a hand over her mouth, stifling a giggle.

"'He gazed at Angela with passion dancing in his burning red eyes. Holding her hand to his chest, she knew that she would never feel a heartbeat in his gorgeous body. Undead, but not unlovable. She would teach him how humans loved. He bent to brush away a strand of her long chestnut hair, whispering that she was more beautiful than any creature he had known, vampire or human,'" the tween read dramatically. "'He was hers forever. Her vampire. Her immortal lover.'"

Arlonne smiled crookedly, shaking her head. Gina erupted into laughter alongside Laini, who was nearly crying.

"I can't believe I own all these," Gina wheezed. "It all sounds so stupid now."

"'Undead, but not unlovable,'" Laini said dramatically, between bouts of laughter. "This sold a *million* copies?"

Arlonne checked the cover. "Two million," she corrected.

I grinned as I watched the group. Laini had never looked so animated. I privately suspected that Major Morag, who had teenage daughters of her own, had donated the vampire romances to either get them out of the house or to stir the pot. Maybe both.

"Mission is a go soon," I announced and winked at Kren. "Sorry to break up book club."

"Oh, I think that's all we can handle today," Laini said assuredly. "Now, Lyra—please tell me how to act for this press event, because my undead body evidently lacks a heart."

"Here goes nothing," I muttered as our squad of black Range Rovers drove up. A complex line of security guards waved us along past Canongate until the driver parked in front of the Scottish Parliament building in the heart of Edinburgh. Guards swarmed around us—the security was tight. My gut clenched in a thrill of anticipation. This was it. Everything needed to go smoothly today.

I slid out of the car, my knee-high black boots catching the sun and making the leather shine. Major Morag strode toward our caravan. She looked strange out of uniform, having gone for a black pantsuit today. I wished I'd known that was an option. I felt vaguely uncomfortable wearing a dress for the first time in months. She pushed her sunglasses up off her face. Her gray-peppered red hair was an unruly mess of curls, but it made her look approachable rather than unprofessional. As various car doors slammed around me, I looked around to make sure everyone was accounted for. Dorian, Bryce, Kane, Roxy, Laini, Colin, Sike, Louise, and Tahn had joined our mission today. Tahn was a good noncombatant choice suggested by Kane. He came from the new cohort of vampires and gave off nonthreatening vibes. With short white hair and a long white beard, Tahn's green eyes shone brilliantly in his light brown face as he swept a careful look over the Parliament building and gathered crowd. Today, he wore a scarlet knitted cardigan, tan slacks, and a pair of polished brown shoes. Essentially, he was a vampire grandpa. It impressed me that Kane possessed the social savvy to suggest him. Zach had coordinated the outfit with Gina and Louise's help.

Soldiers styling vampires. Just another average day.

Morag shook my hand, surveying the group gleefully. "Not too shabby, Sloane. Our press conference will love this. The fashion is optimal vampire public relations." Her eyes fell on Kane, who looked especially dapper in a white button-up shirt with a dark green tartan blazer. It had taken an army to convince him to leave the cape behind, but from the way he subtly preened in the car's reflective window, I suspected the look was growing on him.

Morag whistled lowly. "Impressive! The cameras will love you, Kane."

Kane scowled, apparently uncertain whether that was an insult. "Excuse me?"

Roxy snorted. "Precious pretty boy."

I let them have their spat as I glanced around. Our clothing had been planned days in advance to make sure we looked professional yet relatable, capable but also in need of aid, sexy and also reliable as witnesses. It was exhausting.

Laini fidgeted with a pair of gold earrings on her ears. They were only a clip-on costume pair, but paired with her soft pink sundress, they gave her the air of a sweet vampire starlet. Dorian looked the best in my opinion, but I was probably a little biased. His tall frame suited human clothes well. He wore a tailored black overcoat over a white button-up shirt tucked into a pair of charcoal-gray slacks. Sike had surprised everyone by helping with the sewing, turning out to be an excellent tailor. He'd had to let down quite a few hems, as the vampires were, on the whole, of taller builds.

"Prepare for the swarm," Morag told us in a low voice. I stiffened as she led us through a flock of activity. Several reporters shoved microphones and cameras in our direction.

"Mr. Bryce! How are you responding to allegations you've been a secret operative for the Scottish government during your entire time at the Bureau?"

"Mr. Clave, any contributions to the ethical debate about vampire feeding?"

"Do you believe you can get along with humans?" a red-faced man bellowed at Laini, probably misjudging her as weaker than the vampire men. Sike stepped in front of Laini, who had stared curiously at the fuzzy microphone being shoved at her. Louise hooked her arm with Laini's and hurried her along while Sike faced a new barrage of reporters.

"Calm down. You'll get your chance at questions." Morag threw out her arm against a particularly pushy reporter and gestured for security to keep order. They took a massive step back. *Guess you don't mess with officials who have military combat training and a dedicated security team.* Morag hustled us along as she barked warnings at reporters. Members of the general public pushed against the barricades, but I would much rather have the poster-toting fanatics at our throats than the reporters.

From the crowd, a young woman held up a poster of my face with a crown pasted on top of it with the words QUEEN OF THE UNDEAD underneath it. I twisted my fingers nervously. I could neutralize an armed soldier in fifty different ways, but the Bureau hadn't ever given me training on being an international celebrity. More flashes went off from the reporters' cameras. Morag placed us on the makeshift stage behind a fleet of podiums bristling with mics.

I glanced at the vampires nervously, hoping the onslaught of attention was manageable for them. Kane glared as he scanned the crowd but kept his mouth shut. His eyes narrowed briefly. Did he sense darkness? Sike and Laini studied the area similarly. They seemed steady enough. They had fed recently, so I didn't expect trouble from them.

Beside me, Dorian gave a short growl under his breath. My stomach twisted uneasily as I grabbed his elbow. He kept his face tilted down for a moment, avoiding the cameras as shadows swarmed beneath his skin. He was hungry, but he had promised both me and Morag that he could handle this. I squeezed his arm gently, keeping my polite smile aimed at the crowd. Was it a mistake to let him come? Morag and Bryce had agreed to it since, thanks to the livestream, Dorian was the most recognizable of the vampires. But his hunger might place us in jeopardy… again.

If Morag noticed anything, she pretended not to as she stepped up to the large middle podium. She waved her hand at the crowd, and the shouting tapered off.

"We're happy to have you in the crowd today," she announced, her voice amplified through the microphones, spreading out over the decorative pools and floating on the air toward the nearby Holyrood Palace. Kane glared at the microphone. It let out a feedback whine, and Laini winced. A camera crew inched closer to Morag. She nodded to a sharply dressed man, who stepped up. "Our friends at the BBC are currently doing a documentary series on this issue." She winked at the crowd. "I hope they filter me to look ten years younger, but you know how the English are since they lost the greatest thing that ever happened to them."

A resounding laugh rose from the crowd, which drew a good-natured scowl from the BBC host, a pleasant, academic-looking man in his late thirties. Morag probably couldn't care less about her appearance, but she knew how to charm a crowd and playfully tease her neighboring ally. I took mental notes on her posture and easy demeanor, hoping I could mimic them when my turn to speak came.

"Charles Winterford here with BBC1 for our series on vampire-human relations. Since Scottish independence from the UK some ten years ago, the offer for vampire asylum has catapulted Scotland onto the world stage in a profound way. It's a controversial decision." Charles stepped up to the podium, directing his microphone to Dorian. My nerves tingled. "We'd love to hear from the vampire whose cruel treatment at the hands of the Occult Bureau gained the sympathy of many who viewed the now famous livestream. Dorian Clave, can you give your first official statement to the UK media?"

Dorian took a half step forward. His eyes darkened as he visibly fought a snarl. I balled my hand into a fist beside me. *Please, please keep it together.* He blinked twice and stared into the camera before turning back to Winterford, who seemed a little unsure of himself now that he was standing in front of a pack of vampires.

"My people and I are here to seek a new life for vampires. We mean no harm to humans," Dorian spoke. His firm voice spread easily over the crowd even though he was too far from the microphone. "We are grateful to Scotland for granting us temporary asylum. We would like to get to know humans better, as equal species."

Kane looked down, rolling his eyes, and Laini covertly kicked him in the leg, hidden from sight by the podiums.

No harm to humans.

The truth was more complicated than that, but this was the public relations statement we had decided on. The vampires *technically* weren't here to harm humans at the moment. It was the reason they'd stopped feeding in the Mortal Plane.

Winterford's expectant gaze swung over to me, along with his microphone. I stepped forward, grateful to feel Dorian's presence beside me. My arm brushed against Dorian's overcoat. Maybe everything would go okay.

"Ms. Sloane, your uncle is famously in Scottish custody for his alleged inhumane crimes involving planned vampire eradication. Where do you stand on his *alleged* actions?"

"My uncle—" The term was so repulsive to me now that I choked on it. The reporter stared at me, his eyes widening a fraction. No, I couldn't let this be a scandalous moment of news.

"My uncle's actions were deplorable, but our connection is only by blood. It doesn't matter who did this. My official stance is that I would like to encourage the US to stop hunting vampires. The deliberate eradication of a species that came to us in their time of need, seeking a partnership, constitutes genocide of the cruelest kind. Despite the bloodshed between our species in the past, I'm confident that all humans and vampires with good intentions can coexist." I gestured to the group on the stage. "Just as my small team has been doing for some time now."

As I showed off our finely dressed group, I saw Kane curl his lip from the corner of my eye. Was he hungry? Or angry that we were pandering? I cleared my throat as I glanced at Laini.

"In fact, the vampires have prepared their own statements to showcase their linguistic interest in human languages."

Laini stepped forward. We hoped that having her sweet face on covers would show another side to the vampires, who could appear intimidating. She shyly glanced at Winterford and then began speaking in Scottish Gaelic, which she'd been practicing with two guards at the barracks. Winterford looked somewhat puzzled, but the Scottish journalists' eyes widened in delight as Laini delivered her message, another statement about peace between the groups.

Sike came forward after her. "I've been trying my hand at Scots," he admitted to the crowd. He grinned bashfully. "Try not to hate it too much." He began speaking in a language somewhat similar to Gaelic. I grasped a few words that sounded slightly English, but much of it sounded like gibberish to me. Some in the crowd began laughing pleasantly, enjoying Sike's attempt, though it seemed like he butchered some words.

"Lovely," Winterford said, quite genuinely. "Thank you."

Morag turned to the reporters as Winterford and the BBC crew fell back, but his camera crew remained focused on us. "We'll now take questions from the floor. Please wait until I call on you." Gestures flew up from the crowd, hands waving with microphones clutched tightly in their grasp. Morag pointed to a brunette woman in the front row.

"Isabella Smith, *The New York Times*," she said and aimed her analyzing gaze at me. "How can we expect to keep humans safe from spontaneous vampire violence? There have been reports in the United States of rumored attacks."

Rumored attacks were a laugh. They were the work of gossip or invented entirely by the reporter. If the vampires had fellow survivors in the Mortal Plane, they would know. I could answer that well enough, but I knew it wouldn't satisfy her. That was apparently the name of the game in media and public relations. "Congress assured me during my conversations with them back in the US that these reports have been conclusively proven false. I have no more information on the matter. As I'm no longer in an official military position, I rely on what the US government is telling the public, which is that you don't need to worry about spontaneous vampire attacks."

"We expect our US allies to keep their people informed of any pressing dangers, but these are nothing but baseless horror stories spread across social media," Morag added firmly. "Next question." She selected a blonde woman with a red neck kerchief near the back.

"Charlotte Leblanc, *The International Gazette*. We ran a focus group with our readers. One of our top questions was about long-term expectations for vampire-human relations. For example, if we live peacefully, can our species interbreed? Will there be total integration of cultures, despite the inherent threat that vampires apparently pose to certain members of the public?" Her expression was cheerful, but a pang of defensiveness rose up in me. Did anyone outside our group suspect my relationship with Dorian? I squirmed slightly as I stood beside him. As for whether humans and vampires could interbreed, I'd like to know that for myself.

Dorian shifted beside me. Was he hungry or frustrated by the questions? I prayed the conference would end quickly. They said it would be twenty minutes to half an hour, but I was pretty sure it would run long, with this many reporters clamoring for responses.

"At present, we don't have enough information on that," Morag replied. "But I wouldn't suggest setting up any dating websites for vampire partners anytime soon."

The crowd chuckled. *Glad someone is enjoying this.*

"How are you responding to the rumor that tens of thousands of vampires will be walking Scotland's streets?" a man from an English newspaper asked. "Will they be able to coexist if the vampires can maintain themselves by feeding on convicted criminals? Should the public *worry?*" His bushy eyebrows bunched together over thick-framed glasses.

"It's too early to say anything definitively, without research to back it up and time for lawmakers to reflect on their decisions," Morag replied, giving a careful answer that meant nothing. "There will not be tens of thousands of vampires roaming Scotland, however. Future decisions about the guidelines for vampire feeding will be decided among international groups. I foresee some countries differing on restrictions, but perhaps we'll see a creation of vampire-friendly countries that establish strict systems on this issue."

"Won't they just attack us anyway, if they feel like it?" a voice asked from the crowd.

Morag scowled. "Please wait for me to call on you, especially if you're going to shout ill-considered speculation. No, vampires do not attack on pure whim. As we understand, they have a finely tuned internal sense of when a person has done unspeakable harm to others in the past. In fact, we hope researchers can study this ability to develop new opportunities for criminal science."

The next reporter chosen stood. A wiry man with oval glasses peered at us curiously, as though we were lab experiments on display. "Henry Bugle, *The Independent Times*. Do we have a clear idea about what the internal rules are for vampires? Whose rules do the vampires' 'feelings' follow, anyway? Is there any research currently in progress?"

The combined stares made my skin itch. There were plenty of questions we needed to figure out answers to, but we needed time to do that. The public floating the possibility of living alongside vampires was hopeful, but I knew the tide could turn easily if something went wrong. Dorian fidgeted next to me, a soft growl escaping his mouth.

Tahn raised a hand to answer, immediately charming the gathered reporters. "I can't say much, but a lot of us vampires are working with scientists and researchers to answer those kinds of questions in ways humans can understand." His voice was soft and syrupy, with a slight huskiness created by his age. "I must admit, it is fascinating to explore our own physiology in this way."

A square-jawed man with a badly kept black beard surged to his feet, obviously annoyed at not being picked. "Who exactly will pay for these refugees if they're granted asylum? Can we expect the vampires to get jobs and pay taxes? If they don't—"

Dorian jerked beside me, and I grabbed him without thinking. He dropped to the ground on his knees. Sike and Laini quickly stepped in front of him.

"Uh, just a moment," Morag said quickly, trying desperately to speak over the sudden rise of whispers. "One of our fellows isn't feeling too well. Convinced to do a whisky tasting last night, and I think he got into it a little too much."

"Been there," shouted a jovial Scottish reporter in an electric wheelchair. His comment raised a few appreciative laughs.

"See, this guy gets it." Morag waved over a man in a black suit to take her place. She pressed her hand to my back and murmured quickly, "Get him off stage *now* and into one of the cars so we can get him away from here. We'll finish up and follow."

She aimed a smile at the crowd, which was becoming increasingly apprehensive. Kane's head swiveled suddenly toward the nearby Arthur's Seat. Laini surveyed the crowd, her face focused. My nerves burned, telling me to move fast. Something bad was coming.

Morag gasped abruptly as Dorian ripped himself from her and Sike's grasp. He leapt over his podium into the crowd. I froze in horror as I watched his powerful hands swat cameras and reporters to the side. He knocked down a man as he raced down the street.

"He's headed for Holyrood," Morag said sharply into the comm I hadn't noticed she was wearing. "Track him and keep him clear of civilians."

Dorian was already a significant distance away, little more than a black smudge racing across the muted green of the cliff's base. Kane attempted to follow, but he stopped suddenly and hovered on the stage.

Like hot water pouring over great slabs of ice, the plaza in front of Parliament rang with several swift, sharp cracks.

Someone screamed as the BBC camera shattered.

Bullets.

"Get down!" I yelled as a spray of gunfire pockmarked the podiums.

Louise cried out as Sike leapt in front of her, yanking her down. I threw myself off the stage to avoid the spray. A trail of red caught my eye as I dropped into the chaos.

Blood, but I couldn't tell whose.

CHAPTER FOUR

"Get down!" I shouted above the fray.

The crowd erupted into screams across the plaza. Several more shots pelted the ground. A window shattered across the road in The Queen's Gallery. A wave of humans ducked. Someone's sobs rose above the screams. I heard bodies splash into the pools in front of the building.

I risked raising my head and spotted Laini, Sike, and even Tahn across the plaza lifting reporters to their feet and helping the security team direct the crowd. Kane snarled as he looked around wildly, searching for the shooter. His eyes narrowed as the remaining crowd pushed against him, fighting their way back toward the Royal Mile. Police sirens rose in the distance. Laini shook her head, her fangs extending and shrinking back to their normal state as she struggled to restrain herself.

I dragged myself up from the ground, waiting with a thundering heart to hear another shot. My first instinct was to help the vampires, but the crowd made that impossible. People still rushed to get away from the plaza, with emergency response vehicles and curious people trying to push through from the other direction. The security team, including Morag, ushered people into the Parliament building. Some reporters remained glued to the ground, whispering panicked statements into their microphones or cameras.

After another moment passed with no more bullets, I stood up fully in front of the stage to make my way through the chaos. Flashing lights reflected off the metal and glass of Parliament as police and ambulances pulled up in the square. A cold chill ran through me as I glanced toward the Holyrood Palace. Where was Dorian? Had he chased the shooter?

Laini and Kane finally broke free of the crowd and ran off in the same direction he had disappeared in. I followed them as quickly as possible, shoving my way through the remaining crowd. Police officers rushed out from newly arrived convoys. I pushed past them, ignoring their yells for us to either head for the police vehicles or the building, and sprinted toward the palace. Laini and Kane darted into the nearby ornamental park.

I ran as fast as I could, past the ornamental gardens and pools of the Parliament building. Tourists peppered the path up to Arthur's Seat, but they were scattered by Laini and Kane and then me a minute later. Laini and Kane could have moved faster, but they likely held back, not wanting to hurt anyone in the crowd of humans. Many of the faces were confused and anxious.

"Were those gunshots?" a woman asked me in a sweet French accent as she clutched her children close to her.

"Clear the area," I shouted and waved my hands, all I could manage as I raced by. I didn't look back to see if they obeyed or stayed frozen in place. My tone had been official enough that someone could mistake me for an authority figure, but my distinct American accent and frantic pace would be strange.

I pumped my arms and legs. I would give anything to be in athletic gear with some running shoes, but this outfit would have to do. People milled around in the palace parking lot, visibly alarmed and confused. I ran against them like a salmon going upstream. Had Dorian sensed something was wrong before it happened? Was that why he ran this way?

At the base of the steep incline, I spotted movement and a flash of pink in a clump of trees and briars. Changing course, I ran over, my fashionable boots sliding slightly on the damp grass, and was greeted with a somewhat distressing sight. Tousled and dirt-smeared, Kane sat on a wildly snarling Dorian, shoving his knee sharply into the small of his writhing back, while Laini grabbed his arms and pinned them to the ground.

"Dorian," I called out, dropping to my knees close to his head, panting for breath. He didn't respond, only continued to growl and fight against Kane and Laini's grip.

"Nice try, but he's lost it." Kane stooped down to Dorian's ear. "Did you hear that, you fool? You're ruining your own stupid plan. Why can't you follow your own rules?"

Laini glanced at me with a nervous frown. "The sniper left. Much faster than I would expect from a human." Her gaze darted toward the path leading up to Arthur's Seat. "All I can sense from this distance is darkness, an unusual amount for one person."

"We could have run the shooter down," Kane said crossly. "But we kept our word to Dorian to stop him if he lost it, since he's being an idiot about feeding. If he'd killed the shooter, we might have missed our chance at asylum."

I couldn't stop my flinch at his words. We all knew Dorian's refusal to feed regularly was due to not wanting to cause me pain. Kane's words felt like an accusation that wasn't altogether misplaced. Dorian's hunger made him feral. Luckily, it also made him weak enough to be restrained by Laini and Kane. I understood why he'd asked them to keep an eye on him. I just hated that it was necessary.

"The shooter is farther away," Laini reported, closing her eyes for a moment. "I don't understand how they're moving so fast. If they were somewhere up on the hill, it should have taken them far longer to get back to ground level. Every path is very steep and precarious."

"It wouldn't be a problem if they weren't human," Kane said ominously. Not human? They'd used a gun on the crowd, which didn't seem supernatural. But a human couldn't run like that...

"What can I do?" I asked. My lungs ached from my run, and I couldn't rip my eyes away from Dorian, who began to calm slightly.

Approaching footsteps sounded behind me. I turned to see five soldiers in black combat dress running up to our group—our Scottish military detail.

"We've secured the plaza," the leading officer said with a steady nod. His eyes fell to Dorian, and he frowned uneasily. "We'll escort you back to the major and the convoy."

"We can help you look for the shooter," I said, gesturing toward Arthur's Seat. "But we have to hurry. They're already nearly out of the range of the vampires' senses."

The officer shook his head. "I have orders to escort your group back. You're not Scottish law enforcement, so we must treat you as civilians. You can't be part of the investigation. Sorry, Ms. Sloane."

Ms. Sloane. The words felt like a slap across the face. I was no longer First Lieutenant Sloane of the Bureau, was I? Here I was, a highly trained soldier, and I could do nothing to help Dorian or my friends.

"Understood," I managed tightly. This feeling of powerlessness sent a wave of frustration through me, but these officers were just doing their job. I couldn't argue right now. It would only slow them down.

"We can carry the problem child," Kane added dryly, grabbing Dorian's legs and securing them with a rough motion.

The officer's face relaxed slightly, though his lips never moved an inch. I could recognize tightly concealed discomfort in a soldier. How often had I felt the same way myself? It was a relief for the officers not to have to restrain a vampire.

We headed back to the plaza, our pace slowed on the return journey by Dorian's weight, until he recovered enough to stumble along with us. An ambulance siren wailed in the distance, and my stomach filled with ice. The shots had injured someone, possibly multiple people. I remembered the blood on the ground. I hadn't seen who it belonged to.

"Any fatalities?" I asked the officer.

He shook his head. "Don't believe so, Ms. Sloane. Someone is down, though." He tapped his comm. "Major Morag called for medics."

I hurried alongside them. The scene had changed drastically in just the last several minutes. The crowd now stood in a cordoned-off area to talk to police officers, who were covering people in emergency shock blankets. A circle of guards surrounded the plaza area where we'd held the press conference. The officers helped us get through, citing their orders.

I hurried to the stage, where I found Roxy and Colin huddled around Sike. Sike sat on the ground, clutching someone. A numb sensation came over me when I saw the end of a tidy strawberry-blonde braid. *Louise.*

Sike cradled Louise, who stared at him in a daze, moving her mouth slightly with nothing coherent coming out. Roxy knelt beside him, pressing her folded coat to Louise's left shoulder. Blood stained the faded denim and dripped down Louise's arm.

"You'll be all right," Sike whispered shakily. "I need you to keep your eyes open, Louise. Please."

Louise blinked blearily up at him. She twisted her mouth painfully. "My head hurts," she breathed. Her weak voice alarmed me, and I looked around, trying to see if paramedics were close. Police officers stooped by several other wounded people who were strewn about the plaza and on the road. A camera lay smashed on the ground. A poster with a heart drawn around Kane's face slowly turned to mush in a pool of water. Sobs and babbling voices drifted through the air.

Bryce was tying a tartan handkerchief around his sister's arm. Major Morag leaned against the podium, cradling the arm with its bloodied blazer sleeve. There was only a small amount of blood, meaning she'd likely been grazed, but Bryce was wearing the brittle smile he wore when he was afraid and trying to hide it.

Somewhere nearby, vehicle doors opened. A voice shouted to make way through the crowd.

"That'll be the paramedics," Morag announced. Despite her

injury, her tone was solid as a rock. "We need to get Louise to the hospital right away," she said, talking directly to Sike, who held Louise against him.

"If you hadn't pushed her away in time, it would've punctured a lung or worse," Roxy muttered. Sike's usually tan face was pale, but he nodded. Louise moaned in pain but kept her eyes open. I felt a swell of fear inside me. I couldn't watch another member of my team die.

"Major Morag! What do you have to say about this situation?" a reporter cried out behind me. I turned, unable to stop my glare as a towering man with sparse blond hair attempted to shout over the guards. Kane slowly turned in the man's direction, his fangs still fully descended. The reporter's face immediately paled.

"My comment is that I've just been hit by a bullet, so I need a minute," Morag snapped. "Guards, keep the media at bay. See that they don't pester the public too much."

The guards fanned out. I watched as the men and women in their intimidating black clothes stepped farther into the crowd, pushing the media back. Most of the reporters fell back, but a stubborn woman with disheveled hair attempted to yell requests for state-ments. The officers only parted to let half a dozen first-responder paramedics rush through. Two headed toward us carrying a stretcher, while the other four fanned out to the other wounded.

"We're here," a red-headed woman said as she rushed over to Louise. "We'll take her to the Royal Hospital. It's the closest hospital with an emergency center."

Morag nodded. Sike reluctantly released his grip on Louise as the paramedics carefully moved her onto the stretcher.

"Wait," Morag muttered to her brother. Her pale face twitched with alarm. Bryce helped his sister to her feet as she clutched her blazer to her bloody wound. "They haven't caught the shooter. I want to send guards in a car after the ambulance."

"We'll send them," Bryce promised Morag. "We can transfer her to the compound's med bay once she's in better shape."

"Understood," the medic said. "But they'll have to explain to hospital security themselves." They ferried Louise off the stage on the stretcher with Sike sticking close to her side. Morag barked into her comm, and three guards followed the medics through the crowd.

"Our turn," Roxy said and grunted. She rolled up the bloody coat underneath her arm, a grisly souvenir from our press conference.

With Bryce beside her, Morag managed to give commands to the guards. They helped us fight through the reporters, gawking members of the public, and a barrage of police cars and ambulances to reach our black Range Rovers. As soon as everyone was in, the doors locked and our convoy of cars peeled out, heading toward the airport.

Sitting in traffic snarled by the incident, frustration choked me in the quiet interior of the car. I couldn't speak. I ran my fingers across the sleek interior of the seat beneath me, trying to ground myself as my body surged with adrenaline. Dorian sat beside me, now fully in control. He appeared stormy about recent events. The light shadows beneath his skin moved. He watched me carefully with his sharp gaze.

It pissed me off that I could do nothing. Lieutenant Sloane reduced to an onlooker, barred from the hunt for the sniper who shot my friend and wounded innocent civilians. I dug my nails into my thigh, irritated by the very presence of a dress on my body instead of military fatigues.

The Bureau's restructuring had left our careers and lives in a tumultuous limbo. The government *had* offered us our jobs back, but at the request of my team and the vampires, I'd asked for more time to decide, citing the uncertainty of our situation with Scotland. They had agreed, saying that we could negotiate for other positions within the reformed Bureau, take up our old jobs, or leave voluntarily to pursue other opportunities instead of being fired as the original board intended. Since I was no longer employed by the US government and I would serve as a witness, I had zero sway over the investigation into the Bureau beyond giving an occasional testimony. Temporary asylum in Scotland was good, but I had no real authority here. I was a liaison and consultant for vampires, but not a soldier. The Scottish government paid for our human presence in terms of room and board here while it was still useful. But how long would that last? How long would *I* last in a position that offered me no real way to wield my strength and assets for our allies?

Others now protected me when I should be working alongside them. I couldn't stand for that much longer—I would have to be useful in whatever way I could. I might not be able to be a pair of boots on the ground in the physical hunt, but maybe I could offer something just as valuable: knowledge. Someone had to know something. Someone with a vested interest in making sure our press conference failed dramatically.

Alan's face and his ominous parting message at the end of the Chicago battle immediately appeared in my mind's eye.

"I need to see Alan," I muttered. "He might have had something to do with this."

Dorian squeezed my hand, then let go after a moment. "You'll have to do it alone," he said grimly. "After this, I'd be even more tempted to kill him than usual."

I stared at his face, at the pale shadows moving sluggishly across it. He was clearly joking, but also hungry enough for that to be a real concern.

Fine. I would go alone. I hoped the three board members were ready to talk, because I was ready for answers.

CHAPTER FIVE

T he helicopter flight from Edinburgh to the VAMPS compound felt longer than ever before. Barely anyone spoke. As we trudged into the compound in the bright afternoon light, the rotor blades of the choppers slowing to a halt, I spotted a few people gathered at the entrance to the barracks. News of the attack at the conference had apparently preceded us. I wondered if everyone back here at camp had watched the news in silent horror.

I steeled myself for the onslaught of questions. Luckily, the gathered vampires focused on Dorian, Laini, and Kane. Tahn trailed behind them looking weary and shaken. I wanted to shake my head over the time and effort we'd put into his outfit in preparation for this event. Who could've predicted a shooter?

Zach and Gina barreled out of the communications trailer, and I gave them a quick wave to let them know I was all right before I slunk away to let my other teammates tell the tale. There was somewhere I needed to go first.

On the side of the compound, there was a stone building with its own concertina wire fence. The military had originally used it to store munitions and weapons, but over time it had become a mock prison for interrogation practice. There were three holding cells in the building. Three prisoners, three cells—it was perfect for our needs.

A guard with a neatly pressed uniform greeted me at the front.

"I'd like to speak with the prisoners," I told her.

She nodded and opened the door using a complex pin system on the heavy-duty lock. The steel door opened. She followed me inside, her rifle held loosely before her.

Alan and the other two board members lived here now, in confinement. Each concrete cell had a bed, a desk, a chemical toilet, and not much else. The prisoners were taken one at a time every other day for a shower in the communal block, then marched straight back to their quarters. I scowled at the small TV mounted opposite the cell doors, a new addition to the bare walls. They didn't deserve access to television. Even letting them watch a small slice of the outside world through a bulletproof window in the door was too much luxury, if you asked me.

Alan sat at his desk. He glanced at me with a perfectly neutral expression. No surprise. No anger. No remorse. No misery. In return, I felt like he was a stranger to me. No rage. No grief. No love. The guard pressed a button on the side of the door, and a crackle sparked in the small speaker embedded in the wall.

"I saw the news," Alan said, and though his face was bland, his voice was smug. "Shame about your little press conference." He gestured with a small remote toward the news coverage that was currently playing.

The guard cleared her throat. "They can't make a weapon from the devices," she assured me.

That was naïve thinking. Alan needed nothing but his mind to be a weapon. I doubted anyone was willing to take that away from him.

"You know why I'm here," I said, finding I was angry after all. It simmered beneath my words. "What do you know about the attack?"

Alan shrugged casually. "Nothing at all. How could I?" He gestured to his cell with a feigned expression of interest. "I'm being denied basic human rights here. Doesn't that sound familiar?"

There was no internet, no phone. Yet with the television, he was still getting news. If he'd had safety plans in place before we took him into custody, one of his operatives might be continuing his work. I could easily see Alan planning events and attacks months in advance.

He tapped his fingers on his desk. "Is being treated like a performing parrot for the benefit of vampires getting old yet?"

I stepped away from the door. I wouldn't get anything useful out of him now that he'd started his mind games. My goal was to slowly teach him that manipulation meant I would leave. If he wanted to talk to another soul, he'd have to behave himself. I was tempted to question him until he said something useful, but that would probably be futile and frustrating, and I'd ruin whatever progress I'd made with him. I could try again later.

The guard swiftly cut off the speaker, and we made our way to the next door. On the other side of the window, the elegant figure of Elena Bradley sat on her bed. She was writing in a small notebook with a pencil. Her long dark hair looked dull and tangled. She refused to look up.

"Ms. Bradley," I said after the guard pressed the button to talk. "I'd like to ask you some questions about the conference today."

She waved her hand in the air, dismissing me. "I don't know anything."

I narrowed my eyes. "Was there a Bureau backup plan to sabotage any potential vampires' reception?"

Bradley lifted her gaze to mine. Heavy bags rested beneath her eyes. She sighed heavily. "How could I even have known that you and your traitors would blast news of the supernatural all over the world?"

"Noted," I said crossly and pressed the button myself. Funny how prison only seemed to make their attitudes worse. I'd thought yanking them from their fancy Bureau offices and lives of powerful luxury would be enough to break them.

The wiry man, Calum Jones, was next. When I looked through his window, he was sitting at his desk. I pressed the button. He leaned his head on his hand and stared blankly back at me. There was no confidence, no careful dignity like Alan or even resignation like Elena Bradley.

"I don't know anything about the press conference," he said, correctly guessing the reason for my visit. He pressed his lips together. If he wanted to add something, he'd found a reason not to. I tapped my toe on the bare concrete floor. What else could I ask him?

"Do you still have colleagues working for you?"

His eyes flashed dangerously. "You don't understand. It doesn't matter what I tell you. My *allies* have power beyond belief." He paused, and his eyes drifted to the television. The screen flashed with more coverage about the press conference. "I wouldn't be surprised if they're waging war against the vampires in public."

"Your immortal allies?" I pressed. The guard shifted beside me. It wasn't good to visit them for longer than necessary.

Jones stood slowly, then walked closer to the window. His dead blue eyes stared at me, holding me fixed with their hollowness. "The dark energy weapons were just the beginning. You'd think me a fool if I told you the truth. I may not know everything, but I know what's important." He scrunched his face into a disgusted snarl. "The vampires are a scourge on this earth. They'll do anything to get what they want. And you know what? You got what you deserved for getting involved with these creatures. Creatures who are, and always will be, subhuman."

A cold anticipation ran through me as Jones leaned on the windowpane, his breath fogging up a spot.

He pointed an accusatory finger at me. "Whatever is coming for your friends, more will come soon." His blue eyes widened. "And it'll be worse than a few warning shots at a press conference. I promise you that."

I tried to get more details out of him, but he refused to say anything useful, instead devolving into insults and vague threats.

I switched off the intercom and forced myself to walk away despite his bone-chilling warning. It could be a mind game. It could be the ravings of a madman who was used to power and privilege. Due to their powerful positions, no one had ever denied these people anything before we took them to task. Why should I trust them?

Well, that was wonderfully unproductive and anxiety-producing.

The guard opened the door, and I walked out into the honeyed light of late afternoon. Everyone had moved inside, and the camp had gone strangely silent, as if recovering from the events of the day. No one was at the shooting range. No sounds of sparring drifted from the open windows of the gym. The sound of Corporal Fraser banging on her pan to announce dinner hadn't come yet.

In the silence, fatigue finally sank its claws into my skull, and I wanted little more than to sleep and forget about today for a few hours. My brother found me on my way back to my room.

"Are you okay?" he asked, his eyes searching me for injuries. I nodded wearily.

"Exhausted." I squeezed his arm. His watch beeped. He glanced down at it with a frown. He had a meeting with Bryce for a public relations statement. I promised to catch him up later, and he left, assured that I was alive and well. I hugged him tight before he went.

I snuck the rest of the way back to my quarters, but when I arrived at the plain green door, my hand hovered over the knob, unable to turn it. Louise wouldn't be there. Her sensible sunset-yellow flannel pajamas would still be folded on her pillow, and the book on FBI history she was reading in hopeful preparation of securing an interview with them would still be lying open and face down on her bedside table because she always lost her bookmarks and preferred to bend the spine than dogear the pages. The thought of her hooked up to beeping monitors in a narrow hospital bed with a weary Sike holding vigil at her bedside made me drop my hand and back away from the door. Even small actions I took somehow reminded me of what I had lost and what I stood to lose.

There was someone who would understand what that felt like. I knocked at Dorian's door. We could do with one less lonely room.

Dorian opened the door to let me in. "That frown tells me you're thinking. I take it nothing useful came from talking with the board?"

"A cryptic warning about allies, but nothing much." I threw myself onto the narrow couch next to the door and instantly regretted it. Cushioning and comfort weren't the military's specialties.

Dorian joined me. There was limited space, so his leg pressed against mine. The contact sent an excited thrill through me for half a second. I hoped that in another life, I would be able to act on feelings of desire *before* discussing matters of life and death.

"I'm frustrated as hell," I blurted. I needed a proper vent session. "I have no power. No real purpose. I couldn't go after that shooter today. I couldn't help Louise. I couldn't get anything out of the board. There's nothing I can do."

His jaw twitched with his own frustrations. "'Nothing' is better than actively making the situation worse. We might have caught the shooter if I'd just held it together. I managed with the crowd, but then this huge dark presence came out of nowhere. It completely overwhelmed me." He shook his head with glazed eyes, probably recalling his deranged chase to Arthur's Seat. "I could feel the shooter getting away, but their darkness was so strong it incapacitated me. And the speed was too fast to be human."

"Unless they had some kind of transport close by?" I wondered aloud. Silence fell between us. I didn't want to blame him for losing control, but anger burned me up from the inside out, seeking a target. I took a deep breath. *Get a grip. No one expected a shooter today.* But everyone else had been prepared to the best of their ability. "The Bureau won't let us help, either, because it would be a conflict of interest. It's not just the Scottish government or Congress."

He glanced over at his desk. It was low enough that I could spot an atlas open on the desk. He'd circled the Canyonlands.

"I'm itching to get back to the Immortal Plane," he confessed. "Even before what happened to Castral and the rumor about a vampire group in hiding, I knew we needed to get back there and search for ways to fix this. To end this. The tear is getting bigger each day. We have no idea how much time we have before the planes merge and explode."

I thought again about the shooter. "Could the immortal allies Alan mentioned be responsible for the shooting?" I asked. "He said he had nothing to do with it, but he could be lying." I shook my head tiredly. "Honestly, I have no idea why I thought any of them would tell me anything true, let alone useful. They're determined to be as unhelpful as possible." Jones's ominous warning about his allies made me scowl bitterly. Most frustrating was that while Jones had admitted he didn't know everything, that suggested he at least knew *something*. Unfortunately, whatever intel he knew had convinced him vampires were evil.

"Immortals can't cross through the circles any more than you can," Dorian assured me, slinging his arm across the back of the couch behind me. "They can only come through the tear, and even if they did, they would starve very quickly and have no way to feed. They can't survive without the ambient energy of the Immortal Plane. I doubt they'd be able to cross the ocean to find us." He dragged a hand down his sharp jawline. "I've got some other news. Morag is on her way back. They patched her up, and she should be back in the barracks tonight. She, Bryce, and I had a video call, and we agreed that she should contact Fenton. There will be a meeting with him tomorrow. I don't know what Morag and Bryce will be hoping to achieve, but my goal is to get as much information out of the revamped Bureau as we can."

"Revamped," I echoed, and cocked a smile. "Interesting choice of words."

The corner of his mouth tugged upward. "I'm adding to my vocabulary. Sike tells me puns are funny to humans. He said they're charming."

"Are you trying to be charming?" I laughed, shaking my head. "Keep that up, and you'll have the heart of every poster-holding fangirl in the world."

His glacial eyes sparked with interest as he lifted a brow. "Worried that I'll leave you for a woman who pledges her undying love to me through arts and crafts?"

I suddenly registered that he still wore his human clothes. He'd removed the overcoat and unbuttoned the top two buttons of his white shirt, the once-crisp material now marked with grass stains and mud. My mouth went dry.

I didn't want to talk about the world outside anymore. I gave him a wicked smile.

Dorian tensed as I moved toward him. "It's not exactly under the best circumstances, but it'd be a shame to waste our time alone," I told him.

He slowly smirked and wrapped an arm around my waist as I climbed into his lap, my dress sliding up my thighs. "Great minds think alike. Sitting around moping won't help, so why not... release some stress?"

I kissed him hard, relishing the knowledge that nobody would walk in. My head buzzed softly with pain, but I ignored it as Dorian pushed off my leather jacket, then skimmed his hands softly down my sides. I moaned, enjoying the feeling of him pressed against me. This was the benefit of him starving himself, the flip side of the earlier disaster. Was it worth it? The selfish part of me said *yes.*

I wanted to kiss away all the worries of today. If I could touch him, I knew he was real and safe. Nobody could take him from me in this moment. There was no danger here except the rising tension between us.

He bit my bottom lip softly, and I smiled against his kiss, enjoying the swelling desire inside me. I ran my hands down his powerful arms, fingertips tracing the corded tendons and curlicues of shadow. He brought one hand up to press against the back of my head, deepening our kiss. His other hand skirted the hem of my shirt. I pressed the wandering hand against me, inviting him farther in.

My head felt light, but I melted beneath his touch. His fingers, feather light, traced a line on my naked skin beneath the shirt, rising slowly but surely toward my breast.

The pain inside my chest spiked. My head spun. I gasped, pulling back and nearly sending myself off his lap. His hands grabbed me firmly around the waist to keep me from falling. The humor and desire on his face had vanished, replaced by concern and guilt.

Seriously? Even when he's this weak?

"Are you okay?" he asked, stroking my hair gently.

I nodded, trying to ignore nausea as I felt my strength return. Dorian maneuvered me onto the end of the couch so I could lean against the cushions, putting a safe amount of distance between us.

"I guess our truce only partially works," I said and rubbed the skin over my heart in slow circles. It did nothing to help, but the dizziness gradually disappeared. The burning in my chest faded to the original buzz.

I sighed and glanced at the bed. "I'm guessing cuddling is out of the question now?"

He shook his head firmly. "We can lie next to one another," he said with a wink. "But if you try something, and Zach catches me dragging your unconscious body back to your room, I'm sure the Immortal Plane will look like a safe haven."

"Hands to myself," I promised, then eased onto his bed. He took the opposite side, staying as far away as possible on the narrow frame. I leaned my head against my arm as I reclined. It was strange to see Dorian like this. It felt even more intimate than kissing. What would it be like to wake up to him every morning? My breath caught at the thought.

"Do humans always like to cuddle?" Dorian asked suddenly.

"Many do," I said, managing a shrug. "It feels good to be close to people."

"It's a bit like pack animals huddling together," he said, amused.

I rolled my eyes. "What? Vampires don't cuddle? Are you too tough for it?"

"We embrace," he replied easily. "Obviously, vampires are much too tough and deadly for such things as cuddling, though. There are other ways of showing affection beyond cuddling." He winked.

I stared at him, wondering what other things besides cuddling he'd done before. And who he'd done them with.

"What?" he asked. "I see those studying eyes, Lyra."

I might have been new to relationships, but I was pretty sure asking about exes was a no-fly zone.

"Do you want to learn how to cuddle?" I teased. "I mean, do you guys even know about big spoon and little spoon?"

He raised a brow. "I'm sorry. Why are we talking about silverware?"

I laughed so hard I had a coughing fit. He patted my back gently with a mocking tut. I smacked his hand away, still laughing. When I got my breathing back under control, I explained.

"It's usually when the taller person lies behind the shorter person. Basically, the big spoon holds the little spoon, and it's comfortable and kinda cute."

He stared. "I've never thought of you as a spoon. But you are very cute."

I pressed a hand over my embarrassed, warm cheeks. "Never mind." I peeked at him through my fingers. "It's always good to expand your skillset, you know."

We talked for a while longer, about everything and nothing, ignoring the dinner bell when it rang, preferring to stay in our quiet little bubble of contentment. If he was going to starve to be with me, it was only fair that I returned the favor. The soldier part of my brain wanted to use this opportunity to ask about the vampires' enemies in the Immortal Plane, but I knew that it would spoil the moment. I'd asked before, of course, unable to contain my curiosity after the revelation on the Bureau rooftop. But Immortals were painful for the vampires to talk about. Dorian had tried to give me details, but apparently it was hard to know where to start, and the attempt always darkened his mood for hours. Right now, I just wanted to rest instead of prying.

He told me about the letters that had begun to arrive for the vampires from fans all across the world. The Scottish government wasn't happy about all the fan mail that had been pouring into their office, so they'd apparently set up a special address for people to send letters to. The first three sacks had arrived the previous day. Impressed and amused, I was nevertheless slightly concerned about the growing vampire craze and said as much.

"It could benefit us," Dorian reminded me. "I'm assigning people to write back."

"Sure, sure," I said with a yawn. "You just love being a celebrity."

He smirked and gestured to his face. "I was made for fame, obviously."

I snorted a laugh. "You've been watching too many trashy reality shows." I yawned again and sat up reluctantly. "I should probably head back to my room and actually go to sleep."

He nodded and feathered a kiss on top of my forehead. I slid off the bed, and he followed me to the door, keeping a perfect distance between us. Neither of us wanted to part ways, but it would be difficult to sleep next to one another.

"Goodnight, Dorian."

His eyes were soft, a sweet emotion I treasured. "Goodnight, Lyra."

I left him and felt the pain fade as I put distance between us. The pain was strong even though he was so weak. That was something to consider. I sucked in a deep breath as my body returned to normal.

Louise's empty bed greeted me when I got back to my room. I faced away from it, staring at the wall until I fell asleep.

CHAPTER SIX

The next afternoon, we gathered for the meeting with Fenton in the communications trailer. He arranged to call after three p.m. to accommodate the time differences of the various Bureau offices. I helped Zach connect the flat-screen TV to the computer we would be using for the conference call. Everyone felt Louise's absence as we wrestled with cables and tried to sync the software.

"It's this blue one," Zach insisted and waved the end of the wire in front of me with a grin. "Man, do you remember when we spent six hours setting up our Christmas gift when we were kids?"

His chipper energy was infectious, earning a smile from me. "Then let's try it," I said as he fiddled with the TV.

Bryce cast a sympathetic look our way, but computer tech wasn't one of his strengths. Morag flipped through her notes again and again. The bandages on her arm peeked out from the cuff of her purple button-up shirt. She pushed her reading glasses up on the bridge of her nose and scowled, underlining something on the page.

As the time for the call drew closer, those who had been invited began trickling into the trailer, gathering around the weathered conference table. The Bryce siblings were front and center since they were in charge of the details. Dorian, Kane, and a few other vampires, including two I had met briefly and knew as the elder lore-keepers of their group, sat on one side of the table. Dorian reintroduced them as Dorsa and Torran.

Dorsa appeared to be in her sixties, but knowing little of the vampire aging process, I had no idea how old she really was. She looked a little like Arlonne—they had the same copper-toned eyes and rich brown skin. She wore her thick dark brown hair braided in a circle around her head, and she was friendly enough despite her tendency to purse her thin lips. Torran looked to be in his seventies. He wore a thick blue wool sweater he'd adopted from the collection of donated clothes, one of the only vampires to abandon their classic cloak in favor of human clothes. The color offset his silvery hair, grayish skin, and long white beard. He stroked his mustache occasionally, the heavy lines on his concerned face adding a serious edge to his aura.

I settled into my seat beside Zach. Everyone was a little tense as the software connected us to Fenton and the rest of the meeting.

When the audit of the Bureau began, a panel of congressional representatives had appointed trusted government workers to review the Bureau's conduct. Because of the CIA's collaboration with the Bureau, although it was apparently only limited to a few individuals, Congress strived to select the auditors from as many varied sources as possible to ensure increased accountability.

They had appointed interim board members inside the Bureau during the reformation. Fenton had also gotten Congress to reinstate many of the members who had been fired by the original board for their pro-vampire sympathies. We would be meeting with the resulting interim board today. Among their ranks were Bureau middle managers that had been promoted and rising stars from various Bureau branches outside of Chicago. They'd appointed Captain Clemmins to the board, but I didn't see his face on the call.

On the TV screen, several boxes showed different people, along with their respective time zones. I studied the new faces.

Captain Abbas, a Middle Eastern woman from New York in her early forties, wore a Bureau uniform and a black hijab, her expression alert and pleasant. Next to her, Captain Ruiz from the California office stared into her computer with confidence, the large cup of coffee on the desk beside her betraying the fact it was barely eight a.m. there. She was a Latina woman with her dark hair sharply cut into a bob. I pegged her at late thirties. The FBI had agreed to transfer her to the Bureau, though there were rumors that she was a spy and serving as a government oversight plant. Not that more oversight from the Bureau would be a bad thing.

The rest of the faces—from Phoenix, DC, and a few other regional offices—blurred together in a sea of hazy memory. I recognized many of them from various meetings I went to before coming to Scotland, but so many people had changed positions, it was difficult to keep track.

Fenton, in the Chicago office, occupied the main screen. After the usual exchange of pleasantries, Fenton dove straight into the main issue at hand.

"We haven't been able to apprehend any of the original board members yet," he announced. "After the majority of them escaped in the first helicopter, they disappeared. Many have gone abroad, with the last trace of them being at airports or accessing their bank accounts to empty them."

"Guess we were lucky to get three of them, including Director Sloane," Bryce said, drawing his arms across his chest.

Morag scrawled something in her notes with a neutral frown. "|Do you think they could be responsible for the latest attack?" she asked bluntly.

"It's possible," Fenton admitted. "There are warrants out for their arrest, but it's not impossible that one of them made their way to Scotland. Or hired a professional."

"It would be irresponsible if the Scottish police weren't able to keep the ex-Bureau board members out of the country after everything that's happened," Captain Ruiz broke in sharply. Morag lifted an eyebrow a fraction. "It's more likely they're trying to maneuver behind the scenes and are dispatching people to do the dirty work for them. We've frozen their accounts, but as Fenton pointed out, many of them emptied those accounts before we could reach them. And I imagine they have the ability to secure funding elsewhere."

Captain Abbas cleared her throat. "Several are independently wealthy, either from other positions they held in business or through inheritance."

"I wasn't the only person on that board with a trust fund," Fenton added wryly.

"Perhaps we should look into local sources for the sniper first," Ruiz added. "Vampires have many enemies among the human public. Someone in the criminal sphere over there could be responsible."

There was a subtle buzzing on Fenton's desk as his phone rang. Fenton, slightly embarrassed, snatched up his phone. A shadow of tired worry crossed his face. "I have to take this," he muttered as he answered it. His shoulders sank.

I drummed my fingers on my knees anxiously. It was important.

"Yes," he said. "I'll connect you right away."

A new box appeared on the call. The text display introduced the newcomer as Director Runyard from the Bureau office in Fort Worth, Texas. His wispy brown hair and glasses gave him a stern look. If I recalled correctly, the office in Fort Worth was one of the largest in the Southwest. He was currently in charge of organizing the ground forces near the tear.

"I don't mean to interrupt," Runyard apologized. The subtle alarm in his voice made me sit up straighter in my chair. "It's been quiet for a few days, but last night something new came through from the Immortal Plane. I'm at a loss for how to handle it. Moab is in serious danger. The rest of Utah and western Colorado might not be far behind if we can't figure out how to stop these things."

I leaned closer to the screen. Runyard looked like he hadn't slept all night. Whatever came through the tear, if the Bureau couldn't handle it, had to be bad. This is what we'd warned the government about. There would be more creatures as long as the tear kept growing.

"This is the first moment I've been able to tear myself away from organizing our defenses. I'm requesting authorization from the board. I desperately need vampires to help with the tear." He scrubbed at his eyes. "Is anyone willing to come immediately? Humans, vampires, anyone with experience of the Immortal Plane. I can figure out a way to pay you for your services, if necessary."

Dorian leaned forward with a composed face, but his jaw was clenched tight. "I would love to help you, Director, but it's difficult," he said with a touch of sympathy and paused. "The US government won't allow any vampire presence in the Canyonlands. I've already asked multiple times and been denied. They told me it will have to wait until after the summit in four days."

I concealed my surprise at Dorian's claims as something clicked in my mind. What was he playing at? He was going to get us back to the tear, come hell or high water.

"Four days?" Runyard sucked in a sharp breath. "We don't have four days. I have men and women risking their lives. I have civilians at risk."

"Four days if the vampires agree," Dorian said, unblinking. "Your government has repeatedly turned down my requests to aid you from the beginning. Now I find myself disinclined. Why should we risk our lives for your sake?"

He was being harsh, but it was for a purpose. Deep down, Dorian wanted to help, but the Bureau couldn't come waltzing back and requesting things like this lightly. If they had allowed us to be at the tear after the Chicago HQ business, we might have been able to prevent this. Morag glanced at me with a calm but suspicious face. Dorian was playing a dangerous and clever game.

Runyard's cheeks grew red with frustration. "You can't be—"

"Wait. I can offer you something," Dorian interrupted. Dorsa and Torran watched him carefully. The rest of the vampires did the same. "I have vampires who are ready and willing to help save human lives, but we've grown tired of waiting for the government's precious approval. I see you're a man who cares about his country. I will personally take responsibility if the US government doesn't comply, but I have conditions."

The conference call transformed into a negotiation just like that.

I sank back, watching Dorian work. He had learned a lot about human politics by watching everything around him.

"Name them," Runyard said.

"I want to form a task force to go into the Immortal Plane to find the cause of all these problems and try to stop it from the other side. It will help both our species." He drew himself closer to the web camera, taking up more of our screen. "I want to remind everyone that if the tear grows larger and allows the Immortal Plane to merge with the Mortal Plane, this situation will become exponentially worse. It could *explode*. That is not a probability but a promise. We can't wait on politics for this."

Bryce covered his smile with his hand. Morag lifted an impressed brow, leaning back in her seat. For a moment, I thought the screens were lagging, as there were no responses, but Dorian's sudden outpouring of words had simply stunned everyone into silence.

"I'm in favor," Abbas said abruptly. She lifted her chin with a determined air.

Ruiz nodded. "Same here. If Fenton supports this measure, I think it could help save lives."

"I'll authorize your departure," Morag said. "But I'll be losing my PR stars."

Fenton sighed wearily but nodded. After a moment, a small smile played on his lips. "Well, if anyone can pull off a near-impossible feat, it's this group." He sucked in a deep breath, fortifying himself before going on crisply. "We'll get it done and arrange what's necessary. The board will try to handle the politics. We'll let you guys save the day."

CHAPTER SEVEN

For the rest of the afternoon following our conversation with Fenton, I was restless. I ran laps around the compound to work through my thoughts—Morag had nixed any plans to travel farther outside the guarded area. Dorian's proposal to go back to the Immortal Plane was risky, but we needed to do it. When he originally told me his plans after the Chicago HQ chaos, I was a mixture of terrified and excited. That hadn't changed. My fidgety nerves demanded movement.

After the run, I did combat drills in the gym, finishing off by sparring with Drinn, the burly vampire from Kane's crew who'd been on the last mission to the Immortal Plane. We grappled, and he let me practice my takedowns. He was climbing to his feet for the eighth time when Roxy appeared at the door. She watched as I feigned left then right then left again, Drinn shadowing my movements, then dodged under his punch and took his legs out from under him. He landed gracefully and gave me an approving thumbs-up. As his left hand was missing several fingers, I grabbed his other hand to pull him to his feet before turning to my teammate.

"You telegraph your moves too clearly," she commented, taking a step into the room, her vibrant red hair catching a ray of sunlight through the window. "And you don't stay loose enough in your stance."

"Thanks for the tips," I said dryly, chugging from my water bottle. "Are you here to train too?"

She shook her head. "I've been looking for you. Louise just got back from the hospital. They're putting her in the medical trailer for a few days. Thought you might like to go check on her."

I wiped the sweat from my face with my T-shirt. "Sure. I'll clean up, then go. Have you seen her?"

"Briefly," Roxy said as she turned to leave, her tone strangely blank. "But they took her in very quickly. Figured she needed some time to settle, and I was afraid the nurse might turn me away if I tried too soon. So I let her be."

I frowned at her quick retreat and looked at Drinn. He shrugged his broad shoulders silently. I returned the gesture and left the gym, hurrying through a shower before gathering Louise's favorite sweatpants, book, reading glasses, and toothbrush. I wrapped them in her blanket and headed to the medical trailer.

I knocked on the plain white door. A heart-faced nurse with freckles answered a moment later.

"Are you here to be seen?" she asked politely. I shook my head, cheeks warming, embarrassed that I apparently looked that frazzled. *Should probably have an early night and get some sleep.*

"No, I was hoping to visit Louise. I was told she'd returned from the hospital in Edinburgh, so I brought some of her things over to make her more comfortable."

The nurse nodded. "She's on some pretty intense painkillers, so don't expect scintillating conversation. But I can let you visit as long as you don't tire her out." She waved me in. For our needs, we had one nurse and a few medics on call. There were also a few vampires from Kane's group that served as healers for any vampire illnesses. The two groups were apparently swapping information as part of the ongoing research at the camp.

"She only got back a few hours ago, so she might be napping," the nurse said and pointed to the tiny white-walled corridor. "First door on your right." The clinic only had a few rooms, which were carefully cleaned and organized. The trailer smelled strongly of disinfectant and the strong tea favored by the Scottish staff.

I gently slid the first door open and peeked inside. I hoped the stark clinical surroundings coupled with the strong painkillers didn't trigger Louise's memories of torture at the hands of the Bureau's old board.

Inside the tiny room, Louise lay propped up on a narrow bed with a plain blue blanket tucked around the lower half of her body. She was wearing a hospital gown made of starchy cotton, and her left arm was cradled in a medical sling. I tried to keep my gaze neutral, but all I felt was pain and frustration as I looked at her. She was a vibrant woman sequestered in this tiny room, shot by someone who hadn't yet been caught. It wasn't fair.

I sat in the small chair next to her bed. She stirred as the flimsy plastic and metal groaned noisily.

"Lyra?" she asked sleepily. Her eyes were glazed over, sharpening only slightly when she found my face.

"How are you?" I asked slowly, worried she might be too out of it for a real conversation.

She yawned and winced when she tried to raise her hand on the injured side to cover her mouth. "My whole body feels like garbage," she said with a shake of her head, her voice slightly dreamy. "I don't recommend being shot."

I had to stifle a laugh, wondering if she was okay to talk about the event. Her loopy voice made it hard to take her seriously. White bandages covered her shoulder and part of her collarbone.

"My butt is sore from sitting so much," she complained. She sat up straighter, and I helped her fluff the pillows behind her back for better stability. "I really hate having a sore butt. Have you ever heard of a sadder thing?"

"Never in my life," I said, deadpan. She grinned back at me, her eyes slightly unfocused.

"Major Morag agreed to bring me back when she realized I would be safer in a facility full of vampires. She said vampires would be better at protecting me than hospital security if the shooter came back," Louise relayed.

She'd grown more coherent, but then she delivered a silly grin that encouraged me to smile right back.

"Do you remember what the doctor told you?" I asked.

Her smile faltered for a second. "Oooh, yeah. He frowned the most I've ever seen a person frown before. It was hard to understand his accent. He said the bullet missed my tendons but still screwed up a bunch of tissue." Her hand hovered over the bandages. "The nurse said it'll be a long and hard rehab for me, but it could have been worse." The grin returned. "But as soon as I can use a computer again, I won't be totally bored. There's plenty of hacking I could do to help the cause via an internet connection."

I chuckled, resting my elbows on my knees. It was good to see her in fine spirits. "I'm glad Sike was there to push you out of the way in time," I said. If he hadn't, I might have been speaking to her in a coffin instead of a hospital bed. "He was quick."

Louise frowned. "Yeah," she mumbled and began picking at her blanket. "He's great."

I studied her. She'd been carefree on painkillers just a second before. "Louise, is everything okay with Sike?" I hadn't seen him since yesterday.

She began to nod but stopped. "Well, yes... and no." She licked her lips nervously. "I've started to feel a strange burn in my chest when I'm with him. I hadn't thought much about it. I barely noticed it. But then Sike pushed me out of the way when I was shot. Now, every time I'm around him, the pain... it's almost unbearable."

Heat pricked my skin. Silence fell over us. I processed her words over and over.

Surely Louise knew what this meant. Everyone in our group had watched the dramatic construction of my relationship with Dorian. The pain was the centerpiece of everything. I had seen Sike and Louise getting closer over the past few weeks, but for the most part I suspected a flirty friendship that *could* veer into more. It was hard to picture anyone wanting more than that after seeing me and Dorian together.

Her confession made my body lighten with an odd sense of relief mixed with sadness. I wanted to cry about the shared pain of the curse and mutter my thanks at the same time because I didn't feel so alone anymore. Some part of me had expected to be the only one to ever experience this pain, to live with this complicated relationship. There were a million things I could say to her. I didn't want to tell her what to do or to warn her against a relationship with Sike if her feelings were strong enough. It would be hypocritical, the same thing Halla had done to me. Louise already knew the dangers because of my issues with Dorian. She and Sike were both adults. They could make their own decisions.

"Do you want me to tell you what I know?" I prodded. "If you feel up to it, that is. It's not much, but it could be something."

Louise drew circles on her blanket using her good hand, nodding. "You might need to remind me when I'm not out of my head on painkillers, but I want to hear it now."

I tried to organize my thoughts. It was difficult, considering I'd gained my knowledge in bits and pieces and was still learning as I went. "It seems to happen because of the vampire's feelings, not ours. The vampires have a theory or two about why they *think* the pain happens, but I don't know if any of those stories are true. Or testable. They mostly seem like folklore."

She relaxed against her pillows, her brows wrinkling together as she considered my words. Memories of Grayson's obvious crush on Louise came back to me. She'd never considered him more than a colleague. If she felt the same for Sike, it would be a little more difficult to brush aside.

"Do you *want* Sike to feel this way?" I asked.

Louise gave a frustrated sigh. "If things were different," she said slowly, "I could see Sike being perfect for me. He's smart, goofy, a good listener, and just so freaking cute... especially when he smiles." Her cheeks grew pink.

I smirked to myself. *Sounds like she likes him to me.*

"But"—Louise grew serious again—"I don't know how you stand this kind of pain. It's impractical, Lyra. How could I ever function like this? If this mess ever clears up, I want to go work for the FBI. How can I do that if I risk falling into a freaking coma every time I go near Sike? I know what happened to you. I saw them carry your limp body into an emergency medical helicopter, and you were gone for three days. Sike is wonderful, and I like him a lot. He's really interesting, and we've grown closer over the past few weeks." Her head slumped back against the pillow, exhaustion overtaking her. "But I can't live my life in pain or waiting for the next time I fall unconscious. I don't know what to do."

I considered my options. Should I tell her that Dorian and I were looking for a way to break the curse? That we were experimenting with delayed vampire feeding? I couldn't give her false hope, but I wanted to support whatever she decided.

"It's difficult but worth it for me. I still have doubts sometimes," I admitted. "I guess that's most people in relationships... but this situation is a lot harder than most. It requires a level of sacrifice that I'm confronting on a daily basis. It takes work." Especially when you found yourself hunted by your former employer and thrown into an international dispute. Dorian and I had forged much of our relationship during stolen conversations in our rare private time and through mutual admiration for the other's courage and determination in the face of overwhelming odds. None of it had been easy—most of those conversations had been incredibly hard—but it was worth it.

Louise said nothing. Her eyes looked distant, blinking slowly. The drugs were beginning to make her drift away from the conversation.

I quietly stood as Louise closed her eyes, worried for her and Sike both. I hovered beside the bed for a moment, watching as she drifted off to sleep. The painkillers were powerful. She should rest peacefully. I thanked the nurse on my way out.

Taking several deep breaths of fresh mountain air to help clear my head, I drifted aimlessly around the camp, trying to find some focus for all the frustrated energy generated by my inability to take practical action.

Statically hoping had never been my style, but right now I wished for so many things my head hurt. I wished Louise weren't injured, so I could share with her, with anyone, my worries about my relationship with Dorian. Most of all, I wished I had answers to questions raised by the vague bits of folklore I'd picked up involving humans and vampires. Reporters and politicians and the public kept asking me if humans and vampires could comingle, and I wanted to shout back at them that I had no idea. I was still trying to figure that out for myself.

I wandered out of the gate toward the shooting range. It was inhabited by several soldiers and vampires, though they weren't shooting right now. They were instead learning how to disassemble, clean, and reassemble a pistol. Kane was there, face creased in concentration. The resemblance brought Halla's pinched face to my mind. I distinctly remembered every part of our conversation—no, her lecture—about the curse. I shoved my hands into my pockets and kicked a small reddish rock. I had put off seeking Halla out because it would be unpleasant, and there had been more pressing issues than vampire folklore in the past few weeks. Dorian and I had wanted to go together, but he was too busy prepping for our upcoming journey. I would tell him later... I would also tell him about Sike and Louise at some point, of course, but only once I was confident they were comfortable with more people knowing. *I'm not here to spill secrets that aren't mine.*

Now that Louise was suffering too, it was doubly important that we get to the bottom of the curse. It was strangely validating to realize that the pain I felt with Dorian wasn't some wild fluke. Human-vampire relationships had consequences, and not just for me. Could we study the effect? Perhaps I could pose the question to the Scottish scientists Morag had brought in. Maybe some of the other vampires would know something more. Somewhere out there, someone had to know.

Turning back to camp, I searched the barracks for Halla. She generally avoided humans, so I rarely saw her out and about in the camp. I looked everywhere, eventually finding Eskra in the library reading a book about the Loch Ness monster to her son Oten and the two preteen vampire girls, Ayless and Kren. All three children were enraptured, and I felt bad as I knocked softly on the doorframe.

"Sorry to interrupt," I apologized. "Do you know where Halla might be? I need to talk to her."

If Eskra was surprised by that, she didn't show it.

"She shares a room with Sabal in the east barracks, across the hall from Kane," she said. "There's a sigil painted in white on the door. You can't miss it."

Someone had mentioned to me before that Halla spent a lot of time with Sabal. Maybe it had been Kane? I vaguely remembered our first or second night at dinner when he'd loudly mentioned how happy he was to be sharing quarters with Neo. Apparently it was for the best, as Halla's crabby caretaking method seemed oddly effective for Sabal. Sometimes we even caught the lone twin smiling for a moment or two, a rare event ever since her sister had gone missing in the Immortal Plane during the failed attempt to rescue Rhome's family.

"Thanks, Eskra. Enjoy the story, guys." I left and headed toward the east barracks.

Once there, I scanned each door. I passed Zach and Gina's room, hearing the low, unintelligible hum of conversation from behind the door. A little farther down, I saw the sigil Eskra had referred to. The majority of the chipped green paint was covered in a complex design done in white paint. Sharp lines that reminded me of Viking runes flanked dots and curves that flowed like Sanskrit across the wooden surface. It was beautiful and intimidating.

I gathered my courage and knocked on the wall instead of the door. After a moment, Halla answered, wrapped in a shawl. She drew herself to her full height as she regarded me with a somewhat cold expression. Sabal hovered behind her.

Halla cleared her throat. "Sabal, go lie down. It's your turn to feed soon. You need your strength."

Sabal's mouth twisted into a sour pout, but to my surprise she floated to the other side of the room and vanished from my sight. It must be good for her to have someone to tell her what to do now that her sister, Myndra, was missing. They used to do everything together. I couldn't imagine what she must be going through. Zach and I weren't twins, but if anything happened to him, I would probably need Halla's kind of tough love and badgering to keep me going.

"Yes?" she asked shortly. No hello or greeting, but I hadn't been expecting one.

"I'd like to ask you a few questions, Halla," I said. "Are you available for a few minutes?"

Halla's lips twitched into a scowl. "I know what questions you're here to ask. I won't give you any more advice if you're just going to keep ignoring it." Her eyes narrowed. "Dorian is making a terrible decision, not feeding just for the chance to... well." She slowly looked me up and down in disapproval.

I forced a rude response to the back of my throat. She seemed to take my silence as a temporary victory.

"Dorian is a fool," Halla muttered with a pitying shake of her head. "The pain will never be worth it."

My irritation won out. "You've never been in love, if you honestly believe that," I snapped.

She stiffened and fell quiet. Offended, or stricken by my response? I'd bet offended. I sucked in a deep breath, trying to regain my calm. "I'm sorry for that. I'm here because you have knowledge and experience that could help not only me, but many others. In this new world we're heading into, who knows how many people will be affected by the same problem as Dorian and me? If we can figure out the cause and find a way to reduce or stop it, then we'll remove another barrier between vampires and asylum."

Her shoulders lifted. "And I'll have you know that I loved my husband, Kane's father, very much." She paused for a moment, and her gaze dropped. "He was murdered by humans seeking revenge."

I swallowed the grit in my throat. "I'm sorry to hear that," I said genuinely. "Actually, I'm sorry for a lot of things. For my words and for everything humans have done to harm vampires. I imagine you've lost multiple loved ones to humans."

Halla regarded me carefully.

I steeled myself. "I know that there's no way for me to make up for that, but I'm trying my best." And I meant it. I didn't bother trying to hide the exhausted frustration on my face. *Let Halla see I mean it.* "Truly, I am. Even in the situation with Dorian, although you may not believe that. His strategies for dealing with the curse are hard for me to prevent." How could you stop a vampire from starving himself?

Halla simmered quietly and crossed her arms. A brittle silence passed between us. I wondered if I had lost her. She twisted her lips and sighed suddenly.

"I suppose I regret some of my actions, as well," she confessed slowly. "In my mind, it's hard to separate humans from the people who killed my husband. Sometimes I see them when I look at you. It's not on purpose. I know that Kane respects you, and I should probably trust his judgment more than I have been."

He does? I resisted jumping on that fascinating tidbit. It was nice to hear it from Halla, since she knew Kane best.

"You've made sacrifices for us when you didn't have to," the older vampire said. "I respect that."

The agitation and unease inside me softened. I'd expected this conversation to go much worse than it actually was. Funny how anxious expectations and reality often panned out differently.

"Thank you. I appreciate it. And really, I'm worried for Dorian. I agree with you that he's a fool for not feeding," I said, shaking my head with a huff. "I've told him repeatedly that I don't want him sacrificing his strength for me."

Halla rolled her eyes. "Kane can display a similar stubbornness. I sympathize." She opened the door wider and gestured for me to enter.

As I did, my eyes traced over the patterns once again.

"It's a sigil of remembrance and protection," she said, carefully closing the door. "I had Dorsa paint it to bring Sabal some comfort and hope about Myndra."

"It's beautiful," I said. "I didn't know vampires painted things like that."

Halla raised an astute eyebrow. "There is a lot you don't know about vampires."

I sat on a couch similar to the one in Dorian's room, but this one was covered in a red-and-gray tartan blanket. Sabal sat on her bed on the other side of the room, but she stared without saying anything.

"That is definitely true," I admitted. "Which is why I have a question about vampire folklore. It seems unlikely that Dorian and I are the first couple to experience this problem. I'm ready to hear hard truths, but I need to know all the details. How do you know that I'll die if I stay near Dorian?" I spread my hands helplessly.

Halla sat on the bed on the left side of the room, and her gaze relaxed. "I don't know why it happens, exactly… I told you about the theory of emotional auras because that was the best explanation we had in my time. If you want to know more, I would advise you to seek out vampire scholars in the Immortal Plane." She frowned bitterly. "If there are any left, that is. They may have all been killed by now. War doesn't tend to favor those who hold old knowledge. I've heard that vast quantities of vampire relics were lost or destroyed in Vanim, our largest city. It was the one closest to the tear, which damaged much of it, and whatever was left was destroyed." Her eyes grew pained, and she paled, the emotional toll draining her energy.

"Are there any other examples, folktales?" I pressed. "I want to learn more, but I don't know where to look."

"I only know the story I already told you," Halla said listlessly, apparently too exhausted for any of her usual waspishness. "I don't know any more about it. If I did, I would have said something."

I swallowed the other questions I'd come up with. Apparently, there was nothing more to be gained from this conversation, other than wasting her time.

"Thank you, Halla," I said, feeling a wave of guilt for making her relive her past during this visit. "I can let you get back to your day."

"That would be good," she muttered. "I could use some rest."

I stood, and she followed me to the door. Before I could leave, however, Halla reached out to grab my arm.

"Wait," she said. Strange. Her grip felt soft and caring now, almost like my mother's might. "I know I've been harsh, but I want you to know that I meant to protect both Dorian and you. I'm a stubborn woman. I still stand by my advice that you end your relationship and try to forget each other." She cleared her throat roughly. "I would hate to see one of you get irreversibly hurt."

Her advice used to infuriate me, but I understood her a little better now. She still hadn't convinced me, but I felt a surge of warmth when I looked at her. It startled me to realize that I liked this irritable, dour woman.

I rested a tentative hand on her thin shoulder. "Thank you. And if you ever want to talk with someone, just come and find me."

She didn't say anything but nodded before gently closing the door.

I left the barracks. Having Halla of all people open up to me sent a strange new wave of energy through me. *In the Immortal Plane, maybe we could find more information about the curse.* The scholars might know something. I wanted answers. No, I *needed* answers, and now not just for Dorian and me.

I was halfway to the dining hall when a thought occurred to me. I stumbled to a halt.

I'd accused Halla of never being in love without realizing what that meant for me. In asking her... it was practically a confession of my own feelings.

Was I truly in love with Dorian?

CHAPTER EIGHT

Fenton's confirmation that we'd been given approval to travel to the US to help in the Canyonlands arrived just after midnight. I found out when Zach gently shook me awake and said that we needed to pack and leave as soon as possible.

Lights shone from various windows across the camp as the other selected humans and vampires were similarly roused. In less than an hour, we were all gathered in the cold night air outside the camp's gate. I hitched my gear bag up onto my shoulder, looking around at the assembled team. The other humans were Bryce, Roxy, Zach, Gina, and Colin. Swathed in their thick cloaks, Dorian, Kane, Laini, Bravi, Arlonne, Neo, Drinn, and Sike stood nearby. Sike's desire to go along had surprised me. He'd volunteered with visible determination back at the VAMPS camp, though in the past he often avoided missions likely to involve combat, preferring situations that involved flying or stealth.

Two more vampires had come along, but not as combatants.

Kane stood protectively by Torran and a vampire named Riven. The latter, I learned, was a scholar who looked to be in her forties. She had a willowy face framed by thin braids of brown hair on either side. Dorian no doubt hoped their superior knowledge of the Immortal Plane would come in handy.

There was a strange tension as we walked toward the helicopters that would take us to a military airfield where our plane waited to fly us out of Scotland. The airstrip was empty except for our plane, which had just landed, and the chopper at the end. A sense of loneliness stole over me, despite being among my friends and teammates. Morag solemnly waved us off, looking uncharacteristically vulnerable as she stood there in her striped robe, her feet shoved into combat boots. Bryce was the last one into the chopper, lingering to give his sister a final hug.

We landed at seven a.m. local time on an airstrip along the Colorado border after a ten-hour flight. The cool tarmac beneath me felt like stepping on a piece of home now that I was back in the States. I inhaled the dusty breeze as it struck my face. Our exhausted group of vampires and humans gathered and headed for a waiting chopper, lugging our gear bags.

Even as my head ached from lack of sleep and confusion from the time change, I felt a certain euphoria to be back in the US and finally allowed to do something useful. Assuming the government didn't stop us first. Fenton had assured us he would work things out, but I had so much doubt now when dealing with government agencies. I half expected the chopper to whisk us all away to prison. With vampire assistance, though, that would be only a moderate inconvenience.

"Everyone's accounted for," Bryce muttered. He took up position at the back of the group to ensure that everyone boarded the large military helicopter.

"Where are we headed?" Zach asked, half asleep against Gina's shoulder.

"Moab," Bryce replied, having been the one to coordinate with the pilot. "It's a small city outside the Canyonlands. According to Director Runyard, it's the one most affected by the Immortal Plane tear."

The chopper took off, limiting the conversation to what could be said over our comms.

After another hour or so, I glanced out the window. We'd crossed into Utah and the Canyonlands and were now approaching Moab. My breath caught. Beneath us, the land looked like a war zone. Giant plumes of smoke drifted upward from the smoldering remains of a fire. The pilot maneuvered us through the columns but ultimately had no choice but to dive right through the smoke.

The midmorning sun glinted off Moab, the first city to suffer in the wake of the barrier's destruction. *The first.* The chilling thought made my hope melt. If Moab fell, others would be next. The Immortal tear could take out countless cities. And when the planes finally merged—utter devastation.

"We're heading down now," the pilot said over the internal comms. "Get ready to disembark."

We touched down on an eastern hill that overlooked the town and scrambled out of the chopper, the already scorching sun particularly harsh because I'd acclimatized to cool Scottish days. It must be in the nineties already. I felt like I'd stepped into Hell's oven.

A narrow concrete road wound up the steep hillside toward us from Moab. Around us were a spattering of campsites with fire pits.

Camping families had probably used the sites before, but now military personnel occupied every open spot. I saw the Bureau's symbol on a few uniforms before we approached. Trucks, tents for soldiers, and a medic station filled my view.

"Is that what I think it is?" Zach asked, pointing to something up above. In the west, closer to the Canyonlands, a swirling mass of swollen black clouds gathered in the sky. Lightning flashed across the brewing storm, bright green and purple bolts.

It had only been a few weeks since we'd last seen the tear, but the lightning we'd witnessed previously now looked tame by comparison. And the smell... I gagged. The air had a sour, acidic flavor. This place no longer felt like Earth. The hairs on the back of my neck stood to attention.

I glanced at Dorian, knowing the clouds and lightning were merely the symptoms, that only vampires could see the actual tear. Did he see anything different in that sky? His paleness could have been from lack of feeding. It was hard to gauge his emotions as he looked at the pulsing rift, though we all knew that if we got what we wanted from the Bureau, Dorian's next step involved traveling through that monstrosity in the sky.

Bryce jogged down the hill a few yards and approached the nearest group of soldiers. "My name is Nicholas Bryce. We're expected on invitation of Director Runyard," he shouted. "I need to talk to whoever is in command."

The soldiers studied our chopper as it took off once more, but the tallest nodded to Bryce and took off running. Was Director Runyard here already? Or had he entrusted our mission to someone else we knew?

I surveyed our group as everyone gathered around. The human

side was fueled by a restless desire to see some action. For the vampires, I imagined it was more personal—their fate on both planes depended on the results of this mission.

Sike grunted as he switched the weight of his gear bag to his stronger arm, the other obviously still slightly weaker from his gunshot wound a few weeks earlier. I'd have thought he'd stay behind, especially with Louise injured. The fact that Kane had joined us didn't surprise me, though he claimed Dorian had dragged him into it. Nice try. He'd waited for the chance to stop the tear as impatiently as the rest of us.

The soldier from earlier came running back with Captain Clemmins behind him. Clemmins's dark skin shone with sweat. He wore a Bureau captain's uniform, but dirt and streaks of dried mud marred the fabric. Bryce stuck out his hand. Clemmins clapped a broad, scarred hand into it and gave it a healthy shake.

"Good to see you, Bryce," he said with a grateful nod. His curly black hair, though cropped short, looked like he'd been running his hands through it in frustration. It also contained more gray than I remembered from our last meeting.

"Let's head over to command." He led us down the hill and through the bustling encampment into a large tent.

It was interesting to see the Bureau's supplies in a new light after getting used to the Scottish camo and color. They were using the latest improved desert pattern from the Bureau line of technology, darker browns and tan to blend into the scenery. They'd organized the tent around a table with a screen built into it, currently showing a digital map of Moab. Splotches of transparent red covered much of the city graphic.

"Points of contact with our enemies," Clemmins said and tapped the screen. The red disappeared. "This was our situation two nights ago, before all this happened. Nothing. The first night." The screen popped up with red, slightly less than before. "And the second night." The original amount appeared, staining the city.

I cocked my head. "What was it that came through?"

Clemmins waved over a soldier. The soldier picked up a cooler, the kind you would use to tote cans of soda to soccer practice. He opened it for us.

An egg-shaped rock sat in the cooler. I squinted, stooping closer. The rock was about a foot long with several grooves running across it, as if some grand creator had formed it from interlocking pieces of futuristic armor.

Roxy huffed a laugh. "You're getting your asses kicked by rocks?"

Clemmins flared his nostrils. "You're independent contractors here, but you were Bureau soldiers not so long ago, so I'll give you this reminder only once," he said tightly. "While you're not technically part of my troops, you will still treat superior officers with respect. No swearing in my tent."

Roxy quieted and dropped her eyes to the stone in embarrassment. I felt a twinge of sympathy. I might have made the same mistake without thinking. After all, we'd become used to a loose command structure among our group of rebels and vampires, because we'd created the arrangement ourselves. Things had been similarly informal at the VAMPS camp. Our old roles in the Bureau might not fit as comfortably as they used to.

Clemmins pressed on calmly. "These rocks are actually creatures. They curl up like this at sunrise and stay that way until dark. Last night, these were stony creatures that looked like insects, one and a half feet long. They eat everything in sight and can fly for short distances."

"Creatures?" Bryce echoed.

"Thousands," Clemmins said grimly. "They poured from the tear two nights ago. We alerted Director Runyard. I believe he called you the first chance he got once we'd dealt with the first night's situation." He shook his head, his mouth set in a firm line. "That was the last time we got any rest. Last night was a little better, but the creatures exhausted our forces as we tried to beat them back. We fought them away from important infrastructure, especially the power systems."

"And the fires?" Bryce asked. "How many types of monsters have you been dealing with?"

Bryce's presence made me thankful. He'd maneuvered easily back into the swing of things and focused on the most salient questions. I was worried about the smoldering fires too. The tear's presence had led to wildfires across the surrounding states in the last few months. As I understood from intel given immediately after the fallout of our takeover of the Bureau, immortal creatures had caused those fires. The old board had tried to blame gas leaks and redbills, but I wondered if these creatures were actually the ones responsible.

"Just the bugs, so far," Clemmins responded. "They downed power lines, which caused most of the fires. Our team was stretched too thin, so unfortunately, we couldn't salvage the power system. The creatures seem to crave the metal in the electric grid." Clemmins glared at the dormant creature in the cooler. "The one thing we *have* learned about these creeps is that they have some kind of sensitivity to light. We spent the better part of today sourcing and setting up giant football stadium-style floodlights and generators to protect the remaining parts of town."

Neo crouched and studied the stone up close, as if it would offer up secrets. Riven hovered behind him with her chin in her hand. Her studious gaze swept over the object.

"We can slow them down and dictate their path somewhat, but we don't know how to destroy them," Clemmins said. "Their stone armor deflects bullets. They can *eat* your gun and anything else you try to get them with. They don't seem to be interested in consuming humans but will definitely bite you if you try to pick them up. They can take an arm off."

From the look on his face, I assumed a soldier had found that out the hard way.

"Never seen something like this before," Neo confessed. Dorian and Kane nodded in agreement.

Well, that wasn't good. I worried Dorian might have misjudged and been overly confident. He'd based his ploy to get what he wanted from the Bureau on the assumption that he'd be able to help. A tense moment passed.

"No," Torran remarked suddenly and stepped forward. "I recognize that creature well enough."

Riven cleared her throat loudly. "If you're all finished trying to do my job, this *is* why I spent ten hours on a plane to get here. The closest name for them in your language would be 'the empty swarm.' They're like your locusts here in the Mortal Plane," she explained and ran a nail across the hard surface of the creature. "They only swarm occasionally, but when they do, they prey on stone, metal, and wood. They seem to skip over leaves and flowers, usually attacking just the bark. Luckily, their appetite doesn't include animals. They're incredibly destructive to cities, as you might imagine. Their combined efforts and insatiable desire to feed can take out sophisticated structures in mere days."

Clemmins twisted his mouth. "I'm afraid I've seen that for myself."

Torran nodded. "Urban vampires won't recognize them, because the cities had magic items that warded off the empty swarms," he said. "Out in the rural areas, we had to hang special charms made from certain immortal stones, but we still saw them from time to time."

"Magical items," Clemmins muttered, his eyebrows raised as he glanced skeptically at Bryce. The officers hovering nearby stared doubtfully at Torran and Riven. This piece of information apparently went one step too far for them to believe. *We're standing next to literal vampires, people.* They could see the storm around the tear as well as I could.

Dorian had mentioned the concept of magic to me once or twice before in passing, but he never went into detail about how it worked. I got the sense that even in the Immortal Plane, it wasn't an everyday occurrence for vampires. I studied his face for any reaction, but his calm stare homed in on the empty swarm creature in the cooler. To him, this was just one more challenge to overcome. None of the vampires looked particularly concerned, which went a long way toward reassuring me.

"The good news is that, as you've already discovered, the creatures are sensitive to light of any kind," Riven confirmed.

Clemmins stroked the stubble on his chin. He obviously hadn't had the chance to shave today.

"But artificial light only frightens them. It won't wound them."

Riven looked to Torran for confirmation, and he nodded. "I believe sunlight could be more effective. The creatures have never felt the sun in the Mortal Plane. It would probably burn them up if we could find a way to get through their tough outer shells." She paused, looking somewhat bashful. "I must admit, I've never actually faced these creatures before. The empty swarm is a rare thing in the Immortal Plane, and the city I'm from was far from the areas they usually frequented."

"So, you're not entirely certain how to defeat these things, and you don't know more than we've already discovered ourselves," Clemmins summarized stonily, obviously not impressed by the lack of certainty.

Bryce and I exchanged a concerned look. How could we beat a creature with impenetrable skin?

"I can only offer the advice that I've read," Riven replied, a touch defensive.

"You need to understand," Laini said. "Many of the threats you're facing from the Immortal Plane are little more than myths, even to us. Our world is dangerous, yes, but the creatures you have fought with us, like the soul-scourger or the shrieking decay or the empty swarm, are rarely sighted. They mostly live deep in the earth or in the wild wastes far from our cities. We'll tell you what we can."

There was a loaded silence in the tent for a moment or two before Clemmins spoke again.

"Well, I guess we should just be thankful we're not fighting a shrieking decay, whatever that is. It sounds horrific."

"It is," Roxy and I said simultaneously, sharing a look as we remembered our desperate struggle to bring down the monstrous, acid-breathing flying lizard.

"What about corrosive substances?" Gina suggested. "Does the Bureau have anything heavy-duty on hand, or something you could bring in before everything goes to hell again this evening?"

"Battery acid might do it," Zach said. He tapped his foot on the ground in thought.

"How could we shoot it at the empty swarm?" Neo glanced at the weapons strapped to the soldiers' chests. "Do we have weapons that shoot acid?"

"No, that's illegal," Clemmins said firmly. "But we're used to being resourceful for the sake of our nation's safety. We can figure something out." Despite his confident tone, it sounded as though he were trying to convince himself.

Neo had a point. Even if we had acid powerful enough to cause damage, how would we strike the creatures en masse? I stared at the screen and the angry red splotches of destruction on the map. I was finally on the front lines again, but I had no idea how I could help.

Dorian cleared his throat. "I would like to gather some redbills to survey the area from the air. There are likely some hanging around near the Canyonlands. We can get a better idea of what's going on more quickly and safely than drones or scouts in helicopters. Especially if the empty swarm eats metal." The assembled vampires nodded, looking more somber than when they'd walked in. This would be more difficult than we'd hoped.

Clemmins nodded his assent, but his grave face said everything. He was nervous, and understandably so. They'd brought in the vampires as a last resort.

I exchanged a look with Zach.

Where did that leave the human volunteers?

The next several hours were filled with finding where we would be most useful. Our human team helped any way we could, which primarily involved rounding up the few civilians left in town and helping construct the line of defense. The vampires had gone searching for redbills, returning around noon mounted on several they'd procured from a flock hiding in the nearby Canyonlands. By mid-afternoon, we humans were feeling the effects of the jetlag and piled into a dusty, hot tent to grab some fitful rest in preparation for the coming attack. We squeezed in beside groups of tired soldiers weary from their long night.

By the time sunset came, the scene in Moab looked more like a post-apocalyptic hellscape than Earth. It was as if the Canyonlands had a nightmarish sister dimension. Gathered with the humans from my team and a group of Bureau soldiers near the Moab Visitors Center, I stared at the scorched sky, marveling at the thick smoke still staining the air. The sun, a burning dark red ball, sank toward the hazy orange horizon. And over it all hung the sizzling, snapping tear. The lightning pulsed in psychedelic shades. An even stronger acid smell burned my sinuses, drifting in from somewhere in the town. Something strange, a scent I couldn't place... something not of this world. I shivered despite the heat. Utterly alien was the only way to describe it.

"Attention, soldiers," a pleasant but firm voice called. "Listen up." A man stepped to the front of our cluster. He had brown hair and a thin, patchy mustache clinging to his upper lip. He had a slightly anxious air, and his smile came off as more twitchy than reassuring. I guessed him to be a year or so older than Zach. Clemmins had briefly introduced him earlier as First Lieutenant Paulson. Although we were technically suspended from our roles in the Occult Bureau, we'd been told to hover nearby, ready to coordinate with his unit.

"We are the main body of tonight's defensive line. I want you to protect this power system with everything you've got," Paulson said, surveying every soldier's face, his hooded eyes narrowing slightly as he passed over me and my group. "These lights could be the only thing that keeps this town alive tonight."

How could we forget? Everyone had pitched in at some point today, helping set up the line of giant floodlights to surround the downtown area. Our aim was to protect as much of the town as possible. If I craned my head, I could see the line of lights receding into the distance.

Circling above on the redbills, the vampires worked on aerial surveillance. Once night fell and all hell broke loose, they would report news of where the empty swarm was heading via their comms. Clemmins had mentioned something about possibly procuring lights for the vampires to carry on the redbills to shine from above, but I didn't know if anything had come of that idea.

I stared at the currently unlit bulbs of the floodlights nearest to me. Nothing in my time at the Bureau could have prepared me to screw in industrial lightbulbs to help defeat an army of stone bugs. Life continued to be full of surprises.

Some things never changed, though. The first thing Clemmins did was institute a structure for us. After Roxy's quip, he probably felt the need to whip us back into shape. Zach and I would supervise our team but answer to First Lieutenant Paulson. Roxy grumbled quietly about how we'd just returned to the status quo, but we followed orders. Paulson and Clemmins provided us with comms that were patched in to command. They also provided us with weapons... sort of.

In the parking lot of the Visitors Center were the piles of makeshift weapons, many of which were desperate improvisations to compensate for the fact that regular weapons were off the table. The first pile offered small explosives, flare guns, and a curious number of firecrackers and sparklers. I wondered if they'd raided a teenager's illicit collection of fireworks.

The second pile was more promising but rose to sillier proportions in some of its offerings. A few grenades, a limited stock of the shock patches we'd once used on redbills, some crowbars, sledgehammers, a gas-powered hedge trimmer, a few golf clubs, and several baseball bats. It looked like a very threatening garage sale. I debated over my weapon. The hedge trimmer looked fun, but growing up in a high-rise in Chicago, I'd never used one before. It might be best to leave that for someone else. I pictured myself squinty-eyed, swinging a crowbar like a video game character, but realistically a sledgehammer could deliver more force. On the other hand, the shine of the golf club wedge beckoned to me the way grenades beckoned Zach.

I've gone insane during my time in Scotland. I tested the weight of the club in my hand as Paulson cleared his throat. When we first met, the slight sense of discomfort he gave off at being pushed into this intense leadership role reminded me of myself only a short time ago. Remembering myself that way felt so alien now. Perhaps because I was the face of a vampire refugee movement, had been suspended from my job, and currently clutched a golf club, while he wore an official Bureau uniform and his voice wavered just the slightest bit when addressing the troops.

"If you try to hit the bugs with explosives, aim only for the mouth," Paulson announced. "If you use metal for your weapon, I advise you to aim for anything *but* the mouth, since they snack on metal. And might take your hand along with it if you don't move fast enough." He shifted his weapon, a battered-looking flamethrower, in his hands.

Roxy gave a low whistle—too quiet for the first lieutenant to hear, thus avoiding any complaints about insubordination—before continuing to dig through the piles of tools. She clearly wanted the flamethrower. Maybe I did, too. Just a little. It did look really cool.

"I guess this will do," Roxy muttered with a grunt. She held a sledgehammer in one hand and a collection of sparklers in the other, a crowbar hanging from her belt. "Maybe I can stab their insides with a sparkler if the sledgehammer breaks the outer shell."

"One can only hope," I whispered dryly and pulled down my Bureau strike team visor. Right now it helped reduce the glare from the setting sun, but when night fell it would shift to dark vision. Thank goodness they had extras for us. Fighting an army of all-consuming stone bugs in the dark sounded objectively terrible. A few of Paulson's soldiers nodded to us. Although a few still carried normal weapons, they didn't seem too confident even with their guns. They'd seen things these past two nights that had deeply unsettled them.

"The coolest thing about this fight is that we get to use the latest night goggle technology," my brother said as he selected a hefty wooden baseball bat from the pile and tried a swing.

Gina counted the number of fireworks and explosives among the inventory. She frowned worriedly. Would there be enough for us to hold through the night?

Over the next few hours, shadows gathered in pockets of the town, growing until the floodlights above us turned on. I squinted under their bright light, the intensity burning my eyes. No wonder the bugs hated it. The generator roared to life. Paulson nodded in approval as he surveyed the area.

I stood beside Roxy, my club raised. Nothing happened. She cocked her eyebrow and glanced at me expectantly. *Where are the bugs?*

"What's the chance hundreds of Bureau soldiers lost their minds in the desert heat and hallucinated these things?" she asked in a low voice.

I shook my head. "We saw the rock in the cooler. Riven and Torran said they recognized the creatures."

Roxy grumbled something about how she'd just been making a joke and fell silent.

Five more minutes passed. Roxy checked her watch and twirled the sparklers in her hand. She tapped her foot. Another minute passed. She sighed. I used to call this background noise the Roxy soundtrack when we went on missions together. She hated to wait. As she opened her mouth to complain of boredom, our comms crackled to life.

"Scout reporting in," Neo said, tension humming through his voice. "We've got eyes on the swarm. They're uncurling and heading toward town. All teams should be on high alert. It's about to begin."

CHAPTER NINE

I waited with bated breath for the empty swarm. A hum of uneasy silence surrounded us. I gripped the golf club handle until my knuckles whitened, grinding the wedge head against the asphalt. The nearby soldiers muttered under their breath to one another and held their guns tightly.

Roxy scanned the sky with a scowl, swinging the sledgehammer impatiently, pendulum style.

After weeks away as a civilian, I couldn't deny that I was happy to be back in the fray. Here, I could do something to help, unlike back in Scotland. My years of finely tuned combat and strategy skills were of little value if I didn't get to use them. I bounced on my feet and strained to listen for the approaching swarm. Nothing.

The communication line sprang to life with a sudden buzz.

"I just flew over the main quadrant to see if we had any bugs over there," Bravi relayed gruffly. "No bugs yet, but there's a person lying in the middle of a street, not moving. Are you sure all the residents were accounted for?"

Paulson pressed his comm against his ear. "A person?" He scowled and stared out into the darkness past the lights, as if to glare at the oncoming swarm. "We need someone to check that out." He dragged a hand down his face and anxiously stroked his sparse mustache.

I nudged Roxy gently. "Do you want to go?" I asked and stepped up to Paulson. His appraising gaze swept over us, and I could see his internal struggle on his face. Send his own soldiers or the recruits? Zach and Gina talked quietly to Bryce as I dragged Roxy up to Paulson.

"We'll do it, sir," I said. Roxy nodded. I prayed she wouldn't add a smart comment about how she would do anything to break her boredom. Paulson had already pegged us as troublesome.

I wanted to be useful. This person might be dead, but they could also be injured or drunk. And the trip would also be an opportunity to scout for the first signs of bugs. Although the vampires were watching from above, they couldn't see everything on the ground. If Roxy and I caught the bugs earlier than the defense line, we might stop more of the empty swarm. Technically, we would still be within the safety perimeter of Paulson's operation.

Paulson mulled it over, pressing his lips together. His eyes flashed to the floodlights and the darkness beyond and then back to my eager face. "Fine, but report back as soon as you find them, and take them straight to the medic tent."

"Understood, sir," I said, and he nodded, dismissing us. I turned to Roxy. "Ready?"

Roxy nodded, a small grin on her face. Although I could tell she was uneasy about scouting for the mystery body, she was also ready to do something besides just wait. Paulson had plenty of strong soldiers near this line, our other teammates included.

We jogged away from the group, and while I was pleased at our side mission, I was unimpressed that no one saw us go. Instead of paying attention to their surroundings, everyone had their eyes completely trained on the floodlights. Lieutenant Paulson should really be engaging more with his troops, instructing them where to keep watch. On the next block over, I spotted a half-devoured street sign. Main Street sounded promising.

Roxy followed me as I maneuvered between abandoned cars, stopping only to stare at the chunks missing from the devastated machines. The swarm had torn through the frames easily, consuming massive quantities of metal. I passed a van that closely resembled a piece of lace. A shiver ran down my spine, from both exhilaration and unease at not knowing exactly where the threat awaited us. Clemmins had given us some idea of what it would be like, but I wanted to see it for myself.

"God," Roxy muttered as she hopped over another pothole. "They've eaten the streets."

It was true. Potholes marked the road like Swiss cheese. A fallen tree at the side of the road had a gaping cavity through its center. What had once been a drive-through coffee shop was now a crumbling shell. A front door swung on its hinges in a local hardware business. Half-eaten nails and screws littered the sidewalk out front. The streetlights remained dark, unable to offer their services after the grid went down. The empty swarm had consumed everything in its path.

After a few minutes, the sound of rushing water reached my ear.

A stream ran alongside Main Street with a quaint bike path next to it. A grove of hardy trees shifted in the breeze, relishing their survival. In the slowly dimming light of dusk, I could see that their leaves had curled and yellowed at the edges. Could they have been poisoned by the smoke in the air? I didn't know how trees worked. I grimaced at an abandoned half-eaten bicycle wheel lying on the path.

There was something else near the path, a human-like form lying face-down in the grass. Something about it seemed odd as I loped toward it, careful to keep a wary eye on our surroundings.

"Are you kidding me?" Roxy asked as I came up to the object. "It's a *mannequin*." A mannequin in a pale gray suit, which covered most of its body except for the plastic hands and hair. It was easy to see how Bravi could have made the mistake from a distance.

"There may have been some looting the past few days," I said with a grimace. "Doesn't look like the bugs have a taste for mannequins, at least." I prepared to call Paulson; he would want to know it was a false alarm to calm his nerves. A twig snapped in the distance.

Insidiously, a buzz began to swell around us, starting low and building. Roxy sucked air through her teeth. I froze. The sound came from everywhere at once. It was a terrible creaking sound, like an army of monstrous cicadas. Something flickered beside me, and I turned sharply toward it. A shadow slipped past us low to the ground, disappearing into the hazy night. I glanced at Roxy as if to say, *Did you see that?* She nodded, and even in the half-light that didn't quite activate my dark vision, I could see her face tighten. We steeled ourselves and crouched slightly, ready for anything.

A moment passed. Nothing happened. We moved as rapidly as

we could toward the source of the sound, farther inside the thicket of trees. The whining increased. My skin erupted with goosebumps. There was something unnatural about the sound.

Dusk rapidly darkened the surrounding area. The dark vision in our visors switched on, turning everything to ghostly shades of green and gray. Shadows shifted around us. A skittering to the left drew my attention, and I turned toward the motion. My breath stopped in my throat.

An empty swarm creature was perched on a nearby tree branch. It looked like a stone cricket, except it was nearly a foot and a half long. A thick head connected to a disturbingly hunched back. It had eight legs, haphazardly assembled slices of jagged rock. Its black eyes sat upon two wandering eyestalks. And the worst? A gaping round mouth full of lamprey-like teeth.

The creature turned its terrifying mouth toward us. The teeth began to whirl, making a grinding noise. The source of the buzz. My heart slammed against my chest. Roxy swore.

Our comm lines crackled and activated. "Paulson, calling for reinforcements," he barked. "The floodlight we're protecting is malfunctioning. We need all the help we can get."

Roxy and I turned without hesitation, but a sickening crack made us freeze. I wheeled around to see that several other bugs had gnawed through the base of a tree. The bark creaked as the trunk split. It fell between us with a groan, sending up dust and leaves and forcing us to jump apart to avoid being crushed.

As I leapt back, a heavy weight slammed into me from the side. I lost my balance and fell awkwardly in the dry grass with a pained gasp. The whirring sound began again, closer this time, as a swarm creature clung to my left arm and side, practically pinning me down. It was heavier than I'd imagined, twenty pounds or more.

Scrambling backward, I tried to throw it off. The creature moved its eyes toward me, operating the stalks like antennae, the movement almost curious. The mouth stopped whirring. It didn't appear to want to bite me. From my belt I grabbed my small flashlight, shining the sharp white beam directly into its face. Beyond a slight recoiling of the eye stalks, it seemed unaffected. My heart sank.

"Here's some breakfast!" Roxy shouted and slammed her sledge-hammer into the monster. With a stony chitter, it let go of my arm and rolled to the side, twitching briefly. However, despite the force of the blow, there was no visible damage to its armor.

She hovered over it and spat in the grass. "This thing is one ugly SOB. Let's get out of here."

"I couldn't agree more," I groaned as she helped me up.

The buzzing sound grew behind us and then all around us. Before we could register what was happening, more trees began to shake and fall. We ran for the edge of the grove. If we wanted to live, we had to get away from the trees.

"Repeat, I'm calling for reinforcements!" Paulson bellowed into the comms.

Roxy and I ran, dodging falling branches and leaping over those already on the ground. How many of these monsters were in here with us?

I sucked in a sharp breath as something yanked me to the side. My flashlight fell from my hand, and the dark vision visor slipped sideways, leaving me with only one eye able to see out of it. I fell into a crouch from the force. Horribly close to the flesh of my thigh, a creature greedily gnawed on the end of my golf club. I yanked it back from the ugly monster's mouth, but the bug had already eaten the head, reducing the club to a stick.

As I scrambled backward on the uneven ground, the creature tensed its back legs and hopped, aiming above our heads. I jammed what was left of my club into its underbelly to knock it off balance, and Roxy swung the heavy sledgehammer with a grunt, slamming the bug back as hard as possible. It rolled away, tumbling into the creek below. Immediately, a grisly sucking sound rose from the water, as though the bug were trying to suck up the water like a vacuum cleaner. It stopped after a few seconds, leaving only the regular grinding of the empty swarm around us. We exchanged a glance, then darted down to the creek and away from the trees. The creature lay submerged in the water, eye stalks moving with the current. Otherwise, it was completely still.

"Could water—?" I said, cutting myself off as I turned to Roxy.

"I think so," she replied.

We might have something! Triumph surged through me. This trip wasn't a complete waste of time.

"I've got a giant swarm coming toward Section F," Dorian said into the comm.

My heart lifted upon hearing his voice.

"That's us!" Paulson shouted.

"Lyra Sloane, reporting in—" I started, but Paulson cut me off.

"Just get back here, now!"

Returning to action, Roxy and I hauled ass back toward the Visitors Center. Bugs hopped past us left and right, no longer tempted by our tiny metal sticks with a feast of abandoned cars before them. One bit into an unlit lamppost, and I leapt aside as it fell. The lightbulb shattered on the ground, sending shards of glass across the mauled street. The air teemed with buzzing. The empty swarm moved like grasshoppers, but I spotted a few of them gliding with transparent wings. Those wings didn't seem capable of supporting their stone bodies, but I'd seen stranger things.

We rounded a bend and spotted the line of floodlights. The areas covered by the bright rays remained free of bugs.

Paulson's shouts carried through the night, a note of panic evident in his voice. A team of techs gathered around the base of the light directly above the first lieutenant's group. My team would be nearby. The light flickered briefly. The techs shouted to each other.

"It's the base!" one cried as he bent over a panel in the pole.

These things could destroy the entire city if the lights went down. The destruction would ruin people's lives. And it was only a matter of time before they moved on to the next town like a pack of unstoppable locusts. How long until they ate their way across the country?

"Don't let them near the extension cord or the generator," Paulson snapped on the comm. His voice was high and tight, the carefree attitude long gone. "It'll cause a chain reaction and destroy all the lights connected to this generator. We can't afford a huge hole in our defense, so don't let them get close!"

I ran up to the group. Zach and Gina had their backs to the techs, protecting them from any oncoming threats. The light flickered in and out.

"There's thousands of these things," Zach said, shaking his head in frustration. "And they're heavy as hell."

"Sir," I said, addressing Paulson. "We found a way to kill the bugs. If we drown them—"

"Do you see any water around here, Sloane?" Paulson said, exasperated. "Forget that and keep them off this light." He turned back to the techs, dismissing me.

The soldiers were barely holding the stone bugs at bay. Colin smashed a crowbar into one, but the creature reared and ate half the bar in one bite.

"They keep eating our weapons," he snapped, visibly frustrated even though we'd been warned of exactly that. He grabbed his backup weapon and shot a flare into the open mouth of the same creature. It reeled backward from the hit and skittered on the ground, knocking over two oncoming members of the swarm.

This strategy wouldn't work. In a game of exhaustion, supernatural stone locusts already had the advantage of their natural physiology and numbers. The empty swarm would easily overwhelm us. The floodlight above us flickered. My nerves burned with determination. Using water was a strategy that held potential. I pressed my comm into my ear.

"This is Lyra Sloane calling for Captain Clemmins," I said firmly. "I have a lead on how to stop these things."

The line crackled. Paulson looked around angrily. "Stay off the line, Sloane!" he yelled. "We need to keep it clear for command."

"I'm trying to help you!" I shouted back.

"Clemmins is busy," someone else said on the line. "He doesn't have time to talk to you."

Another voice chimed in to say something to the same effect, but all I could hear was my frustrated blood pumping through my head. Roxy sidled up beside me, launching a firecracker she'd snagged from the ground at an oncoming creature.

"Nobody is going to listen about the water," I told her.

Her face contorted smugly. Was she about to point out that this was how she felt under my command? Because this *really* wasn't the time. Instead, she slapped a hand on my shoulder.

"If they won't listen, we'll just have to blow these little creeps up all night long," she said with a mad grin. "You light the firecrackers, and I'll throw them in." She tossed me a full pack of the red firecrackers.

I nodded and got out my lighter. There were a few abandoned cars near the floodlights, and the bugs that were feasting on them inched toward us in the shadows.

"Light up as many as you can." Roxy chucked her firecracker at one bug that scuttled toward us, its gaping maw whirring. Unfortunately, she didn't see the one behind it. I quickly threw another right after hers. The fireworks sparked and exploded, ripping those particular members of the empty swarm apart. It was only a temporary victory, however, as four more moved in to take their place.

Our only advantage, except for the nearest fading floodlight, was the bright light shining behind us. Although the light didn't hurt them, the bugs certainly preferred to stay out of it. But if the lights failed...

I had to try Clemmins again. Firepower wouldn't work. I lit another firecracker while Roxy threw two more.

"Please, I need to speak with Captain Clemmins," I said on the line. "I found a way to stop the swarm."

Again, a chorus of officers told me to stay off the comm. This time I understood the tone underlying their dismissive words: distrust. They brushed me off as a meddling dissenter instead of putting aside the fact that I was a suspended Bureau soldier and listening to what I had to say. I scowled.

"Better to ask forgiveness than permission," Roxy said, having overheard the exchange along with everyone else on the line. She clicked her tongue when she saw how few firecrackers were left. The vampires remained quiet on the line, but I guessed they were reluctant to interfere in the human hierarchy. It was hard enough for them to be involved already. I could only imagine what Dorian must be thinking about this.

Despite our best efforts, the swarming creatures grew closer, and we pulled back to the generator. Paulson's team hovered around the base, shouting for us to hold our ground. We would, but we were running low on things to fight the stone bugs with.

Colin lured an insect toward him with the promise of a golf club, and Gina stepped in to fire a flare gun straight into the bug's mouth. Zach was doing something similar with Bryce. Our former captain baited a line of hopping swarm monsters by waving around the remains of another crowbar. When they opened their mouths and hopped forward, Zach tossed grenades down their throats.

A bug hopped toward a tech, slipping past Zach and Gina on the left. I smashed it straight in the mouth with Roxy's sledgehammer as it zeroed in on the light's base, briefly knocking it back.

"Duck!" Bryce bellowed. I did as he said, and he rammed the whirring blade of the hedge trimmer into the bug's mouth. There was a hideous shriek of metal as the blades met the bug's grinding teeth, but the bug rolled backward from the force and stopped near an abandoned car. Its oncoming comrades paid it no mind as they continued to hop past. They had no sense of one another. As long as there were enough to swarm, they would continue to do just that.

The buzzing grew louder and louder. Shots rang out. Soldiers fired at the impenetrable creatures, but the bullets only grazed the bugs' stony skin or ricocheted back dangerously. A soldier nearby screamed in pain as a bug took off one of his fingers along with his metal knife.

We couldn't fight much longer if the enemy kept eating our weapons.

Clemmins's staff could dismiss me all they wanted, but I saw what happened to the bug back in the creek.

"Dorian," I said into my comm. "I have a plan. When Roxy and I fought one near the creek, it fell into the water and completely stopped moving. We think water kills them, or at least makes them still."

"Sloane!" Paulson yelled. "What did I tell you about using the comm?"

"Paulson, get your chatterbox vampire fans off the line," someone bellowed. "We don't have time for this."

"Water," Dorian echoed, ignoring the interruption. "I hear you. Okay, what do we need to do?"

"Have you or anyone else seen any ponds or streams on your scouting? Something deep enough to submerge them?"

A lit firework fell from Roxy's hand as she fumbled to avoid Colin. He was forcing back another bug with a baseball bat, his swing powerful enough to have led to a home run in any other scenario. I swiftly kicked the sputtering explosive into an oncoming monster's mouth.

"We're not going to last much longer with our limited supplies," I warned Dorian. "This needs to happen fast."

"I saw something when I swept over the south of town," Bravi said suddenly. "A pond on a farm, I think. We could try to herd them there."

"We can use the lights," Dorian said.

A male voice I didn't recognize came on the line. "Hey! If we need water to stop these things, the Colorado River runs north of town."

Clemmins didn't have time for me, but at least his soldiers did. After this was over, I would probably get a lecture that would go down in history for both length and intensity. Roxy and I looked at each other.

Worth it.

"Do whatever you can," I said. "I'll communicate with First Lieutenant Paulson."

Roxy covered my back as we made our way over to Paulson, who was close to the right side of the base.

Paulson was trying his best with his massive flamethrower. He tried to scorch an oncoming line of nearby bugs, but his fire was useless against their closed mouths.

"Roxy, get ready with some sparklers," I said. I snatched up a discarded soda can and threw it in front of the monsters. They opened their mouths upon sensing the metal. As they did, Roxy threw a bundle of sparklers into Paulson's oncoming spray of flames. The combined effort created a small series of explosions, forcing the bugs back.

It was too dangerous to stop to talk, but Roxy and I worked alongside Paulson to try to keep the insects back.

We fell into an exhausting routine as the swarm thickened: bait with metal, throw firecracker, defend against any bugs that slipped through the firepower. Our supply of explosives dwindled.

Around me, soldiers' faces were marred with grime. The oncoming swarm of the bugs was never-ending, their terrifying faces displayed in the night vision visors with a demonic glow.

"We might have something," a tech shouted excitedly.

Directly above us, the floodlight sparked to life for a blissful moment. The bugs stopped, then retreated as the added light shone on them. Then the floodlight popped and went black. A tech swore. For a horrific second, my entire body went numb.

"Nice try, bugs!" Kane roared somewhere in the sky.

In an instant, beams of light fell on the surrounding area. I looked up to see Kane and Dorian atop two redbills, bright flood-lights strapped to their underbellies. The bugs scattered back into the darkness for safety.

Dorian and Kane swooped down, expertly maneuvering the redbills to push back the monstrous insects. Dorian swept past, and the sight of his triumphant face filled me with a fierce surge of joy.

"There's a creek past a bike path and a tree grove," I said into the comm. "If you can start pushing them back there, it's a start until we can herd them to the river."

"Got it," Dorian said. "I think it's working. Sorry we couldn't get here sooner. We were outfitting the redbills with stronger floodlights."

Thank God you did.

Harassing the bugs with the portable lights, Dorian and Kane pushed the creatures farther into the darkness toward Main Street.

"We need to hold until dawn," Paulson muttered next to me, in his weariness apparently forgetting his irritation at how I'd ignored his commands. "If your water idea works, we can throw all the dormant bugs into the Colorado River and drown those suckers."

I stared at Roxy. Her brow was coated with sweat, and she met my gaze with already tired eyes.

Dawn would be a long time coming.

CHAPTER TEN

"I feel like hell," I said, rubbing the blooming bruise on my arm. The bug that had attacked me in the grove earlier had left a parting gift.

"You look like hell," Roxy fired back. That was as good as a heartfelt, "I feel your pain, friend," from her. She rolled up the leg of her uniform and placed a cold bottle of water against a scrape on her shin.

I stared at the raw flesh with a frown, still processing what we had just been through. Adrenaline was a mighty drug when it came to combat. It was only when you came out the other side that you understood how intense it had been.

Dawn was seeping across the sky, and we were now back in the command tent, battered and bruised but alive. I sat perched on a gear box opposite Roxy and Colin while Zach, bags under his eyes, leaned his head on my shoulder. I expected to hear a snore any minute now. Gina rested her head in her hands, her usually sleek blonde hair hanging in greasy, dusty strings over her fingers. Between the jetlag, blinding lights, and fighting all night, our bodies had seen better days.

One of the soldiers on Clemmins's staff offered us black coffee in small cardboard cups. Zach took two gladly, nursing one between battered hands and handing the other to Gina. I declined. The caffeine would morph my weariness into jittery nerves. Bryce took a cup as he walked up to our group. He sat on Roxy's other side.

"Nothing like battling stone insects to keep you young," he said dryly and lifted his cup to us. He drained it in one go, apparently immune to its heat.

"You're like a walking advertisement for energy drinks," Colin mumbled, sipping slowly on his own coffee.

"I hope the vampires come back soon," I said, scanning the pale sky through the door of the tent for Dorian and his team.

With the powerful torches on the redbills, the vampires had managed to keep the empty swarm from causing too much damage to downtown for the rest of the night. Moab had been saved by the skin of our teeth. I imagined Clemmins was thrilled that Director Runyard had brought us in time.

While Dorian and Kane held back most of the swarm attacking our area, Bravi and the others had used the redbills to herd the rest of the bugs toward the edge of town, forcing the empty swarm toward the Colorado River. Many of the disoriented bugs attempted to hop out of the water, only to get pushed back in by others trying to escape the floodlights.

It wasn't entirely clear what it was about the water that disabled the bugs, but we believed they drowned. They certainly didn't come back up once they were in the river. When dawn broke, any creatures still loose in the city curled up into their shells again. Now Dorian and the others were helping spot any lying dormant in the city. Clemmins had sent out groups of soldiers with construction equipment to collect and drown bugs in any available water source. Whatever they needed to get the job done, however inelegant. Somewhere, some poor kid's inflatable pool was probably being used for supernatural pest extermination today.

The bank of floodlights, aside from our broken one, held through the night. Unfortunately, anything unprotected by the light appeared to have sustained damage, including most of the property in residential areas. I rubbed at my tired eyes. Moab would have to rebuild, but at least we'd discovered a way to stop the empty swarm before it erased the whole town from the map. My heart hurt for all the displaced people. Nobody should have to worry about their home being destroyed.

"How's your leg?" I asked Roxy, not letting myself get too caught up in what we hadn't been able to save. We'd done our best.

She shrugged. "It could be worse. I'm just glad those freaks weren't flesh-eaters." She yawned without covering her mouth and spread her arms wide as she stretched.

Paulson eyed us stonily. I'd pegged him as fatigued at first, but now I wasn't so sure. He seemed resentful, especially toward me and Roxy.

Clemmins, his uniform jacket hanging open and stained with dust, entered the tent, and we all got to our feet, respecting his wishes to follow Bureau protocol.

"What's the report for last night?" he asked, looking at Paulson. A soldier offered Clemmins a cup of coffee. He took it, his hand steady.

"We were able to contain all the bugs throughout the night," Paulson replied. "The vampires herded them back, and we're in the process of drowning any stragglers."

Clemmins downed his coffee and nodded with a flicker of stern approval. "Excellent work." He hovered near the planning table. His eyes swept over us. "Thank you for the help last night. We appreciate it."

Paulson stepped up to Clemmins. "Captain. I'm sure you've heard that Sloane and Taylor were a great help last night, but they clearly don't know how rank works. They disobeyed my direct orders," he said stiffly. "They made their own decisions instead of immediately calling in for backup. If they are to continue working with us, I request that they learn to treat officers with some respect."

I said nothing but was so angry I had to grind my teeth to stuff down several choice comments about officers who let their swollen heads get in the way of accomplishing mission objectives. However, Clemmins—now staring blankly at Paulson—had already reprimanded us once. If Lieutenant Paulson's complaint was strike two, I didn't want to inadvertently provide strike three.

The captain's lack of expression morphed into a serious gaze, and he crossed his arms. "Paulson, you are aware that all these people, including Sloane and Taylor, are former Bureau soldiers, yes?"

Paulson blinked, caught off guard by the question. His face fell at the realization that Clemmins wouldn't be taking his side. "I believe I was aware of that, sir."

Clemmins nodded once. "And are you also aware that they were involved in the crucial and justified uprising against the corrupt Chicago board? I know you'll be just as pleased as I was to learn that they took part in numerous active missions removing redbills from civilian areas prior to leaving the Bureau."

"I... uh... no, sir. I was not fully aware of their previous experience."

Roxy and I shared a slightly smug look as Clemmins continued relentlessly. I hid my small smile behind my hand, and Roxy dropped her eyes but grinned.

"How long have you been an officer, Paulson?" Clemmins asked. "How many successful missions have you led?"

"Well, um," Paulson stuttered, "I was promoted a month or so ago, sir, and... well... I think last night could be considered a successful mission to some degree—"

"What rank do you think these two women held?" Clemmins demanded, cutting the other man off. "And how many successful missions do you think they've been a part of?"

"Uh." Paulson flushed. Clemmins gave him an inquisitive look, clearly expecting a response. "I didn't actually think to ask."

"Exactly." Clemmins exhaled through his nose, his tone softening. "I'm dismissing your concern and you, Paulson. Go get some rest today. You need it. We'll have a lot of work to do again tonight."

Paulson slunk away without another word. He didn't need to know we were currently suspended. We may have broken rank, but we'd also saved Moab.

I barely had time to savor my sweet victory. Dorian walked into the command tent with a victorious but battle-weary air, his cloak worn around the edges. I marveled that it was still able to become even more tattered, after everything we'd been through, without falling apart. Laini, Bravi, Sike, and the others followed him.

"Thank you for your service," Clemmins said, stepping forward and shaking Dorian's hand. "We appreciate your hard work."

Dorian nodded, a bemused twist to his mouth as he returned the handshake. "We did our part, Captain. We scouted from the air and directed the soldiers to any locations with eggs. I don't think we missed any."

Clemmins smiled appreciatively. "What do you vampires plan to do next?" he asked. "I have a few ideas."

I exchanged a curious look with Roxy, who raised her eyebrows without attempting to hide her surprise.

"Such as?" Bryce asked, another half-finished cup of coffee in his hand.

"Based on this performance, I'd be happy to offer you positions in the Bureau," Clemmins said, his tone warm. "For the humans, this could mean major promotions, should you choose to return to the Bureau." He looked to the gathered vampires. "I'd like to employ vampires, too... when the politics are sorted out."

Zach straightened his back, all ears for both the praise and Clemmins's offer. A small swell of pride came through me. Although the last board's actions had left a bad taste in my mouth, Clemmins was a man with high standards. We had impressed him, and that meant a lot.

But a job at the Bureau? My palms went clammy as reluctance made my body sink. At some point in the past, my old self would have taken that offer easily. I didn't know if going back to the Bureau would be the right choice for me. It felt wrong... like a sweater that used to fit perfectly but got laundered wrong and now pinched and chafed. Our recent adventures spoiled me with a break from hierarchical command structure, the kind that Paulson preferred. The collaborative process between our groups while we were on the run was more chaotic, but it meant everyone had a chance to voice concerns. Could I follow orders barked at me again? My sense of respect for authority deteriorated completely after the Bureau's corruption came to light. If I returned to my job at the Bureau, it might suffocate me.

"We look forward to that day, but in the meantime I'm moving forward with my task force to the Immortal Plane," Dorian said firmly. He turned to face the room. "Who's coming to the Immortal Plane with me? I'd advise you to get your things. We're leaving from here. As soon as possible."

He thought he was going to drag us off to the Immortal Plane without any rest after we fought through the night? I didn't know whether I wanted to kiss his stupid face or punch it. His tenacity was unmatched. After a transcontinental flight, fighting stone creatures, and leading a search group on redbills, Dorian still wanted to move forward. Did he think we were going to hold hands and skip off to battle baddies in the Immortal Plane? Vampire bodies might require less rest, but human bodies had to prepare for a journey.

As hot as my vampire Superman was... I was completely exhausted, and so was the human side of our team. Though I wanted to see the Immortal Plane again, it would take time to gather our strength, not to mention any supplies we might need.

"Now?" I asked, my voice rising with stress. *Take the hint, Mr. Charges Ahead.*

Dorian nodded. "It's perfect timing. We're already here. The sooner we find the surviving vampire community, the better. They could help us avoid our enemies and help us get into the Immortals' city to gather information about the tear *and* how the Immortals first contacted the Bureau."

Clemmins was silent, then snapped his fingers and gestured for his staff to leave. The three Bureau soldiers left the tent, letting the canvas door swing shut behind them. "I admire your focus, Mr. Clave, but such an endeavor will require extensive planning, as well as authorization from various members of the Bureau board and likely Congress," he insisted. "We'll need official confirmation. There are five people I can think of off the top of my head that I need to call before I can even consider beginning the process."

Thank God for bureaucracy.

Dorian stared at him, unbothered. "I'm not asking for permission. I, and any others who choose to join me, will be leaving as soon as we can. We will rest, gather supplies, and then we need to jump on this opportunity. We're right here by the tear. It's grown, now low enough to the ground that things like the empty swarm can pass through. Trust me, there are much worse creatures on the ground that even vampires prefer to avoid. We need to stop the problem at its source. Somebody needs to figure out what's happening in the Immortal Plane, and we are by far the most qualified for the task." He paused. "Do you want more cities like Moab to fall?"

"We need at least twenty-four hours," I argued. He wanted to go, but I refused to let him rush us even if he was motivated. "We can't just rush through this, Dorian." His eyes met mine, and he seemed to consider this. He gave a tiny nod of acknowledgement.

"And what about the summit?" Bravi asked, her voice strangely flat.

I wondered whether Dorian had failed to tell her of his plans. The hardness in her eyes seemed to suggest so.

"Not all of us can go to the Immortal Plane," Kane said. "We need to keep the group small and stealthy. Whoever doesn't go on the mission will represent our cause at the summit." He raised a hand. "I'm going to the Immortal Plane," he added, hastily claiming his spot.

Bryce crumpled his empty coffee cup with a laugh. "Captain, they're on the right track. It wouldn't be hard to throw this mission together." His face flickered with excitement. "I mean, we're already independent contractors. I'd be happy to go, as an experienced human operative, to oversee the mission in the interests of the board."

He was on board, too? It would be good to have him along. I looked around the room, judging faces. Zach stared at the ground, thinking deeply. Gina and Colin exchanged hesitant glances. A wild grin spread across Roxy's face.

Dorian glanced at me with confidence. "So Kane and Bryce are joining me and Lyra in the Immortal Plane. Anyone else?"

He hadn't even questioned whether I would go with him. It warmed me that he knew I was as eager as he was to figure out the mysteries of the Immortal Plane. I'd wanted to return ever since he first showed it to me.

Bryce clapped his hands together. "I wouldn't miss this for anything. Another world? Count me *in.* Morag will be sick with jealousy."

"Well, you guys can't have all the fun," Roxy said with a laughing huff. "I'd like to see how well my combat training fares against these Immortal goons."

"I'm in," Laini said. I tried hard to suppress my surprise. I figured Laini might want to stay behind, but... Dorian was her only remaining family. She probably would rather risk it together than apart.

"As am I." Arlonne stepped up beside her.

"We can probably only fit two more on the team," Dorian warned, glancing over everyone impassively. "We leave tomorrow morning. The rest of you can discuss which two will come to the Immortal Plane and who will attend the summit."

"Neo and I will stay here," Drinn said, sharing a look with the other vampire. "We saw what happened to Castral, and we barely escaped with our lives last time. We'd rather go to the summit, then return to help our clan in Scotland."

"Well, I'm coming," Bravi said, stepping closer to Dorian. "As if I would let you go on your mad schemes without me."

"Actually," Dorian said, placing a hand on her stocky shoulder, "I have a more important request for you."

A more important request than going to the Immortal Plane? It must be big if he could only entrust it to Bravi.

Her eyes narrowed. "I don't like where this is going."

He grimaced. "I suspected you wouldn't," he said. "I need you to act as the head of the clan back in Scotland. Take Riven, Torran, and the others to the summit, then take them back to Scotland. Find a new portal to send groups through for feeding. Work with Morag on the asylum claim. Keep everyone working together and training."

Bravi gave him a sharp look. "Oh, so you're dropping all your responsibilities on *me*, so you can go and be a reckless fool in the burned-out shell of our homeland?"

"No," Dorian said, giving her a serious look. "I am doing what must be done if any of us want the chance to return home and rebuild. I ask you to care for the clan in my absence because there is no one I trust more."

Bravi blinked several times, and I swore I saw tears briefly, but they never left the confines of her bright green eyes.

"Fine," she said roughly, shrugging off his hand. "But if you die over there, I'll find you and kill you again myself."

Dorian grinned, his appreciation for her loyalty showing clearly on his face. "Understood, dear friend."

She nodded stiffly, then stepped into the background, clearly unwilling to engage in the conversation any further.

Clemmins looked around. Faced with our combined resolve, he slowly nodded with a sigh. "I see," he said. "Well, I guess it's time for me to use *my* board privilege. I will authorize your mission and source your provisions, as long as you report back during your journey." He furrowed his brow and looked questioningly at the vampires. "If that's even possible."

"Unfortunately, communication is difficult in the Immortal Plane," Dorian explained. "We did some basic tests while we were in Scotland, taking human technology through to the Immortal Plane to see if it still worked."

"It didn't," Neo said succinctly. "We tried, but human technology can't communicate through the barrier between planes."

"In fact," Dorian said, eyes narrowing as he recalled the unfamiliar information, "according to the human researchers back at the VAMPS camp, any technology that uses electricity or... electromagnetic waves"—he glanced at me for confirmation, which I gave with a short nod—"won't work in the Immortal Plane. The same way that magic doesn't work in the Mortal Plane."

"So, there will be no way of communicating with the Bureau

while you're gone?" Clemmins asked, sounding unenthused by the idea. "No backup, no extraction plan, limited resources, and the risk that even if you do find useful intel, you'll have no way of getting it back to anyone at the Bureau who could then use it to help close the tear or fight the creatures coming through it before you die horribly?" I blinked at the length of his monotone deconstruction of our plan.

"Your concerns are justified, I won't deny that," Dorian said. He looked at Clemmins squarely, and they exchanged the look of two leaders who knew they only had bad cards to play. "But we can't simply do nothing. We vampires have our ways of getting information out, and we will get it back to you however we can. We both want the same thing: to save both vampire and human lives. Right now, you're fighting fires as they spring up. We have to go find the source."

Clemmins interlaced his fingers with a solemn look of understanding. "I know." He sighed deeply. "I envy you. You get to go on the offensive while I'm left playing defense, stuck with all the politics and paperwork." He ran a hand over his short curls, pursing his lips thoughtfully. "All right, I'll arrange things on this side. We'll get you to the Immortal Plane."

Hope and fear swelled inside me, the feelings warring with one another. On the one hand, the prospect of finding answers thrilled me. We could save the world. Literally. But danger and unspeakable power waited for us in the Immortal Plane. Could our team survive it?

My eyes softened as they landed on Dorian and the rest of the gathered team. We would figure this out together.

CHAPTER ELEVEN

C lemmins pulled out his phone and stepped out of the tent.
With a smile, I sat back down on the box next to my brother as the others began to talk quietly among themselves. Zach frowned and flicked my knee.

"Don't get too excited to jump into bizarro land," he chided me. "You may be capable, but that place is lethal."

I studied his face. "You're not coming with us?" I'd assumed he would take one of the empty spots.

Zach looked at his dusty boots. "It's not that I'm afraid to go... well, I mean, I am. But it's not just that." He glanced at Gina, and she shuffled closer to sit beside him. "The group needs to stay small, and there's nothing I bring to the group that others don't already provide. Roxy is better at combat and survival. You've got leadership and strategy covered."

I began to protest, but he held up a hand.

"Honestly, Lyra, I'm not fighting fit again yet." He massaged his thigh where he'd been shot just a few months before. "My leg is nearly healed, but I'm not ready for a fast-paced, rough mission. Especially if the Immortal Plane is as bad as everyone says."

"We both think we'll be of more use here," Gina chipped in. Apparently, they'd engaged in telepathic communication, the way couples sometimes did. "We can be the human face of the group at the upcoming summit. After all, Zach spearheaded the public relations campaign with Major Morag, and I'm prepared to take on more public speaking duties."

Unfortunately, they made a lot of sense. My shoulders fell in disappointment. "I'd feel a lot safer in there knowing we had each other's backs," I said, "but I understand."

Dorian drew everyone's attention with a sharp whistle. "If you're coming with us, get some rest. Those who don't need it can come gather supplies right now," Dorian said. "Even if you're not joining us, please come help us prepare."

A shiver of apprehension ran through me. We only had twenty-four hours to prepare ourselves. Who knew when we would return? I needed to talk to Dorian about this mission. There was a lot we needed to cover before we set off for the Immortal Plane.

Sike, rubbing his arm nervously, went over to Dorian. "I'd like to go, too."

I cocked my head and stared at him while he faced Dorian. His plucky sense of self seemed changed. What had happened? I remembered Louise's uncomfortable expression during our discussion of her pain.

"Are you sure?" Dorian asked with a pointed look. It wasn't unkind, but it seemed he'd thought Sike would stay in the Mortal Plane. "This is going to be very dangerous, and we'll be moving fast and quiet. I thought you would want to be with Louise while she recovers back in Scotland." I hadn't told Dorian about their situation, but apparently he'd found out somehow.

A shadow of pain flickered through Sike's eyes. He shook his head. "No, she… it's too difficult. She doesn't want to see me. She's in pain when I'm around."

Bravi frowned at Sike, but her eyes were soft. "What do you mean?"

"What, she doesn't like you anymore?" Kane asked gruffly. "Did you offer to murder her enemies? Women love that."

Laini shot a weary look at Kane, who seemed completely serious in his romantic advice. Roxy snickered but caught herself and turned it into a cough upon seeing Sike's face fall.

Remind me never to let Kane give Dorian relationship advice.

Sike rubbed the back of his neck. "It's complicated." His voice turned harder, more passionate. "Look, I don't know if she even wants to be friends or what anymore. I just want to help out, and I can't sit still right now. I know I'm not the strongest fighter, but I'm smart, I'm quiet, and I can be practically invisible when I want to be, which is ideal for this mission. I won't be a burden."

Louise's rejection had wounded his pride, but he lifted his determined face to Dorian. I felt my heart squeeze with compassion for our friend. He just wanted to make Louise happy… even if that meant leaving her and discovering his own destiny in combat.

Dorian squeezed Sike's shoulder roughly in a brotherly fashion. "Of course, Sike. Nobody thinks you're a burden. You can only improve a team."

The smaller vampire broke into a relieved grin. "Thanks. I'm ready to get to work."

The air shifted. Sike's impassioned declaration sent an electric charge through the room. Who could resist the charm of a guy ready to take on the world to prove himself?

Bryce smacked his fist into the palm of his hand. "I think everyone's ready for a new adventure."

I nodded in agreement. My muscles felt lighter as I stood and stretched. Although my body was sore and still woozy with jetlag and crashing adrenaline, the upcoming mission into the Immortal Plane eclipsed the pain.

"Maybe we'll even be able to bring the vampires that are in hiding back to Scotland with us," Laini said hopefully. "And if they've been evading detection this entire time, perhaps they can help us infiltrate the Immortals' city."

"If they exist," Kane chimed in.

Laini's theory was sound enough, though Kane had a point. If these refugee vampires did exist, I just hoped the Immortal enemies weren't counting on us to lead them straight to the hidden group. In the back of my mind, I wondered whether the surviving vampires existed and whether they could help us unlock the mystery behind the Bureau board's connection to the Immortal Plane. What I did know was that I was going to have to use every bit of my strength and wit to find out.

Filled with new energy, I began helping with preparations.

"Get some rest," Gina told me, but I couldn't be persuaded. I stifled a yawn. Okay, maybe I could be persuaded, but I would help as much as possible before I passed out on a cot.

My body might have been tired, but my mind was alive with ideas and wondering what awaited us on our mission. *Who* awaited us. As the day wore on, I passed Dorian several times as he delegated instructions. I liked that he was taking over for a moment, and I even appreciated a few lines of advice from Kane. They knew the Immortal Plane best. I was happy to help, but I itched to discuss our plans together.

After a good six hours of sleep, I woke in the late afternoon to join the others. I united with some of my human teammates and a few Bureau soldiers for a decent meal over a fire in the evening. Scraping up the last of the rations, I headed to the mess station to rinse my dingy metal tray and placed it with the other dirty ones on the side. I wiped my hands roughly on my uniform pants. My mom might not have raised a lady, but she did raise a soldier.

"Decent food?" Dorian asked behind me, his voice nearly making me leap.

I shrugged as I faced him, trying to keep my racing heart calm. "Military grub. Can't complain, though," I said.

He gestured over to a small stony rise beside the camp. "Care to join me?"

I nodded and followed him as he headed out into the soft night. The murmuring of voices faded behind us as we climbed up to a small collection of rocks nestled in the hillside's edge. It gave a perfect view of the city... and its destruction.

We'd tried our best in Moab. I only hoped our best would be enough in the Immortal Plane.

"I'm nervous about leaving behind all our tech," I admitted as we settled on the smooth surfaces of the large rocks beneath us. "It's scary to think we'll have no way to communicate with the Bureau or even each other."

Dorian offered a confident half-smile. "Well, at least your guns will work. It's not a hopeless situation in there, just very different."

"The guns will be useful for as long as we have ammo," I said dryly. "And if our silencers malfunction or break, we won't be able to shoot without drawing the attention of everything for miles around." I looked toward the strange greenish glow, backlit by burnt orange, that outlined the rippling thunderclouds concealing the tear. The smoke from Moab had mostly dissipated throughout the day, clearing the air enough to allow us to admire the strange phenomenon.

When Dorian first took me through the tear back when we first met, there were no thunderclouds—the tear hadn't been visible at all. That felt like a lifetime ago. When I thought about pre-vampire Sloane back in the Bureau, I hardly recognized her. When Clemmins had offered us our jobs back, even offered promotions, part of me knew I should have been happy. Instead, the idea of going back now —maybe of going back at all—felt wrong. It certainly wouldn't help further our goals to gain the vampires' asylum and bring about a peaceful world for humans and vampires. The Bureau was in the process of changing, but Congress would be watching it like a hawk. I could probably get more done if I circumvented all that bureaucracy. If it were up to me, I'd get a Fenton-like donor to bankroll an independent mission to fix this mess. *Maybe I can buy a lottery ticket before we go.*

The best way I could help our cause was by going to the Immortal Plane with Dorian and our team, even if it looked terrifying from our current vantage point. Would the little that Dorian had told me about the Immortal Plane be enough to prepare me for being there? Not just for a few minutes in the sky, but *really* being there? We had no clear idea how long our mission could take—it could be days or several weeks. I needed to know more.

"What can I expect in the Immortal Plane?" I asked quietly. My hand feathered over his long fingers, the cuts and calluses of his hands comforting me. He was silent for a long moment, gathering his thoughts. I didn't rush him.

"I'm not sure what I can say that'll prepare you for it. The Immortal Plane is... so very different from everything you're used to," he confessed, the lightning from the tear illuminating the sharp lines of his face. "But not everything is like these creatures coming through the tear. Not everything wants to kill you on instinct. Things can be beautiful in a strange way over there."

"Cool," I said. "And what about the things that do want to kill me?"

He smirked. "Don't worry. You're *you*, and I'll be there."

I was somewhat skeptical that not everything would want to kill me, especially when I mentally catalogued every fight I'd been in with an immortal monster. The soul-scourger with its burning mist, the shrieking decay and its acid breath, and now the empty swarm and their almost indestructible stone shells. The monsters inside the Immortal Plane certainly wielded advantages.

Dorian smirked at me, and I realized I was staring off into space, letting my mind run wild with thoughts.

"You're plenty tough enough," he assured me. "I wouldn't bring you if I doubted you for a second. I wouldn't want to do this mission without you."

I studied the shadows beneath his skin, barely visible in the dim light of the tear. He needed to feed before we waded into treacherous territory. He caught my frown and nodded, understanding immediately.

"I'll feed whenever I can while we're in the Immortal Plane, don't worry. Being at anything less than full strength in the Immortal Plane is far more dangerous than here. The dangers we face there will be tough on everyone," he said. He squeezed my hand tightly. My chest buzzed with a dull ache. "You're right about my recent feeding habits. It took me a while to realize it. I must admit, I can be a little stubborn."

He was right about that. A warmth bloomed up alongside the hollow burn in my chest. Even though he could be as stubborn as they came, moments like these told me I'd made the right choice. Our struggles together would be worth it if we worked together.

"A little?" I replied, raising a brow and pursing my lips.

He chuckled, and I wanted to trace the laugh lines at the corners of his eyes.

"Very stubborn," he amended. "But this time, I know I have to support our team to the fullest on this next mission." He scowled irritably. "Unfortunately, I also know that means I won't be able to steal you away to kiss in spare moments."

I smiled at a few memories. There was nothing I wanted more than to be close to him, but the Immortal Plane had no mercy for romance.

"Not that we're likely to have spare moments in the Immortal Plane," I pointed out reluctantly. Keeping things professional for our mission would help both us and our team. There would be no romantic breaks in an entirely new dimension filled with danger.

That meant our last moment for the foreseeable future was now.

I leaned my head against him, enjoying the way he stroked the back of my hand with the rough pad of his thumb. For a moment, we stayed like that. The distant sounds of camp became a dreamy soundtrack in the background.

Dorian pushed my chin up, and our noses brushed. Why waste a perfectly good opportunity? I smirked, leaning up to kiss him. He murmured approvingly as his kiss burned against me. I raked my hand up his neck and wove my fingers into his dark hair, pulling his lips against me harder.

The pain swelled in my chest. I pulled away an inch and sucked in a sharp breath. Dorian's eyes lowered in disappointment, but there was understanding there, too. My memory of discussing love with Halla swam to the forefront of my mind. A pleasant heat washed through my body, soothing the pain. Although we hadn't named the feeling yet, there was the beginning of love here.

But the curse hung over our heads like a determined storm cloud. I looked up and ran my hand lightly over his strong jaw. His cheekbones had grown sharper over the last weeks. My heart burned, and I pulled my hand back to myself.

"I'm worried about you," I breathed. "It might be hard on my body while you're at full strength in there. I'm not sure you'll be able to handle it." Still, hope flickered right alongside the burning sensation in my chest. With Dorian, I always felt a sense of the impossible, that we could do anything if we were together.

"The distance created by feeding will be temporary, just for while we're in the Immortal Plane," Dorian said. "And I will not admit defeat with us. Once we get back to a place where we don't have to worry about safety, I *will* go back to fasting if it means we can… spend time together."

His determination sent a shiver of pleasure down my spine.

"Well, maybe I'll be less judgy about you starving yourself after being deprived of your touch for a few weeks," I joked. I was pretty sure I wouldn't be, but there was no point arguing now, when he intended to feed the next chance he got.

His smirk twitched, but his eyes turned serious. He squeezed my hand for a second. "Our relationship—our *thing*—is important to me, even when we need to prioritize other problems."

I laughed, pleased by the little moment of budding romance in the midst of our lives filled with action and war.

"I didn't realize we had a *thing*," I teased and winked. "I feel the same way, Dorian."

The warmth overtook the pain almost completely. I inhaled his cedar scent, hoping it would overwhelm the lingering acidic odor from the tear. I wanted to enjoy Dorian in this moment, while we weren't in combat or immediately strategizing to save lives.

I leaned my head against his chest again. "We can be close once we're out of combat."

It was as much of a promise to myself as it was a reminder for him. But I couldn't forget that it could be a long time before we found ourselves free of conflict. At least we could share that sobering worry together.

Dorian wrapped his arm around my shoulder. "We'll be together, even if we can't be close like this. There's no one else I'd rather have beside me."

In only a few hours, we would journey to the Immortal Plane. I hoped his confidence would prove justified. I squeezed his cloak between my tight fingers and forced myself to appreciate our tiny moment of peace for the night.

Tomorrow brought a new, dangerous adventure.

CHAPTER TWELVE

T he smoke had entirely cleared from the air by dawn the next morning. I rolled from my cot with a groan. Stepping up to the door of the tent, I took the clearer air as a positive sign. Our group had rested, restocked, and prepared for our journey. Well, as much as one could prepare for an adventure into a treacherous supernatural world. I'd slept like a baby as soon as my head hit the pillow last night in the tent I shared with Zach.

During our quick breakfast of instant grits, Bryce insisted we couldn't leave without informing our families. We had to say our goodbyes. After all, if we didn't come back…

I wouldn't have dreamed of leaving without calling my parents, though I suspected they would be upset. After a few days in Chicago with them, we'd left for Scotland, and now I had to leave on shady vampire business again. Yeah, they'd be thrilled.

I hovered beside Zach as he called from his cell phone.

"Hey, Mom," he said with a smile. "Yeah, so we've had a slight change of plans… yeah, we only just got a free moment to call. So, basically…" He briefly summarized the plan for my parents. There were benefits to not being on the Bureau payroll anymore. He didn't give them exact details, but it was a hell of a lot more than we ever could say when we were soldiers. My parents were understandably worried, since Zach and I'd had to leave right after we returned from our harrowing adventure on the run.

As was often the case, I was grateful for his easy way of speaking. The recent media training had helped him in all areas of life, including the best way to gently break the news to our parents that their only daughter was headed off on a long-term mission. The fact that he was going to briefly visit them after the summit before heading back to Scotland would hopefully help to lessen the blow.

I checked my watch. If it was seven thirty a.m. for us, then my parents would just be sitting down for their usual eight thirty a.m. breakfast.

Zach offered the phone. "They've got you on speaker so they can both hear you."

I took it from him. "Hey, guys."

"Oh, Lyra," my mother said, her voice pinched. "Your father and I saw that press conference. We've been worried sick. Why didn't you call us?"

The oncoming guilt trip was well earned. I should have called, but time fell away from me as we prepared for our journey. International calls were abhorrently expensive, too, and my bank account was in no place to charge international fees. I hated that I'd made my parents worry. "I'm sorry, I should have. International calls are a little difficult at the camp though."

"We understand, kid," my father said. "Looks like you handled the situation like a pro, from what we saw before the cameras cut off."

I stifled an awkward laugh. Dropping to the floor and hiding was not only what you were supposed to do when guns went off, it was the only thing I *could* do, as a technical civilian. Still, it was a little embarrassing. "Yeah, it was madness. The Scottish police did an excellent job of securing and managing the scene, even though the shooter got away. I was glad to have them there." I didn't let myself bitterly add that I'd been unable to actually contribute myself.

My mother cut in. "You looked so collected and confident during those questions. Who taught you to speak to the media like that? I was so proud."

I cringed inwardly. Did they see the question about Alan? I nearly flubbed that one. I bit my lip as I stared up at the sky over Moab, which was blissfully free of any stone insects.

Even though I knew my parents were unhappy that I was continuing with the vampire missions, they were still proud of me. Zach shot me a smile, and I turned away from him, hiding my red-rimmed eyes. How many times would I have to say goodbye to my family? It was the nature of the work, but almost losing them once had been the worst experience of my life.

"Guess I must have picked it up from my talks with Congress," I said, using an exaggerated humble brag to hide my actual feelings. While they were heaping praise on me, why not mention that, too?

"Lyra," my dad said, his tone serious, "I'm obviously worried about you going on this mission. Your mother is, too. I'm sure it comes as no surprise that we would rather you didn't go into an unexplored, separate plane of existence inhabited by terrible monsters. Of course we don't agree with everything you do, but we do respect that you're fighting for what you believe in."

"I second all of that," my mother said. "We know that you're tough and smart and brave and that the people... and the vampires around you will keep you safe, just as you will keep them safe."

Part of being a Bureau family meant that letting your child go on dangerous missions was par for the course. I doubted it made it any easier, though.

I felt my throat tighten with rising emotion. "Thank you. I love you guys."

"Come back in one piece, okay? No extra teeth, if you can help it," my father said wryly.

I heard my mother huff and a brief thud on the line.

"And you'd better take that seriously," my father said with a hint of laughter in his voice, "because your mother just swatted me for that joke."

"I'll try," I said and glanced toward Zach. "I'll put Zach back on, okay? I love you." I passed my brother the phone and rubbed my eyes. I missed my parents dearly. They'd suggested in certain subtle ways that they didn't approve of my relationship with Dorian, but they knew without a doubt that he would do everything he could to protect me on this mission, even with his life if it came down to it. Perhaps that was some small comfort.

Zach ended the call and wandered back to me. "Tough call, huh?"

I nodded and stared at him in the early morning light. "You're sure you don't want to come with me to the Immortal Plane?" I attempted a half-smile, but it fell flat.

He smiled tightly and nudged my arm playfully. "The slots filled up too fast," he teased. A pensive frown crossed his face. "At least one of us should be here to keep things moving. We need our Scotland group in top form after that press conference. Besides, I feel pretty good about all the work I've been doing with Major Morag. She's a beast with military strategy and diplomacy. I'm learning a lot."

I felt a pang of happiness for him, mixed with the bittersweet realization that this would be our last reunion for some time. My brother was growing in ways that were taking him away from me, but I was excited for him... even if it made me sad that he wouldn't be beside me this time. I'd taken his constant presence for granted.

"I like my place in life," Zach said with a genuine grin. "I have my hands full. I'll keep up the investigation into the Edinburgh sniper and keep working with Fenton and Clemmins to make sure the Bureau stays on track."

I nodded with a soft smile. "You can come on the next Immortal Plane adventure," I promised him. "When you've toughened up and have two working legs again."

Assuming my party comes back safely...

He hugged me suddenly, squeezing tight. "Keep your wits about you, Lyra."

"I will," I whispered and thumped him hard on the back, grateful for his comfort.

Over Zach's shoulder, I spotted Sike hovering awkwardly nearby. He waved, afraid to break up our familial moment.

"Sorry to interrupt," Sike said, "but could I borrow the phone?"

There was only one person Sike would want to call on a phone. Zach handed it over without a word.

"I don't know if she'll even pick up," Sike admitted as he took the phone.

It struck me how bizarrely small it looked in his gangly hands.

He pressed something on the screen and frowned. Music began playing. "Uh, how do you find the dialing thing again?"

I sidled over beside him and helped type out the number in the phone app. He was the vampire with the best grasp of technology, thanks to Louise, but most of his experiences were on computers with large screens. A smartphone was too much.

Sike pressed the phone to his ear when it began to ring. Zach shuffled back into the tent, busying himself with double checking my food provisions. He couldn't fool me—his eyes were also rimmed with red from oncoming tears. Would he be okay with me shipping off to the Immortal Plane? I wanted to throw my arms around my brother, but something about the stiffness of his shoulders told me not to come closer. He needed a moment alone. I stayed by Sike.

I can't exactly leave Sike with the phone. I stepped back, making it clear that I was on hand if he needed any technical help but trying not to eavesdrop. I hoped his call wouldn't upset Louise. Should I have stopped him?

"Hello?" Sike pressed the phone closer to his face, talking directly into the microphone. "Yeah. It's me. Sorry." He pressed his lips into a flat line as Louise said something.

It was impossible not to hear bits of the conversation. I couldn't hear exact words, but Louise didn't sound happy.

"It can't work."

I heard Louise's strained voice, then it grew muffled. The air felt suddenly hot. I glanced up at the sky, wondering if I should comfort Sike after the call or if he would prefer to be left alone.

A pause followed. "It was a tough mission. Yes, I'm okay," Sike muttered.

He quieted as she said something else. "I understand, Louise. Good luck. I wish you well, even if I can't be next to you. I only wanted to say goodbye. Just in case."

Sike ended the call and handed the phone back to me. To my surprise, a broad grin broke out on his face. Then I saw the tightness around his eyes. *Poor Sike.*

"I can't wait to get to another plane," he quipped, then quickly walked a few steps away, signaling that he didn't want to talk about it. He put his back to me, facing the outcropping where our chopper had landed the day before. It was our designated meeting point for the mission.

Roxy tapped me on the shoulder. "I just need to make a call real quick." I handed the phone over to her. Sike hovered nearby, but his eyes were trained on the desert landscape with a wistful look. I wanted to ask him more about his situation, but I held back. It wasn't my place to over involve myself.

"Mom, stop trying to talk me out of it," Roxy said tersely, her conversation drifting to my ears. "I want to do this. Period. End of story. Now, hand the phone over to Jacob and Suzy. And then the rest. Yes, *all* of them." There was a long pause. "Jacob? Tell Mom to stop crying." She turned away from us.

I tucked my hands beneath my arms, feigning a chill on them so I could actually hug myself tightly. Something about Roxy's call made me want to cry more than calling my own family to say goodbye.

"Yes, I will try to come to your ballet recital when I get back," Roxy muttered with a shake of her head. "No, Suzy, I *can't* bring my gun to show off to your friends. I'll just have to impress them by flexing my muscles."

I flattened my lips tightly to keep from laughing, knowing that would earn me a punch in the arm from our fiery teammate. Despite her tough outer shell, I could see what an amazing sister and daughter she was. Her family didn't approve of her becoming a Bureau soldier or her dangerous lifestyle, but she made it work by proving her worth over and over.

"Jacob, stop interrupting," Roxy snapped and then composed herself. "Come on, honey. I already told you that I love you. Yes, I think you'd be a great soldier, but don't tell Mom. We'll talk about it when you're older. For the love of—let Georgie on the phone before he starts hysterics. I can hear him starting to wail in the background. Did you guys take away his action figures again? Karate Steve is *not* to be touched while I'm gone."

Kane tapped his foot in the red dirt impatiently. I raised an eyebrow as he stared at Roxy with his lip curled. Did he think we were weak to call our relatives? Or did he hate that the human woman who often matched him in sparring talked openly about attending a dance recital?

"I want to use the human phone," he admitted through gritted teeth when Roxy finished. "To call Halla." He struggled with his confession. It was as if both the phone and his need to call his mother made all the cells in his body riot. Roxy stared at him, her face and eyes pink from her emotional call. She wiped her cheeks roughly and smirked.

"You can have it, but only if you admit you're a big old mama's boy," she taunted. He huffed.

"It's not shameful to have a good relationship with your parents."

He lifted his chin proudly. "At least she knows better than to beg me off a mission."

Roxy rolled her eyes and dangled the phone in her fingers in front of him. "Well, we can't all have monstrous mommies that are happy to send us off on mysterious missions in alternate dimensions."

He said nothing, only extended his hand expectantly with a stony look. To my surprise, Roxy sighed wearily and moved to stand next to him. "Here, let me show you how to do it. She should be at the barracks, right?" She muttered in a lower voice, "You big baby."

I snorted and shook my head at their antics. Behind them, Bryce talked on another phone. It might've been the same burner phone that he used in our wild missions on the run. He bent his head as he spoke. I could see the word "Morag" on his lips. I turned away to give him a moment of privacy.

Everything was too intimate out in the open, but we had no choice. These could be our last calls for a long time... possibly forever. I swallowed the grit in my throat as my stomach sank. My gaze landed on Dorian and Laini, who stood next to each other.

"I'm not sure how long we'll be," Dorian said into the phone. He must be talking to the vampires left at the barracks. "Bravi will be there with you soon. Trust Morag with everything." There was little emotion in his voice. All business, all leader-Dorian.

He didn't need to call family. His only family member was coming with us to the Immortal Plane. Laini rolled her neck and watched the landscape, just as Sike did. Did they find their new home beautiful? Or did they look forward, in some nostalgic way, to seeing the familiar landscape of the Immortal Plane?

Arlonne sat beside them with her chin in her hand. There would be nobody for her to call. The sour taste of melancholy entered my mouth as I forced myself to turn away from her. This moment was yet another reminder of how much the vampires had lost, how little we had to call back to, and how tightly we had to cling to what we had left.

We all had our reasons for going to the Immortal Plane.

Zach joined me. He wiped his nose on his sleeve. "Allergies, right?"

I smirked. "I love you too, Zach." I slung my arm around him. "Even your *allergies*."

"You know, you still snore," Zach teased as we gathered my gear and began to head out of the camp.

Instead of being annoyed at his teasing, I felt only overwhelming love for my brother.

"It's payback for your gas," I said snarkily, but I couldn't look at him. If I did, I might cry. Zach and I had cheered each other on through every step of our training and gone together on practically all our missions once I joined the upper ranks. This would be the first time I faced danger without him. When would I see him again?

The sunrise was magnificent today. I sucked in a breath of cool morning air as I stared out at the desert, deliberately not looking at the tear for a moment. As we reached the summit, we found the vampires gathered nearby with a small flock of redbills. I cheered inwardly upon seeing Dorian's sassy redbill, Drigar. We'd come a long way since he tried to eat me and I threatened to turn him into chicken wings. The last time I saw the large bird was before the Chicago HQ mission a few weeks ago, when we'd had to leave him behind because of his injury. We'd left him here in the Canyonlands with the other redbills to recover, and it seemed he'd done just that.

We planned to take four redbills, two people to a bird. Laini and I would take one together. Dorian would ride with Bryce, Roxy would go with Arlonne, and Sike would join Kane.

Dorian stood in the center of our group, his arms folded. He seemed better after some rest, but I wanted him to feed soon. His expression was determined, but the hollows under his eyes worried me.

"We should go over some basic ground rules for the Immortal Plane before we take off," he said. His glacial eyes studied the human volunteers, including me. "Never *ever* assume anything in the Immortal Plane is friendly. I don't care if it's sapient, animal, or plant. Most creatures will leave you alone if you don't bother them and stay out of their way."

Roxy clicked her tongue. "So, they're more afraid of us than we are of them?" she guessed hopefully.

Kane let out a sharp laugh. "Not a chance. Always assume that you're in the way of *something* and be on high alert."

"He's right," Dorian said gravely. "Immortal creatures will likely leave you alone if you're smart, but there's no guarantee. Every creature could be harmful to you. Since this is the first time we'll have humans inside the Immortal Plane, we can expect the learning curve to be steep. Very steep."

I scooted a pebble in the dirt, fidgeting as I took in his words. The empty swarm had perfect camouflage for rocky or dark areas. If there were more creatures like that, we would have to be doubly attentive to our surroundings, as Kane had said.

"Second rule is that humans do not wander off anywhere without vampires. Ever. There are no maps and no familiar landmarks for you when we go in there. There will be no sun, stars, or

technology to guide you. You will be in completely unknown territory, so if you need a bathroom break, one of us is coming with you.
Sometimes things… change." Dorian said the last part slowly.

I wrapped my hand around my naked wrist. It felt strange to
leave my watch behind with everything else. There would be little to
link us to the human world and nothing to help us orient ourselves.

Kane smirked beside him and shook his head, casting pity on all
of us gathered humans. "What he's trying to say is that the landscape
can shift sometimes. If you *do* get lost, stay exactly where you are. A
vampire will come and find you."

Laini jumped in. "And don't listen to voices from people you
can't see."

"Well, that's not ominous in the slightest," Roxy muttered.

It all sounded so *alien*. Anxiety and excitement filled me.

Bryce scoffed. "Come on, now. We're soldiers, not babies."

"You should heed their warnings," Arlonne said with a tiny
smirk. "In the Immortal Plane, you are indeed little more than
babies."

Bryce gave no reply but a slight nod of respect at her words. I
noticed he often seemed impressed by Arlonne. *Interesting.*

We waited until Clemmins joined us on the hill, his eyes
concealed behind aviator sunglasses.

"I can't say I'm entirely happy about this," he said grumpily, going
down the line to shake our hands. "But if anyone has a chance to
make this madcap mission work, it's this group."

"I appreciate your belief in us, Captain Clemmins," Dorian said,
inclining his head in thanks. "I hope the board and Congress don't
give you too much hassle for this."

Clemmins shrugged his lean shoulders. "They need me too much to fire me again. Perhaps a bold move is what's needed to fix this problem." He looked up at the flickering, pulsing tear, the lightning reflecting in the mirrored surface of his sunglasses. "Remember, though, this is a surveillance mission. I know you all have something of a hero complex, since you volunteered for this. But please try not to be too reckless. We need you back alive."

Bryce took his time shaking the captain's hand. "I'd promise to bring them all home safe," he said, his brogue thickening with emotion, "but I can't guarantee that. And I don't want my final action on this plane to be a lie."

Clemmins nodded in understanding. "Just do your best, Bryce. I'll make sure I keep your sister in the loop."

I hugged Zach one last time, then hugged Gina just as firmly. "Look after each other," I said, wiping away a stray tear but not letting the rest fall. "I'll be back before you know it."

CHAPTER THIRTEEN

Our redbills soared through the sky, their powerful dark wings propelling them swiftly upward. The military encampment shrank away, and the Canyonlands unfolded beneath us, riddled with chasms and silvery lines of water, dusted with patches of scrub. Far below, the partially ruined city of Moab was just beginning to awaken, tiny specks of soldiers scurrying through the streets on various tasks. I waved a silent goodbye to what could be my final glimpse of humanity and looked ahead to where the tear crackled with energy, roiling with bruised clouds.

I can't believe we're willingly headed into this thing.

I leaned on Laini's small but sturdy frame as the redbill increased its speed. To my right, Dorian flew on Drigar, Bryce sitting behind him. I was envious because I didn't get to fly on the big, sassy redbill myself, but I smiled at the sight of him and Dorian reunited.

"Brace yourself," Laini said, her voice tight with caution. "We're heading into the storm. It will be uncomfortable."

I tensed for freezing wind and lightning. Instead, syrupy darkness and heaviness enveloped us. I couldn't see even an inch in front of me. The sound from the redbills' flapping wings disappeared. There was... nothing. A complete absence of all the tiny things our senses would usually latch onto to assure us that we were alive and well. It was as if we'd stumbled into a vacuum. The sharp smell of ozone struck my nostrils, followed by the scent of decaying leaves and damp copper. I shivered. These clouds weren't like clouds from the human world—these were of the Immortal Plane. They weren't bound by the physical constraints of the human atmosphere. Who knew what I was breathing in?

My vision increased to a smoky haze. As if from far away, I heard a whooping sound from someone. Bryce? Kane's loud, distinctive cackle followed.

Blinding light exploded in front of me. Static electricity in vibrant greens and purples and blues crackled wildly in the air. I shielded my eyes. This was it. We were passing through to the Immortal Plane.

I'm not sure what I expected.

Past the intense illumination of the tear, it was dim. I could barely see, only able to make out the vague silhouette of Laini's head and the black wings of the redbill propelling us through the empty foreign sky. Humid air wrapped around us. It smelled of scorched cedar, an ashy, harsher version of Dorian's scent.

As my eyes adjusted, a flash of movement drew my gaze upward. Above us, the sky swirled and rippled like charcoal dropped into water. It blended with faint highlights of glowing amber. On the horizon, barely visible in the jaundiced light, was a smattering of green, yellow, and purple smudges, but I couldn't see much more.

"What's up with the sky?" I asked Laini, unable to keep my curiosity at bay. "It wasn't like this before, when I came through with Dorian."

"This is the darkening," she explained calmly, sending our redbill drifting up toward the swirling clouds. "In a way, it's the equivalent to your human twilight, but when it falls here is dependent on the weather. The sky changes often, with little rhyme or reason. Everything here does."

She turned, and I could make out her delicate profile as I watched her stare at the passing flecks of amber.

"The soul-lights get blown across the sky by powerful winds that affect only them," she said. "It's like a spiritual push in the sky. The light changes as the winds move the soul currents. Everything depends on the number of souls in the sky. Sometimes areas stay light for what you would consider several days or even weeks. If there aren't many around, it can be dim at any time and last just as long. When the sky is at its darkest, even vampires have a hard time seeing. We're not sure why it happens. It's just the way it is." She sighed, almost wistfully.

"What?" I asked, curious.

A small smile came to her lips. "When I was a little girl, I used to make wishes on them. The way mortal children do on stars," she said with a soft laugh.

"Is it always so erratic? Is there any kind of cycle?" I wondered. "Like a timeframe?"

She hummed and reflected. "Yes, it's very erratic. When it's calm, I would say the light can stay the same for maybe… twelve to thirty-six hours. Then it transitions to the next stage, often very quickly.

The currents are quite strong right now, so it's likely to get dark in a few hours. Who knows how long the souls will stay?"

Last time I came here, it was plenty bright enough to see the devastatingly bizarre area. I sucked in an awed breath as the amber currents twirled above us, buffeted by the wind to move across the sky. I could easily see how Laini could've taken them for magical, wish-granting oddities. The light brightened the area slightly. I couldn't tell if it was actually growing brighter, or if my eyes were merely adjusting.

Then I processed what she'd said. "Wait, these are *literally* souls?" I asked. Souls were a big deal. I had one inside me, presumably, but I felt nothing more than an odd admiration for the pretty lights above me. Nothing called out inside me as I looked at the amber lights. Could I touch the souls if they got close enough?

In the dim light, I felt rather than saw Laini nod.

"They really are souls," she said. "It's beautiful, isn't it?"

"Whose souls are they?" A million questions tumbled into my head. "How do they get here? Are they just human souls? Or are there vampire souls there too? What about the Immortals? Do they have souls?"

Laini took a breath to reply but then stiffened. "Hold on. I sense something." The controlled alarm in her voice made me tense up.

From the shadowy surroundings, I saw Dorian and Bryce swoop nearby on Drigar. Bryce saluted me with a tight smile. Drigar flew strong. His wing had healed nicely.

"You sensed it, too?" Dorian asked Laini with a knowing gaze.

"I did," she replied. "But whatever it is, it's too far away to get a good read on it."

Dorian nodded. "Too far to bother us, I hope. Still, we should hide sooner rather than later."

Scanning the horizon, I noticed the green, yellow, and purple lights swelling larger. They were now a defined streak that flashed with white lightning in the distance. They continued to grow at an alarming rate.

"Dive," Dorian said abruptly.

Laini nodded. She yanked my arms around her waist. "Hold on, Lyra. Don't worry about hurting me. Just don't let go."

Suddenly, the redbill tipped into a dive with the rest of the flock. My stomach flipped from the motion, and I obediently clutched Laini for dear life as we rapidly lost altitude. I'd been on many redbill rides, but diving maneuvers had been blissfully uncommon. The force stung my face like it had during my first trips on Drigar with Dorian.

We plunged down, and the light faded as we left the souls high above. Closer to the ground was an inky fog—I could barely make out the lines of some dilapidated ruin in front of us. The redbills weaved back and forth, so low to the ground that I could sense the solid surface below us, even if I couldn't see it. Nausea clawed at my throat as we twisted between and around structures that were little more than looming shapes in the gloom. I didn't know how long we dashed around like that, but eventually we landed. Laini grabbed my hand, pulling me off the redbill, and in a gap in the fog I caught a brief glimpse of the rest of the team slithering off their own redbills.

"Let's go," Kane said, his voice cutting through the darkness.

I couldn't see him, my eyes still adjusting. Laini kept hold of my hand so I wouldn't get lost in the fog. The ground was uneven and rocky, sending me stumbling every few steps. The thick air tasted different in my mouth—sour and hot like our first day in Moab. If I'd been alone in this fog, I would have immediately become lost. Or worse. I now understood Dorian's insistence that we didn't go off without a vampire companion. It was incredible that they could see through this darkness.

"Don't shove me, I can walk," Roxy snapped somewhere ahead.

"You'd wish I'd done it more if an Immortal found you trailing behind," Kane argued.

"Quiet," Dorian demanded.

The fog was thinner here. My vision adjusted slowly, and Laini released my hand. We stood under the shelter of a leaning wall in the remains of an old building.

Dorian, his cloak bunched up around his neck, dropped his voice. "Get down and stay there."

We obeyed, flattening ourselves into damp, ashy mud. My anxious pulse hammered inside my ear. Roxy crouched next to me on my left, Laini on my right. I could hear their soft breathing as we tried to stay quiet.

Overhead, I heard something like the hum of a jet cutting through the air high above. What were they? More soul-scourgers, the mist-based creature we'd tangled with near the ski resort hideout? No, that couldn't be right. Dorian had ordered an emergency nose-dive for a reason, but the alarm in his voice sent a wave of worry through me. We'd handled a creature like that before, so it must be something else. Whatever this was, it was even more dangerous.

Roxy nudged me and pointed upward. I followed her line of sight. The wall we had taken cover under had several destroyed windows, the wooden frames still clinging to slivers of an amber, glass-like material. I adjusted my position slightly to look out at the barest hint of the swirling sky through the narrow spaces. Then, something cut through the murk.

Intermittent green and violet lights flashed, followed by a blink of yellow. The edge of a pair of leathery wings stirred the fog. Something, a dark green shape in the fog, twisted sinuously. There came a cry—a horrifying, gurgling wheeze.

The sound sent a dreadful shiver of recognition through me. In an instant, I envisioned Grayson's body tumbling to the ground. I saw the shrieking decay and Finley's melted body. Every muscle in my body tensed as I willed myself to take steady breaths. Something, not just the shrieking decay, was up there. Any movement could cost us our safety.

I counted my slow breaths and reached eighty before the terrible shape began to fade away. Something passed overhead and came back, over and over. If they suspected we were in the area, they didn't seem to know where. If an Immortal was up there, I wondered how heightened their senses were. How had they known we'd crossed through the tear? There was more flapping of wings and another wheeze, this one much more distant than before, but I still didn't dare to move or even risk letting out a relieved sigh.

In the dim light, Dorian held a finger to his lips. No talking. Minutes ticked by. The sound of wings faded. Whoever it was, they took their sweet time leaving.

Finally, Laini let out a ragged exhale.

"They're out of range," she said, her voice still in a whisper. "If we can't sense them, they can't hear us."

"Do you think our little convoy caught someone's eye?" Arlonne asked, wedged into a corner beside Sike. "Or that they just routinely patrol near the tear?"

"I think just patrolling," Kane said, peering through the broken window at the soul-lights, which had been blown into new patterns by the passing monster. "But I'm concerned by the fact that they seem to have a shrieking decay as part of their defenses now."

We slowly made our way out from under the overhang. After I became acclimated to the light in our hiding spot, it was easier to see our small group… and the anger on the vampires' faces.

Dorian scowled at the sky as if his glare might strike his enemies down. Whoever it was, he hated them.

Which means I'd probably hate them, too.

"What was that?" Bryce asked. "An army of angry souls?" He rubbed his face as his eyes glanced from the hideout to the sky. I could see him trying to work out his own theories. Our period of terrible quiet and stillness meant we'd had more than enough time to dream up terrifying conclusions.

"Those lights weren't souls," Dorian breathed. He sounded like a furious dragon, the words rumbling low in his chest. I half expected flames to burst from his mouth. "We sensed the presence of monsters, but that wasn't all. I felt wildlings and… an Immortal ruler."

Roxy blinked twice. "So, that was like your Immortal president coming to find us?" she asked. "Should we be flattered?"

"Not the president," Laini corrected gently before Kane could say something mean. "Everything in the Immortal Plane has a purpose. The Immortal rulers are a species, like vampires. We usually refer to the Immortals as being of a different caste."

A specific purpose for everything in the Immortal Plane. "What's their purpose, then?" I asked. Dorian had danced around my inquires during our time in Scotland, but his reticence hadn't seemed malicious. More that he wasn't ready to explain the Immortal rulers—they were obviously difficult for him to talk about. But now we *had* to know the situation. It could be the difference between life and death for us.

"The Immortals are designed to rule the Immortal Plane. They have no other name or purpose. They hate vampires," Dorian said darkly. He ran a hand through his hair, tugging it slightly as he thought. "And it looks like they're herding immortal creatures through the tear."

My hands went numb. "You mean… they're purposefully sending the monsters through?"

His deadly serious gaze landed on me. Normally, his glacial eyes sparked some kind of comfort inside me, but not this time. We shared the cold realization that our situation was more sinister than we'd ever imagined.

"If they've organized creatures to patrol the tear, it's likely that they've had a plan in place for a while. They knew something came through, and they were on us in moments." Dorian shook his head in frustration. "Not only do they know about the tear, but they're actively attacking the Mortal Plane."

Laini hummed. "That explains how the empty swarm came through. It bothered me how the bugs had managed to fly high enough to reach the tear on their own. You saw their flimsy wings. That kind of physiology only allows short gliding at best. But the Immortals could have taken the swarm to the tear and pushed them through, letting them glide down to Moab."

Roxy grunted irritably. "These guys sound like the worst. Are they the ones who initiated contact with the Bureau and told them about the Immortal Plane?"

Alan's smug face flashed in my mind, his cryptic mentions of allies sending a new surge of adrenaline through me.

"That's what we're here to find out," Dorian said firmly. "We won't stop until we do."

CHAPTER FOURTEEN

The Immortals had gone, but they left a heavy tension in their wake. We had to get moving.

Laini's grip tightened on my hand. The vampires pulled us humans along through the thick fog, which grew denser in some areas than others. Sike led Roxy beside me, while Arlonne helped Bryce. Dorian and Kane took point and scouted just ahead.

It was hard to describe the Immortal Plane, or what I saw around me. The fog moved like a living entity, forcing my eyes to continually readjust.

I had never taken recreational drugs, but I'd spent my fair share of time hopped up on painkillers in a medical bay, and they'd sometimes given me the slight sense that reality was temporary. This was a hundred times worse. Every time I felt my vision stabilize, the yellowish shadows shifted, and I was off balance once again. My stomach rolled with nausea. There was a tinny ringing in my ears.

Worse, the fog was *heavy*. The air brushed against me with slimy fingers. Every molecule seemed designed to drag my body down.

Laini's pale skin glowed in the darkness like a beacon, beckoning me. I tried not to stare at her hand in mine. The shadows beneath her skin flickered and shifted and swirled more rapidly here, almost taunting me. It made her figure appear to shift in the darkness. I shook my head and tried to focus my eyes. Sike's skin, though not as pale, shifted in the same way. My eyes found Roxy's queasy face, the only normal thing in this primordial fog. She looked as green as I felt. Or was that yet another trick of the light?

After perhaps ten minutes of walking, my eyes acclimatized to their new fate. I began to see more details, noticing patterns in the shifting of colors and light. The human brain was a powerful thing, even thrown into another dimension. Dorian had assured me I would adjust, and he'd been right so far.

I began to see the faintest outlines of amber light again, which occasionally dispersed into the sky. A hazy horizon, also dotted with amber, came into view. Dark shapes danced ahead, and I rubbed my eyes, but the shadows on the horizon remained steadfast, becoming a tree and a creeping vine.

This place will either give me a seizure or a nervous breakdown.

Nobody spoke as we moved through the world, for which I was grateful. If I opened my mouth, I was afraid I would start spouting nonsense or throw up from my slight vertigo. I glanced down, hoping the ground would offer some solace.

A soft amber light glowed beneath my feet, and I stumbled sideways. I looked around me. Beneath the drifting fog, the landscape emitted a dim tawny glow. The dirt beneath me grew brighter, illuminating more of our surroundings.

Laini guided me over piles of rock, but it was smoother than the previous landscape. I could feel the stones beneath my boots, like cobblestones. It felt like a street. I looked up and realized the faint outlines ahead were actually the broken and torn remains of buildings. I narrowed my eyes, trying to get a better view. More of the faded angular lines appeared in the distance. There was a city's worth of ruins here.

I sucked in a sharp breath. We were in the demolished vampire city, the one that Dorian and I had flown over during my first visit. Laini squeezed my hand but didn't turn around. When I glanced to the side to catch a glimpse of Sike, his eyes roved over the ruins without expression.

God, this plane used to be their home.

The vampires were quiet to evade detection, but the silence served another purpose. Dorian, Kane, Sike, Laini, and Arlonne mourned as they led us through the wrecked remains of their old lives.

The Immortals did all this? I studied the broken path beneath me. The pavement had once depicted an intricate pattern of rust-red stones, but now there were holes and broken pieces scattered everywhere. The wind picked up, singing eerily as it passed through the rubble, almost conjuring voices.

The houses surrounding us were small and burnt, the yellow glass in the windows either broken or hung from the frame in melted brown strings. As we traversed a side street between two tumbled walls, my foot struck something that clattered across the path. Looking down, I shivered with disgust when I recognized it as a heap of bones. Out of the corner of my eye, I had thought they were jagged stones. The pile wasn't alone. Skeletons in various states of wholeness littered the ground. It was as if everyone had dropped during their day and had simply been left to their fate. How many vampires were out there, unable to mourn their loved ones because they'd had to run for their own lives?

A large group of souls floated by, and the sky briefly lightened. Taking the opportunity, I studied the buildings we stood among. Strange. I knew what buildings devastated by bombs or gunfire looked like, but these structures looked like they had been *sliced*. The building closest to me had neatly lost a quarter of its construction. A house on my left looked like a cutaway dollhouse, the front wall completely erased. These structures were stone. What could have done this? I knew the breath of the shrieking decay could melt stone, but it was messy and volatile; this was so precise.

I puzzled over a building where the roof and upper floor had been removed as if with a knife. The ground floor was untouched, except for weather damage. Questions burned inside me.

"Where are we?" I whispered to Laini, wanting to put a name to this place.

She looked back. "This was once Vanim. Our home."

I went to speak again, but she shook her head. There was such pain on her face, I didn't push.

The quiet weighed on me, almost unbearable. The area grew lighter as we walked. Still, Laini clutched my hand, but now I supported her instead of the other way around. Her eyes stared ahead with a strange distance to them.

New colors emerged around me as the sky lightened. A weed with dusky pink flowers crawled up a broken fencepost. Iridescent blue mushrooms bloomed on one of the skeletons. Under the dirt and smoke damage, the walls of some of the buildings had obviously once borne murals or signs, and hints of color peeked through the grime. Looking up, the fog now somewhat thinner, I saw that the sky revealed a strange texture in the distance, like waves rippling above us. Around the city, I suddenly made out the jagged silhouettes of mountains that surrounded the ruins with towering heights. It felt like the mountains leaned in, sagging toward the city from the weight of their massive existence. The rippling sky made the sensation even worse. The Immortal Plane pushed on us from all sides.

"We'll break here," Dorian said abruptly. His short command broke the silence, but it did nothing for the tension.

We stopped by an old stone bench next to a tall building made of crumbling black bricks. I sat precariously on the bench, hoping it wouldn't transform and bite a chunk out of me.

The vampires gathered together nearby. Dorian, eyes weary, rubbed his hands across his face, leaving streaks of soot on his forehead and cheeks. I wished I could brush the dirt from his face. I hated not being able to do anything to comfort him. This was the wreckage of his life. Laini leaned against Sike for a moment. The walk had taken a lot out of her. Kane muttered something gloomy, but I didn't hear it, nor did I want to. They grieved.

Bryce sat beside me and said nothing. He opened his mouth and shut it a few times. I knew what he meant. The distance between our two groups weighed on me. How could we help them? The echoes of so much horror filled this place, so much pain it was impossible to find words for it.

Roxy leaned against the building's stone wall, taking a long drink from the water skins we'd brought with us. Immediately, her face froze and she began to sob. Loud, powerful cries wracked her body. She slid down, her back to the building, burying her face in her hands as she wept. I jumped to my feet, but something about her body's severe shuddering made me freeze. Roxy didn't cry like this out of the blue. Could I even touch her? Or would that make things worse? Dorian and the vampires stared for a moment, caught off guard, but Roxy's cries soon yanked them from their dreamlike state.

Laini's eyes widened sympathetically as she took a step forward, but Kane was faster. He marched over to Roxy and grabbed her shoulders, yanking her away from the building. She stumbled against his chest and peered blankly into nothing for a terrifying minute. Then, the color came back into her face. She pulled herself back, and Kane jerked away at the same time. Roxy dropped her gaze, clearly embarrassed by her outburst. Kane shuffled in place, obviously in shock of some kind.

"I heard voices," Roxy muttered abruptly. "Terrible, terrible voices. They told me awful things. Death and destruction. I could *feel* what they felt." She rubbed her hand against her chest and made a motion like she wanted to rip out her heart.

Kane turned to me and Bryce, his face tight. "Yeah, don't touch the buildings here. They have plenty of stories to tell, and they're usually not nice." He forced his tone to be casual, but the hollow humor chilled me to my bones.

"The stone, it remembers," Laini added. "It tells you things that you don't want to know. Memories are... very powerful in this place."

"It was so real," Roxy said, breathing hard. "What happened here?" Her voice was small, so unlike her usual rough confidence.

I scooted to the edge of the bench, dreading what the vampires would say next. They had a story for these ruins, and it was no fairytale. My skin erupted in goosebumps as apprehension welled up inside me. Another story meant more pain, but I owed it to them to witness their history.

Dorian inhaled slowly. The somber light in his eyes wavered between hesitation and something else. Something stormy and overwhelming, a feeling that might be impossible for us to understand. Arlonne kept her mouth firmly shut, and Kane seemed stunned to silence. Something about Roxy's desperation had pushed him too far. His tough-guy attitude had melted away into the clearing mist.

"I'll tell you," Laini breathed. Her earnest gaze turned toward the buildings. "This used to be our home. Vanim was once a great vampire city, but between the damage caused when the tear first opened and attacks from our Immortal enemies, it has been destroyed. Everyone who lived here has fled or been killed or captured by Immortals."

My shoulders sagged under the weight of Laini's sadness. I hated seeing the vampires in pain. I hated that they had to drag us through the decaying remains of their pasts. I hated knowing that I couldn't help Dorian and our friends with this.

"Vampires always had a special relationship with the barrier," Laini explained. "We can move through it, but it takes an incredible amount of energy unless we're at the special stone locations. Sometimes, the effort needed to push ourselves between the planes without a portal can kill us. But we are the only creatures that can interact or move through it, except at the tear." She paused. "The Immortals have always disliked us, begrudging our role in society, but they used to tolerate us. The last two hundred years saw a massive rise in hostility toward our kind. This disdain grew into undisguised hatred. Our numbers prevented them from outright attack, but they forced us out of their Immortal cities, banishing us to the mountains and deep into the forests. And so, we sought a way to protect our new homes. We needed a safe place to exist, to hide our sacred knowledge and continue purifying souls in both the Immortal and Mortal Planes. Our finest scholars conceived an idea. My mother told me that it seemed perfect at the time. We never imagined it would bring our downfall."

Dorian averted his eyes, glaring at the ground. Was he thinking of his brother? His parents?

Laini's voice wavered, but she continued. "Our finest minds devised a way to construct the city so that it became *part* of the barrier. Since no creatures but vampires could cross the barrier, Vanim was safe from attack. We built doors into this half-plane, to conserve our energy. Our lights and magic were powered by the energy of the barrier."

I hadn't realized the barrier was capable of all that—I'd been thinking of it as a wall between rooms, but it seemed to be more like a crawl space, an interdimensional bubble.

Laini went on, "With the buildings anchored between worlds, we were protected from our Immortal enemies' awareness. They couldn't find what they didn't know was there. But… something went wrong. Something gouged through the barrier, creating the tear you're all now familiar with." Her chest rose and fell quickly as her breathing became strained. "The damage to Vanim was unimaginable. Buildings lost their foundations in mere moments. Portals collapsed, a few exploding out into the city and destroying everything around them. In some areas, the energy released from the ripped barrier sliced through stone." The last word barely made it out of her mouth. Telling us was a painful task. She pulled herself together and forged on.

"Most vampires inside the buildings… the shock and ensuing damage killed them. Since our powers are linked to the strength of the barrier, the survivors all weakened. We lost over half the population in the first few minutes. The city had lost its protection from the Immortals, who took advantage of our weakness to launch a large-scale attack that devastated our remaining population. We held out as long as we could, protecting the city for almost a year. It wasn't enough." She shook her head. "They created new weapons and blasted down what was left of our walls. Wildlings rounded up monsters, some of which you've seen, most of which you haven't, and used them against us. Hunters wore magical armor with strong protections. It was impossible to fight when we were already so weak. It happened so fast. Vanim was reduced to this, and we lost most of our surviving population. We couldn't take care of our dead. The bones you see scattered about are our comrades, left to rot where they fell. In the aftermath, it wasn't safe enough to return and properly burn their remains." She looked around. "Now, they're the only vampires who remain in this city."

My heart broke. I wanted to scream a promise to those Immortal cretins, that they would pay for the suffering they had brought on the vampires. An equally loud cry rose up in the back of my mind, reminding me of the human cruelty that brought us to this point. The Immortals had hardly done this alone. Somewhere, Alan sat in a cell, content to be a cog in this murderous machine. I'd once been an unwitting participant in this sick game. Never again.

"Did you have magic among your people?" Bryce asked gently.

"Sometimes for large community projects, like to light our cities,"

Laini replied, "but vampires tend not to use magic in our daily lives, especially for combat. It's never been our way. The rulers never allowed other castes to learn those arts very much. It all makes sense, now that I think about it. They wanted it to be a slaughter." The distant look in her eyes shattered as she stumbled again on her words.

"Thank you, Laini," Dorian whispered tightly. "Save your strength."

She gave a grateful nod.

A sadness as sharp as a knife's blade twisted in my core. Those bones were once loved ones and friends to the vampires. I shut my eyes for a moment, trying hard not to imagine what it would be like to walk among the remains of the people I loved.

"My brother Lanzon was a warrior and a scout," Dorian said, his voice carefully neutral. He refused to give away his emotions. "I was part of the group assigned to protect the civilian vampires fleeing the city."

Dorian once told me that vampires had a rich variety of occupations and were not just warriors. They had been scholars, healers, teachers, even entertainers. Yet so many of the vampires I had met were warriors who'd survived the hard times better since the tear thanks to their skills. Those who hadn't been trained for battle... I swallowed as tears pricked my eyes. Most of those unfortunate souls lay around us in piles of abandoned bones.

Horror gripped me. I could practically feel the dread like a rope knotting around my throat. I couldn't breathe. There was so much pain in this place.

"I'm sorry," I managed in a wavering tone, unable to keep the tears out of my voice. "I'm so sorry."

Bryce nodded gravely. "No creature deserves this."

Roxy rubbed her arms vigorously, as if to banish chills. Her eyes were red from tears. I hated to imagine what she had heard from the voices of that building.

I had known the vampires' story would devastate us, but hearing it from Laini and Dorian sent everything over the edge.

"Thank you," Laini said as her strength returned. She smiled, bittersweet. "Now you know why we fight so hard. The memories of everyone we left behind live on in us."

Kane brushed his nose roughly with the back of his hand. "We all lost people, many of them arguably greater than us. My grandmother was the strongest woman I've ever met. I watched a building come down on her." In the dim light, his lean body tensed at the painful memory. He carried a great burden. They all did.

"My entire family," Sike mumbled and kicked at a nearby rock. It ricocheted off into the distance, striking a building. "Parents. Brothers. Sister. Grandfather. I was all alone. I was lucky to find Dorian and the others, in the aftermath."

Laini sucked in a sharp breath. "Lanzon wasn't the only death for me. I lost my aunt, uncle, and cousins that same day." Her voice went high and fragile. "They all survived the tear. We thought it was a miracle." She pressed her balled-up fist against her mouth. "I'll never stop until we get justice for them."

Never. I felt a surge of determination course through me. Roxy wiped her wet eyes roughly. Bryce didn't bother to hide the tears streaming down his face as his gaze lingered on a child-sized set of bones.

"My father," Arlonne whispered. It was all she said. It was all she needed to say.

For a moment, a silence fell over our group as we honored the fallen. I pressed my fingernails into my palm, relishing the sharp pain that reminded me I was alive. I was in the Immortal Plane, and I would be damned if I gave up looking for a way to right this terrible wrong with my friends.

Vanim was where it had all begun, and it was here that we began our journey to end it.

CHAPTER FIFTEEN

We picked our way through the dark fog for hours. Or rather, the vampires moved forward and helped us along. I wondered if Roxy and Bryce felt like babies too. Arlonne had been right about that.

After our stop in Vanim, I was grateful for silence again. Laini helped me when the path became too dim in certain spots. Sometimes, when she held my hand, I tried to imagine giving her as much comfort as possible, like a psychic hug.

The redbills had left us long ago at the vampires' request, but we occasionally heard them call to one another as they followed us from above. Fortunately, the number of wild flocks prevented that from giving us away.

I could make out the thin, winding path ahead sometimes when the fog lifted in areas, revealing strange trees clad in thick blue-and-green moss that I didn't dare touch. Although we occasionally saw the faint outline of a ruin in the distance, we never stumbled through another town or settlement. The surrounding landscape began to skew toward what I assumed was a more rural part of the Immortal Plane. Although I had no concept of how far this place stretched, in my mind it went on forever.

Sound traveled oddly in this plane. Roxy nearly tripped at one point, and her startled gasp sounded as if her mouth was right next to my ear one moment and then a hundred feet away a moment later. It was impossible to calculate distance. Everything echoed and whispered or stopped altogether, as if the warm pressure swallowed it up.

"It gets better," Laini assured me.

She and Dorian were both strangely confident in a human's ability to adapt. Maybe, after growing up here, they'd found the Mortal Plane to be just as strange at first as the Immortal Plane was to me. They assumed that since they'd adapted, so could I. I hoped they were right. I needed some good news after leaving the devastated city behind us.

Sike's form became clearer in front of me, Roxy walking beside him. For a moment, I thought Laini was right and my brain was starting to figure things out. Maybe I had gotten used to it. Looking ahead at the horizon between the sparse trees, however, I realized the amber soul-lights in the sky had merely grown brighter, helping me see farther. I could see now that Dorian was leading us along the edge of a forest, following a steady ridgeline farther into the mountains.

I felt for the stone, Lanzon's stone, that was in a leather bag on a cord hung around my neck. Those could be the mountains this stone had come from.

A long way off, a multitude of tawny lights broke off from the main current, drifting lower and lower. They slowed as they descended, dimmer than their companions higher in the sky. It was beautiful.

I craned my neck to see the sky full of those slow, drifting lights. They moved like stately, celestial jellyfish through water. After the brutal feelings earlier, I felt oddly peaceful.

"Incredible," Roxy breathed as she stared in awe.

Bryce's eyes glittered. The amber color reflected on his face, as it did on all our faces, basking us in an almost magical glow. They reminded me of the childhood storybook about fairies and fantastical adventures that my mom used to read Zach and me. I wanted to reach out and touch one of the lights, a tiny, childlike part of me hoping it would fill me with magic. The vampires appeared nonplussed by our reaction. Kane stared at us blankly, looking at the lights and then back at our stupefied faces, obviously wondering why it was such a big deal.

Dorian glanced back to see what the fuss was about and met my gaze. A half-grin crossed his face. "It's good that the sky is getting brighter."

"The lights are souls, but you may already know that," Sike said.

Bryce and Roxy nodded next to me. Apparently, we'd all been filled in by now.

Sike's tired face transformed as he smiled serenely. His features looked especially handsome in the yellow glow. "They're both human and immortal, but most come from the Mortal Plane."

"How do they get here?" I asked. The lights filled me with awe. *To think that something this beautiful could exist in the Immortal Plane.* And here I stood, from the Mortal Plane, looking up at human souls coming from my homeland. This landscape was a collaborative work of beauty between our planes.

"When people die, their souls are pulled into this plane. If the souls are full of light energy, they pass straight on, peacefully, to the afterlife. If they have too much dark energy, though, they have to be purified. It's almost like they're too heavy... they stick to the darkness in this plane and remain here until they're purified," he explained. "That can take a long time, since there are so many. Which is why a vampire needs to cleanse them before they get to that point, or else it's up to the harvester. It's not the best gig, but someone has to do it. Otherwise those souls would be stuck here for far longer than they already are."

"You're all Kharon," Bryce muttered in astonishment.

Sike gave him a confused look.

"Kharon is a character from one of the ancient mythologies of our plane," Bryce explained, eyes still on the souls. "He was paid to ferry souls across the River Styx, which divided the land of the living and the land of the dead."

"Yeah, well," Kane said, swiping at a trailing strand of moss that tickled his face, "we don't get paid."

I brushed my finger over my lip in thought, finally hitting the life-changing realization that had been inevitable from the moment we arrived. Souls existed. There was an afterlife, both good and bad. Vampires were the ones who helped send souls onward to the positive afterlife. How much further did this story go? Although we'd agreed to keep our distance, I desperately wanted to speak to Dorian about this.

I took a deep breath, feeling like my head was about to explode.

Laini caught my eye and shrugged apologetically, sensing that I was struggling to take it all in.

"It's hard to believe," she acknowledged. "But it's true."

"Funny how you're all in awe." Kane chuckled. "I never considered that you humans would be so fascinated by something so ordinary."

"Ordinary?" I echoed, aghast. He couldn't be serious. I pointed to the light closest to me, unable to contain myself. "That's a *soul*."

He just blinked at me as if I'd pointed out a firefly.

"So, this place is kind of a purgatory on the way to a good after-life?" Roxy wondered aloud. "I thought vampires were bizarre enough as a concept, when the Bureau recruiter told me." I some-times forgot that not everyone had grown up with dinnertime tales of vampires over pasta. Our Bureau family had openly discussed vampires since Zach and I were young, before we could even consider going into the Bureau as soldiers. My mother would often report her strangest reactions from potential recruits when she delivered the news. If they couldn't handle it, the Bureau made sure to keep them quiet with an aggressive legal agreement.

Dorian cleared his throat. "We should get going." Despite his serious tone, he failed to hide his amusement, obviously suppressing a grin. Why did the amber glow make all the vampires look so beau-tiful? Dorian's lean face positively radiated in the ochre light. His glacial eyes took on a golden edge. Laini's features, too, sharpened in all the right places under the lights.

They were made for this place. Made for this land.

We continued, and I dropped my mental line of inquiry on how flattering amber looked on the vampires. We had a mission. The sky lightened to an odd twilight. Our footsteps changed, or at least the sounds of them did. My steps sounded solid as we walked, but I could hear them echoing softly in the distance.

"The souls remind me of fairies," I confessed, hoping to stir the conversation in a lighter direction as we walked. The brightening sky brought a feeling of hope with it. Laini smiled.

"Aye," Bryce said. "I know what you mean. My ma used to tell me of the little folk in the fey realm, where sprites and brownies and will-o'-the-wisps live."

"Oh, we've got something like fairies in the Immortal Plane, if you're interested," Kane said wryly. "But I warn you, they eat eyeballs."

I grimaced at the image. Kane had officially killed my fairy comparison.

"They're not that bad," Sike corrected. When he saw that he had our attention, he unraveled like a true storyteller, pleased to have an audience. "Most things here are just trying to survive. Animals and plants in the Immortal Plane follow the soul-light, like birds in your world follow the weather. The plants grow when it's light out. When it's not, the plants use their roots deep in the soil and stone, to feed off the energy of the darker souls that sink into the ground, or settle into rocks or inanimate objects—"

"Be careful picking up a discarded shoe in the forest as a young vampire boy, is all I've got to say," Kane muttered.

I raised an eyebrow, but Sike continued. We would hear about Kane's disastrous shoe story another day.

"Sound is also super interesting in the Immortal Plane. It can tell you a lot. For example, it's important to be silent during the darkening, like it was when we arrived, because when creatures follow the soul-lights to feed off blooming plants, it leaves empty dark areas,"

Sike explained, his face animated as he showed off his knowledge. "The sound echoes through dark areas, since there isn't much to buffer the sound. So, words and movements can be heard more easily and travel much farther in the dark."

Dorian threw a teasing look at the smaller vampire. "That's why we only let Sike talk this much when it's light."

Roxy and Bryce laughed, but I stayed quiet. Sike bringing up the sounds made me think. First, the surrounding sounds disturbed the heck out of me. They were the opposite of comforting. Second, they sounded strange, even in the increasing light.

Growls and grunts echoed from the undergrowth as we walked. A shrill bird sang a stilted song. I swore someone cackled in the distance, but nobody looked left when I did. The worst was the breeze. It hissed when it rustled through the tree branches, like hundreds of angry serpents slithering through the air. Trees shouldn't sound like that. I shivered.

The Immortal Plane was always going to be weird, Lyra. Cool it.

The hissing wind brushed past my face, carrying a strong scent of cedar that hid something dank and musky. I once went mush-room hunting with my father as a child. He warned me to stay away from areas that smelled of pack animals. This smelled the same but more metallic. Unfortunately, I could *taste* it in my mouth like acidic blood.

The sky continued to brighten, but a haze hung before my eyes. I couldn't see perfectly. The trees, different from the mossy ones, leaned in strange directions. The world wobbled slightly in my peripheral vision when I turned to look elsewhere.

"These trees are weird," I muttered, mostly to Laini. The bark was slate gray. Disheveled fuzzy needles covered their spindly branches like thick, coarse fur. When the breeze pushed against the branches, they hissed again. I strained. No, not quite a hiss. There was something underneath it. Something like a sigh, or a whisper. My throat tightened as an unsettled sensation passed through me. It sounded like people talking about uncomfortable subjects from a long way off.

"I kinda want to pet them," Roxy said, staring at the trees with interest. I could see what she meant. The fuzzy needles looked appealing, in their own way.

Kane shot her a look. "Don't touch *anything.*"

Tiny creatures scampered across the forest floor, appearing like bits of soot and cinder running before my feet. If I tried to focus on them, they became blurrier and ran off. Vines grew up from the ground as I walked. Occasionally, I felt a tug on my boot laces. Were the plants mocking me?

"Where are we going?" Bryce asked, a tremor of unease in his voice. The forest probably put him off just as much as it did me.

Dorian slowed his pace and hung back closer to us. "Most Immortal cities are roughly west and north from these mountains," he explained. "We'll eventually head to Itzarriol, the capital. It's where the Immortals control their politics across the entire plane. Where they declared war against vampires."

I raised a brow. Eventually? What was first? And were we just going to waltz into Itzarriol?

"If there's a conspiracy to push things through the tear and use the Bureau to destroy vampires in the Mortal Plane, that's where we'll find evidence," Dorian assured us. "On the way, I'd like us to carefully make a stop around Lake Siron and see if we can find any evidence of vampires, even if it's just so we can tell them how to get to Scotland. We should find out if there are any truths to the rumors and warn them that the Immortals have heard of them."

"Hopefully without leading the hunters to their door," Arlonne muttered.

Dorian nodded acknowledgement. "We can't fly on the redbills yet, since the Immortals will be scouting the area near the tear. But the redbills are following us until we find a proper place to mount up again. Then we can move faster. We need to set up surveillance, maybe plan a few trips into the city to gather information. The less time we spend out here in the open, the better. If we manage to find the other vampires, they might even be able to help. They could be great allies to help with the infiltration. Maybe they're already infiltrating the Itzarriol."

Bryce grinned. "A ballsy government coup in two dimensions? Why, Dorian, you're making my day."

I snorted, pleased to see my old captain excited.

"Not so fast," Kane said with a fierce scowl. "You said that you're going to tell them about Scotland. Why bother with that place if they already have a stronghold themselves? They've managed to evade capture from the Immortals so far. Maybe we should join them here."

Would it be a stronghold, though? I got the impression that the vampires had managed to *evade* capture, but how much longer could that last?

"It's too early to consider that," Dorian fired back. "Besides, it's too much work to move our group from Scotland back through the tear. Our people would starve before they made it back here."

Not to mention Kane's group had just left the Immortal Plane with their tails tucked a few weeks ago. Would they want to return so soon?

"You've got ulterior motives," Kane complained sourly.

Dorian lifted his eyebrow. "Maybe, but my motivations also benefit our people. I'm confident that this group could help us."

Arlonne cleared her throat, setting her hand on her hip. "*If* such a place even exists."

She had a good point. We had only heard rumors about these vampire survivors up to this point.

Dorian opened his mouth to reply, but his face froze suddenly with alarm. Something echoed in the distance, a ringing cry. It sent a jolt of startled electricity straight down my spine. Arlonne hissed beneath her breath as she looked up to the sky.

"Dark energy is approaching fast," Dorian said for the benefit of the humans. His eyes darted to the forest. "Everyone get to cover! Now."

CHAPTER SIXTEEN

We scrambled to hide in the forest. There were plenty of trees but hardly any underbrush to duck behind. My hopes sank as we rushed through the ominous woods. The trees whispered softly as I ran past them. I tried to keep up with Laini as best as I could. Her hand wrapped around mine tightly. But the forest wouldn't work. The lack of undergrowth meant the Immortal rulers would see us immediately.

"Past the trees," Dorian commanded. "We'll find something."

I forced my eyes to focus even as a wave of lightheadedness came over me. Laini let my hand go as our group managed to catch up with one another in the trees. Good thing, because she might have dislocated my shoulder if that's what it took to escape the Immortal rulers fast enough. I could see an opening in the trees toward our left, but only more of the towering trees before us. Our choices were left, forward into the forest, or back the way we came.

Bryce muttered something foul and chose left. He shouted, "Here! Over here!"

Laini weaved through the thicket of trees to a streambank, and I followed close behind. Bryce jerked his head toward the stream. "What are you waiting for? An invitation?"

Kane leapt across the stream, splattering the mud on the other side. Dorian had already jumped, one of his legs narrowly missing the murky violet water. He pointed at Roxy and me.

"Don't touch the water."

I wasn't planning on it. The stream stank of burning tires. The water looked like dark souls that had been left to liquefy and run together. Murky shadows danced in the rushing liquid. I stepped carefully alongside the running water, moving as fast as possible behind Laini and Sike. They came to a point where it would be feasible for the humans to jump to the other side of the bank. They leapt over the water easily. I followed suit. A splash of water flew up and singed my boots, leaving a tiny burn. I wrinkled my nose. *Okay, definitely not touching the water.*

Behind us, the sound of flapping wings came closer and closer.

Dorian led the group, keeping close enough that my chest had a tiny dull buzz. Well, I couldn't tell if the burn was from our proximity or my heart working from the sprinting. Roxy and I nearly collided as we rushed up the other side of the bank. Kane waved us toward what looked like a mass of rotting plants.

We came to the small underside of a cliff. Through amber-tinged dirt, the hardy roots of vines pushed through the earth and dangled to create a bizarre curtain. The moss-covered roots reached all the way to the ground. It would be perfect to hide under. The plant tendrils twitched as we ducked under them. Kane swept them aside using his cloak and herded the humans into the center, keeping us away from the roots and the hanging greenery that covered our weak hiding place. The moss had thorns, now that I studied it up close, desperate to peek between the few cracks to see what was happening outside.

This place would work for now, but if our pursuer crossed the stream, they would easily be able to spot us.

"Quiet," Dorian muttered.

The vines trembled softly as wings flapped nearby. I crouched along with the others, thankful for the natural cover of the hanging moss, even though it stank of deteriorating plant matter. I held a hand over my nose.

Something terrible hissed and landed nearby with a weighty thump above us on the cliff. The force shook a few loose bits of gravel from the underside. One pebble dropped onto the toe of my boot. Kane scowled when a wad of dirt fell onto his head. Above us, the creature stomped its legs, and something—or someone—slid off. I heard two distinctive points hit the ground. Heavy boots? It sounded like metal against earth. My mind dreamed up images of a knight in shining armor stamping across the dreary grass and dirt. I tried not to breathe, afraid that it might bring attention to us. I glanced at Roxy beside me, her hand also clamped over her face. Dorian nudged Laini and Arlonne. They exchanged silent looks. Kane would have been in on it, but the clump of dirt on his head prevented that. He couldn't move without it falling and drawing attention.

Arlonne jerked a thumb to herself and used her fingers to act out her running. She wanted to lure whoever followed us away if we got caught. It was a definite possibility, with the poor coverage of our hiding place. Dorian nodded. If it came down to it, Arlonne would lead a distraction and the rest of them would attack from behind.

The steps faded slightly, but a low voice rang out.

"What can I do for you?" the speaker asked. The voice sounded a touch feminine, but the tone brimmed with brasslike growls. It sounded like someone had taken a regular human voice and dragged it over rocks while lowering the bass.

"I saw movement but couldn't sense an aura that matched it," another voice said firmly. Immediately, I realized *this* voice was in charge. "Have you seen any vampires around? There's a rumor that they've been sighted near here." This speaker was closer to us. I couldn't tell if it was a man or a woman. There was a strange pull to the voice. If I closed my eyes, the thrall of the voice seemed to wrap around me. It *enchanted* me. It must be an Immortal.

"No," came the rocky voice simply.

"Are you sure?" the Immortal asked, some irresistible and cruelly cold note in the question. "I've heard another rumor that wildlings are *helping* vampires in this area."

A wildling? I glanced at Laini, but she merely listened with a tense face. Kane carefully maneuvered the dirt off his head, then looked at it as if he didn't know what to do with it.

"No. I haven't heard or seen anything," the gravelly subordinate replied. It had to be the wildling. Its voice was slightly strained, as if it were unable to stop itself from talking. "My patch of forest has seen no vampires."

"You should think again," the hunter said, beckoning with a soft voice. It softened and rolled out of the hunter's mouth in a perfect manner. A woman. I was sure of it now. "You can and should tell me anything." The demand echoed out into the air.

"I have seen nothing," the wildling answered easily. "Nothing at all." It sounded tired all of a sudden.

The ground above us abruptly shook as the hunter, I assumed, beat her foot into the ground. "Useless," she hissed angrily. "Why do you lot even exist?"

The wildling let out a cry of desperation. I briefly saw a flash of teal outside through the moss. The air filled with a low, growling scream of absolute agony. A sound of flesh being punctured reverberated through the air and created a bone-chilling scraping noise that ended in sudden silence.

A shiver ran down my back as I held in my strangled breathing. Something heavy fell to the ground above us. I suspected the wildling would never give another answer again.

"Ugly beast," the Immortal said with disgust and thumped across the ground. Wings flapped again after she had mounted whatever beast she brought with her. My pulse staggered as we waited. The moss shivered as a sharp breeze spread out over the area. The beating wings faded away. I dropped my hand and pulled in a shallow breath.

Dorian lifted a hand for us to wait. Kane snarled silently as he stared ahead, glaring blankly. Laini's lips twitched, livid. The Immortal's merciless nature submersed us into a pool of fury and outrage. Dorian dropped his hand, and we dispersed, fleeing from the claustrophobic hiding place.

"That wretched—" Kane grunted and ended in a low whisper,

saying something much nastier. The air tasted metallic, as if blood hung in it.

"Let's check to see if the poor thing is alive," Laini cut in and scrambled up the cliffside with Dorian. I rushed after them, horrified to see a dark shape lying lifeless in the dry grass. A pool of inky blood formed beneath the wildling, who looked like a lump of shaggy fur. She *had* been a tall creature with horns and bushy hair, now bleeding out from a blade to the throat.

"What the hell just happened?" Roxy asked. Bryce scanned the area around us as we circled around the wildling's twitching body.

"A hunter happened," Kane said sourly. "A rotten, wasteful use of space."

"We should've ambushed her when we had a chance," Arlonne said with a snarl, glaring at Dorian.

He shook his head. "No. There was no way we could've known the situation would turn to violence. She was cooperating, answering the questions."

"She's still alive," Laini said somberly as she crouched beside the creature. The wildling shivered, her body stiffening as she groaned in pain. Laini closed her eyes and took hold of the knife stuck in the creature's throat. "I'm sorry. This is the only way I can help you." She waited for the creature's nod, then dealt the finishing blow to put her out of her misery. The wildling gave a jerk and let out a pained sigh, sounding almost relieved. As I watched, a small, pale soul rose from her chest and floated away, like dandelion fluff. There would be no more agony where she was going. I sucked in a sharp breath as Laini stood, blinking back tears.

"Needless violence," she muttered, shaking her head. "She wasn't even dark. The poor thing. She was doing her job."

I tore my eyes away from the sickening pool of wildling blood. The murder was another cold injustice of the vampire hunters, more proof that the Immortals wielded immense power against anyone they deemed beneath them.

And everyone, it seemed, was beneath them.

CHAPTER SEVENTEEN

"We've got to keep moving," Dorian said.

I tore myself away from the wildling's fallen body. Kane snatched up the knife from its throat. Roxy gave him a disgusted look, and he huffed.

"She can't use it," he argued. "And we need it. Who knows what this world is going to throw at us next?"

With that chilling notion, we started walking again, and I tried to think over Dorian's plan from before our horrific detour. Every snap and crunch beneath our shoes made my nerves surge on high alert. It was as if my body expected to hear that terribly hypnotic voice call out from the woods again. We made our way back through the trees without a problem, but Bryce sometimes stopped to stare up into the tops of the trees before Kane shoved him gently to keep going.

We went back to our original path.

"Keep close to the trees in case we need to hide again," Dorian said. I hoped we wouldn't have to. We would head next for the lake and then the strange city of Immortals. A place filled with cruel beings who wielded horrific power.

I couldn't picture Itzarriol, the Immortal capital city. Would it be a living version of the vampire city? I somehow doubted it. My daydreams conjured marble temples that looked a lot like the ones from my high school history textbook, from the chapter about Rome. From the ruler's voice and actions, I suspected the architecture would reflect a culture of beauty and cruelty combined. I tried to ignore my aching feet. From the tear to here, it could easily be ten or fifteen miles, I guessed, but it was hard to estimate distance in this world.

After what felt like twenty more minutes of walking, Dorian stopped our group again. "Let's make camp somewhere around here," he suggested. "Keep an eye out for places while we walk."

The edge of the forest offered few options. We could go deeper into the trees, but I wanted nothing to do with the hissing branches. Still, it might be preferable to sleeping out in the open, vulnerable, with rulers hunting us. It was difficult to think about sleep when "night" was so bright. It felt like morning, but my internal clock yelled that it was time to rest. Weird. I rubbed my eyes.

The sound of agonized sobbing drifted from somewhere in the distance. I kept walking but strained to listen. It came again: a high-pitched wail of distress. I looked around at our group. Nobody was crying. I worried about my sanity leaving me. *I must be really tired.*

"Did you hear that?" I quietly asked Roxy, who was walking closest to me. I didn't want to alert the others if I'd only imagined it. "The cry?"

The vampires should've heard it too, but they said nothing. I wiggled my ear, wondering if somehow the elevation of this world had plugged up my hearing.

Roxy shook her head. "No, all I hear is that weird groaning."

I didn't hear any groaning. In fact, the cry had turned to mocking laughter and pained shrieks.

I studied the surrounding trees uneasily. "Dorian warned us we shouldn't follow voices in the Immortal Plane. I guess it's a trick of the distance, or the wind, or something."

Roxy flinched, and I wondered what she had heard. "I hope so."

We fell back into stride and silence with one another. Occasionally, the cry came back to me, but I desperately tried to ignore it. Dorian, Kane, Laini, Arlonne, and Sike gathered together in the front of our group. They appeared calm and steady in their movements, unbothered by the voices in the trees.

Bryce took up the rear of the party behind Roxy and me. I wondered if he'd heard things, too.

Before I could ask, Bryce stopped dead and sucked in a sharp breath, causing us all to turn and face him. "The girls," he cried, his eyes bulging. "We need to help them. Now!"

He took off into the trees and slid down a slope before we could react, disappearing into the forest. My panicked heart slammed against my chest. Bryce was *fast* when he wanted to be.

"Follow him," Dorian snapped. "What the hell is he doing?"

The vampires sprinted after Bryce, but they were slower than usual, not wanting to lose me and Roxy. Laini kept glancing back over her shoulder to make sure they hadn't lost us. We followed them as fast as we could.

Was this about the voices? Had Bryce heard them too?

"Don't let him out of your sight," Dorian shouted to us. I veered around a thick tree toward the left, while the vampires went right. Kane and Roxy ran with me, her heavy breathing right behind me, his lithe form tearing through the forest just ahead. Dorian and the others ran far ahead.

Kane groaned. "I got stuck with you slow losers."

I ignored him and pumped my arms, trying to catch the darting shapes of Dorian's cloak ahead of us. Bryce had a head start. He was a fast runner, but geez, never this fast. Maybe he was in a magical trance that increased his pace. Somewhere deeper in the forest, Bryce shouted something incomprehensible. What had happened to my ex-captain? I just prayed this little detour wouldn't draw the wrong kind of attention.

The forest emptied into a clearing, where a massive tree with red bark grew. Bryce rushed around the base of the giant tree in circles. I slid down a small slope to reach Dorian and the rest, joining them by the tree.

"Where are they?" Bryce demanded. "I heard them crying. They're hurt!"

Laini grabbed him by the shoulders. "Bryce, it's not real! It's in your head. These redwood trees pull up a lot of pain and distress from the dark soul energy in the soil. It's just an echo of things that have already happened."

"Those don't look like the kinds of redwoods we know," Roxy said accusingly between panting breaths.

Kane shrugged. "There are lots of things here that might share a name with something in the Mortal Plane but nothing else."

"Why would it do that?" I asked, shaken. Betrayals by rulers were bad enough without the greenery adding to it. "It's a tree."

"It isn't trying to do it," Dorian explained. "It naturally reflects the pain and darkness it feeds on. It can disorient you if you pay attention to it. We learned to deal with these things as kids. This was my fault, for not warning you clearly enough. I hadn't noticed any young redwood trees." He scowled, angry at himself.

This was a *young* tree? I marveled at the towering height.

"But I heard them," Bryce snapped. "Listen, they're calling again!" He looked around for the source of the sound, frantic.

Laini slapped him hard across the face. I gasped at the suddenness of it. Laini was the last person I expected to slap anyone. Bryce reeled to the side and pressed a hand to his startled face. The clarity came back to his eyes in an instant.

"You hit me!"

Kane let out a peal of laughter.

"Sorry," Laini said with a guilty look. "That's what my grandmother told me to do when I was a kid."

Noted: Laini has a killer slap game.

"Don't run off like that," Kane grumbled, his mirth short lived. "The rules aren't jokes." It seemed that Halla's lecturing nature had rubbed off on her son.

Bryce nodded solemnly. "I know. I'm sorry."

Dorian looked thoughtfully up at the smooth-skinned bark of the tree. What was he thinking? Up close, I realized the red skewed more to a rust color, the texture closer to leather. Nothing like our redwoods at home.

"Follow me," he said simply. We continued down another slope, which led to a cliff that looked out onto a valley below, choked with the enormous redwood trees. The scale of the massive trees made the landscape look like a surrealist painting, where everything was the wrong size. The treetops in the valley were nearly level with our group as we stood on the cliff. The tips of their branches had to be several stories from the ground. The foliage, dense clumps of thick green needles, looked menacingly sharp. I whistled in awe. This was a good place for us humans to go crazy in.

Dorian gave a satisfied smile. "We can use the thorn canopy as cover to fly safely. It can provide shelter, too."

Arlonne let out a short, sharp laugh, startling me. Sometimes, she was so quiet I forgot about her presence.

"Your side trip turned out to be useful, after all," she said, slinging a grin at Bryce.

Bryce proudly pressed a hand against his chest. "I meant to do it all along," he announced.

I studied the incredible forest before us. We would pass our first night in this untrustworthy dimension in a monstrous forest that transmitted the pain and suffering of dark souls trapped in the ground.

I suspected it wouldn't be the most restful night of sleep.

CHAPTER EIGHTEEN

Ensconced high in the redwoods, transported up by the redbills, we camped in a large hole carved into the dense trunks of purplish black thorns. Before we bedded down, a few of the vampires had gathered the redbills and taken them for a short trip up into the trees to check for any hidden creatures that could do us harm. The redbills naturally sought out this area, drawn to it like a magnet, and moved through and around the hostile trees with ease. Numerous tunnels wound outward from our little cavern, and Laini explained that wild redbills had carved this area earlier, which our birds could sense. From the direction of the new growth, the thorns pointing every which way, the old flock appeared to have moved on some time ago.

The thorns—each around the length of the two daggers I had sheathed in my boots—overlapped from tree to tree, blocking out any light that might have crept in from below. It created a curiously springy yet solid surface upon which to spread our mats and sleeping bags. When anyone moved, the woven floor creaked enough that I was concerned we would fall to our deaths while we slept, but it held steady beneath our weight. Although gear bags and clothing snagged on the needles in a few places, it was oddly comfortable to sleep on, since it distributed our weight evenly. It was like a charming bed of nails. Throughout the night, however, the redwoods had whispered to me. I imagined they whispered to Roxy and Bryce too—a constant low chatter of pained voices speaking of deep grief and lost chances in life.

When I woke up after an unknown amount of time, the sky was once again dark outside our strange camp. Part of my brain wanted to suggest this was morning, but in reality I had no concept of what time it was. I stared out the narrow opening of the nest from my sturdy sleeping pad, studying the gloom outside, my eyes now accustomed to the lack of light. There was little to see except more of the redwoods stretching away. I knew if I crawled to the doorway I might see the jagged peaks of the mountain range lit by whatever souls were caught in the sky right now. But it was wiser to not make myself a target for creatures with far better eyesight who might be looking for food or a prisoner.

On the far side of the nest, Dorian rested beside Sike. I felt a pang of disappointment, missing his touch. It would continue like this for the rest of our journey, especially after he fed. I shook myself to dispel my low mood. The voices didn't just mess with your head by calling to you—it seemed as though they had crawled into my psyche, leaving me unsettled and sad. This was a mission, and I needed to concentrate... for everyone's sake. I rubbed my hands, reminding myself that I was alive and well and would learn to ignore the voices. We had survived our first night in the Immortal Plane. That was what mattered.

Roxy and Bryce stirred beside me, slowly coming to consciousness. Roxy flicked on a lighter, the solitary flame letting us see a fraction more of one another and the space around us. In the orange glow, Bryce's eyebrows scrunched together as he examined the unforgiving trees.

"It feels like there are eyes on us all the time," he said, keeping his voice low.

My spine tingled with an unnerving sensation. "I know what you mean."

Roxy peered through the foliage to the shadowy sky, still kneeling on her sleeping pad. "It's all shadows," she muttered after a moment. "There's no light to focus on."

Bryce nodded.

The vampires began to move around and gather their packs, their forms little more than sound in the dim light.

"Let's get ready to go," Dorian said. "We're going to be spending most of the day flying through these tunnels, so make sure everything is strapped down tight and won't get caught on thorns."

The air in the nest moved as Drigar gently flapped his wings. The flame from Roxy's lighter caught the proud glint in his eye. Reuniting with Dorian had made him happy.

"The redbills created the routes we'll be taking over a lengthy period of time. Thousands of years, maybe," Sike relayed to us as we packed up our beds. We humans nibbled on some dry rations.

"They'll spread throughout the entirety of this tangle," Kane said. "It's a concealed route, but it's not the fastest. The redbills will have to fly slower because of the space constraint."

"It's the safest way to travel," Dorian said with an air of assurance. "Even if it's not the shortest."

The forest was massive, but it was a better bet than facing threats on land or in the air. As odd as these tunnels felt, I was glad the thorns hid us so well. It would be harder for the hunters to find us.

"You never know where the tunnels will take us, though," Laini told me with a low chuckle. "Unfortunately, sometimes their tunnels veer off into dead ends or lead to bizarre places. The redbills have minds of their own."

We finished our rough breakfast and made sure we hadn't left anything behind. Laini no longer had to help me mount her redbill, even in the blackness. I could see the bird's general shape, and I'd had plenty of practice climbing onto redbills over the last few months.

We set off, and I quickly found that with my vision practically useless, every sound became more intense. It didn't help that the dense canopy around us trapped all sound—the redwoods made sure we heard every shadowy complaint of unknown souls. After a while, I heard Sike sigh under his breath, the exhalation weighted with emotion. Could the vampires be feeling it too? I'd assumed they were immune, since they were used to it, but it was doubtful they'd had a reason to spend this much time in these tunnels before, even if they'd previously explored them on occasion.

More than once, a dagger-like thorn sliced at one of our group. My scalp burned where I'd been scratched, and I heard both Roxy and Dorian let out sounds of pain. The blood matting my hair was hot, almost hotter than it should be, and I swore the whispers got louder. The world swirled with no point of reference to cling to.

"Laini," I croaked at one point, thirsty but too afraid to reach for my water skin in case I fell off the redbill. "What happens if you get caught on the thorns? I think I'm more susceptible to the echoes after being scraped."

She guided us around a dogleg in the tunnel, a fraction of light catching her rich hair. "Getting wounded by the thorns can have that effect," she said quietly, "but it's temporary. Just hold on. We'll be out soon."

How many hours has it been?

Occasional slivers of sepia light slipped through pockmarked gaps in the thorny cover, revealing what passed for daytime out in the wider world. I tightened my grip on the redbill feathers. Every single muscle in my body buzzed with restless energy as the voices grew louder. I sucked in a breath, tasting the musky air inside the passageways.

Up ahead, a yellowish glow burned like distant firelight.

"The exit," Laini muttered with a grateful sigh.

We must have traveled miles across the valley and possibly beyond, but I had no way of gauging how many.

The redbills stretched their wings in the open air with apparent relief but kept low over the trees to avoid detection. The treacherous mountain peaks still surrounded us. I'd taken dozens of redbill flights across the US, but the landscape passed much faster there. The Immortal Plane seemed never-ending.

The trees began to thin out, and the terrain became sparser, filled with jagged rocks and small patches of strange vegetation. The intense effects of the redwoods began to fade as we got farther and farther away. I slowly regained my senses and lost the heady sense of dread I'd been wrapped in for... well, who knew how long. A short while later, a large lake came into view, surrounded by deep green grass and a few stony outcroppings of gleaming black rock. Nestled in the mountains, the surface of the water was coated with a thick bluish mist through which iridescent bubbles appeared, floating up through the air like jellyfish without their tentacles. The bubbles were massive. Up close, I estimated they were at least six feet wide. They rose from the water and never popped, only continuing to lift into the sky. The almost luminescent water and the stone and grassy area around the lake made me think of prehistoric Earth. Could this be where the surviving vampires had hidden?

"Welcome to Lake Siron," Laini said, then clicked to our redbill, who chirped softly in response.

The group of redbills descended as one, weaving through the bubbles. The giant spheres floated by, moved gently by the breeze the same way the soul-lights high above were.

The redbills flew carefully in wide circles above the area. I watched the ground with interest, as did the vampires. Their vision allowed for more precision, but the strangeness of the world gave me and the other humans an advantage in spotting something they might gloss over in a landscape that was familiar to them.

As we passed over a wider stretch of grassland, I felt Laini stiffen in front of me.

"There is darkness here," she said, inhaling sharply like a dog that had caught a scent.

I glanced to the side and saw Kane's fangs lengthen slowly. The darkness was powerful enough to evoke a response, even from here.

Dorian snarled, the shadows beneath his face shifting. He hadn't fed since our arrival, and his face was gaunt. I wanted to reach out to him and calm him, but it was impossible right now. Drigar flew between our hovering redbills, allowing Dorian to speak to us over the low wind.

"Wildling," he said.

Kane nodded. "Definitely."

I couldn't help my surprise. He was reacting so differently to this wildling than the one we had mourned in the redwoods. It seemed that not all wildlings were as gentle and innocent as that one had been.

Below us, a small hill overlooked Lake Siron. A pack of creatures moved across its grassy surface, almost blending in with the shifting plains.

"It's herding the velek below," Sike noted.

"The what?" Roxy asked from behind Kane.

"The wildlings are the caretakers of the forest creatures," Arlonne said from my other side. "Velek are creatures of the plains and the forest. The wildlings move them from place to place to manage the vegetation and pests."

"It's a bit like the connection we have with the redbills," Sike said, "but dark wildlings like the one down there actively control the herd, rather than communicating with the velek to understand what they need. Dark wildlings can be very cruel to the creatures they're meant to be protecting."

I peered down, squinting in the amber light. At first, the velek looked like mortal deer. Nostalgia settled over me as I remembered my time with Dorian and the elk traveling through the mountains, but these creatures moved differently than elk or deer—they darted and weaved, sometimes leaping for no clear reason. Their faraway outlines struck me as odd and strangely proportioned. The horns sprouting from their heads looked subtly wrong, but it was impossible to make out details at this distance. I couldn't see the wildling at all.

"Aren't you worried that thing will sense us?" I asked, looking between the vampires' faces.

They didn't seem to hear me at first. Laini scratched the back of her neck, eyes unfocused. Kane pinched the bridge of his nose, his fangs glinting. Dorian watched the herd below and shook his head with a low growl, a few pieces of his dark hair falling over his crystalline eyes.

They're all hungry.

He leaned forward, the lines of his face deepening. "It won't be able to sense vampire auras. None of the immortal creatures can," he assured me. "For all intents and purposes, we don't have auras here. Even in the Mortal Plane, your technology can have a hard time picking us up if you don't know specifically where to look."

"But you can sense each other?" Bryce asked. "If we get separated, are you able to find one another?"

"Vampires can sense one another's auras just fine," Laini said, brow furrowed as she tracked the velek. "And human auras will just feel like a powerful soul-light to any Immortals who might notice you."

The Immortals could sense our souls? The thought made me uncomfortably aware of my body, as if I were a radio tower giving off waves.

"They can't tell the difference between a soul with or without a body?" Roxy asked intently.

"No, it's actually very hard to differentiate," Dorian explained. "Especially for Immortals who have never been to the Mortal Plane. And as long as we stay out of the wildlings' sight, they shouldn't notice anything amiss either. We need to be vigilant, however, and not just about the wildlings. If the vampires do have a camp around here, I expect they've set traps and magical protections in the surrounding area."

At a silent command from the vampires, the redbills headed for the far side of the lake and landed behind a stack of large, fractured boulders. The rocks were like obsidian and cracked along sharp lines to form bizarre geometric shapes. The area stank of blood and sulfur from the water. I covered my nose for a moment, but the scent burned into my nostrils. Roxy gagged. Bryce pulled a face.

I couldn't agree more.

I slid off my redbill with Laini, alert and prepared, mentally reminding myself where every weapon was on my body. Bryce's face tensed as he surveyed the area. Roxy's hand hovered near her holster. None of us spoke above the slightest whisper for fear of drawing attention.

"Are you going to feed on the wildling?" I asked Dorian quietly, looking around for the incoming herd but seeing nothing.

He shook his head. "If it were on its own, yes, but the velek would outnumber us. We could get stampeded if the wildling called on them for aid. Now," he addressed the group, "let's spread out and look for signs of the settlement. A vampire goes with a human. Humans keep watch while vampires search for anything that seems routinely disturbed or very purposefully placed."

"Be stealthy," Kane added.

Like I would start stomping around with a dark wildling about.

"And stay within sight of the lake," Dorian instructed. "We don't want to get too far from each other, especially if those velek come this way."

Leaving the redbills tucked behind the rocks, we split into groups. Kane, Arlonne, and Bryce walked away from Roxy, Sike, and Laini, spreading out along the bank of the lake, our dull clothing blending in with the rocks and grass and grayish dirt. I went with Dorian, not giving him the chance to disagree. He would have to feed soon, and then we would truly have to keep our distance. I wanted to take advantage of the time we had left. Everyone kept their eyes trained on the ground or the horizon, looking for clues and trouble.

Up close, the lake was a multicolored quilt of madness beneath the mist. In the area closest to us, it bubbled mint green. It brightened to yellow several yards toward the center, then darkened to orange, then red. It was odd to see bright colors in the usually drab landscape of the Immortal Plane. Some part of my brain convinced me that the water was whatever this plane's equivalent of radioactive might be. My stomach rolled queasily. I pressed my lips together and tried to ignore the rotten-egg smell, but it only grew worse as we continued onward.

In a small dell filled with fuzzy, tangled vines a few dozen feet from the lake, thin white trees with mustard-yellow leaves dotted the area in a rough circle about forty feet wide. They looked like the Earth aspens I saw every fall. The leaves melted together for a moment, then jumped back. I rubbed my eyes. The grove flickered and refused to stay still, as if it didn't want me to look at it. One second it looked like a proud circle of healthy trees and the next a ruined, rotten jumble. Another trick of the Immortal Plane.

As one, Dorian and I headed for the grove, keeping a respectable distance between us and the trees, stopping at the edge of the matted vines.

"I'm surprised to see a circle to the Mortal Plane here," Dorian said quietly. "Whatever you do, don't touch them."

Instinctively, I curled my fingers into my hands. "Why?" I asked, my throat tight. After the redwoods, my trust in trees was running dangerously low.

"The hunters often set magical snares in the circles," he said distractedly, casting his glacial eyes over the trees. Did they move for him? His eyes were focused as he searched for any sign of such danger. "This portal has been made inactive, and they've also trapped it."

"How can you tell?" I asked, looking closer only for the trees to shimmer and waver. Dorian had warned us that this plane would challenge our human senses, but I felt frustrated with my reduced abilities in the Immortal Plane. It was like being a rookie on my first mission all over again.

Dorian dropped his voice. "This place was once a portal between the Immortal Plane and the Mortal Plane, like the stone circle in Scotland. But hunters have poisoned some of the trees and uprooted others. Concentrate and look closer at the trees. They're long dead."

I looked. Somehow, hearing him say it made it easier to see the grove. For an instant, as if catching a glimpse through the still water between rings of slow-moving ripples, I had a clear image. Most of the trees were rotten and twisted, others cracked in half like dispos-able chopsticks and left scattered in the open space of the circle. The reality of what I was looking at sent a chill of dread through me. The warm air did nothing for my goosebumps.

"So, we can't use it anymore?" I asked.

He nodded. "The circles have to be whole and linked to both planes correctly, or they won't work. The objects that form the circle, usually rocks or trees, exist in *both* planes at once, linked by the portal. They act like anchors or coordinates, allowing us to travel between planes safely." His jaw tightened angrily. "The ruling caste knew these places were important for vampires. They set out to destroy or guard every single one, to catch and exterminate vampires coming and going."

He tilted his head, then pointed. "Do you see a bluish rock at the base of one of the trees? It might take you a minute to find it."

I looked, blinking to focus my vision, trying to see between the ripples like I had before. Eventually, I saw it—a small glow at the base of the largest tree. "I see it."

"That's part of the trap they've set on the circle. It powers a magical glamor that makes it look untouched. I imagine you're struggling to see anything other than a perfect version of the grove, yes?"

I nodded. "It's like it doesn't want me to look at it too hard."

"Exactly," Dorian said. "The glamor makes it look like the circle hasn't been tampered with, but if we were to step in there, we'd trigger a trap and either die immediately or be captured in something that would hold us until hunters arrived."

I quietly considered the broken trees as I reflected on his words. This was a world with genuine magic, and it was used for evil like this. A seed of grief grew inside me.

"However," he said, "it's often possible to recognize when a glamor has been set on a circle. Can you see a kind of flickering?"

I nodded, twisting my mouth with uncertainty. "It's like the edges of the trees here are off… like I'm looking at a regular image with 3-D glasses." I took a beat, wondering if he would know what I meant by that. "Like I'm seeing a trick image."

"It's because the planes closely align in this area, so the barrier is thin here. You're seeing *through* the barrier to the Mortal Plane for a fraction of a second, then focusing back on the Immortal Plane. All of that messes with the glamor and makes it flicker. It's only dangerous if you're not paying attention."

It was a strange feeling to be so close to my plane yet unable to touch it. I tried once more to see the circle as it was here on the Immortal Plane—the broken version covered by the glamor—but I only managed it for a moment before the mix of magic and different planes exhausted my eyes and I had to give up. My nerves danced. Every fiber in my body felt like a small traitor. What kind of soldier was I if I couldn't study my surroundings properly? *I have to adapt and find out, I guess.*

Dorian moved in my peripheral vision, his cloak like one of the dark human souls drifting to the ground.

"Lyra," he said, his voice suddenly urgent. "Crouch and follow me. Head for the three rocks covered in vines."

I turned to see him moving low to the ground toward three of the glass-like black rocks back near the lake that were slowly being covered by vines similar to those in the dell. I followed his lead, feeling a small sense of satisfaction as my training and skills kicked in. He wedged himself into a hollow at the base of the rocks, tugging me in at the last second before the velek herd crested the hillside. A shadowy figure moved among them.

I peeked between the wooly leaves, trying not to touch the vines. The velek, deer-like creatures that varied in size, made low rolling hums as they moved. One was the size of a small pig, the next the size of a buffalo. A baby and an adult? It was hard to tell. Their shaggy pelts were made of gray, green, and tangerine moss. The resemblance to deer ended dramatically at the head. I studied their extra-long snouts, their wide mouths full of sharp canines and flat molars. I remembered what Arlonne had said about the velek being used to manage vegetation and pests. I suspected that while they mostly ate the grass and various things from the trees, given the chance they would eat anything else that didn't move fast enough.

Their heads were topped with giant branching antlers like those of a moose. The antlers' ends weren't sharp but rounded like pieces of coral. I squinted to make out the shapes on the tips of the antlers and immediately wished that I hadn't. Their antlers held human faces. It was as if a deranged sculptor had carved expressions of agony, grief, anger, and cruelty into the surface of each antler. Just below the antlers on the creatures, furry eyestalks extended from their strange snouts. Each stalk had a beady black eye at the end of it.

I instinctively pressed my fingers to my lips, making sure no sound of surprise escaped. Dorian tensed beside me as the herder came into view.

The wildling, a squat and stony creature that perhaps came up to my shoulder, moved through the herd. Nature had crafted the wildling from something that looked similar to the stones we were hiding between right now. The black glassy stone of its flesh would easily blend in with the shards of rock that littered the plains, making it difficult to spot.

The herd passed us. Beside me, Dorian's hand brushed mine as we braced ourselves behind the vines, barely breathing. He dug his fingers into the ground, his lean face pale with hunger, resisting the urge to feed from the wildling only forty feet or so from where we were crouched. There was a pulse of heat against my chest as the leather bag containing Dorian's stone began to warm. I winced, fumbling to pull it to rest outside of my shirt. There was no light, but the bag continued to grow hotter. I looked to Dorian, confused, but his eyes were clenched shut, his fangs descended out of a desperate need to feed.

One of the larger velek close to us—this one the size of a healthy horse—abruptly lifted its head. Unlike the other velek, it had a small teal gem embedded in its forehead. The surrounding flesh was swollen and raw, weeping a green ooze. Its eyestalks waved back and forth as it turned toward us, setting its snout to the ground. My stomach clenched. It sniffed along the exact path Dorian and I had taken to hide behind the vines.

Dorian said our auras should be invisible to the creatures. Was he wrong? A bead of sweat trailed down my neck as the creature grew closer, snorting. Dorian growled beneath his breath as the wildling also inched closer with the moving herd. It was filled with dark energy. Could Dorian control himself?

The approaching velek stopped a few feet away and gave a pealing bay similar to a bloodhound. It made no move to attack us, just stood, its creepy eyestalks twitching back and forth as it tried to get some visual evidence of us.

More of the herd pulled away from the moving current and headed our way. None of them made noise, but our original betrayer continued his baying, getting more and more frantic.

Please be quiet.

It was a lost cause. The dark wildling turned its head toward us, revealing a golem-like face that looked like it had been poorly carved from rock, all jagged edges and odd angles. My body froze with foreboding. Could it see us? Dorian hissed something like a command, but the velek with the gem continued baying, and its comrades continued to accumulate around our hiding place. The wildling reached for something that hung around its neck on a thin cord.

Dorian growled and exploded into movement, rushing toward the wildling.

It was too late. The wildling produced a horn, and the sound resonated clearly in the heavy air, seeming to grow and fill the entire valley. It was a sound I hadn't heard since the first time I came to the Immortal Plane.

Dorian's angry snarl sent a wave of dread washing over me.

Despite not knowing what this sound would unleash, I knew one thing for certain.

It meant trouble.

CHAPTER NINETEEN

The blast from the wildling's horn faded slowly, the echoes slipping out of the air like oil off water.

Dorian's eyes flashed with hunger. His fangs descended fully as the last ounces of his self-control disappeared. I lunged for him, but he was faster. He vaulted around the velek toward the dark wildling with another rabid snarl.

I rushed after him, but the velek were stubborn. Instead of scattering like I expected from herd animals, the velek lowered their antlers and began a chorus of bays and bellows. The ones closest to Dorian charged him. A velek in front of me knocked me back with a toss of its large, impressive antlers, the distressed faces in the bone mocking me as they slammed into my side and shoulder. I darted out of the way of another oncoming velek. I needed distance or altitude, since they would likely overwhelm me if I tried to run. I scrambled up the rocks we had been hiding between, clinging to the thick vines and thankful they didn't cut or poison me. *So much for not touching anything.*

Another velek rammed the rock, breaking off a plate-sized slice. I clung to the vines, jamming the toes of my boots into cracks in the otherwise smooth rocks. From this vantage point, I watched as Dorian dodged the oncoming velek. The herd slowed his pace, but he expertly avoided their intimidating antlers. He bounded like a skipping rock between the charging creatures, each move taking him closer to the squat wildling. It turned to run, releasing a panicked cry before trying to blow its horn once more, but it was too late.

Dorian tackled the wildling, cutting the blast off suddenly. A grating scream, like rocks grinding together, filled the air as Dorian's fangs sank into the wildling. Apparently, the rock-like flesh was only a shell of some kind and was easily punctured by vampire fangs. The velek herd immediately stilled, milling around aimlessly, except for the one with the gem in its forehead. It reared abruptly and tore off over the hill, baying all the way.

The vampires had mentioned that the wildlings controlled the creatures. It had been making it harder for us by pinning the herd against us, but now the wildling was helpless. I had to look away toward the shivered edge of the aspen circle as Dorian drank from its rocky form.

Pushing through the wandering velek, Kane and Arlonne ran up. Arlonne immediately joined in the feed, while Kane hung back with an amused smirk.

"Oh, good. I didn't need to help you take care of one wildling," he said. "As soon as we heard the horn, we thought you'd lost your edge. Imagine struggling with a little stone goblin."

"Where are the others?" I asked, scrambling down from my perch up in the rocks, my throat tightening with concern. Had the horn called more wildlings or something worse?

Kane pointed up. "Sent the humans up on redbills with Sike guiding them. We have to keep our humans and non-warrior vampires away from the action. It's better that they're ready to fly at a moment's notice."

I tried to ignore Dorian and Arlonne's nearby feast, instead focusing on Kane's words and face. As the other two vampires fed and the source of darkness was drained away, I noticed that Kane's brow relaxed.

In the sky, two redbills carrying the rest of our team circled, close enough to land if they needed to. As I considered the distance, a shriek caught my attention. Drigar let out another war cry as he flew toward our group, a second redbill in his wake. He whipped past us, and Dorian jerked his head back with a sudden grimace. The wildling's bronze blood dripped from his mouth and chin. The shadows beneath his skin darkened with his new strength.

"They're here," he breathed hoarsely. "We need to move. Now!"

A hazy, sinuous shape rose and fell through the swirl of clouds and soul-lights. There was the far-off sound of beating wings. Kane let out a sharp whistle to call down the redbills carrying our team.

I spotted the shrieking decay first, its terrible body contorting as it flew—not as fast as our two unmanned redbills but still very fast— through the sky toward us. This one was smaller than the one we'd fought in the Mortal Plane at the ski resort, but it was still double the size of a very large crocodile and covered in black scales. It twisted toward the redbills, and Drigar screeched angrily.

Sitting atop the shrieking decay were three figures. The wildling was obvious, with its onyx rocky form, but the other two were more difficult to make sense of. Their silhouettes shimmered in a similar way to the glamor around the tree circle. I couldn't see features or weapons, but just their presence was enough to send a pulse of raw fear through me.

I couldn't feel darkness in a soul, but with these creatures, I didn't need a vampire's senses. The menace and ill intentions were easy to pick up on. I knew without a doubt that these were the Immortal enemies the vampires had been so reluctant to talk about.

My eyes registered long bluish hair whipping in the wind before our redbills attacked. Suddenly, a flash of teal light blazed through the air from the back of the shrieking decay. The smell of burnt leaves rose up before it struck Sike and Bryce's redbill clean in the side. The redbill cried out—a terrible, shrill sound of pain—and tumbled from the air. I heard Bryce and Sike scream as they plummeted toward the ground, still clinging to the wounded redbill's back.

"Hunters." Arlonne jumped up, snarling, her face marred with bronze blood. The wildling beneath her and Dorian lay lifeless on the ground.

My fear of the shrieking decay's riders was a flickering shiver of dread, as fast moving as the trees in the grove, but now it turned to cold anger. I was not letting anyone on my team die here by this stinking lake in the middle of nowhere, a world away from my home. It was not happening—not on my watch. My head cleared, and I felt my analytical mind kick in. Maybe I wasn't a soldier of this plane, but I was still a soldier. It was time to do my job.

From my last tangle with a shrieking decay creature, I knew their spine was vulnerable if we could get to it. The teal light obviously consisted of some kind of magic. The laser-like consistency of the beam reminded me of the X-75s. The hunters riding the shrieking decay were the source of the magic, so I needed to find a way to take them out somehow. Maybe they needed a weapon to fire it that we could try to destroy.

Bryce and Sike were still on the redbill, sprays of black blood scattering into the sky around them from their wounded mount as it fluttered erratically toward the ground. I saw a brief flash, and the shrieking decay gave a gurgling wail, tossing its head as something struck its thick neck. It seemed Bryce had gotten lucky with a silenced shot from one of his guns, before their redbill fell into the gleaming black boulder field. It looked like it would be a messy landing, though I didn't see where they came down. My fists clenched. I hoped they were all right.

"The redbills can't handle a shrieking decay, especially one with two magic-wielding riders," Kane warned with a growl. "I'm sending the ones with no riders away. We'll need them down here." He waved his hand, and one of the redbills heading for the monster peeled away, but Drigar craned his head back and kept moving toward the fight.

Blood dripped from Dorian's mouth as he scowled, sucking in a sharp breath. "Drigar knows better than to keep fighting," he growled. The glacial color of his eyes darkened. "Ranged attacks are their specialty, and he's heading straight for them."

As if to prove his point, more lights flew from the back of the shrieking decay, toward Drigar. Terrible flashes of teal and black streaked through the sky. The shrieking decay dodged the rising bubbles expertly as it crossed the lake, hunting its downed prey with an otherworldly shriek. Drigar answered with a battle cry of his own, avoiding the rays and continuing to advance. Alongside Lake Siron's bubbling, misty surface ran the velek with the gem on its forehead, faster than even Dorian could run. It had led the hunters here.

At least it's not spewing acid yet. I pulled the rifle sight from my belt and squinted through it, trying to make out as many details as possible. The beast wore a more complex and sturdier version of the saddle and muzzle that had failed during our fight with the shrieking decay on the Mortal Plane. The Immortals had perfected their design. It actually did as the riders intended, meaning that they didn't want it to spew rot yet. Right now, the beast was skimming lower on the other side of the lake, toward where Sike and Bryce had landed. Looking through my scope, I caught a blur of movement as one of the hunters leapt off the back of the shrieking decay, landing in the grass behind a shard of rock thrusting up out of the plain.

"One of them is on the ground," I said, putting my scope away. "I think it's going to hit Sike and Bryce." We had to help them, even if it meant facing down Immortal warriors feared even by vampires, on the back of a shrieking decay. *Oh, is that all?* I felt a hysterical laugh swell in my throat, but I swallowed it. I'd long ago come to terms with the fact that I could die on the job; I hadn't yet. I could panic when it was over.

"We need to move," Dorian said, roughly scrubbing the blood off his face with his sleeve. He stared at me, brow furrowed, something feral back in his face that I hadn't noticed had been missing. "Use your gun if they get close enough, but otherwise you need to hang back. These hunters carry magical weapons."

In other words, I currently lacked the skill set to deal with them. Fine. I trusted Dorian's judgment. I had no experience with magical weapons and no training in how to avoid them or what would happen if they hit me. That wouldn't stop me from helping any way I could.

"What can I do?" I asked urgently.

He glanced out over the lake, seeing Laini and Roxy retreating from the shrieking decay on their redbill while Drigar harried the beast's underbelly with his talons. "You can sneak around to the other side to help Bryce and Sike get clear of danger, but stay out of this battle," he instructed evenly. "Laini will call one of the other redbills back and get you all out of range until this is over. We'll try to get close to the hunters so they can't use their long-range weapons, and we'll wear them down enough that we can get away."

Arlonne grunted in agreement, black swirling into her eyes, her skin teeming with fresh shadows from her feeding.

"Leave the magic to us," Kane said firmly.

I nodded shortly, ready to run as soon as they gave me the word. I had my orders.

Dorian, leading the way, took off with Kane and Arlonne around the lower half of Lake Siron and toward where the hunter had leapt to the ground.

I followed more slowly, slipping from one patch of cover to the next in the boulder field. According to what Dorian had said about how Immortals picked up auras or frequencies, they wouldn't be able to distinguish my aura from the surrounding stones. No frequency scanners existed in this plane, thankfully. A part of me hated to be left out of the action, leaving the fight in the hands of others. I knew I was outmatched, but I hated the feeling of being helpless on the sidelines. I wanted to understand the magic so I could rise against it. But I knew I had to be practical, and running recklessly into a fight when I didn't understand its mechanics wouldn't benefit the mission or the team.

Bryce and Sike falling from the sky flashed through my mind, and I scanned the air for the wounded redbill. Seeing nothing, I picked up the pace, desperate to make it to them before the hunters did.

The grass on the plains was longer here—almost up to my shoulder—so I was able to move more freely, running in a crouch with my hand hovering over my holster. My lungs burned as I took an erratic path to throw off anyone I couldn't see who might be trying to shoot at me. My back felt bare and vulnerable as I imagined one of the magical blasts hitting me between the shoulders.

A large boulder up ahead looked like a promising place to pause and take stock of the situation before I jumped in. I should be close to the fallen redbill and my friends by now. I peered out from behind the boulder as someone let out a cruel, melodious laugh. My muscles tightened. A flash of blue hair caught my eye just before the scene lit up.

I dodged back behind the boulder as teal light blasted past my hiding place. A sensation of strong static electricity lingered in its wake. I pressed against the stone. Had they spotted me?

"One day you'll learn accuracy that matches your vanity," Kane shouted. Arlonne grunted.

"I'll cut out your tongue, vampire," a cold voice snapped.

There was a note of the same musical taunting I'd heard before.

It was a woman's voice. I stole closer, confident the hunter hadn't seen me. Behind a boulder with a scraggly tree growing beside it, I looked through the leaves to get a better look. Any knowledge of an enemy was a good thing.

The first hunter I saw was the one who had jumped off the back of the shrieking decay. I could tell from the way the hunter stood that she was in command of her team on this mission. She stood easily over seven feet tall. Pale blue skin pulled tight over the defined angles of her face. She had oceanic blue-green hair piled atop her head in a complex series of braids all woven into a bun, secured in place by two glittering hair sticks with shining skulls carved into the ends. Bright silver chain mail covered her from her neck down to her feet. Her boots appeared to be made of a worked metal that should have been too heavy to lift and featured gem-studded soles. When she stepped forward, they slammed into the ground. Her right arm was heavily protected by sharp overlapping scales of a lacquered turquoise material. She wore gauntlets of the same material, with silver and gemstones worked into the design. A teal gemstone, matching the one in the velek's forehead, sat in the middle of her wide brow. Unlike the velek, the skin around her gemstone shimmered.

I was partially in awe of her stature, partially envious of her armor, and fully worried as she took on Kane and Arlonne. Kane leapt toward her and attempted to strike her head, while Arlonne went for her legs.

The woman rolled her eyes. "When will you bloodsuckers learn?" she roared.

In a swift movement, she countered Kane's attack easily by bringing up her armored forearm to slam into his chest. He flew backward with a gasp as the air was knocked from his lungs. In the next second, she smashed her hand into the ground, aiming to crush Arlonne under her fist. Arlonne threw herself out of the way just in time. The hunter grunted and yanked her hand back, bringing up chunks of the ground with it. Crumbling rocks and dirt fell from her hand, and as she shook off the debris, I saw another teal gemstone embedded into the palm of her glove.

A knife made of jagged black glass glinted in her other hand, but she didn't use it yet, instead lifting the hand containing the stone toward Kane. He yelled something incomprehensibly foul as a blast of teal exploded from her palm. I gasped as Kane dove out of the way, pushing Arlonne out of the blast's path as he went.

The woman grinned, showing off an unsettling number of small, sharp teeth. Her glee rolled from her in waves. She leapt and dodged easily as Arlonne and Kane attempted a counterattack. She laughed in delight when Arlonne tried to strike her head, swatting the vampire away with a savage blow from her armored elbow. The fight was an elegant dance, and I hated that she was winning. Sweat collected on Arlonne's brow, and she breathed heavily. Kane gnashed his teeth, fangs flashing. No more trash talk meant this was serious. The woman tilted her head back and laughed again, a cruel smirk on her face.

I tore my gaze from the intimidating woman. There was more than one fight in this battle. The shrieking decay floated near Sike and Bryce's fallen redbill but was kept at bay for now by Drigar and Laini's redbill harassing it from front and back. Dorian skidded to a stop on the shore of the lake, chips of black glassy rock flying up from beneath his feet. He called Drigar, and the bird instantly dove toward him. In moments, Dorian was mounted, and they flew back toward the shrieking decay. There was a new aspect to the fight now—the beast's riders would have to rethink their plan of attack.

While the towering woman who was attacking Kane and Arlonne emanated a cruel power, this immortal's face was rounder and more youthful. Silvery braids fluttered in the wind as he pulled the shrieking decay out of the way of Drigar's claws with a powerful movement of the reins. His metallic golden skin sharply contrasted with his black eyes as he glared murderously at Dorian. Apparently, color coordination was a big thing for Immortals. His armor was black metal, crisscrossed by seams of golden inlay, with white gems patterned down the arms and across the backs of his gauntlets. It was hard to tell from my position, but I guessed he might be shorter than the woman.

As Dorian dive-bombed the Immortal, striking out with a knife as long as my forearm, a creature I hadn't spotted before snapped sharp teeth in Dorian's direction, like a dog defending its owner. It sat on the shrieking decay's head in front of the golden Immortal and was definitely shorter than the other two. A small, goblinoid creature covered in scaly green-and-red skin, it had a pair of leathery wings on its back. I had absolutely no idea what this thing was, but it appeared to be a companion of the younger Immortal.

Dorian swung at the younger Immortal with his knife again as the shrieking decay tried to move closer. The blade scraped off the armor, sending up sparks, and the hunter glared at him, brow knitted with contempt and impatience. His haughty eyes said this was beneath him. From the other side, Laini and Roxy attacked on their redbill. The redbill clawed the inky side of the shrieking decay, which bucked backward to avoid both birds' talons. Dorian fell flat onto Drigar's back, narrowly missing a giant bubble that reflected the shrieking decay's ugly grimace.

I took a chance while the female hunter was preoccupied with Kane and Arlonne and dashed out across the final stretch toward Sike and Bryce. As I ran, my body mostly concealed by the grass and my lack of aura, my eyes went to the harness contraption on the shrieking decay. Dorian tried to get close enough to land a hit on the younger hunter, dodging out of the way as the beast swung a spiny wing at him. For a moment, I saw the shrieking decay in perfect profile. The harness the Bureau had used had definitely been modeled after something they'd learned from the Immortal Plane... except the immortal harness worked. It was sturdier, made of a high-grade material I couldn't identify, and the design fit so well it was practically a part of the creature. A ripple of worry flowed through me. It was unsettling to find more proof of a full-blown conspiracy between the higher-ups of the Bureau and the Immortals. How else would the Bureau have produced that kind of technology?

It was a small blessing that the Bureau's harness hadn't worked back in the Mortal Plane. While the Bureau had modeled it after the Immortal Plane's technology, they'd failed. We didn't know the creatures as well as the Immortals did. But these Immortal rulers had given the Bureau enough information to perform the basics. Who knew what other secrets and knowledge the Immortals had shared with unscrupulous board members? It would be tough to gain the upper hand. Even with all their strength and speed, I wondered what the vampires could do against magic weapons.

I made myself focus on the task at hand, holding my breath as I ran beneath the belly of the shrieking decay, eventually coming to hide behind a tumble of rocks covered in more of the hairy vines. Beyond Dorian's fight, I saw the crumpled redbill and had to suppress my curses against the hunters. I couldn't see Sike or Bryce in the wreckage. The redbill shifted slightly—or were those merely the feathers rustling in the breeze? A spike of fear stabbed through me. It rose to my throat, where it turned to white-hot anger. My friends were somewhere out there, and I would protect them any way I could.

The hunter's voice rose again, cutting the tense scene with her mocking laugh.

"What a pleasant surprise to find so many worthy vampires. I was right to linger by the lake," she gloated. "Thank you for the amusement, but it's time to end this. I have a party to attend." Her last statement had a punch of finality to it.

Her voice carried strong resonance, seeming to bellow around me from all sides. It must be able to cross great distances.

She tapped her boot impatiently. "You should just surrender," she said, her voice growing louder. The boulder beside me vibrated slightly at the timbre of her tone. She looked expectantly at Arlonne and Kane.

The two vampires glanced at each other and laughed, the next moment leaping into a run to attack once more.

She scowled and huffed. "Fine. Onder, finish this!"

The little onyx wildling nodded on the back of the shrieking decay. It had stayed so still on the saddle that I'd forgotten it was there. Dorian snarled and swung Drigar around, crouched low on his bird's back to prepare for the oncoming attack. Somewhere on the back of the other redbill that now circled to the rear of the beast,

I was positive Roxy was giving a rather explicit description of exactly where she would like to shove the female hunter's knife.

The wildling shoved the little winged creature out of the way as it scampered up onto the head of the shrieking decay, then raised its hands. It made a few sharp movements in the air with its short charcoal fingers, then slammed the fist of one hand into the palm of the other.

Thorny red vines, far more vicious than the ones I was close to now, broke through the ground beneath Kane and Arlonne. I held back a gasp. What power was this? Wherever the vampires stepped as they ran, vines sprang up and coiled around their legs. The thorns tore into their bodies and held them in place as they struggled. Arlonne growled and tried to rip the vines from her body. They tore, the sound like ripping leather, before the vines wound up her arm with frightening speed. Blood began to drip down her arms where the thorns sank into her flesh. Laini rose higher on her redbill with Roxy, obviously worried that the vines might strike out for the birds. It was smart, but it left me with fewer options for how to escape with Bryce and Sike when I finally reached them.

Urging Drigar on, Dorian dove for the wildling, his mouth open in a roar, fangs exposed. The rocky creature dove to the side with a sound like an enraged piglet, and the vines temporarily slowed their growth.

Kane grunted angrily and took advantage of the moment once the wildling wasn't concentrating on controlling the vines. Pushing himself up from his position lying face down on the group, he ripped through the spiny net by sheer force of will. The thorns sliced into him and created thin rivulets of shadowy blood. One vine snapped like a tight rubber band, and another reeled back for a moment but ultimately snared both his hands behind his back. The hunter smirked. She gave a laugh as sharp as broken glass.

Suddenly, Dorian leapt from Drigar's back onto the shrieking decay, his fangs flashing in the light. I had never been so happy to see vampire fangs. He launched himself at the Immortal, who cried out as Dorian struck him across the face with the blade of his knife. I couldn't imagine the hunters were used to physical blows actually connecting with their pretty faces. He tussled with the hunter for control of the shrieking decay but was attacked from behind by the little winged goblin creature. The three of them wrestled in the broad saddle while the wildling regained its balance and threw its small arm forward with a grating chattering sound. The serpentine monster drifted toward the ground at the same time as the vines crawled higher, seeking Dorian. I wanted to scream for him to watch out, but Laini did it for me.

"Dorian!" Her cry, mixed with Roxy's behind her, echoed terribly over the clearing.

The hunter stepped toward a trapped Arlonne, raising her right hand with the embedded jewel. The woman grinned as she prepared to unleash an energy shot straight to Arlonne's face, elongating the moment to toy with her victim. To her credit, Arlonne met the hunter's gaze with an unpleasant scowl. She spat on her boot, unable to move any more. The hunter's glee faded for a faltering moment, quickly replaced by disgust and annoyance.

The vines tightened around Arlonne's body. Blood leaked from the many thorn punctures all over her, matching the tears that began to spill from my eyes. I slowly pulled my pistol from its holster, ready to lose my cover and invisibility if it would be enough to maybe help in the fight.

The jewel began to glow. The older Immortal narrowed her eyes, her lips lifting back into a haughty smile. She knew she had Arlonne right where she wanted her. I raised my gun, aiming for the center of the Immortal's palm.

Movement fluttered on the lakeshore and from under the crumped redbill's wing, Sike leapt from his hiding place.

"Hey! Over here, you ugly giant!"

CHAPTER TWENTY

"Sike, stop!" Dorian shouted in a strained voice from the shrieking decay.

Too late.

For a moment, everything froze except for Sike. He sauntered from the redbill with a limp. Blood leaked from his nose, the telltale shadows dancing in the brilliant red liquid. His long, thin limbs moved slowly. He wasn't a warrior like the others, but he certainly knew how to plot a dramatic twist.

Dorian wouldn't be able to protect Sike. None of them could while tied down with the vines. There was only me and maybe Bryce, with our gun that I wasn't even sure would pierce the Immortal's armor if I fired on her. I crept beneath the tail of the shrieking decay where it floated some ten or fifteen feet above me, watching the scene unfold as I tried to get to Bryce. Sike was giving me a chance to get my former captain out of here, and I had to take it.

Strangely, the red tendrils didn't rise up to grab Sike. I looked to the wildling and found it watching the hunter intently. She held up a single gloved finger.

Dorian snarled in fury as he clashed with the other hunter, who was still trying to get control of the shrieking decay. The hunter stepped forward slowly. The wildling chirped.

"No, don't bother with the vines for this collection of bones," the older Immortal drawled. Her melodic voice dripped with cold disinterest. "This one is weak. I'll happily snap him in half myself when this is over. I think his strange little skull would look excellent in my collection."

God, I had never wanted to rip out someone's cold eyes so much in my life. I let my rage simmer in silence as I paused behind a cluster of spiny bushes. I had to keep my position hidden if I wanted to try anything.

"Whose skull are you calling strange?" Sike asked, a twinge of fake offense in his voice. "I know you guys are all so hideous you spend ridiculous amounts of soul energy powering your glamors, but... really? You're poking fun at how I look?"

"Speaking of soul energy, tell me," the hunter said in her carrying voice, "where has your group obtained all that wonderful fresh soul energy? I saw one of you use it to power some kind of weapon when you attacked my mount at the beginning of this fight."

My heart leapt to my mouth. Bryce had fired at the shrieking decay. She had seen him.

"I can sense so much fresh energy all around us yet can't find a specific source. What are you storing it in?" She sucked in a breath for a moment. Her eyebrow twitched with annoyance. "I've never felt anything like it before. If you tell me, I'll break your legs instead of your neck and let you go free."

Sike swayed slightly on his feet but stared back with his chin tilted high. "Still sounds like a crappy offer, so no thank you," he said with a grin. I knew it was forced, but to others it would appear cocky.

His attempt to be brave in the face of danger made my heart swell with pride.

Her nostrils flared angrily. I could almost hear her thoughts. *How dare someone so weak be so defiant?*

"Very well," she snapped. "Your neck it is then." She leapt forward, her feet moving far faster than her giant boots should have allowed. In mere seconds she was within range and brought her fist swinging like a club toward Sike's face.

To my delight, he managed to dodge, twisting nimbly out of the way as the metal-clad force came rushing by.

She immediately wheeled around, her dexterity as impressive as her power, and dealt a backhand strike with the handle of her knife.

I recognized her strategy. She was feeling out his weaknesses and trying to determine whether he had any hidden weapons powered by the soul energy. He swung his arms upward, taking the brunt on his forearms to protect his head. Kane cheered with a jarring laugh until the vines squeezed him, causing him to hiss.

While I was inwardly cheering for Sike, the female hunter was now almost directly next to the fallen redbill. There was no way I could get to Bryce without her seeing me.

The hunter scowled—apparently deciding that there were no hidden threats—and began to swing at him harder, moving faster despite her massive armor. Sike managed to defend himself for another few moments, but not only was she bigger and stronger, she was clearly more agile and better trained. Sike cried out in pain as the hunter's fist struck his side. He recovered, but the hunter circled him quickly. A moment later a kick sent him sprawling. The knife slashed through the air, and he barely rolled out of the way in time, the blade sinking five, six, nine inches into the ground. The scent of blood reached my nose.

The wildling chirped again, its voice a panicked flurry. Arlonne groaned through gritted teeth as the vines wrapped around her more tightly. We couldn't fight a battle without two of our best fighters. The wildling needed to go. The Immortals hadn't noticed my presence yet, but that couldn't last forever.

I aimed at the wildling, years of training moving me smoothly through the motions, and sucked in a ragged breath. I had one shot, one chance to get this right.

I fired, the silenced pistol making little more than a soft cough as the bullet zipped through the air. The wildling cried out, but the sound cut off in its strange, rocky throat. It slid from the shrieking decay and tumbled the twenty or so feet to the ground, where it landed with a meaty thump. The vines immediately sagged. Arlonne gave a grateful gasp as she sucked in air, before she began tearing at the plants. Kane stooped over. Blood poured down their bodies. He smashed the vines beneath his feet.

Sike's pained gasp made me turn. I froze. The hunter held his arm at a painfully unnatural angle. It was the same arm he'd injured before. His face contorted as he drew in a ragged hiss. He tried to struggle out of her grip, but it was useless. She was too strong.

And now she was staring directly at my hiding spot.

In a horrifying show of casual cruelty, she snapped Sike's arm like it was a piece of straw. He screamed, the sound echoing across the steaming surface of Lake Siron.

Without a care, she released him, and he crumpled to the ground.

"No!" Kane bellowed, careening toward her. She whirled into a kick that hit him with such force that he fell like a stone and lay on the ground gasping desperately for breath. In a blur of speed, she appeared in front of the boulders that I was hidden behind.

Keeping a cool head, I fired twice with perfect form, once at her chest and once at her head. One bullet ricocheted off her chain mail armor, and she sidestepped the one I'd sent toward her head.

She literally just dodged a bullet.

The display of speed made me lose concentration, and before I could evade her strike, the hunter smacked the gun from my grasp. A jarring complaint reverberated up the bones and muscles of my hands and arms, and my fingers went numb from the force of the blow. I barely registered my wrist twisting and the gun falling to the ground before the hunter grabbed me by the front of my camouflaged uniform and hoisted me into the air.

"What the hell are you, little bug?" she asked, her tone laced with both interest and contempt. "And where did you get all this purified energy?"

Kicking and swinging helplessly in her grasp, I couldn't help but stare at the glowing gem in the middle of her forehead. It had the same effect as when I'd been looking at the grove—like everything was shimmering and rippling—but it was less intense. The signal for this one was stronger somehow.

Something burned against my chest, and I choked back a startled gasp as Dorian's stone burned white hot against my shirt. It didn't alert the Immortal at all, however. She just kept turning me this way and that, then poked at my fallen gun with her giant boot.

I heard Dorian snarl somewhere above, and movement stirred

behind the hunter's shoulder as a redbill flew through the air, but I blocked it all out. I needed to keep her attention on me, and for that I would need all my wits.

"If you put me down, I'll tell you," I said hoarsely. My hands wrapped around her armored arms as I swung my legs for momentum, hoping to get close enough to strike. When I tried to kick her, she sighed wearily. I was playing a losing game, and we both knew it. I couldn't touch her, thanks to her long limbs. How could I break free from her grasp?

I looked squarely into the hunter's cruel green eyes. Up close, she was even more startlingly beautiful. The sharp lines of her face made her appear almost elven, but the vertical pupils gave the impression of a snake. The cold interest behind them wasn't lost on me, but it was fading as she found my form increasingly disappointing. Her mouth twitched irritably as she sized me up, as if she'd expected something more interesting. How ironic that someone so utterly beautiful could be so horrible. In the Mortal Plane, ancient people might have worshipped this woman.

The hunter narrowed her eyes as my legs swung at her once more.

"That won't work. Don't do it again," she said.

Her tone took on the same echoing resonance as before. It fell over me like a warm blanket. My muscles relaxed. She was right... I should stop struggling. I loosened my grip on her arms and hung there compliantly. The hunter smirked, pleased. I felt drugged as I stared into her eyes. They consumed me, threatened to swallow me whole.

"Answer my question," she demanded. "Where did you get all this purified energy?"

I blinked slowly, trying to comprehend the sounds as they left her moving mouth. Her lips were the same purple as grape jelly, I realized. The comparison seemed very funny to me in that moment, but I got the feeling if I laughed she might shake me.

"I don't know." It was the honest answer. It slipped easily from my mouth.

The hunter shook her head and glared at me. "Tell me what you are, creature," she commanded.

The echoes of her speech wrapped around me. I wanted to tell her. I opened my mouth, trying to remember why a small voice was screaming at me to keep it closed. This woman was clearly nice. She just wanted me to answer her question.

"I'm… I'm… I'm a soldier," I sputtered. *I was, wasn't I?*

Her mouth curled downward in rage, her teeth bared.

Oh no, I accidentally made her mad. I tried to remember what she wanted to know, anxious about disappointing her.

Her anger consumed her, so much so that she failed to notice the oncoming attack before it was too late. Laini and Roxy's redbill streaked across the field, smashing into the hunter's shoulder with its razor-sharp beak.

I broke out of my trance immediately, swinging my knee up. The hunter lurched forward, and my knee connected with her tough chin before the two of us hit the ground. The resounding contact sent a numbing tremor down the entire length of my leg. Her hand left my shirt as we tumbled together down toward the lake. When we rolled to a stop, she halfway straddled me. She wheezed, pained, and I shoved her off me with so much force she rolled almost into the water. She and her armor were bizarrely light, maybe twenty pounds at the most. My bicep curls were heavier.

I scrambled back, and the hunter looked up at me, dazed for a moment, before she leapt to her feet. She flexed her fist again and pointed her palm toward me. Her arm shook slightly. I dove out of the way, but nothing happened. The warm breeze swept over us. The scent of sulfur and spilled blood burned into my nostrils.

"What?" The hunter stared at her palm. She shook her gloved hand as if hoping to dislodge the magic. It was strangely satisfying to see the arrogance drain from her for the first time. Instead of sick delight, a genuine shadow of confusion passed over her face.

"Sucks for you," Kane snapped as he wrapped his arm around the hunter's neck and pulled her backward to let Arlonne leap on the hunter as he dragged her away. The female hunter snarled and swung her blue blade through the air, but the vampires had the upper hand now that her glove no longer worked.

The body of the flying goblin creature plummeted from the back of the shrieking decay, Dorian's knife lodged in its throat. Looking up, I saw him still trading blows with the other hunter. Dorian would be at full strength after feeding, and he wasn't a mild opponent. But it appeared neither was the hunter. Laini, circling close to the monster's back, dropped Roxy off to join the fray with Dorian, which she did with a fierce whoop, trying to find a gap in the black-and-gold armor for her knives to slip through.

I left Arlonne and Kane to their revenge and Dorian and Roxy to their fight, and rushed toward Sike. His crumpled body on the ground reminded me of my original orders: get to Sike and Bryce and get them out of harm's way. I hadn't done such a good job of that.

My stomach turned as I fell to my knees at his side, surveying the damage. He bled from multiple wounds across his skinny torso where the hunter had slashed him. His nose also appeared to be broken, and I suspected his arm was snapped in several places. Digging into my pack, I brought out pads of dressings, finding the worst slash and applying pressure to slow the flow of blood.

He took a shaky breath and opened his bleary brown eyes.

"Sike, are you with me?" I asked, leaning down toward him.

He nodded slowly and painfully grinned up at me, blood coating his teeth. "Worth it," he croaked weakly.

I shook my head, part of me wishing I'd stepped in earlier to save him this pain but the rest of me knowing I'd at least done what was needed in time to save his life. "Not worth it, you idiot! You could have died before any of us could do anything." But the relieved smile on my face belied my anger.

"I saw you with your gun out," he said between gritted teeth. "Knew you'd take the shot when you needed to." He glanced toward the fallen redbill, grimacing as he tried to move toward it. "You should check for Bryce. I'm worried he might be pinned."

I glanced around quickly, unwilling to leave the badly wounded vampire vulnerable even to go and find Bryce. The tide of the battle had turned as Kane and Arlonne overtook the magicless hunter. Was it safe to leave Sike to fend for himself for a few minutes?

Laini's redbill swept low, and she dismounted before it landed. Her pale face boiled with anger at the hunter. "Monster," she breathed before joining the fight. She darted forward and nearly succeeded in knocking the knife away from the hunter.

The hunter's blue hair, now torn from its fancy arrangement, splayed around her beautiful face as her panicked gaze moved between the three vampires. *She knows she's screwed.* Good. I never wanted to hear her echoing voice compulsion again.

The shrieking decay let out an alarmed cry as it attempted to retreat, but the golden hunter tried to pull on its reins. He rammed an elbow into Roxy's face as he and Dorian struggled for control of a long, curved knife.

"Inkarri, we need to retreat!" the young hunter bellowed.

Inkarri. A fitting name, since it was beautifully exotic with a rough edge.

Inkarri scowled as she tossed her knife into her other hand, weighing her options. She could choose to fight three vampires with zero help from magic. The wildling was dead. The winged goblin was dead. The shrieking decay wailed as it contorted, trying to escape and remaining only through the control of the hunters. The golden Immortal pulled hard on the reins, causing the creature to jerk upward in a nearly vertical movement.

Dorian leapt from the shrieking decay's back just in time to avoid falling into the bubbling lake, taking Roxy with him. The creature swung back around, its spiny jointed legs hanging down. Inkarri snarled and ran toward the monster, trying to join her companion. Arlonne, Kane, and Laini pursued her, all of them moving almost too fast for me to track.

"Where are you going? We're not done playing!" Kane yelled and attempted to lunge at her, but Inkarri was too quick.

She moved with blinding speed and caught up to her mount. Dorian tried to cut her off, but she hit him in the face with her armored elbow and spun away from his grasp. In moments, Inkarri successfully scrambled up the trailing legs and onto the saddle of the shrieking decay. It fled, its whipping tail soon a distant shadow in the sky. Laini glanced at her redbill hovering nearby. If she pursued the hunters, there was the risk she would end up flying solo into a group of Immortal reinforcements. It was too dangerous. Besides, we needed to leave as soon as possible.

"I almost had him," Dorian growled in frustration. He dragged his nails through his hair and shook, the adrenaline and dark energy still coursing through his body. "If it hadn't been for that magical armor and those stupid protection charms..." He trailed off, his face swarming with fast-moving shadows. I was struck again by the rugged beauty in the lines of his face. The desire to reach out and touch him came right up alongside a small voice reminding me that Dorian had just fed. I shifted, and his gaze immediately flickered to me and then Sike.

"He's alive," Dorian said, a fierce smile spreading over his face.

He rushed toward Sike, and I stepped forward to meet him halfway without thinking. He was five yards away when the throbbing buzz began in my chest.

The ache tugged at me like a hook had been jammed between my ribs and my sternum. I opened my mouth to warn him, but the burning quickly overtook me. I might as well have jumped headfirst into the steaming lake. All that came out was a choked gasp. The pain burned white hot in my chest. I steeled myself for the oncoming lightheadedness.

Suddenly, Dorian faltered. Surprise turned to confusion, then his mouth twisted in pain, and he fell to his knees. He clutched his chest, releasing a wild snarl.

"Dorian!" I wheezed. What was—? No, he was hurting too. How was this possible? It was only supposed to be me.

The pain seared my chest, flaring out into every nerve of my body. One leg buckled, and I braced myself on the remaining one. I couldn't collapse onto Sike and hurt him even more. I tried to angle my fall with the last bit of my strength. Someone caught me and lowered me to the ground, but I wasn't sure who.

My vision crawled with darkness. I struggled for consciousness. *Not Dorian, too!* Why was this happening? I curled into a fetal position, my body working instinctively to cope with the pain.

"Those idiots," Kane shouted somewhere in the distance. His voice echoed, reminding me of Inkarri's terrible power. "Someone drag them away from each other before they kill themselves!"

"Got it," Arlonne said with a grunt.

I felt a strong hand wrap around my upper arm and drag me over the ground. Everything seemed to float away from my body. The sensation of the dirt and rocks and grass beneath me faded. I slipped in and out of darkness. My vision began to bleed over with white and flashes of color.

"The hunters are out of range."

Was that Laini? The voice was soft.

Kane snorted, frustrated. "For now. How long until they're back with reinforcements?"

Water splashed. Where? *You're near a lake, Lyra. Don't forget.* The edges of my thoughts frayed. The pain washed over me with a terrible promise. I struggled against the agony.

I tried to mumble something, to ask if Dorian was okay, to ask if Bryce was beneath the redbill, but darkness swallowed up the white light around me.

And then I was gone.

CHAPTER TWENTY-ONE

I couldn't find Dorian.

Everything was shifting mist and fog. All I could feel was the distant pulse of a heartbeat, though I wasn't sure if it was mine or someone else's. Maybe it was the Immortal Plane itself? Each beat, each thump-thump, triggered my training, my soldier's instinct. Move faster. Look harder. Do better.

Broken walls and ruptured cobblestones slid between banks of gray clouds. My foot struck a hairline crack in the street that ripped open into a crevasse filled with smoke and bubbling yellow water. I flung myself backward but landed on nothing, falling... I blinked and found myself standing in front of a partially collapsed building. A shutter hanging crookedly off a window repeatedly smacked against the wall as a breeze passed by, clearing the fog. My surroundings came into focus—Vanim, in all its ruined glory.

I was looking for Dorian, right? I had to find Dorian. He was hurt. I had to help him. I pushed forward. My limbs were heavy, as if encased in cement. Despite my best efforts, I couldn't move in a straight line. It was like I'd forgotten how to walk.

The ground lifted and undulated, as if I were trying to run across a pool when the cover was on. I blinked and tried to rub my eyes, but my hands were too heavy to lift. As if the city pushed me back with an invisible force, my vision tunneled, and I was pulled back through the winding streets.

"Dorian?" I called, scrabbling for purchase with feet that didn't feel like my own. The desperation in my cry echoed back from the foggy landscape, his name unfurling from my lips like smoke to drift in the air in scraggly written text. It wrapped around my throat like a noose, then disappeared.

I needed to find him. We needed to rescue Bryce and get Sike some help. Wait... why did Sike need help? What had happened? I only remembered a bluish knife and flashing light, writhing vines and gurgling screams.

With a yell, I flung my arms out, stopping my rushed backward travel by clinging to the corner of a halved building. For a moment, my body flew horizontally, like a flag in a gale. Then I was on my knees, my fingers bloodied from holding onto the rough stone for purchase. As I watched, the wrecked building began to morph back into a fully formed structure beside me. The walls sucked up the surrounding chunks of stone and wood and mortar dust, growing into perfect supports, and the roof blossomed like a flower to stretch and cover the top of the home.

I stared at the homey little cottage, so out of place in the devastation of the city. Beside it, another building began to develop—returning to its original state—then another and another. The city was rebuilding itself, yet it all felt unreal, like another glamor effect. The perfect buildings crackled and shifted as I watched them grow, snapping between destruction and creation.

I hurried backward, the two simultaneously occurring phases of existence sending a wave of nausea through me. Turning, I began to run, the *weight of my limbs still unnaturally heavy but reduced enough that I could move. When I pressed on, the road began to turn sideways, but I followed it, my feet never leaving the ground, even as it flipped me completely upside down, sending bones and bricks and a curtain of dust plummeting away into the upside-down sky with a dreadful whispering like the redwoods. Gradually, the road became flat once more, though whether I was the right way up was impossible to tell.*

In the distance, a figure stepped onto the cobblestone path ahead of me. Something about the shape of his shoulders, the dark hair, the alertness of his posture made me think of Dorian.

He turned to face me, but it was not the face I knew so well. His eyes were dark, like a Scottish peat river, and the black hair was cropped shorter, furling into soft curls. He was leaner, almost to the point of emaciation. His shoulders, which I knew had carried so much weight during our journey, were much narrower. That's not Dorian.

Next to him was a vampire woman with long dark hair. I could only see a sliver of her face, but it was enough to see that she was beautiful. Had she always been there? I hadn't noticed her appear.

She lifted her hand to brush his cheek, the movement soft, sweet, intimate. I blinked, and she vanished. This didn't seem to worry him. His only reaction was to stare into the open space ahead of him, but not vaguely. He was looking at something. Stepping closer to him, I followed his gaze and saw that the horizon burned red. The smell of sulfur haunted me.

Fear filled his face, and he looked around frantically as if finally registering that the woman had disappeared. His fangs extended, and he snarled at something in the distance. Sensing the urgency, I drew parallel with him, following his eyeline. In the distance, a cluster of green, blue, and yellow lights grew like a thunderstorm on the horizon. They mirrored the lights I'd seen, which had pushed creatures through the tear when we first arrived in the Immortal Plane. Was it Inkarri returning to claim her revenge?

I tried to stay by his side, knowing we needed to work together as partners and soldiers in this coming conflict. I had to help protect the city. Dorian was in among its tangled streets somewhere, and I needed to keep him safe. We were survivors.

Letting him know I was here to help, I reached out to touch this wraith-like twin of Dorian. To my horror, teal energy seeped from my hand as I stretched it out. He reeled back, hollow, dark eyes widening with betrayal. More beams of light struck him from all sides, a barrage of beams that I couldn't stop.

His skin bubbled and burned away, the flesh beginning to rot like he'd been struck by a shrieking decay. Bile rose in my throat as I watched him melt into nothing more than a pile of pearly bones scattered on the ground, like so many of the piles I'd seen around Vanim.

I rolled over, desperately swallowing as my eyes flew open. I retched onto the floor. Dim shapes came into focus—a bedframe, a three-legged stool made of soft green wood, an arched hole in the wall not covered by a door or a curtain. I pushed myself into a sitting position, squirming away from the vomit on the light brown, papery-looking floor. Disoriented, I clutched my pounding head, the scent of sulfur still lingering in my nose. My legs and waist were tightly wrapped in rough linens that tugged at me. They were nothing like the soft fabrics I was used to in the Mortal Plane.

Something rough dug into the palm clutching at my shirt. Well, it wasn't *my* shirt. It was made of a heavy yellowish fabric and laced up the front with a green cord. It smelled a little like bog water.

Opening my hand, I found it clutching the small leather bag that held Dorian's stone. Even through the bag, it warmed my skin uncomfortably. I scooped out the stone and studied it. It was hot and glowing amber—I understood why I'd felt it warm against my chest several times since we'd arrived in the Immortal Plane.

The stone burned in my hand, the contact too much. I dropped the stone onto the covers, where it cooled quickly and darkened to its normal color. I took a long breath and wiped my damp forehead. Trying to calm my racing heart, I began to check in with all my senses in an attempt to figure out where I was. The stone was the least of my problems to solve right now.

What did I remember last? A splash. I remembered water before I passed out. Dorian on his knees. Sike bleeding. The retreating Immortals. I was in the Immortal Plane.

I stilled, tuning into my senses to get an idea of where I could be, wondering for a terrible minute if I had found my way into the depths of some Immortal prison. Looking around, I took stock of my unfamiliar quarters. The most important detail was that another person was sleeping in a similar bed on the far side of the chamber. The broad body looked familiar in the soft light. Bryce?

I broke free of the constricting sheets to kneel on the bed for a better view, feeling a wave of weakness roll over me. His chest rose and fell beneath a cocoon of coarse linens that wrapped up to his waist. A light snore trickled into my ear. Bandages were wrapped around his chest and arms.

He's alive. I pressed a grateful hand to my face. The sweat had mostly dried.

The rounded chamber had no windows and a ceiling that sloped gently downward, every surface the same brown as the floor, all with the same waxy, apparently papery texture. It was high enough that Bryce would be able to stand comfortably, but not much more. The upper parts of the plain walls and the ceiling were broken up by patches of pink, green, and blue lichens that lit the room with a soft bioluminescent glow. I marveled at the illumination. The stinking sulfur of my dream had faded, replaced by the smell of citrus and an earthy musk I couldn't place, but the memory of my ghastly dream sent a tremor through me. Closing my eyes, I listened intently, trying to glean some clues about where we might be or whether there was anyone close by. There was almost nothing. A very faint buzz of what were possibly voices or maybe the wind in the strange trees, but very little else. It was as though the walls soaked up all external sound.

I shivered and pulled the sheets back around me—but the scratchy fabric made me itchy. My head swam and ached dully. The dream had left me disoriented. I rubbed my hand against my sternum, hoping to calm myself. I had a sinking feeling that I'd lost someone, but I couldn't remember who.

Although he was apparently safe in the bed next to mine, I couldn't shake the fear of not knowing if Bryce was alive beneath the crumpled redbill body. Was that my last memory? I twisted my mouth, trying hard to think. There was Bryce, the memory of a splash. My breath hitched with alarm, heart rate rising once more. No. My last strong memory was of Dorian's face, warped with pain as he fell to the ground. Dorian had *felt* that pain. I knew the sensation, how the body tensed when the chest pain arrived.

I pawed at my face, pressing the heels of my hands into my eye sockets. I hoped Dorian was okay. How long had I been out?

I needed to figure out where we were. I inhaled to calm my racing mind, settling my breathing.

One thing I knew for certain—this was definitely the Immortal Plane. There was something about this place, a heaviness to my bones that meant I wasn't home. It meant we were either captured in enemy territory, hidden in neutral territory, or had found allied territory. The only potential allies I was aware of, however, were the mysterious group of vampires that we'd found no trace of so far.

Immortal hunters would not have tended to our wounds and placed us in pleasant rooms with open doorways and no guards. I frowned up at the ceiling. Unless this was a mind game? Were these lights secretly leeching my every memory of the Mortal Plane before they disposed of my body in a shrieking decay's food bowl? Or was some gladiatorial-type combat waiting for me on the other side of the open doorway?

"Hard pass," I mumbled, swinging my legs over the edge of the bed, carefully avoiding the vomit on the floor.

I had to find Dorian. Had he passed out, too? He must have if he'd been in as much pain as I had. Concern flooded me with guilt close behind. Even though I knew it wasn't my fault, it still felt terrible to be a liability to the person I cared for. Brushing off my own pain was almost easy now. When Dorian described his distress at seeing me hurting, I'd thrown his concerns to the wind, knowing I could handle my pain. For our partnership and relationship, it had been a burden I was willing to bear. Now? I knew exactly how Dorian had felt when he saw me wince or pass out from pain. The thought occurred to me that maybe I'd been too dismissive of his concerns.

Something had changed since we came here. I failed to understand why he would suddenly begin to feel pain like me. Maybe the pain was always more severe in the Immortal Plane. Maybe it was because he'd fed so recently. Maybe it was because our relationship was growing stronger than ever. Who knew? It wasn't like we had a manual on human-vampire relations.

Fresh beads of sweat dotted my brow. Even the small effort of sitting up had taken a toll. I wiped them away roughly.

First things first. I had to find Dorian and the rest of the team to make sure they were okay. I glanced at Bryce, who still slumbered peacefully. Did it mean anything that they, whoever they were, had separated the team? I slid out of bed, grimacing at the strange texture of the floor under my bare feet. My body protested the entire way. My muscles ached, dull with lack of energy. *Okay, not off to a great start.* I plucked Dorian's stone from the bedclothes and placed it back into the bag around my neck before tucking the bag into my shirt. It stayed cold. I almost wished it were warm for some comfort.

Along with the shirt, I wore a knee-length pair of soft brown shorts. I couldn't see my boots or any other kind of shoes anywhere. Stepping carefully, I crept to the chamber's uncovered entrance and poked my head out, tensed for any attack or unexpected trap.

The corridor stretched before me with a similar rounded ceiling as the room, the same glowing lichen lights growing along the walls and illuminating everything in a lavender shade. Seeing and hearing no one approaching, I stepped out of the room, revealing the full length of the corridor. At the far end to my left, some fifteen or so feet away, another door was cut into the wall, marking the end of the hallway.

Glancing around for some kind of weapon, I saw a rough broom leaning against the wall near another doorway to my right. Picking it up, I clutched the smooth handle as I began to step cautiously down the corridor, eyes searching for any shimmer or strangeness that could indicate a trap set behind a glamor. I'd nearly made it to the door when a woman popped out of it, alarming me enough that I brought the broom handle sharply up toward her face. In a swift movement, she caught the handle. Curly brown hair fell against brown skin, and startled amber eyes narrowed at me.

I blinked, finally recognizing her in the dim light. "Arlonne," I whispered hoarsely. My voice was as weak as my muscles.

Arlonne raised an eyebrow. "Doing a little cleaning to thank our hosts?"

I sagged against the wall, my energy temporarily sapped. "What happened to Dorian?" I blurted, concern ringing in my voice.

Arlonne chuckled. "Hello to you, too, Lyra," she said sarcastically. "Precious Dorian is in a meeting right now, so I don't think it's good for you to rush over there." She visually assessed me, as if trying to gauge my condition. "He's okay now. After the battle, he was out for three hours."

Three hours! I pressed a relieved hand against my heart. Perhaps we hadn't lost much time.

"How long was I out for?"

Arlonne frowned, setting the broom aside. "You've been out for three days. The healers did what they could, but they have limited knowledge of your funny human anatomy and internal workings. They weren't able to do much besides ensuring you got some rest and monitoring you."

Three days? It seemed to be my magic number.

Silence passed between us as I processed the bad news. I'd

known the curse was difficult to deal with, even if I didn't know that Dorian could feel the pain too. At least he had only passed out for three hours.

I'd told myself the curse was manageable, but I hadn't been exposed to its full strength lately. Dorian's lack of feeding had afforded us a false sense of protection—of hope. A feeling that was falling away from me now. I wondered if my heart had stopped this time. Had Dorian been afraid as he lost consciousness, wondering how long it would be until he woke up, *if* he was going to wake up?

I abruptly realized Arlonne was staring at me, her brow furrowed with concern. I shook myself free of my manic thoughts and snapped back to the present. The lavender lights fell across her broad face, the color softening the scars and making her skin gleam.

"Where are we?" I asked.

The corner of her lips lifted into a small smirk as though she'd been waiting for me to ask. "They call it the Hive."

"You found the refugee vampires while I was unconscious?" I asked as I rubbed my temple. Arlonne's style of speaking was blunt and often lacked details.

"They found us, actually," Arlonne added. "The vampires here have formed an alliance with aquatic wildlings and watched our fight from the lake."

"Aquatic?" I echoed, trying to imagine the funny stone golems underwater.

She nodded. "With their help, the Hive scouts were able to hide under the water during the battle. They emerged afterward to offer assistance." Her face pulled into a disapproving scowl. "The cowards."

"But they helped?" I insisted. I knew she valued action and

courage, but they'd likely had their reasons for not wanting to get involved.

She gave an unimpressed huff. "After they let us struggle. They wanted to save their own skins. With their help, we could have killed those hunters. No one would know we were on this plane, but now the Immortals know there are strange vampires and unknown creatures loose near Lake Siron. We're *all* in danger, thanks to their hesitation." She exhaled slowly from her nostrils, her anger fading slightly. "The Hive scouts brought us back here, but they had the nerve to blindfold us while they were at it. And now... they're not exactly helpful."

That didn't sound promising for Dorian's hope that the vampires in hiding would aid us. Technically, they already had to some extent, by patching up our injuries and sheltering us here. And now Dorian was facing the problem without me.

The crunch of approaching footsteps sounded near the doorway behind Arlonne, and a moment later Roxy marched through the rounded threshold. She spotted me and gave a wicked grin. Either ignoring or not noticing the tension from the conversation she'd interrupted, she barreled over and wrapped me in a hug.

"Hello, lovebird!"

The force of her embrace nearly sent me into the wall, and I had to brace myself with a hand. "Good to see you, too, but I'm not exactly at a hundred percent right now." Though I was beginning to feel stronger, being on my feet.

Roxy whistled, looking over my unsteady posture. "I can see that, but I'm glad you're up. I'm sick of being the only conscious human in the Immortal Plane." She offered her shoulder for me to lean on. "Kane sent me to grab Arlonne for the council meeting. He's acting all grumpy and demanding again, like a royal pain in the ass. He wants us immediately. Dorian's going to try to convince them to help us in Itzarriol. If you're up for it, you should come with us."

Arlonne hesitated at first, evaluating me, then nodded in agreement. My muscles wanted me to go back to bed, but with the news that the Hive vampires were being unhelpful, I couldn't afford to be out of the loop any longer. I needed to see this so-called council meeting for myself and catch up on the situation.

I wiggled my naked toes. "I need to find some shoes... and I might have puked on the floor."

Arlonne wrinkled her nose. "I always forget how much humans are like babies."

Roxy snorted. "Nonsense! We're as tough as nails—when we're not in love with vampire boys who make us swoon." She winked with a snicker. "I've got your gear bag and weapons, but I put your clean uniform and boots under your bed. I doubt they moved. As for puke," she looked around, "I'll... find someone to deal with that."

I went back into the room, crouching to grab my boots and uniform from where Roxy said they would be. I changed quickly, somewhat uncomfortable with my former captain on one side and an open doorway on the other. Once again dressed in my camo uniform, I cast one last glance at Bryce. He continued to sleep peacefully. The lights from the chamber cast a pastel glow on the stark white bandages around his injuries.

"What's the word on Sike and Bryce?" I asked, joining Arlonne back in the hall and keeping my voice low. Bryce deserved to sleep.

"Sike has made progress in the past three days, but he's still a mess from his idiotic bravery," Arlonne said with a curl of her lips. She was frustrated, both with the Hive scouts for not helping in our battle and with Sike for drawing the hunter's full attention. "His arm is broken in four places, and he was stabbed and slashed several times. He also broke his nose and is growing back at least three teeth from the beating he took. The healers are fussing over him, which he's rather enjoying. He'll heal up fine and pretty quickly." She looked toward the room I had just exited. "Bryce will require much more time. He's been conscious, moving around a little, but he has broken multiple ribs and one arm. He's probably bruised a lot of his internal organs as well, judging from the amount of pain he's in when he's conscious, but the healers can't be sure about that because they have no experience with humans. We have no idea when he'll be in fighting condition again, since humans heal so much slower than vampires. He's alive, though." She shrugged. "That's what matters."

I needed to stop passing out for three days at a time. I always ended up missing so much.

"Bryce is tough," I muttered. "He'll be back to kicking ass in no time."

Arlonne gave me a knowing look. "Oh, I know all about that one. When I tried to haul him out from under the dead redbill's wing at the end of the battle, he was ready and waiting with his gun. Almost mistook me for a hunter. I thought he was going to shoot me in the face." She rolled her eyes wearily, but there was also something like amusement and admiration in the expression, in a half-formed smile.

Maybe she was beginning to warm up to the humans in our group. After everything that happened to her at the hands of humans at the Bureau, I didn't blame her for taking a while to trust us. All the humans on this mission were ex-Bureau, and I was directly related to the man who had arranged the experiment that involved amputating her arm without pain medication when she was little more than a teenager. It was good to see her reservations slowly disappear, though.

Roxy reappeared as I pulled on my boots and knelt to tighten the laces.

"I found someone who will clean up your puke, so we're all clear to go to the meeting." She tapped a nonexistent watch. "I'm not getting yelled at by Kane. Come on."

"I'm almost done." I hurried my pace, fighting with stiff fingers over the long laces of my combat boots.

Arlonne cleared her throat. "You know, it was your quick thinking during the battle that probably saved us all," she said.

I looked up, surprised to see that her gaze was warm. She looked… impressed.

"Taking out the wildling with your gun freed us of those vines." She traced a finger down the length of her collarbone, pointing out the divots in her brown skin where the thorns had torn her flesh. The wounds had scabbed and healed over already, thanks to fast vampire healing, but they were still a reminder we'd been in a very tight spot that could have ended very badly.

"Thanks," I said and waved my hand to brush away the praise. "I was just doing my job."

Roxy helped me up, making sure I wasn't going to sway and fall before she let go of my arm. Arlonne simply gave a nod of thanks, and while I could tell the conversation was over, pride bloomed in my chest. Her respect meant a lot to me. This might be the longest I had ever personally spoken with the quiet, proud vampire.

"The *meeting*," Roxy stressed, jerking her thumb toward the hallway door.

"Fine, fine, let's go." I followed her as quickly as I could manage. My boots felt too heavy for my feet, an unpleasant reminder of my strange dream, but I pressed on.

My momentary pleasure at Arlonne's kind words faded as we headed to find Dorian.

I needed to figure out what had happened between us and what was unfolding in this hive of hidden vampires. I had a feeling I wouldn't like what I found.

CHAPTER TWENTY-TWO

As Roxy led the way to the Hive council meeting, I studied my surroundings as much as possible to glean any hint about what kind of characters made up the Hive. How different were they from the vampires I'd met through Dorian? Arlonne already thought of them as cowards.

Like elsewhere, the walls, floors, and ceilings consisted of the same thick, papery material, and everything was lit by the glowing lichens. We took a sharp right turn, ducking through another rounded doorway into a wider hallway with numerous doors in the wall on the right-hand side. Here, in addition to the lichens, light was provided by lanterns made of the same amber glass as the windows in Vanim, affixed to the floor every few paces. For a moment, I was concerned by the idea of having flame anywhere near the likely flammable material of the Hive, until I recognized the familiar glow. With a sense of awe, I crouched down by one. The casing was about as tall as my shin, the panes of golden glass held together with strips of dull bronze. Inside, floating like a lumines-cent jellyfish, was a soul. It was difficult to get a sense of its shape as it pulsed and drifted within the confines of the lantern, a mixture of bright light and swirling darkness. Somehow, being unable to define it seemed fitting, considering that this was the soul of a once-living being. This person had had a name, a job, a family, a first pet, weird habits, a song that made them cry—they'd made mistakes, obviously, or they wouldn't be trapped here in the Immortal Plane, but who knew how they'd reached that point in their life, or whether they wished they could go back and undo those mistakes.

Carefully, I put my fingers against the glass, part of me expecting it to be hot, but both the glass and the casing were room tempera-ture. Something Inkarri had said during our battle came back to me. She'd mentioned bottling soul-lights and asked Sike how he'd managed to contain so much. I assumed she had been talking about the human energy brought by Roxy, Bryce, and me, but now I knew why she had been so interested. In the Immortal Plane, the energy created by souls was more than just supernatural calories. They could provide literal power.

"Pretty amazing, huh?" Roxy bent to examine another lantern. "Not going to lie, they do creep me out a little."

"I don't think they're creepy," I said, standing slowly, taking a moment as a rush of lightheadedness overtook me. "It feels more like they're… I don't know. Sacred, I guess. The essence of a whole life lighting our path."

Arlonne said nothing in response, and Roxy just scoffed, but I noticed her paying a little more attention to the lanterns as we continued.

The corridors curved in a dizzying repetition of brown walls, floor, and ceiling. It was nearly impossible to tell the corridors apart. Roxy's knowledge of the hallways both impressed and unsettled me. I was relieved that she knew her way but upset that she was three full days ahead of me in terms of exploration. I'd definitely need a guide to get around, and I didn't like losing my independence like that.

At one point, we passed through a hall with windows to the outside. Pausing for a moment, I peered outside to see a vast, dim cavern below us. I reeled from the sheer scale of the area. How much weight could this papery material hold? Far below, yellow-and-blue water rippled, glowing the same shades as the lake. The colors lit up the cave, the steaming water several stories beneath us, while the top of the cave was lit by more of the familiar lichens. I couldn't see the edges of the massive cave through the haze. It could go on for miles.

"How are we suspended up here?" I asked.

Arlonne chuckled. "This is literally an abandoned hive that the vampires took over," she explained and pointed at a large teardrop-shaped construction hanging from the ceiling of the enormous cavern we were in. I hadn't noticed it at first, as it was at the very edge of the illumination provided by the water and the lichens. Its exterior was a pale yellow, like whipped butter. "That's what it looks like from the outside."

I saw dozens of large winged shapes flitting around the other hive. "Are those what build the hives?"

Arlonne nodded. "Jaspeths. They're like giant versions of your world's wasps. No need to worry about them, though. Any that get too close are usually just a little lost, smelling the pheromones."

The thought of running into an enormous wasp lost in these passageways alarmed me more than facing down another Immortal ruler. I had rested my hand on the sill of the window, but I withdrew it. Was I rubbing giant wasp romance hormones all over myself?

Arlonne smirked. "Can you smell it? The vampires collect and spritz themselves with it," she explained. "They did it to us, too. The jaspeths live in a new hive closer to the mouth of the cave, but they feel less threatened when we're covered in pheromones. The odor prevents them from attacking us."

I sniffed the air. "I have to admit the citrus and musk smells a lot better than the lake," I said. "It's almost nice enough that I'd wear it as perfume."

"You think that, but wait until you see how they collect it," the vampire said vaguely.

"What does that mean?" I looked at Roxy.

"Don't ask," Roxy told me with a raised eyebrow. "Trust me. Now come on, or we'll be later than we already are." We hurried on until we came to another chamber doorway, this one double the width of the others and covered by a set of thin white curtains. From the passing scenery through the windows, I was pretty sure we were now at the top of the hive. Ducking through the curtains, we entered as quietly as we could. The council meeting was already in session.

At least forty vampires filled the chamber. It was well lit, more so than the rest of the hive that I had seen so far. Dozens of large soul-light lanterns, some containing possibly four or five souls, created a circle of light that was almost theatrical in its arrangement. Outside the circle of lanterns, most of the vampires leaned against the walls or sat on simple rugs on the floor as spectators, hovering close enough to hear the discussion. They didn't look too different from the vampires I knew from the Mortal Plane. I saw shades of copper, brown, and pale skin among the crowds, and a full rainbow of hair colors, although many wore their hair cut short. All of them wore thin cloaks made of some kind of rubbery, water-resistant material. That made sense, considering their proximity to the lake and connection with the aquatic wildlings.

In the center of the circular chamber, within the circle of lanterns and beneath where the ceiling rose into a point that likely marked one of the spots where the hive was attached to the roof of the cave, a panel of four elderly vampires sat on ornate woven rugs of greens, golds, and blues. Everything about their posture and how all eyes were on them told me that this was the council.

They all appeared to be at least in their sixties—though I knew they were likely far older—and had the lean, spry physique I'd come to expect of most vampires. The first elder gave me the vibe of a martial arts master. He stroked the bottom of his long white beard reflectively, sharp gold eyes focused. A woman sat beside him, one of her eyes closed by mangled scarring. The other was open, shining like a wet black stone. She had shaved the sides of her silver hair, the central section tied into a braid that reached the nape of her neck. A man whose long limbs reminded me of a spider rested to her right. He appeared to be the youngest of the three. Instead of a severe or overly focused expression, he smiled gently at nothing in particular. Eggplant-colored marks about the size of a penny dotted the tan skin of his face, neck, and exposed arms.

The last elder, likely the eldest of all of them, was a short woman who radiated a fierce intensity of personality. Seated, she didn't reach the shoulder height of the rest of the council. If she stood, I was certain she wouldn't be over three feet tall. She had short white hair and bright cerulean eyes that suggested she saw much more than people might expect.

"Mandola is the one with the beard, Pyma is the one missing her eye, and Glim is the one with the lanky legs," Roxy supplied for me as she leaned in close to my ear. "The tiny woman is Mox."

I nodded, only half listening because Dorian stepped forward through the ring of lanterns into the center of the room. He looked healthy and steady on his feet.

Roxy gestured for me to follow, and we moved to the back as far from Dorian as possible, leaning against an unclaimed patch of wall. The lichen here glowed amber, which combined with the warm light from the lanterns to give the whole chamber a sepia, honeyed feeling.

A few eyes flickered to our presence, many of them narrowing in suspicion or widening in curiosity, but they soon returned to the elders. There were a few mutters but not enough to cause a disruption. There were more important matters at hand than our presence.

A weight fell from my shoulders as I studied Dorian. He stood tall and relaxed in the center of the circle facing the elders. He bowed at the waist, the respectful motion fluid and natural. There was no sign that he was feeling weak or dizzy like I was. It seemed as though he'd regained his strength by resting and from his recent feed on the wildling. Still, I would keep as far from him as possible while he made his case—I didn't want to cause him any discomfort during this crucial meeting.

Across the chamber, I spotted Sike sitting on the floor wrapped in a cloak several sizes too large for him that looked suspiciously like Kane's. He leaned against Laini, weak but upright, his broken arm held protectively across his body by a sling. He looked terrible, one side of his face still swollen and bruised, but he'd apparently been determined to attend. I raised a hand subtly in greeting, but he missed the movement, entirely focused on Dorian as he began to speak.

"As you are aware, my companions and I have traveled a great distance from the Mortal Plane to find your colony, both to offer aid and request assistance," he said, his voice rich and clear.

"Where in the Mortal Plane have you come from?" Mandola, the elder with the beard, asked.

"Scotland," Dorian said slowly, pronouncing the word as if it were magical. "It is the northern part of an island in a politically significant region of the Mortal Plane."

It was odd to hear human lands being described as though they were exotic. I noted the shimmer of interest in Glim's eyes as he regarded Dorian carefully.

Dorian continued. "We were offered asylum there by human allies and have established a camp in the mountains. Members of my clan and other survivors of Vanim's destruction are now living there safely under the protection of humans who believe in our cause to return balance to the planes. We're attempting to establish a haven for vampires there, one that we are eager for you to come and join."

There were a few murmurs and a sharp, disbelieving chuckle from somewhere in the chamber. Pyma snapped her fingers and made a harsh sound in the back of her throat. Silence immediately fell, but I'd caught the tone of the room. Arlonne's dislike of the clan began to make more sense to me.

Dorian kept speaking, apparently unfazed. "We are preparing to make the Immortals answer for the devastation they have brought down upon us, regrouping and growing our numbers. In the meantime, we need more information regarding the immortals' involvement in the attacks on the Mortal Plane. Monsters such as shrieking decays, soul-scourgers, and empty swarms are being sent through the tear to wreak havoc on the human world."

"Forgive me if I sound callous," Pyma interrupted, her voice pleasantly husky. "But what does the destruction of the Mortal Plane have to do with us? What have humans ever done for us that we should risk ourselves to help them? We are scraping out our survival here. Are you suggesting that we risk a massacre at the hands of the Immortals in order to help a species that is equally intent on our destruction?" Her hand hovered instinctually toward her ruined eye. "If they suffer now because of the tear, that is only justice. They *are* the ones who created it in the first place."

I felt Arlonne shift beside me, the stump of her arm an unspoken acknowledgment of the point. A deep weariness washed over me. I now understood the uphill battle we faced, because Pyma was right about humans. My own uncle, sitting in his bare cell back in Scotland, was testament enough to that. But there was so much more to it than that. Look at Dorian and me, connected by deep affection and loyalty despite the literal pain our relationship brought. Or that we three humans had come to this plane, a place not meant for human life, to try to help these vampires fix the problems plaguing both of our planes.

Dorian took a moment to think, then respectfully inclined his head to Pyma. "I understand your caution, Master Pyma. But the danger posed by the tear threatens more than just the Mortal Plane. The tear is ever-widening and starting to blur the boundaries of our two worlds." He briefly addressed the room, focusing on the vampires. "The very purpose of our existence is to maintain balance, both here and in the Mortal Plane. Right now, everything is out of balance. Immortals brutally kill the wildlings at whim. Monstrosities that belong deep in the bowels of the Immortal Plane are being driven to the surface to be used as mounts for the Immortals and to attack the Mortal Plane. The redwoods are crying louder than ever before as too much darkness saturates the ground." He pivoted, appealing to the other side of the room, his eyes briefly passing over me with a spark of recognition, despite my face being masked by shadow. "If we want to prevent more tragedy in both the Mortal and Immortal Planes, we need to find a way to halt the growth of the tear and then close it. That is part of the reason my team of humans and vampires came to this plane—to gather information on how to fix the breach in the barrier between our worlds. Information I believe can be found in the Immortal capital, Itzarriol."

A grumble ran through the gathered onlookers, their voices tight with fear.

Glim spoke, arranging his gangly legs so he could rest his elbows on his equally bony knees as he did so. "Our scouts risk their lives on every trip to Itzarriol, but it is a danger we accept out of necessity. If we do not feed, we die. You seem to think this mission you pose is of equal necessity?"

"I do, Master Glim," Dorian replied.

"And you ask for aid from Hive members, despite the aforementioned high level of risk?"

I looked between the council and Dorian, knowing that this was the real question all these vampires wanted an answer to. This was where they needed to be convinced to risk their lives for us. As Dorian paused, I couldn't help the flutter of nerves in my throat. Our trip to the Immortal Plane would all be for nothing if he couldn't get the council on his side.

"I ask for your aid, Master Glim," Dorian said, weighing every word as he said it. "But I assure you I do not make such a request lightly. I ask because inaction in the name of self-preservation will only protect you for so long. The Hive has scouts and resources that could significantly improve our chances of successfully gathering information about a possible remedy to the tear. The council and your people have important intelligence on the Immortals and how Itzarriol operates. If we work together, we could get to the heart of this conspiracy."

A wave of pride came over me as I watched him work the crowd, using logic and charisma to overcome their resistance. My entire body grew hot with a deep surge of affection. We had come so far in our journey. I felt so lucky to have ended up with someone this impressive. I'd had the honor of witnessing his moments of laughter, joy, vulnerability… and the harder moments, when he'd put on a tough face for the world.

My pride dampened as I remembered how fragile our situation was in the present moment. Was he putting on a brave face right now? He might still feel weak and sore, like I did. Our proximity was now nothing but a liability. It was almost certain that if the Hive and the council agreed to work with us, only one of us would be able to go to Itzarriol unless we found a way to dampen the pain without Dorian starving himself. The coming days would be a test of strength and sacrifice like nothing we'd experienced so far.

"And then what?" Mandola asked, spreading his hands in query. "Even if you get the information you seek—which I doubt you will, knowing how secretive and intelligent the Immortal rulers are— what will you do then? Retreat back to the Mortal Plane with your team?"

I glanced at Arlonne with a slight grimace. They really weren't making this easy. She raised an eyebrow in response as if to say, "I warned you."

"Unless an immediate opportunity to strike at the Immortals presented itself, then yes, we would retreat," Dorian acknowledged. "But we would not leave without finding a way to bring your clan with us to safety in Scotland. That I promise you."

"Assuming we wish to go," Pyma rumbled.

"Promises are no more than well-intentioned lies if you cannot guarantee them," Mox said, her voice filled with a note of wise chastisement. "But we hear your earnest request. Give us some time to confer."

Dorian inclined his head in acknowledgment. Nobody spoke. All eyes rested on the elders, who turned to one another after an agonizing pause and began talking inaudibly among themselves. Dorian still stood by, hands clasped formally in the small of his back, slight tension around his mouth the only indicator of his stress.

It was slightly disconcerting to me that some kind of decision was going to be made so quickly, with the discussion progressing in front of Dorian and all the gathered onlookers. Such transparency was so different from the Mortal Plane. Here, the elders didn't hide behind boardroom doors or the walls of private offices. However, regardless of where the decision was made, the question still hung in the air like smoke.

Would they help us and let us help them?

CHAPTER TWENTY-THREE

The quiet discussion lasted around five minutes. While the council talked, I tried to read the tone of the room. Thanks to Vonn, I had learned the hard way to pay attention to individual vampires in a crowd. For the most part, I saw fear and indecision in the stormy faces and knitted brows. A few vampires stared at Roxy and me, and there was a noticeable space on either side of where we leaned against the wall. They furtively averted their gazes whenever they noticed me watching them in return, and there was a pinched look of weary defeat in many of their eyes. As discouraging as it was, maybe Arlonne was right. Perhaps the Hive wouldn't be as helpful as Dorian had urgently hoped.

The only thing that held off my disappointment was the vampires scattered throughout the onlookers, many with fresh wounds or recent scars, who looked eager to accept Dorian's suggestion. They whispered among themselves and looked toward Roxy and me with curious faces, their body language not overtly hostile. It wasn't much, but it gave me hope that we might find a few allies in the Hive.

Across the room, a sour-faced Kane had tucked himself into a little alcove close to Sike and Laini. He kept stealing glances at the younger vampire, who now appeared to be dozing fitfully. However, the bulk of his attention was on the conferring vampire council.

All whispered conversation among the onlookers ceased as Mox stood slowly. Even with her perfect posture, at her fullest height she was only eye level with Dorian's waist. Turning to address the chamber, her blue eyes were unflinching.

"The elders will consider this proposal, but we have a few misgivings that will need to be discussed privately in more detail," she said calmly. Her voice filled the room, impressively loud and strong coming from such a small frame. "First among them is that the Hive is not a place of war. We are a refuge. We preserve our peace by avoiding bloodshed. Our concern is that sending scouts deeper into Itzarriol than usual will lead to vampires being captured. When Immortals capture our members, the likelihood of our location being discovered drastically increases. It would compromise our struggling community. We are not all warriors here."

The effect of her firm words fell over the crowd. Many vampires nodded in agreement, while those I'd noted looking more supportive of Dorian's idea watched in silence, their faces unreadable. Mox turned to Dorian, and he waited patiently for her to continue, though I could see he had clenched his jaw in silent frustration.

"The methods we have developed to travel to Itzarriol are specific, and the protective measures we exercise have been successful so far. However, we can never be too careful." Her tone held possibility, but a warning hummed beneath her cool words. "The hunters we helped you escape from are aware that there are strange new creatures in the Immortal Plane. It will not take them long to realize that those creatures are humans. While the Immortals may not be able to sense our own auras, there is still the risk that the energy of living humans will be noticed, if one knows what to look for."

Although she faced Dorian and had her back to us, her words were somehow targeted at Roxy and me.

"We'll adjourn to discuss it further," Mox announced. "This concludes our council meeting. Thank you for your time."

Dorian lingered for a moment, and I could see the struggle on his face as he decided whether or not to say anything more. However, he swallowed whatever comment he'd intended to make and bowed his head to the elders once more. The elders bent their heads to him in return. Vampires shifted in the room, some standing to leave while others hung around to discuss among themselves.

"Let's go talk to him," Roxy suggested, heading toward Dorian.

A few nearby vampires shot her curious looks as she walked confidently by, still unsure about her presence even after three days. Arlonne followed. More stares were directed at me, but I trailed along behind. How close was too close for Dorian?

Dorian turned to talk to Kane, who had approached faster than we had, obviously eager to discuss the next step. That put his back to me. I stayed several feet away, afraid that at any moment he'd be hit with an unexpected wave of pain. Every second that passed made me understand Dorian's struggle about wanting to be close to me but being terrified of causing pain in the one he cared about. Not to mention that it would look bad if we reacted to one another in front of the Hive vampires. They were already suspicious of humans, so if even a fraction of them held the same prejudices or fears as Halla, we'd make enough adversaries that convincing the council and the Hive to help us with our plan would become nearly impossible.

Before I could warn him or brace myself, he turned to greet Roxy and Arlonne, immediately catching sight of me. His glacial eyes met mine. Heartburn flared immediately in my chest. He winced, his eyes narrowing.

I hoped my face told him I was sorry, that I wished I knew what was happening to us. He held my gaze, and I knew he understood. The pain flared up worse, but if I hadn't felt it myself, I would never have known from his face. The room shrank away from me. Sorrow, desire, pain, frustration—I wanted to push the surging emotions away, but they demanded to be felt.

We would have to find out how close Dorian and I could stand to keep the pain bearable. Our predicament was a huge setback, that much was clear. Would I even be able to participate in group decisions? There was no question about who would have to leave discussions. In the Immortal Plane, Dorian mattered most for decision making.

My burning heart sank in my chest.

Would I have to sit out the rest of the mission?

I rested my back against the wall outside a chamber deep in the center of the Hive, where the council members occasionally met. For privacy, this room had an actual set of doors made of the same soft green wood as the furniture in my room, so there was no hope of eavesdropping. Inside, my group conferred on our next move without me. A pang of frustration settled in my chest, replacing the heartburn from earlier.

It hurt that they had to exclude me, but it wasn't anyone's fault. Things had to be this way right now. I had to think of our mission logically, and if that meant I had to be filled in on developments after the fact to ensure our lead negotiator didn't pass out midsentence, then that was what we would do.

Still, disappointment swelled.

I stared at the wall across from me, letting my vision drift out of focus. We had treated the curse as a short-term, fixable problem. I had learned to manage the pain, and Dorian had learned to function while hungry for the sake of our physical closeness. But now we were back to square one, and all our strategies were worthless. I had assumed that even if there wasn't a long-term solution immediately available, we could manage as we were until we found the time to create one. But I had no cure or even hope for one at this point. There was no way for us to be together here in the Immortal Plane.

The only options in my mind were dismal at best. If the trigger for Dorian also feeling pain was being back in the Immortal Plane, could I really ask him to leave his homeland for me? Or worse, let him starve himself for the rest of his days? Maybe that wouldn't even work anymore. I sighed and leaned my head back. The wall crinkled softly beneath my weight as I closed my eyes.

Sike limped out of the chamber, his white sling in stark contrast to his bruised tan skin and shaggy brown hair. I cringed sympathetically when I saw him catch his injured arm on the doorframe as he shut the door behind him. We had reason to be thankful, though. His collection of broken bones, slashes, missing teeth, and bruises would have incapacitated a human for months.

He smiled when he saw me sitting on the ground.

"Good to see you up and about," he said and struggled to sit next to me.

I jumped up to support him as he tried not to jostle his arm or wounded torso, earning a wave of lightheadedness as I did. I hadn't fully healed yet, either.

He sat with a grateful sigh and leaned his back against the wall, waiting for me to join him on the floor before he spoke. "I've been asked to come fill you in. Ready?"

I forced myself to offer a weak smile. It hurt to be an outsider, but Sike was trying to make the best of it for me.

"I'm all ears."

"We've determined our next moves. Dorian still wants to do a scouting expedition to Itzarriol, even if the council decides not to help us. Which at the moment seems to be the way things are going. However, he's hoping that if he can get one or two of them alone and explain his plan more thoroughly—especially the part about moving them to safety in Scotland—the Hive vampires will work with us to gather information." He shrugged with an amused laugh. "Dorian is good at talking people into things."

"Too good," I agreed with a brief smile. Was Dorian overshooting his hopes with this one? The elders had said they would consider his proposition, but things had taken on a somber tone, for sure.

"Dorian plans to spend the next few hours with Kane, gathering information from the scouts about the route to the city and the situation in the capital to figure out tactical details. I think he's hoping to drum up support with them, too. Laini is planning to canvass the

Hive vampires to ask if they've had any sightings of Kreya or Rhome."

It had been a while since I'd thought about Kreya, Rhome, and their kids. I twisted my hands in my lap. Wherever they were, I hoped they were okay, but my experience in the Immortal Plane so far suggested otherwise.

Sike continued. "Roxy will gather supplies. The Hive is somewhat used to her now. Then, if the council decides they won't help us, Dorian, Kane, Laini, and Roxy will head to Itzarriol as soon as they can manage it. If we do get the support of the Hive, they'll take scouts along." He scowled and dropped his gaze. "I need to stay behind because my injuries won't heal in time. It's the same for Bryce, I guess. And you. You're not able to go because of the whole fainting thing..." He trailed off awkwardly, changing the subject. "They'll spend a few light cycles watching the city, sneaking in if they can. They'll observe anyone of interest, then head back here to pick us up on their way to the tear."

"What about Arlonne?" I asked. I was certain she would want to join the stealth mission.

"Ah, yes," Sike said. "Arlonne volunteered to stay with you and Bryce and me. She wants to gather information about the Hive and try to convince individuals to come with us back to Scotland, even if the whole clan won't come. And if the surveillance group... doesn't return from the city, we'll need her help to get back to the Mortal Plane to inform our allies about what we've learned and to raise a rescue group if necessary."

A sobering but realistic concern. According to rumor, the Immortals had moved on from killing vampires on sight to capturing them, so the idea of a rescue wasn't absurdly idealistic. I knew there would be plenty of vampires and humans ready to take on the Immortal Plane to rescue our teammates if need be. Bravi would probably lead the charge just so she could kill Dorian for being reckless herself.

"Are you okay with being left behind?" I asked, remembering his stubborn determination to be included on the mission.

Sike sighed. "Not much I can do about it," he said, resigned. "I'd only slow them down."

He was right. I drew my legs up to my chest, resting my chin on top of my knees. "Pretty sure I'm in the same situation. My skills are worthless if Dorian passes out every time we have a meaningful interaction." I couldn't keep a note of bitterness out of my voice.

He tapped my knee playfully. "Strong human soldier Lyra Sloane? Your skills are never worthless. Not a chance." But his lips twitched nervously. The humor in his expression drained away. "I'm not sure what will happen next for us."

I let out a sharp laugh. "That makes two of us." I paused, noting how wounded his wide eyes appeared. He looked sadder than I'd ever seen him, and it wasn't just because he was being left behind. "Sike, do you want to talk about anything?"

Sike scratched the side of his neck, hesitating. "I wasn't quite unconscious when you collapsed beside me. Roxy told me what happened with Dorian, but I saw the pain on your face for myself." He sucked in a deep breath. "If stuff like that happens to you and Dorian... I'm worried about Louise and how my feelings could cause her that kind of pain. I don't even know if she cares about me." A pained smile came over his face. "I've never really found anyone who felt right to me, you know? I mean, I've flirted, and that's all it was between Louise and me for a while, but now..."

CHAPTER 23 | 297

"Something's changed?" I guessed, remembering how fast Sike had been to push Louise out of harm's way at the press conference.

He nodded definitively. "Yeah," he admitted. "For a long time I thought it would always just be flirting and a really good friendship. Louise is cute and funny, but she's a human." He held his available hand up in surrender. "No offense."

"None taken... I think?" I replied, feeling a hint of a genuine smile creep onto my face.

"Then the press conference changed everything. She almost died in my arms. It was like the entire world cleared of fog for a moment, and I realized how much she meant to me. How much I would do to keep her safe." He stopped, caught up in the memory. "I knew things had changed after the hospital. I knew from watching Dorian and you that there would be consequences, but it took on a whole different weight when she told me about the pain. Knowing that my affection for her caused her suffering... it's an awful thing to see."

Unfortunately, I now knew exactly what he meant.

"I don't blame Louise for not wanting to see me." He shook his head in frustration. "It's the rational choice. But I can't turn my brain off. I keep wondering things. Like, how can these feelings, especially when I barely realize they're there, continue even when it hurts her all the time? Shouldn't my feelings go away since I hate how much they hurt her? And how can affection have so much power to harm? It makes no sense to me."

I nodded, familiar with the thought process. "It's not fair. Crushes should be pleasant experiences."

He picked at a loose thread in the large cloak he still had draped around him. "You're right, but Louise made her decision. In a way, I respect her for being able to make the hard choices, you know? It was tough to hear, though. Made me restless, as I'm sure you saw. I came with you guys because I needed to do something, but I'm worried that I've screwed things up here, too. Getting hurt and becoming a liability in our very first battle?" He laughed wryly at his own expense, looking down at the sling. It held the same arm that had been broken when we first met.

"Sike, stop." I couldn't stand to hear any more. "You gambled in your battle with the hunter, but it paid off." I stared at his battered face, suddenly protective. "Every single one of us takes risks constantly. What you did was necessary to turn the tide."

Dorian's face flashed in my mind. "And you can't help your feelings," I reminded him, wishing I could say this to Dorian, as well. "The pain Louise feels isn't your fault. It's because of this, this"—I struggled for words, then settled on what felt right—"curse. Not to mention, you *can* be useful here. You already have been."

"How?" he asked. His tone simmered with defeat.

"You're great at getting information. You can make anyone feel comfortable. People feel good talking to you." My voice grew stronger and more passionate as I spoke. "You could ask the other vampires what they think about Dorian's plan, maybe even try to recruit more of them to our side. We can do the same as Kane and Dorian, asking about the Immortals and scouting, but it might be easier for us because we're not the obvious face of the plan." I paused. "Well, it might be a bit tricky for me, but hopefully some of them will be more curious about a human than suspicious." We'd both needed pep talks today, and he'd done his part to reassure me. "You've got real strengths, Sike, so don't put yourself down just because your strengths aren't necessarily on the battlefield."

Sike beamed. "I learned how to use a cell phone *and* the internet.

I taunted an Immortal hunter to her face. I'm too stubborn to quit. Who knows what else I could do? We might as well start now! Maybe we'll even find someone here who knows about the curse."

His sunny change gave me hope. I found myself smiling back at him instinctively, more evidence that Sike was just the person to go with me to track down some information.

Even if I couldn't stand beside Dorian and help him directly, Sike and I would find our own way to help from a distance. If we asked the right questions to the right members of the Hive in the right way, what we learned might change the mission. I wasn't going to give up now.

He offered me his free hand. "Let's go see what we can find out."

CHAPTER TWENTY-FOUR

S ike led me down the corridor, away from the room where our team was still conferring. His pace was less than speedy, and I eyed him skeptically.

"Are you going to be okay walking through the Hive like this?" I asked. "You don't have to power through and make it worse. We can take it slow if we need to."

"Don't worry," Sike assured me. "I'll be fine. We'll just avoid stairs because, as it turns out, one of the side effects of getting beaten up by an Immortal is that you get winded easily. Who knew, right?"

Stairs? Wasps didn't build stairs, so they must have been built by the vampires. I walked alongside Sike as we made our way through the Hive. Occasionally, I thought I recognized our surroundings, comparing the hallways with the ones Roxy had shown me. It was never the case, though, as we'd then take a different turn, or the pattern of lichens on the wall would be wrong, or the windows were on the other side of the corridor.

"How can you tell where you're going?" I asked as we turned a corner on our current route that immediately led to a dogleg bend.

He clicked his tongue. "I'm pretty good at finding my way around after I've been somewhere once. It's why the elders in the library at Vanim always liked me. I could find a book faster than anyone else in the maze of shelves."

"Well, more power to you," I muttered, stepping around a soul-light lantern that stuck slightly farther out into the hall than the others. "I can't figure out the layout of this place, so I'll be sticking close to you."

"You'll start to notice the differences soon enough," he promised. "The lichens are slightly different colors in different sections of the Hive, so that can help you figure out where you are."

"Really?" I asked, trying to recall which colors I'd seen so far and where.

"Really. Decades before the tear, the Hive was established as a secret archive and academic hermitage, and they grew the lichens to be different colors so they could group information together. Like amber was politics and philosophy, which is why the council chamber is lit in that color."

"The Hive is a giant library?" The sacred silence and simple decorations suddenly made sense.

Sike nodded. "I don't know all the details, but when I was training at the library in Vanim, we were told a little about it. When persecution from the Immortals began to worsen, the elders at Vanim asked academics to move the most important documents and experiments and histories somewhere safe to protect them. That way if the city was attacked, we would still have a record of our people and our accomplishments."

"So, everyone here was a scholar?" I watched a group of vampires scurry past. Two of them were barely more than kids, and the other was a pinched- and exhausted-looking man carrying a baby. It seemed things had changed.

"Originally, yes," Sike said. He paused a moment, wincing as he took a deep breath that pulled on his wounds. "But I guess refugees from Vanim must have found their way here. That in itself is pretty impressive, since the location was kept secret from all but a few elders."

"Now it makes sense why they blindfolded our team on the way in," I said, slowing my pace to match his as we continued.

Citrus and musk hung in the air. We passed through a long, wide hallway lit entirely in blue-white light that was simultaneously calming and unsettling. A few steps later, we were faced with a three-pronged fork in the hallway lit in red. Sike took us down the far left path, and we spent several minutes walking under the blood-like shade.

Occasionally, we stumbled across a Hive vampire or two, and Sike always tried to stop them to engage in conversation. Most were friendly, if in a slightly reserved, nervous kind of way. They usually gave me a wary stare and didn't address me—it was as if they didn't quite know what to say. As soon as either one of us mentioned Dorian's plan to go to Itzarriol, they shook their heads and hurried away, unwilling to discuss it.

"I feel like an ant," I muttered after a burly vampire passed us, refusing to even acknowledge Sike's friendly questioning. "Or a ghost. Nobody will look at me."

We were taking a short rest in a hallway that glowed a soft violet, trying not to feel too discouraged.

"They've probably never seen a human up close," he told me. "If they've ever seen one at all. Remember, most vampires don't visit the Mortal Plane to feed, just warriors and scouts who are trained for it. You're like a myth brought to life."

"I guess you guys know what that feels like, huh?" I said ruefully. "Having your existence revealed to the public and all."

A new voice called, "Excuse me?"

We turned to see a short, stocky male vampire approaching. Under the violet light I couldn't tell his hair color, but his skin was almost as dark as the onyx wildling who had been herding the velek.

"Hi," Sike said, giving a welcoming grin. "How can we help you?"

"You're part of the team from the Mortal Plane, aren't you?" he asked. His voice was a deep bass that I felt in my sternum.

"What gave it away?" Sike asked. "The bandages or the human?"

The other vampire chuckled, offering his hand to Sike. "I am Kono, a scout of the Hive."

Sike introduced us as they shook hands. To my surprise, Kono then turned to me. I took his hand firmly.

"It is interesting to meet a human here in the Immortal Plane," he said, keeping hold of my hand for a moment. "Especially one who would come here to risk her life for the sake of vampires. I don't even need to read your aura to know there is very little darkness in you."

Was there anything more uncomfortable than getting praised by a stranger? I murmured awkward thanks, unsure what to say.

"She's risked more than you know to help us," Sike chipped in, making it worse. "Lyra is one of the humans who has been fighting for months to get us asylum in the Mortal Plane."

"I've been to the Mortal Plane many times," the vampire said, golden eyes gleaming, "and I can assure you that such generosity and open-mindedness are rare, in my experience."

I'd experienced generosity and open-mindedness plenty of times, but I supposed it would be different for a vampire, especially one who only visited briefly before returning to the Immortal Plane. I inclined my head in acknowledgment.

"So, you're a scout of the Hive?" Sike asked. "You go to Itzarriol to feed?"

"Close to it," Kono replied. "We rarely dare to get within sight of the walls."

"I guess you're not too impressed with Dorian's plan to visit the city, then?" Sike asked, his face revealing that he expected a negative response.

Kono remained silent for a moment, obviously picking his next words carefully. "I *am* impressed," he said. "And I see the logic behind his plan."

"But?" I sensed the counterpoint he was leading to.

"But we cannot risk this haven for the sake of potentially gathering information that *might* take us a step closer to fixing the rift in the barrier." He shrugged. "Though you've found safety in the Mortal Plane, you must remember the horror of living in the Immortal Plane immediately following the fall of Vanim. We're finally finding a shred of stability. If it were just me, I would join you in a heartbeat. But we have much to protect here. The young. The very old."

"Your history," I said softly. "I promise you, we do understand."

Kono spread his hands, palms up. "This is only my opinion. Others may think differently."

"That's what we're trying to find out," Sike admitted. "Just to get a sense of public opinion, you know?"

"I wish you well in your endeavor," Kono said, bowing slightly to say goodbye.

"We have a question before you go, if you don't mind," Sike said, giving me a look. "We're trying to learn more about an old piece of folklore involving vampires in the Mortal Plane. Do you know anyone who might be an expert in the histories of vampires visiting the other realm?"

"I don't personally." The other vampire frowned but thankfully didn't press for more details. "However, if you go to the central spiral, you should either be able to find someone who can point you to a scholar or the scholars themselves."

"The central spiral?" I asked.

He pointed down the violet hallway. "Keep going until you reach green, then go left until you find pale pink. The core is close by there. If you reach amber you've gone too far."

Sike and I shared a silent look as Kono nodded farewell and continued on his way.

"To the core," Sike announced, starting off down the hall.

More of the Hive's complex structure revealed itself as we walked. The full extent was like nothing I'd imagined. We followed twisting hallways, often coming face-to-face with unexpected dead ends or needing to double back. Finally, after finding the right green path and correct pink corridor, we emerged into an open space that could only be the central spiral of the Hive.

The spiraling structure in the middle of the vast chamber acted as a ramp, providing a walkway for the dozens of vampires bustling up and down in pursuit of their daily life. I tipped my head back to admire the walls, which were pitted with honeycomb cells and doorways carved at various levels. The higher openings of the chamber connected to the central spiral by strings of thin walkways. Some were organic, made by the jaspeths, and others were more recently constructed from wood and rope. I dropped my gaze back down, taking in the dozens of vampires moving about the space. Voices mingled, echoing from above.

"It may not be stairs, but I don't think I've got the energy to make it all the way up there," Sike said, grinning up at the half dozen levels above us. "So hopefully we find this curse expert on the bottom floor, right?"

I nodded, realizing for the first time how many different professions the vampires here seemed to have. A willowy woman in green robes drifted by carrying something that resembled a microscope, though it had a lot more levers and lenses on metallic arms. A man walked past us in the opposite direction, a book open in his hand and a satchel spilling scrolls from the top over his shoulder. When I looked, maps and markings I couldn't understand filled the book. The man caught my wandering eye and frowned, shielding his precious pages from me. I raised my hand apologetically, but he only sniffed, giving me a suspicious look as he hurried away.

"Bravi would eat these guys for breakfast," I mumbled.

Sike stifled a snicker. "Bravi and the others are warriors," he reminded me. "The Hive has always been a place of study and strategy."

I watched his lean form as he hobbled through the crowd, noticing he didn't refer to himself as a warrior. "You've always favored stealth and wits, and you said you worked in the library in Vanim," I said, moving out of the way of a pack of scouts wearing

sleek cloaks—all of them men with cropped hair of various shades—
who shouldered past us. "Would you have preferred to come here
instead of the Mortal Plane?"

He gazed up at the spiral, watching the community of the Hive
swirl around us. "No. This place is important in its own way, but the
Hive is about protecting the past. What we're doing in the Mortal
Plane is about securing our future."

A small boy raced past, nearly taking out Sike and making my
vampire friend chuckle. I shot Sike an amused smirk. An older
woman, presumably the child's mother, ran after the boy.

"Now," Sike said, "shall we ask some folks what they think about
our plan and try to find this curse expert?"

We began flagging individuals down, trying to ask what they
thought of Dorian's plan. The reactions and responses were varied—
some refused to talk to us, skittish about a strange vampire and a
human, while others held opinions similar to Kono's but were reluctant to get close to the Immortals' city. A few were very supportive,
glad that someone was thinking proactively rather than defensively.

Occupied by my thoughts, at one point I almost ran into a
vampire woman. She glared at me, either offended or horrified, and
fled, her rough linen dress brushing the ground.

Sike was right. None of these vampires had ever been around a
non-hostile human. I tried to keep this in mind, but I couldn't help
but feel as though I was constantly being watched, examined,
judged. It was like being a specimen under glass or a butterfly
pinned to a board.

Unfortunately, of the few vampires we managed to speak with,
none were long-time residents of the Hive and so didn't know

where to find a scholar who knew about human and vampire folklore.

"One last guy," Sike promised for at least the tenth time, eyeing an oncoming vampire. "He looks like he might know something about scholars."

A short man with a shaved head bent over a book shuffled toward us without looking up from the page.

Sike stepped subtly into his path. "Excuse me?"

The man lifted his head and blinked round green eyes, pulled from the book's trance. "Yes?"

Sike cleared his throat. "Do you know where we can find vampire scholars? I'm looking for information about history and folklore involving the Mortal Plane."

To my surprise, the man nodded. He gestured back the way we had initially come. "Find the green corridor. That's where all the history scholars gather. Check the last door."

I waited until the man disappeared into another corridor before I clapped victoriously. Finally, some progress.

CHAPTER TWENTY-FIVE

The room of the history scholars turned out to be an interconnected series of small, cozy chambers. The light was mainly provided by dozens of soul-light lanterns, with polished metal mirrors reflecting their light. Shelves lined the walls from floor to ceiling. Judging by the color, I was pretty sure they were made of redwood, though the whispers were thankfully no longer present. Scrolls, papers, and books were packed onto the dark red shelves, and thick rugs littered the floor, with low tables on top of them.

A man sat on one of the rugs—this one woven from various shades of green—with a scroll unfurled in front of him, his pen moving quickly over a separate piece of parchment as he made notes.

"Hello," Sike said cheerfully. "We come seeking a scholar."

The man looked up. His lean face suggested middle age, but his sharp brown eyes looked younger. Graying blue hair stood up in every direction, the color contrasting with his dark skin. When he went to stand, I noted that he was very, very tall. He enthusiastically extended a gangly hand—not to Sike, but to me.

"A human in the Immortal Plane," he breathed with an oddly pleased smile.

I gave Sike a surprised glance as I shook the scholar's hand firmly. His hands were soft, clearly more used to turning pages than to holding weapons.

He turned to Sike. "If it's a scholar you seek, maybe I can help. My name is Echen. I am a history keeper and lore expert."

Sike grinned and introduced us. I recognized the strong scent of jaspeth musk on Echen. It wasn't unpleasant but more overwhelming in such a small room. When Echen moved, his gangly limbs reminded me of an exaggerated version of Sike.

He gestured around the room. "My humble haunt," he said.

I glanced at another set of nearby shelves. Bottles and jars of a strange mustard-colored liquid sat on the shelves.

Echen caught my eye. "I see you're admiring my collection of jaspeth pheromones. Did you know that infant jaspeths release a distinctly different hormone when they're in danger? It causes an adult jaspeth to become enraged. You don't want to mix them up with the type that keep us safe."

Oh. I leaned away. Sike suppressed a chuckle.

"We have a few questions about vampire folklore for you," Sike said as Echen showed us to his small table, inviting us to sit on the rug opposite him.

Papers with diagrams that reminded me of mathematical figures covered the surface. He speedily tidied the area as we lowered ourselves to the ground.

"I rarely have guests," he said with a wink. "People tire of hearing a scholar spout off his ideas, especially in times such as these."

"I think you'll find us eager to listen," I said.

Echen's smile grew at my response. His genuine delight made me feel, for the first time since I'd woken up in the Hive, like I was welcome here.

"We want to know anything you can tell us about contact between vampires and humans," Sike explained. "Especially romantic relationships. We believe something strange happens when vampires have strong feelings for humans." He kept the specific details of *who* to himself.

"There's a painful reaction, usually in the human." I hesitated before adding, "I know this from personal experience. I just came out of a three-day coma caused by that pain."

"Interesting." Echen scratched his head. "Well, there are various tales. The general idea, however, is that it is incredibly foolish for vampires and humans to couple."

"But it *has* happened before?" Sike asked. "Like, what we're experiencing isn't something totally new?"

"Oh, there are various accounts of vampire and human couples, though according to the historical record, it's not something that has happened often. Friendly interactions between our kinds are exceedingly rare." He stroked his cheek thoughtfully. "Many vampires think it's beneath them to study such things, but I've always thought it quite a fun subject. The situation happens. Why ignore it?" He looked between us expectantly with a singular arched eyebrow.

I glanced at Sike in confusion, not understanding his pointed gaze.

"No," Sike blurted, apparently faster on the uptake. "Not *us*. We're not the couple."

I laughed awkwardly before I could stop myself, hoping it didn't offend Sike. From the mock grimace on his face as he looked at me, he was equally uncomfortable with the idea.

"We're just friends," I assured the scholar. "But we're both affected by the issue. I'm with a vampire. He's interested in a human."

Echen leaned back. "Of course," he said smoothly. "And I'm not here to judge. But you should know that there's hope for both of you."

"There is?" I curled my fingers around the table's edge, the anticipation so strong that I went lightheaded. Were we finally going to get some answers?

"Maybe," Echen said, a note of caution in his voice. "There have been records kept of a few vampire and human couples throughout history. As I said, it happens very rarely, since our two peoples have very little contact with one another. The fact that there are potentially two at once right now is... fascinating." He leaned forward slightly, hitting his stride. "Rumor among scholars has it that the most recent vampire-human couple lived together in the Mortal Plane for a few years. They didn't want to submit to study, so there were only ever the vaguest of notes kept. Those notes couldn't be verified, so they weren't brought here to the Hive. They're probably ash in Vanim now." He sighed. "Such a waste."

"What do you remember of the situation?" I asked. "Do you know what became of them in the Mortal Plane?"

"I think there might have been a child," Echen said, grayish brows drawing together as he tried to recall more details. "No, wait. I think that was the one from my father's era. That would be, oh, two hundred years ago now, and I don't believe it was ever verified."

A couple at some point in history had been able to have a child? I sucked in a sharp breath, trying to process it. If true, that was huge news. Still, it was slightly frustrating that we couldn't confirm any of this information.

Sike leaned his elbows on the table as he watched Echen. "Do you know their names?"

Echen shook his head. "No names, unfortunately, or where they lived in the Mortal Plane. Or did they move to somewhere in the Immortal Plane? No, that can't be right..."

My mind raced as he continued to mutter to himself. How had this couple managed to be close enough to one another to live together? In the back of my mind I'd pretty much abandoned the idea that Dorian and I would be able to do something like that. I wasn't entirely sure I wanted children at all—and certainly not for a long time—but did this story mean that maybe it was something we could consider in the future?

"How did they manage to live together?" I asked. "After he's fed, I can barely be in the same room as the vampire who cares about me. Our..." I paused, flushing at the detail I was about to reveal. "Our first kiss put me in a coma. How could this other couple get past that kind of problem?"

Echen laced his fingers together thoughtfully, closing his eyes. "My memories have faded somewhat, and my knowledge only goes so far, but my good friend was the lead researcher on the situation and kept me well informed. Let me think." He was silent for a few moments as he gathered his thoughts. "I seem to recall that the couple shared their blood somehow... joined in a way that fused their auras together." He hummed as he reflected. "Yes, I think the vampire began to drink tiny amounts of the human's blood, leeching the naturally small amounts of dark energy they otherwise wouldn't have touched. The process blended the auras. That was enough to nullify the curse, and the painful effects stopped, or were at least reduced enough for them to... interact."

There were some similarities to Halla's story, but Halla had said she'd heard the story when she was a child, so it seemed likely she was thinking of a couple from much longer ago.

"Do you remember what happened to them?" Sike asked, hope in his wide brown eyes.

"The couple allegedly lived together for some time, so the solution at least worked for a while," Echen said. He looked at us solemnly. "The story unfortunately has a rumored gruesome ending, however."

Sike's face fell, and my eyes shut as though I could block out the disappointment.

"It seemed that the vampire overdid the feeding. The human died of blood loss, killed by the one they loved. Or at least that's one of the rumored outcomes." Echen scowled. "If there was ever an accurate record made, like I said, it will have been destroyed when Vanim fell. It burns me up, really. There's nothing to confirm whether they even existed at all, or if it was just a story."

The tale partially echoed Halla's warning, although her absurd explanation that the vampire accidentally drew dark energy from the human had been off. I should have asked for more details, but it was too late now.

"Was this couple from a long time ago?" I asked. "An old legend?"

Echen shook his head, his gray-blue hair flying wildly in every direction. "I don't know for certain. Might be twenty years or seventy, or more for all I know without the details in front of me."

"And you can't remember anything else?" Sike pressed.

"No, sadly. I wish I did." Echen spread his hands helplessly.

"Could we ask your friend who was the lead researcher?" Sike asked, but I could tell he was clutching at straws. "Maybe they'll remember."

Echen's eyes took on a glassy sheen. "As I said before, dear boy, any record will be ash in the ruins of Vanim. My friend did not make it out of the city when the Immortals attacked."

The reflective sadness in Echen's face suggested it was time to wrap up our visit. I rose from the table while Sike thanked him profusely. I gave him my own thanks as I shook his hand once more, my mind reeling from what he'd told us. Echen, for his part, muttered something about being pleased that he had finally been able to meet a human.

"If it's okay, I'd like to come back tomorrow to speak with you some more," Sike said, looking with eager eyes at the rows of scrolls and books. "I'd love to go through some of these records if that would be acceptable."

Echen nodded, some of his enthusiasm returning. "History is meant to be shared. Come any time, for as long as you're here. That goes for both of you," he added with a wan smile at me.

As he rose to show us out of the chamber, a wave of jaspeth musk hit me, strong enough to make my eyes water. I glanced down at his low table to blink the tears from my eyes, catching sight of a spiked font I didn't recognize.

"What language is that?" I asked, pointing to the notes. "I haven't seen any of the other vampires use it."

Echen looked at what had caught my attention. "Oh, that is the language of balance bringers and scholars. It's almost exclusively used by vampires now, although at one time Immortal scholars used it, too. I'm using it to write a letter to a colleague of mine in the upper echelons of the amber hallways, up by the council, asking for the official record of this endeavor you and your team are putting together so I can add it to our history."

"I've never seen it before," I murmured, looking closer.

"You wouldn't have seen any of your teammates use it, as they speak and write the universal tongue with those from the Mortal Plane. Immortals use it, too, when they choose to speak nontele-pathically."

"Is that why we could understand the Immortal hunters we met?" I'd wondered about that but had bigger problems at the time.

"Yes," Echen replied, ushering us toward the doorway. "Immortals and vampires do not share a language, so they both would have used the universal tongue during your interaction, which, I must say, I am deeply impressed you all survived."

"Not for lack of effort on their part," Sike joked, gesturing to his various injuries.

I noticed that despite his humorous comment, he looked weary. We probably needed to rest.

Finally bidding farewell to Echen, I insisted that both Sike and I return to our respective chambers to sleep for a while. He didn't argue and guided us silently back through the multicolored maze of halls.

The implications of the scholar's story haunted me. Did this mean Dorian and I had no chance of being together? Or could the madhat method of drinking my non-dark blood, if it even worked, be done safely? The human had allegedly died, but he hadn't mentioned the vampire's fate. They had probably passed away, as well, in the time since the tear. But if not, we needed to find them, or at least someone who might know more about the situation than rumors and dead researchers.

I said goodbye to Sike as we parted ways outside the chamber they had given to the vampires. As it turned out, it was just around the corner from the one given to us three humans. I had no idea what time it was or even how long I had been awake, but from the increased quiet of the Hive, most of its inhabitants seemed to be resting.

Both Bryce and Roxy slept soundly in their beds as I crept into the chamber. I wondered if Bryce had awoken at all today and when Roxy had gotten back from the team meeting. All at once, I felt startlingly isolated as it hit me that I was the only conscious human in the Immortal Plane right now. I understood more than ever how the vampires must feel being so far from their home. A sharp longing for Dorian's presence washed over me. I desperately wished I could talk to him.

Inspired by the memory of Echen's writing, I dug through my gear bag for a notebook and pencil. A letter was the perfect way to communicate when necessity compelled distance from the person you wanted to speak to. I sat on the low bed with the notebook on my leg and wrote by the light of the luminescent lichen.

Dear Dorian

I stopped. Was that too formal? Too intimate? It felt strange somehow. I crossed it out, instead writing him a brisk note. There was a lot that I wanted to get off my chest, brought on by the events of the day. And if previous discussions about our complex situation had taught me anything, it was that they often ended with Dorian insisting he knew best. This time, I wanted to write clearly and powerfully, leaving no room for misinterpretation.

Dorian,

Writing seems to be the best option to communicate privately with you. I'm sorry you're feeling the pain too, now. It doesn't feel satisfying that you have to experience what I do. It feels worse.

Sike and I talked to Echen, a history scholar, today. I might have learned a way around the curse, but it sounds risky. I'm not sure it will work, but right now it is my only lead. I'm of the opinion that we should wait until we finish the mission to try it.

I hesitated, imagining his reaction to my next words, but I steeled myself and wrote them anyway. He was going to hate it.

I want us to consider the worst-case scenario if we can't find a way to end the curse. We need to talk about this after the mission. Right now, I know you need to be at full strength for the rest of this journey.

Once again, I hovered over the page until I'd worked out what I wanted to say. Uncertainty wouldn't read well.

In the balance of things, the success of this mission is far more important than whether or not I am involved. There's too much risk that one or both of us could end up in a coma again. Our cause is more important than any of us individually. I am only one part of the team, and right now my presence is more of a hindrance than a help. Maybe it would be best if I wait here with Sike, Bryce, and Arlonne. It doesn't change my commitment to you—to us—but we agreed to go on this mission as soldiers, not as lovers.

I sucked in a breath and reread. Satisfied, I hesitated, unsure how to end the letter. Sincerely? With love? Hugs and kisses? I snorted quietly at the last.

I finally settled on just writing my name, feeling like I'd chickened out. I tore out the page, folded the paper neatly, and wrote *Dorian* on the visible side.

I crept down the hall to the vampires' chamber, not wanting to wake anyone with supernatural hearing. I peered through the open doorway. The last thing I wanted was to trigger any pain if Dorian saw me, but everyone was already asleep.

I spotted Dorian's form in a bed beneath a rough blanket and tiptoed inside. Quietly, I placed the folded letter and the pencil near his bedside. He stirred slightly.

I turned to leave but froze when Dorian turned toward me in his sleep. He didn't wake up, just shifted a little, his breath evening out. My heart stung with sadness. He reached out his hand in his sleep, eyes still shut. I desperately wanted to stay by his side... but I had to leave him.

"Goodnight," I whispered, hoping he somehow heard me.

CHAPTER TWENTY-SIX

The wraith version of Dorian found me in my dreams again. He walked toward me in the ruined city of Vanim, melting into shadows only to reappear behind me. Blasts of teal light burned through my vision. The world grew murkier as fog crawled over me. Screams of fear and pain sounded in the distance.

I woke up staring at the ceiling, engulfed in the same sense of loss that I had woken with the day before. At some point in my distressed sleep, I had kicked off the rough blanket. It sat at the end of the bed in a crumpled heap. I pressed my hand against my heart where it hammered in my chest. There was an emptiness in my hands, as if something had slipped through my fingers.

In the dim bioluminescence, I saw my teammates sleeping. Roxy snored softly beneath her pillow. Bryce's leg stuck off the side of his bed, his big foot twitching every now and then as he shifted in his sleep. My eyes drifted to the stool beside my bed. My letter sat there folded neatly, notebook and pencil beside it. I blinked, disoriented. I leaned over to grab the note and realized that someone had folded the paper so my original note was on the outside. Had Dorian responded? Wide awake now, I sat up and snatched the letter off the table.

My Lyra,

Although there are risks, which I have considered, I need you on this mission. Our team needs you. You may not know how much you matter, but you are part of the glue holding our group together. I trust your skills.

My heart began to beat faster. He'd called me his. He wanted me to go on the mission. However, there was a seed of doubt beneath the flush of affection, because he once again seemed to be ignoring most of my points. My skills wouldn't be worth much if I passed out in the middle of a battle. Worse, now I could take him down with me.

There are ways we can work around our problem so that you can join the mission. For surveillance, it might be wiser to have several small groups. We would be able to cover more ground and gather more intel. You and I would just need to be in different groups. Even when we're not next to each other, we make a great team.

I smiled down at the letter, shaking my head. That point was comforting, but it didn't entirely soothe the anxious feeling in my gut.

I need you to come on this mission. Really, honestly, truly. I don't know how many more words I need to drive that point home. Even when the pain hits me, your presence grounds and reassures me. I have a suggestion to lessen the pain immediately. There are hungry Hive vampires, and I can donate a small portion of my dark energy to them. It might even help improve the goodwill we need to win their support.

I sighed, trying to keep the sound low for my sleeping friends. Here he went again, insisting on weakening himself for me, even at the cost to the mission. I pressed on, unable to escape my need to read more of his words, words he had written for me about how much he cared.

I miss our days on the run, as ridiculous as that sounds. I miss being able to curl up next to you without unbearable pain. I miss your laugh next to my ear. I miss your touch, your kisses, the shape of your body in my hands. You're in my thoughts even when you're not around.

Warmth spread through my body as my breath caught. I pressed the letter to my lips for a blissful moment, closing my eyes against sudden desire. It was amazing, the emotions that a mere letter could provoke within me. It was old school, but it worked.

I need you on this mission. We leave as soon as we can gather a party to accompany us.

The last sentence flung a bucket of cold water over those delightful sensations. He assumed I would go along, no questions asked, just like he had when he first announced the Immortal Plane mission. I dropped the letter to the bed, dragging my hand down my face. He was trying to decide for me *again*. I exhaled. In Moab, I'd found that I didn't fit into a traditional command structure anymore, after the democratic way we'd run our group as fugitives from the Bureau. I had accepted that we couldn't do that here, since Dorian was the expert in the Immortal Plane, but it still left a sour taste in my mouth. We'd mixed business and pleasure out of necessity, and now I found myself in the position of taking orders from a lover. I could see now why businesses and militaries didn't allow that. I didn't want to grow to resent him.

And our future? It stretched before me like the murky path in my dreams of ruined Vanim. He hadn't addressed that part of my letter at all. I reread the beginning line again, annoyed that my heart still beat faster when I read how he called me his. I cared for him deeply, but I wasn't going to let him manipulate me into doing something unwise.

Frustration, love, and desire boiled within me, pulling my heart in every direction. I put my head in my hands, processing everything. There was no help for it: we would have to talk this through in person. Even if it would hurt.

Someone knocked on the chamber wall beside the doorway, and I shoved the letter beneath my pillow, startled.

"Wake up," Arlonne said as she stepped into the chamber. She wore a rough new linen shirt. The warm yellow looked good against her brown skin. Laini hovered behind her, stifling a yawn. "The Hive elders are giving their decision about aid for the mission."

Roxy scrambled from her sheets, suddenly awake. "They've decided?"

I swung my legs out of bed and grabbed my boots. The speed of their decision—less than a working day—could either be a very good thing or a very bad thing. Either way, the next phase of our mission would be defined by whatever was about to be said in the council chamber.

Bryce never stirred. I hesitated. He'd probably want to hear this, but...

"Leave him be," Arlonne said, her gaze lingering for a second longer than usual on the sleeping soldier. "He deserves to rest."

―――――――

There were fewer people in the council room today, though whether that was because of the early hour or because most of the population didn't care about the outcome I couldn't be sure. The room stank of jaspeth pheromones. The citrus needled me today, irritating my nose. Seven Hive vampires sat on rugs in a circle, including Echen, and the four elders assembled at the front. Mox peered over at our group of vampires and humans, which had stayed close to the curved wall again.

Dorian was the only one to stand before the elders, as though he were about to be judged. After that beautiful letter, I wished I could walk up to him and wrap my arms around him, even if we needed to talk about certain aspects of it. He'd find it harder to ignore my points in person. In the meantime, I hated the distance between us and how unnatural it felt.

"We have come to a decision," Mox announced, drawing herself up. Her tiny frame somehow filled the room.

I stared at her stark white hair and fought the urge to fidget nervously in the silence that followed her announcement. Vampires really knew how to drag out the anticipation.

"I'm ready to hear it," Dorian said and bowed his head, the picture of calm respect.

"We will not help you and your team, beyond the sanctuary that we are already providing," she announced in a firm voice. "We will not authorize sending our people to the Mortal Plane, because we simply don't have enough information about your alleged safe haven, nor do we know you well enough to trust you. We will not send any of our people with you to the Immortal city, either."

My gut twisted as I watched Dorian bring his head up, meeting her gaze steadily.

"I regret being unable to provide supporting scouts and firsthand knowledge of the city," Mox insisted. "We all do, but we're not a resistance movement. Our primary goal is simply to endure, to survive, to protect the knowledge hidden within these walls. The

Immortals grow greedier each day. They used to just kill our kind, but lately they've taken to capturing us. Captivity is a fate worse than death, as far as we are concerned. Each capture increases our risk of discovery. We want no more of our people in or around Itzarriol than necessary. The Hive will only journey there for feeding missions. Nothing else."

Her final words fell. The chamber stilled into a terrible quiet. They wouldn't help. The cold of disappointment stung me. I understood why, but I also wished they would consider that being proactive was its own kind of protection. This must be a terrible blow to Dorian. It didn't show on his face, however—he remained outwardly calm and composed.

"However," Mox's face softened, "do not think that we disparage your goals. We have seen too much death and lost too many of our group to join you on the ground. You are more than welcome to stay here, humans and vampires, and become a part of the Hive, for as long as you so wish. We recognize and value the bravery you all have displayed in getting this far, and we know you could be of great service to the protection of the Hive."

"I appreciate the offer," Dorian said, a touch of genuine warmth in his voice despite the disappointment he must be feeling, "but we came to the Immortal Plane for a purpose, one which we intend to fulfill with or without your aid." He paused. "Is there nothing I can say to make you reconsider any part of your decision?"

Mox shook her head. "The Immortals are far too dangerous for our group to face, and what we protect here is far too precious." Her sharp eyes focused on him. "Tell me, Dorian. Do you honestly believe that your mission will help restore balance to the Immortal Plane and our kind?"

"I do," he replied without missing a beat.

"Would you be willing to die if it gave your mission a chance to succeed?"

"I would." There was no hesitation in his voice.

His answer provoked a mixture of feelings in me, mainly pride in his certainty and fear that he might one day soon have to act on these words.

"And the Immortals do not scare you?" she asked, a note of genuine curiosity in her tone.

I glanced at the vampires gathered on rugs in the circle nearby. When she said the word "Immortal", two of them shuddered. An older man dropped his gaze to the ground, a blank look coming into his eyes.

"Of course the Immortals scare me," Dorian said with the hint of a frown. "I have seen the horror they inflict. I lost my home, my family, my city to their cruelty."

"Then surely you understand why we are so wary of risking the Hive's discovery," Mox said. "You know that this is where the last traces of our civilization are hidden away. Most of those who live here are the old, the sick, the weak, the young, and those with no combat training."

The Immortal rulers scare the hell out of these guys. I noted the slumped postures and the nervous glances they gave one another. It was understandable, but how did they expect to change their current circumstances if they wouldn't take up their own cause? They couldn't survive in hiding forever. As Mox had said, the Hive risked everything with each captured scout. I bit my tongue as I tried to soothe my frustration when I looked at the small elder, knowing the burden of leadership she was balancing on her thin shoulders.

Dorian respectfully bowed his head once more. "I understand your reservations. Should your mind or your circumstances change, my offer to move the archives and records, as well as the vulnerable population, to our camp in Scotland is a standing invitation."

From my perspective, I could see the handsome outline of his sharp profile. His lips were set in a serious line, a muscle twitching in his strong jaw. He put on a brave face, but the news had to be devastating. The allies we so desperately needed wanted nothing to do with our cause.

"We appreciate that." Mox looked set to dismiss everyone and wash her hands of the matter.

"As one last humble request," Dorian said abruptly, "I would like knowledge about your route to the Immortal capital. It will be vital to our mission."

Mox regarded him for a moment, as if trying to pinpoint any shadowy secrets, then glanced back at the other seated elders. There was a long moment of unspoken conversation, and I sensed that they were deliberating over something. Each looked from one to the other until Mandola, twisting his finger around the end of his beard, nodded slowly.

"We will allow you to use our route," Mox said, her voice loud after the weight of the silence. "We will ask our allies, the clan of aquatic wildlings, to ferry you through the Gray Ravine." Her gaze fixed onto Roxy and me. She hummed pensively. "We will also, perhaps against our better judgment, give you the location of one of our safehouses near the city that our scouts use during feeding missions. It will allow your humans to hide until some method of disguise has been arranged."

"If your team gets caught and tortured for information, you will almost definitely end up giving them the safehouse location, so please understand the sacrifice we are making," Glim piped up behind her in his thin voice. "The wildlings will give you no information to find your way back, so you won't be able to give the hunters directions to us. If you return, you will need to call the wildlings to get back here again."

"But you understand that this is still dangerous for us," Mandola said. "You know enough that, should you be captured and compelled by a hunter to speak, you could endanger us." He looked from Dorian to the rest of our team standing by the wall. "I do not say this to frighten you away from your task. What you intend to do is noble, and that is why we will help you as much as we can while retaining our safety."

I remembered some of Kono's comments, and the elder's reasoning made sense to me. The Hive had to think about the safety of all those who lived here, even if as individuals some of the vampires supported us. But something about Dorian and our goals must have convinced them enough to provide us with this amount of help.

"We will not give you this information if you intend to go deep into Itzarriol, however," Mox added, her tone rising to a stern volume. "If you recklessly endanger yourselves by attempting to spy on the Immortal council or poke your noses into the heart of the city, you're on your own. It's already dangerous enough to send scouts out to feed in secret."

Pyma cocked her head to the side, her braid not moving an inch, held in place with a thick wax. "In fact, if you get caught... I would advise you to find a way to take your own lives rather than allow yourselves to be interrogated."

Roxy scoffed under her breath, but whether it was at the suggestion of suicide to protect the Hive or that we would get caught, I didn't know. If the elders heard, they ignored it. Arlonne stiffened beside me but said nothing. I wondered if she was remembering her last experience of capture at the hands of the Bureau.

"Delightful note to end on," Roxy mumbled next to me. "But they gave us a safehouse, so I guess I'll consider blowing my brains out if we get caught."

I was only half listening. I was too busy watching Dorian.

"Thank you for your advice," he said. "We deeply appreciate being shown the way and your provision of a safehouse. I hope that we might work together... some day."

The elders acknowledged his final words with a bow, then dismissed everyone. Just like that, the meeting was over.

I hung back while Arlonne and Roxy joined Dorian to discuss matters. Laini stayed beside me, perhaps guilty about my exclusion from the group. Her eyes darted toward them.

"Laini, you should go listen. Can you just let Dorian know I need him to meet me afterward?" I asked her. "I'd appreciate it. I'll head out and will be waiting for him in the conference room you guys used yesterday." It was excruciating to stand idly by while my group made plans without me. Powerlessness was no friend of mine.

Laini hesitated but nodded in the end. "I'll tell him. Just... be careful not to hurt one another again, okay?"

"We'll be careful," I promised.

She worried for us. I imagined the rest of my teammates did the same, but I had to speak with Dorian.

I needed to discuss things with him in private before one or both of us headed out on what might be our most dangerous mission yet.

Somewhere out there, the Immortal City of Itzarriol waited for us.

CHAPTER TWENTY-SEVEN

I waited for Dorian in the medium-sized chamber of the conference room that I had been excluded from before. It was thankfully unoccupied, with nothing inside it but a large round table made of white wood and several matching chairs. I hoped the room would be big enough that we could keep a safe distance between us. A distant hope, considering I didn't yet know what a safe distance was for us.

Here I am, reduced to hoping a room is big enough that I can stay far enough away from my vampire boyfriend that we don't end up in comas.

I kicked sorrowfully at the crinkling floor and got over it. As much as I hated this situation, I had no desire to pass out again. We had to keep our distance to protect ourselves from each other. That was just the way it was.

My eyes traced the natural grooves of the amber moss above me. What details were they talking about in the council room? I wished I could be there instead of resorting to this, but I would have to wait. The universe rewarded my patience after a few more minutes.

Dorian took a cautious step into the room, staying at the edge. "Lyra."

He hovered there and took a few more steps, testing the distance with slow movements. Under the golden light, the sharp lines of his handsome face appeared deeper than usual. The shadows beneath his skin teemed with dark energy. I fought the urge to run up and throw my arms around him. It was impossible.

He reached out his hand, then dropped it when he realized what he'd done. There was no heartburn... yet.

"Thank goodness we're able to use one of the rooms in the Hive that actually has doors," I joked, suddenly shy. We hadn't spoken since we both passed out on the shore of the lake.

The corner of his mouth quirked. "I'm very thankful for the shred of privacy. Doesn't anyone in this place have uncomfortable conversations?"

I laughed, my nerves immediately melting away. "Apparently not."

"I'm glad to see you up and about after your coma," Dorian said. "I'm sorry it's taken me so long to find a moment to talk to you in person. Letters were a good way to work around our problem, though."

I smiled, but the fact that we'd needed to resort to letters was a cold reminder of our circumstances. A letter could never be as good as seeing him in real life.

"If you're trying to charm me, it's working," I informed him. "But I haven't wasted our time apart. I've had a few adventures of my own."

"Sike mentioned that," Dorian said. "But he said you should be the one to tell me details."

"Echen, the scholar I mentioned in my letter, told us a story about a vampire-human couple," I relayed. I paused, swallowing a surge of dread as I debated how to frame the story. I wasn't sure how I felt about it myself. "We have a potential cure for the curse, but it's not guaranteed. It's just a theory." In as much detail as I could, I explained what Echen had told us about the couple and their alleged method for escaping the curse.

Dorian's eyebrow rose with interest and hope as I spoke. The tired lines of his face lightened.

"There's a catch, though," I added before he got too excited. "In their case, the vampire killed the human by overfeeding from them."

He froze for a moment as he processed the news. I knew what he was thinking—I'd gone over the same thoughts in my head as Sike and I had walked back from Echen's chambers. We had no other leads, no other theories on how to stop this pain. The stakes were high. Possible death, if we tried the method of a couple that had possibly never existed. Constant pain and comas if we continued as we were now. Separation—either on the mission or if he went ahead while I stayed at the Hive—in a dangerous land ruled by creatures intent on our capture and destruction. There was no easy answer.

He was quiet for a long time. Then, slowly, the stormy shadow of concern faded from his face, and he took a deep breath. "If you're willing, then I want to try it." He stared at me expectantly, eyes burning with determination.

I felt the pull of his conviction, the intoxicating power of it that set alight my own resolution to not give up. But... two fires only created double the destruction. Right now I needed to be the cooler head.

"I'm not sure that's a good idea," I said. "Not when we know so little. It could be a fairytale."

"Or it could work," Dorian countered.

"Or we could die," I said. "There's too much to do in the coming days for us to rush into this. For all we know, it's just a story."

Dorian furrowed his brow in thought, shaking his head. "No. You're right... I want to try, but we'd need to be smart about it. If I got close enough to feed off you, we might both pass out again." He began pacing, keeping a healthy distance between us. "I could get the other vampires in the Hive to drain my energy off. Maybe I could attempt feeding on you after that."

All the times I'd seen Dorian in his out-of-control, primal state flashed into my mind.

"And what about the other risks? What if you—" My mouth refused to offer up the words. *What if you kill me?*

A touch of humor lit Dorian's gaze. "I wouldn't worry about that. Your blood is so light, I'll have to force myself to choke it down. I certainly won't take more than I have to."

He said that now, but he'd never fed on anyone light before. What if it didn't work that way, once his teeth were in? After all, that human hadn't died because their partner had gagged on their blood.

"What if I bled into a cup?" I asked. "Just to be safe. And that way, we can measure how much is needed." I warmed to the idea; it would take care of the distance problem, prevent overfeeding, and we could even be scientific about how much blood was necessary to have an effect.

So of course, Dorian shook his head. "Once blood leaves your body, it won't contain your aura," he said. "It has to be a direct feeding."

I frowned. "I've watched you feed from blood bags," I pointed out, remembering the party at the facility, after we'd returned from the Amish mission.

"The stain of darkness is harder to get rid of," he said. "But while we were able to nourish ourselves from the blood, it wasn't a true feeding. Because the blood was disconnected from the human, cleansing the blood of darkness didn't affect their auras. We only fed that way because we were starving, and it was better than nothing."

I shook my head, trying to get my thoughts in order. This was such a big decision, and he'd only taken about ten seconds to consider it. "In that case, it's too risky. I don't want you to weaken yourself right before a mission because of an urban legend. We need to research more. Find out if this couple even existed." I sucked in a steadying breath. "I'll stay behind and research with Sike and Bryce and Arlonne. The rest of you need to go to Itzarriol and do what we came here to do, which is gather information that will help us close the tear. Doing that will be easier without the worry of incapacitating each other, and by the time you get back, you should be weak enough that we can get close enough to each other to try it."

He scowled. "As if I would ever accept that."

My frustration bubbled to life. While his insistence on not leaving me behind was touching, it was starting to feel like he was putting feelings before strategy.

He tapped his foot. "Us standing here shows that it's unnecessary for us to be that far apart, Lyra. The group needs you. I need you. Not just for your insights into battles and your skills, but for your human perspective on the Immortal conspiracy. You're the one who has been the deepest within this Bureau mess. You offer a perspective that nobody else has, and you might be able to recognize clues and see what we can't. Even Kane agrees, and you know how prickly he is. You don't have to sacrifice your involvement in the mission for my sake. We can find a way, just like we have before."

His logic mollified me, showed me that he hadn't been thinking entirely emotionally, as I'd thought. But I was still annoyed by his refusal to consider my points. "Is that what you think this is?" I asked. "You think I'm sacrificing my involvement just for you?"

"Don't you want to go?" Dorian asked, a stitch of confusion between his eyebrows.

I huffed, slightly disappointed that I was distracted from my line of thought by how adorable his look of slight vulnerability was. "Of course I want to go! I want to help. But I have to think about whether I'm going to jeopardize the mission. You should, too." I paced away from him, hoping I could make my point clear. "We didn't think through how the curse might change and affect us in the Immortal Plane during this mission. We *should* have. It was irresponsible for us to assume that being in a different plane and having you back at full strength wouldn't change things. We didn't make any backup plans for the curse flaring up, and now we're stuck in an impossible situation." I looked over at him with a wry grin. "I wish I could go back in time and give myself a kick in the ass. Maybe give you a kick, too, while I'm there."

"We've handled it," Dorian replied smoothly. He took up his pacing again. "Fighting for things that shouldn't be possible is how we got this far in the first place."

Something in his energetic walk reminded me of how many groups and teams and individuals he had talked into supporting him and his ideas: the Bureau, his clan, my team, the Hive council to a certain extent, and most definitely me. He was always the heroic leader in the room—a smooth and powerful figure who knew how to bargain, manipulate, and sway. It was captivating to watch.

He stopped, staring at me. "It's how you and I have gotten this far. We've spat in the face of the impossible."

Oh, he's good. I felt myself drifting into his point of view, like I'd just finished the end of an inspiring book. That was his skill. It was how he had survived for as long as he had. He was a trailblazer, out of necessity and dogged determination. Just as quickly, however, I took a mental and physical step back, focusing on what he wasn't acknowledging.

I pointed an accusatory finger at him, but there was no heat to my voice. I wasn't angry at him, not really. He wanted to fight for what he thought was right for both of us, and I felt only fondness toward him for that. But he wasn't hearing what I was trying to say. "Stop. I don't want to hear moving speeches right now about how we've beaten the odds before and can do it again. I know you're good at them." I paused, the root of my underlying issue with his actions coming into focus. "You've been pushing through so many decisions lately without truly thinking about them. You decided to run into the Immortal Plane to go to Itzarriol without any help from the Bureau, barely taking time to gather supplies. You went to the press conference in Edinburgh while starving so you would avoid hurting me at all, when you could have fed a little. You demanded we were brought to Moab to help with the empty swarm without discussing the plan with any of us, not even me. You can push through your crazy schemes all you want, Dorian, but you can't force the universe to side with you because you say so. You push to make things happen. It's what I like about you, and I also find it intensely frustrating."

"Lyra, I—"

"Listen," I said and sucked in a breath. I'd finally hit my stride, and I was worried that if he knocked me off course, I'd never find the words again. "Please listen. You can't keep pushing me, Dorian. I'm not a strategy to be executed. I'm a person. Leave your inspirational speeches at the door. I need to hear what you're really thinking so I can support you, even if those thoughts are hard. I have to be able to talk to you about my concerns without feeling like you're trying to manage me." I closed my eyes for a second, struggling with my next words even though they were true. "I probably shouldn't have come to the Immortal Plane with you. Which is why I'm trying to step back now. In going to gather evidence of the Immortal rulers' involvement with the Bureau, you have greater advantages here than I do. You have a better knowledge of the dangers, greater speed, stealth, and strength. All of which are *useless* if you can't stay conscious when I'm close by, but I have to be close by because it's too dangerous for me to be too far away from you. I'm a good soldier, but here I've had to be coddled and protected and guided almost every step of the way. A good soldier in the Mortal Plane doesn't necessarily translate to a good soldier here."

Dorian's nostrils flared angrily. "You're an excellent soldier."

"In most circumstances, yes," I agreed confidently. "Here? I'm not so sure, but what I don't need is for you to treat me like your *personal* soldier. If we weren't in a relationship, it could be different. I could shut up and follow your orders. But if we are going to work together, as partners and as soldiers, then I always have to have a choice. I can't shut up and follow while you bulldoze through every decision."

He stilled, not saying a word.

"We have to think about the difficult things... like sometimes having to be apart from each other," I reminded him. "Not forever. Just sometimes. It's unavoidable."

Dorian crossed his arms. My hands longed to reach out and brush away the pensive lines on his forehead.

"Everything you said is true," he confessed with a sigh. "I'm tired of feeling like I have to push everyone around me into action. Sometimes, I just want to lie down and curl up next to you for as long as I want. If I can't have that, I at least want to know you're nearby, and not just for sweet and gentle reasons. I trust your skills. I want to know that you have my back."

My heart fluttered. There was still no pain. "I'll always have your back, but I need an equal say in these decisions. And I think that trying to take me on the mission to Itzarriol is dangerous for both of us, for our teammates, and also for the Hive. If we pass out and get captured, we put them at risk. You're so busy trying to convince me to come, you haven't addressed that problem."

He nodded stiffly. "You're right. I'm sorry. I didn't realize I was managing you. The Immortal Plane... I just slipped into that mode without thinking when we arrived. On both professional and personal matters, I just turned into the guy who barks orders." His mouth twisted into a sharp, sad smile. "I loathe having to be apart from you and having to act like this distance is okay."

I smiled softly. "I hate it, too." A sad affection bloomed within me. How badly I wanted things to be different, but life was often unfair. I let out a hollow laugh. "But if we can barely be in the same room together, it's hard to support each other."

"It *does* make matters difficult." He rubbed his hand beneath his chin, eyeing the distance between us. "I have some thoughts. Thoughts that I would like to float by you, as an equal partner. Would you be willing to experiment?"

I snorted. "Our entire relationship is an experiment."

"Fair enough," he said, biting back a grin. "Let's test how close we can get. We can put a number on it."

A number means cold hard data.

"Now you're speaking my language," I said. "We use a scale of pain from one to ten. We stop when the pain gets to a three. That's usually a constant buzz for me. No arguments. I don't want either of us passing out. The team will be furious if they have to drag our unconscious bodies out of here." I could already see Kane rolling his eyes and complaining loudly about lovebirds. We'd never hear the end of it.

Dorian took a step around the table toward me, and I mirrored the movement. My chest began to tingle with the telltale start of the curse. It was a light pain at the most. "One."

Two more steps.

"Two," he said, eyes narrowing.

I felt tiny beads of sweat pricking my forehead with our next steps. I was just waiting for the pain to spike unbearably, the pressure making my breath quicken.

"Three." I winced, the heat crackling in my chest.

"Three," he agreed, eyeing the distance. "Looks like about fifteen feet to me."

Fifteen feet? That wasn't as bad as I'd thought. It was only about as wide as the kitchen in my family apartment back in Chicago. We'd basically just have the kitchen between us every time we interacted. Reflexively, I inched back, and he did the same. A sigh of relief escaped my mouth. It was doable.

Dorian grinned at me. "See? We always find a way." His expression became serious. "Will you at least consider coming on the mission? We can remain separated for the journey there, then go off in different groups." He paused, as if consciously trying to ensure that his words were part of a sincere appeal to a partner and didn't sound like a leader trying to inspire a follower. The sight warmed me. "You have a sharp eye and attention to detail. You're quick thinking and strategic and aren't afraid to make a tough choice if it's needed. I know that if you had to get out of there quickly to avoid capture, even if it meant not getting a piece of information, you'd do it. I can't trust everyone else, myself included, to do the same." He met my eyes.

I leaned against the back of one of the chairs, taking in his words. Eventually, I nodded. "I'll think about it. Maybe talk it out with some of the others to get their point of view. Whatever I decide, I hope you'll respect it and carry on with the mission."

He nodded, face somber. "I will. You're right. Some things are more important than the two of us."

Something had shifted between us, and a stronger sense of respect had grown into the new space. It wasn't shiny or romantic or exciting, but it was real and important. Too bad we couldn't touch or comfort each other after our intense discussion. I had the strong urge to wrap my arms around him and bury my face in his chest. I *wanted* that physical comfort. My skin ached for it. But I would have to settle for talking across the imaginary kitchen for now. Fifteen feet was better than fifty.

"I'm a tad less frustrated with all this now that we've talked it out," I told him. "But only one single tad."

He laughed. "We should probably take a break." He rubbed his chest. "I'll leave first, but... please know that I wish I could stay here with you."

I let myself wallow in my sadness for a moment as I watched him go, clinging to the sweetness of his parting words. As his broad shoulders disappeared from view, my heartburn faded completely. A bittersweet mood settled over me as our conversation played repeatedly in my head.

I headed back to the humans' sleeping chamber after I heard Dorian's footsteps fade away. That conversation had given me hope for us. It meant a lot that we'd been able to talk things through, that he'd given ground and apologized. The curse still lingered over our relationship, but this argument wouldn't be the end of us. Dorian and I had come a long way from where we started, but finding a cure loomed a long way in the distance.

In the meantime, I would gloomily contemplate the luminescent lichen on my chamber's ceiling. But when I got back, I wasn't alone.

Bryce sat propped up on his pillows. He gave me a hardy lopsided smile.

"You're up," I breathed and rushed to his side. "How are you feeling?"

"Fine," he said, waving a hand in dismissal. His face filled with deep weariness as he shook his head. "Eh, what the hell am I pretending for? I crash-landed on a redbill, then had its giant dead body crushing me for what felt like hours. I broke bones and compressed internal organs that were not meant to be compressed. I'm feeling like crud."

If Roxy were here, she would have added that he looked like crud. I was a little less blunt.

I chuckled. "It's hard to pretend everything is okay in this place, but old habits die hard."

"It's a soldier's habit to pretend like nothing is wrong," he said, tutting. "But it looks like I won't be soldiering for a while, so I can be honest."

He held my gaze with no judgment. My ex-captain had the eyes of a man who'd seen too much, and I imagined my eyes looked more and more similar to his as the days went by. It was odd to think that he had been in charge of me just a few months ago. So much had changed, yet I valued his opinion even more now, after all our recent experiences.

"What if I made a mistake coming to the Immortal Plane? I knew the pain could get bad, but not this bad." I hung my head for a moment. It felt like a rookie's tactical error. Was I losing my edge?

Bryce cleared his throat. "Well, sitting in this bed, I feel like a bit of an idiot myself. I thought I knew a thing or two, but those vampires and Immortal creeps are in a different league." He sighed irritably. "It annoys me how much this place unsettles me, but there's no way to prepare for everything. That's a lie only Boy Scouts believe. You just roll with it the best you can." He shrugged.

It was useless to worry about the things we couldn't change. Bryce remained stuck in that bed like I remained stuck fifteen feet away from Dorian. It would be better to discuss the threats we needed to process. The Immortal hunters and their various magics came back to me.

"I worry about the Immortals even more after witnessing them first-hand," I said, recalling Inkarri's powerful fighting skills and how she had wormed her way into my mind in search of answers. "Have you heard that the Hive has decided to help? Well, sort of."

"Oh, I did," he said, giving a somber nod. "I can't say I blame them for not wanting to stick their necks out after building up this quaint wee haven, but a safehouse and a guide to the city are nothing to complain about. At least you're still going to continue with the mission." He looked around the glowing chamber. "It might not be too bad to stay behind. I'm sure I can learn a lot around here while these old bones heal. I wouldn't have chosen this situation, but I'll try to make myself useful."

I started to reply that I probably wasn't going to go on the mission and so would likely be learning alongside him, but someone knocked firmly on the wooden doorframe.

Arlonne popped her head through the doorway, her wide eyes alive with unusual energy. She spotted me, and the spark faded. "I won't interrupt." She turned to leave, but Bryce called her back.

"What is it?" he asked and let out a hacking cough. Sleeping for days meant he wasn't used to talking this much.

"I came to check on... both of you," she blurted.

He cocked a teasing eyebrow at her hesitation. I stared between the two of them, confusion and amusement fighting for control of my emotions.

She drew herself up straighter. "Am I not allowed to check up on my team?"

I clenched my jaw to keep it from dropping. Arlonne had just said *her* team.

Bryce roared with laughter. "Well, you can give us some advice.

Any wisdom for when you're in a situation where you're absolutely outclassed?"

She narrowed her eyes as if trying to determine whether he was making fun of her. Ordinarily, I wouldn't put it past him, and that gleam in his eye suggested it, but... he sounded completely sincere. I watched the exchange with fascination. What was happening here? Bryce waited patiently for Arlonne's reply.

"You have to learn to turn your weaknesses into strengths," she said, then shuffled in place in an uncharacteristically awkward manner. "Glad you're feeling better," she muttered, then left without another word.

I blinked, trying to process what had happened. Arlonne came to check on us? Or... My gaze shifted to Bryce, who seemed pleased with her advice. Perhaps she came for someone specific.

"She's right," he said enthusiastically and placed his fist into his palm. "Time to flip the script, as the kids say."

I didn't have the heart to tell him that the kids didn't say that anymore. Funny to think I used to dislike facing Bryce after our missions back at the Bureau. Zach used to swear Bryce's ruddy cheeks came from yelling at our stupid mistakes.

"Could you imagine having this kind of conversation back when you ran our missions?" I asked with a short laugh. "It would never have happened while we worked together. You would have smacked me with a dozen insubordination write-ups."

"You're right about that, lass," he agreed. "Things certainly have changed, but I can't say I mind it. We've been through a lot together. I won't ever have children, you know, but our motley crew of dissenters is part of my family now."

Pride blossomed within me. I sat up straighter, feeling as though

Bryce, by considering me one of his ragtag kin, had just given me the highest compliment of all. "Right back at you."

He smirked. "Lyra, I want you to go on this mission and give those Immortal jerks hell for me. For me and all my aches and pains. It's your obligation as a soldier to go and kick some ass." He lifted his bandaged arm an inch into the air, suppressing a wince. "Meanwhile, I'm going to do my duty as a soldier and sleep for another twenty-four hours."

I smiled weakly as he settled down to rest again, still unable to tell him the ass-kicking would need to happen without me.

Lying back on my own bed, staring once again at the glowing ceiling, I thought of the hope in Dorian's eyes, the respect for my ability in his voice, as he asked me to consider joining the mission. Arlonne's words played over and over in my head: *Learn to turn your weaknesses into strengths.*

Being unable to be close to Dorian was a weakness. However... I could be close to the other vampires. It was true Dorian and I worked best as a team together, but I also worked well with Laini. If Laini was my scouting partner, then I'd have someone to teach me about the Immortal Plane who wouldn't send me into a coma.

So much in this world was unfamiliar to me, but that also meant I paid close attention to everything happening around me. Perfect for a surveillance mission.

Weaknesses into strengths.

I was a human in the Immortal Plane. I was slower and weaker than practically every creature that lived here. I had no magic. But I did have a gun. Several guns, in fact. Also a few knives. From what the vampires had told me, my aura blended into the rocks and the earth and the trees, like the ultimate camouflage. In this world, I was practically invisible unless they knew what to look for.

I clenched my fist, feeling the corded muscles in my arm respond. *Weaknesses into strengths.* Looking over at Bryce, I smiled again, but this time it was a feral grin filled with confidence.

Who could argue with a soldier's obligation?

CHAPTER TWENTY-EIGHT

"Are we sure this is the right place?" Kane asked.

The Hive hung above us, a swollen papery globe that curved and jutted from the stone wall, its strange beauty barely visible in the dim cave. A few souls studded the walls to provide light. Kane, Dorian, Laini, Roxy, and I stood in the open cave on a small rocky protrusion jutting into the psychedelic water of the lake. Slick, glowing weeds covered the pebbly surface beneath our feet. The Hive vampires had carved a landing platform from the protrusion. Here, the strong smell of citrus had been replaced by a nauseating metallic stench with an undercurrent of burning sulfur. If someone bottled it as perfume, they could sell it as the scent of the devil himself.

"They said the platform," Laini muttered. "It's the only platform I see."

In unspoken agreement, Dorian and I had placed ourselves at opposite ends of the little jetty. Unfortunately, it was barely fifteen feet. My heart burned even as I balanced as close as I could to the narrow end near the water. Dorian's full strength came at a cost.

He caught my eye and gave the tiniest of nods, lines of pain tight around his pale eyes. This was our reality. We just had to deal with it. *Mission mode: on.*

The mouth of the cave yawned in the distance, a great gap of amber fire from the souls that clung to the walls. It both unnerved and soothed me. In the cave's mouth, the jaspeths had built another hive on the side of the wall. They buzzed near their new hive, hazy shapes against the tawny light. The creatures briefly scattered as a large avian shape flew by the hive, circling down toward us. A minute later, Drigar landed by Dorian where he stood by the cavern wall. The redbill chirped worriedly, nudging his lethal beak into his rider's shoulder.

"Don't worry. I'll be back," Dorian said, petting the soft feathers of the redbill's head. The Hive vampires had flown our surviving redbills here, but we had to leave the birds behind. Apparently, they couldn't follow the path we would travel. What that path would be was still a mystery to me. All I knew was that the aquatic wildlings would have to guide us. I wondered if they would be anything like the stony golem Dorian and Arlonne had fed from. I couldn't imagine something of that size and shape doing well in water, but I was operating under the logic of the Mortal Plane. Who knew how things worked here?

Dorian rubbed Drigar's neck affectionately one last time, then gently shooed him away. The redbill took off, going to nest with the Hive's own flock of redbills, who apparently roosted deeper in the cave.

I smiled. After everything that had happened, it was a relief to see

Drigar alive and well. He'd saved my life from the shrieking decay, and I hated to imagine the lively redbill left in a heap on the ground after a tangle with the Immortal hunters.

"Run the plan by me one more time while we stand here like our prom date just ditched us," Roxy said, fiddling with the buckles on a jacket made of the same water-resistant material as the scouts' capes. Both she and I had been outfitted in full vampire clothing, our Bureau camouflage uniforms working against their purpose at this point and drawing attention to us.

Kane huffed. "Wildlings take us through the Gray Ravine. We get to Itzarriol. The Hive vampires have a tiny safehouse on the outskirts of the city that they are letting us use. We get from the Gray Ravine to the safehouse, then spend the next several light cycles watching the city, gathering intel, and maybe, *maybe* sneaking in to try to gather some physical evidence if we're feeling insanely confident that the risk would be worth it." He swatted her hand away from the buckles. "Stop fussing with them."

Roxy punched him in the shoulder but stopped tugging at the unfamiliar garment. I understood her discomfort. It was like wearing historical clothing—the scratchy linen fabric didn't stretch, and the gray, rubbery jackets just felt a little weird. At least we'd managed to keep our sports bras.

I adjusted the pack on my back. We'd switched our original bags for smaller packs better suited for traveling light and for infiltration. They'd been provided by the Hive, who had wrapped them in special waterproof skins to keep our rations and personal items dry. My notebook and Dorian's letter were wrapped securely in a second skin inside the pack.

Laini stooped and began throwing pebbles in the water. In

response, the water bubbled mustard yellow and neon blue, greedily swallowing the fragments of stone. A black toad, smaller than my hand and sporting four bulging yellow eyes, hopped by. It paid little attention to us.

"What are you doing?" Kane asked incredulously.

"They told me to do this," she insisted. She frowned. "The Hive elders were very specific." She tossed in a few more pebbles for good measure. A bubble rose from the steam and popped. I shifted from side to side. Should we all try? I opened my mouth to ask, then saw a trail of tiny shimmering bubbles rise to the surface a short distance away, and whatever was making them seemed to be headed toward us.

The head of a creature with dainty, sleek features that I assumed was a wildling popped out of the water. Gray-brown scales covered her whole head, and she stared at us with pupil-less white eyes, a catlike mouth hanging slightly open to reveal needle-sharp teeth. Fins on either side of her head flapped in the same rhythm as the bright blue gills running down the sides of her throat. A webbed hand rose out of the water and beckoned us forward.

"Friends of the Hive, my clan will transfer you underwater," she said in a burbling voice. "We will travel beneath the mountains and the desert for many miles until we reach the Gray Ravine. Come."

I stared at the proffered hand, then warily at the water. The sulfur smell rose up from the steaming surface. The Hive vampires really used this route? Roxy scowled, looking just as dubious as I felt, but it was too late to go back now.

"Come," the wildling instructed again. "We have little time to waste."

"She seems overjoyed to be an underwater taxi for us," Roxy muttered under her breath.

Dorian took one skeptical glance at the wildling, then waded in at the shallow end of the jetty, walking forward until his dark head disappeared beneath the surface. The only sign of his presence was pain as he passed me. Kane, not to be outdone, leapt past me magnificently and splashed water everywhere. He too disappeared under the water and didn't bob back up. There were only the echoes of his thunderous entrance ricocheting off the cave walls. Briefly shaking her head, Laini sat on the jetty and dropped in, her nose crinkling as the water reached her neck, before she too was enveloped by the opaque liquid.

I walked to the edge with Roxy. None of our vampire friends came back up. I felt my throat tighten. No bubbles told me where they had gone, and the water was too colorful and cloudy to see anything a few inches below the surface.

"You go first," Roxy said with a quirk of her eyebrows. "Ten bucks says those wildlings eat us for dinner once they've drowned us, and the Hive paid them to do it."

I narrowed my eyes at her needlessly grim humor but couldn't suppress the passing thought that she could possibly be right. "No thanks. Why don't you go first? What happened to your tough-girl attitude?" Looking back at the waiting wildling, I saw her staring at us with mild amusement... or at least I thought I saw a bit of humor in those peculiar eyes.

Roxy placed an offended hand on her chest. "I *am* tough, but I'd have to be insane not to hesitate over drowning myself."

Feeling the weight of the wildling's eyes on me, I crouched and dipped my hand experimentally into the water. Despite the bubbles and steam, the water was not as hot as I feared. It was more like a warm bath after a day out in the cold. Somehow, it also felt different from the water I was used to, the texture more similar to oil.

"You will be safe," the wildling promised. "Your friends will be getting concerned, waiting for you."

Swinging my legs around so I could sit on the jetty, I let my legs dangle in the water like Laini. Apart from the fact that I couldn't feel the bottom, the sensation of the silky water was actually very pleasant. I looked back at Roxy, then at my legs, cut off from my sight at the knee, and sucked in a deep breath. Swimming wasn't my preferred form of exercise or leisure activity, but in the Bureau it had been mandatory to be able to swim a mile, so I knew I could do it. It wasn't like I hadn't expected this, since they'd told us we needed the help of aquatic wildlings. Apparently, they would help us breathe somehow, but I didn't have the details on that.

"Here goes nothing," I muttered, then pushed myself into the water, feet reaching in vain for the floor. As soon as I let go of the rocky platform, I dropped like a stone. Somewhere to my left, I felt the water move, presumably as Roxy joined me. A soft webbed hand closed around my wrist, slimy in the way that seaweed and rock-pools were. I kept my eyes tightly closed as I was pulled along, deeper and deeper into Lake Siron.

Something felt... strange. I could feel the water soaking through gaps in my clothes and filling my boots, but my face was completely dry. My eyes sprang open. I lifted a hand to my face and found a soft, pliable forcefield blocking my way.

Around me, everything was magnificently lit by the glowing water. Roxy waved next to me. The light beneath the surface traveled differently than it did above, and although my vision was limited—around ten feet clearly and then another ten slightly cloudier—I could see the rest of our group floating close by, each held around the wrist by a wildling. Their heads were also encased in a giant air bubble, as mine presumably was, giving us all the look of bizarre aquatic astronauts.

Beneath the surface of the lake, the muddied colors of the aquatic wildling scales glittered the same color as the water around them. Only the bright flash of their blue gills and the glow of their white eyes made them visible until they moved. They swished strong fish tails and swam around our group, their webbed hands reaching out to our bubbles.

The one from earlier gently touched my bubble, and the barrier thickened before my stunned eyes. She touched me with her hand and pointed to her shoulders, an action mimicked by the others. We were going to be pulled through the water.

Things just kept getting weirder.

I latched onto the aquatic wildling. Her scales were rougher than I'd expected, like a pinecone before it opened. With a flick of her powerful tail, she propelled herself forward. A current of warm water pushed us along, and soon the pack of us sped through the water. Occasionally, the wildling, her scales shifting color to match the color of the water we were in, reached back to tap the bubble. I spotted Dorian farther up ahead. The distance between us meant no heartburn, but I wished I could see his reaction to all this.

It was probably wrong to be jealous that an aquatic wildling could touch him, but I couldn't help it.

When I looked around, the underwater landscape danced with life. Small fish-like creatures with leopard scales and no visible eyes rode the current with us for a while, breaking off when they grew bored. We passed charmingly weird collections of black-and-crimson coral where mustard-colored eels peeked out at us. When they opened their mouths, long blue tongues curled out and snapped back. Later, a whale-sized shadow lurched out of the hazy surroundings to swim alongside us. The wildlings made no motion to dart away, giving me a chance to admire the hulking fish's dazzling scales, which glowed deep red. Similar creatures joined the giant fish, weaving in and out of the current, some disappearing in a flash of blue light only to reappear several feet away, popping in and out of existence on a whim.

The current carried us faster than we could have swum. Along the way, the wildlings gestured to air bubbles rising from the depths and showed us how to aim our bubbles into these streams as we passed. The rising bubbles helped refill our oxygen, ensuring we had enough air, but stank of sulfur and blood. I tried not to gag at the metallic taste in my mouth, the thought of being stuck in the bubble with my own vomit a powerful incentive.

There was no way to track time under the water. All I knew was that my arms ached from holding the wildling's shoulders, my hands slowly being rubbed raw against her scales. Sometimes, we had to request that the wildlings breach the surface to give our poor arms a break. They only did so in tunnels deep underground, never risking putting us out in the open. We floated in the pitch darkness for a few precious moments breathing air that, though stale and dank, was still more pleasant than the inside of our bubble helmets.

The water shifted to a blue-gray as we went along—the wildlings gradually taking on the same shade—but it never grew colder. It was like swimming through the Immortal Plane's weird sky. I couldn't tell up from down. The wildlings began to move more cautiously, weaving around stone columns that loomed in the darkness. I got the sense that we were reaching the end of our journey.

Finally, we reached a cliff face of rock almost the same color as the water. With no warning or communication, the wildlings pulled us through narrow tunnels winding through the cliff. Scraping against rock in the tight spaces made me claustrophobic, but it didn't last long. My wildling shot to the surface after only a few minutes. The bubble popped around me, and I sucked in a grateful breath of fresh air.

My bearings returned slowly. The wildlings had brought us to a pool where the slate-colored water bubbled around us more softly than near the Hive. Though there was barely any light, I could just see the edge of the pool about twelve feet away, so I swam over to protect myself from Dorian's presence. The glow of the water here was pearlescent and struggled to filter through the mist that lurked around us. As my eyes adjusted, I realized there *was* another source of light. All across the uneven walls, amber soul-lights were nestled in the stone surface. Looking farther out, I held back a surprised exhale as little pinpricks of orange light flickered as far as I could see. The entire canyon teemed with souls that were slowly leaching their darkness into the stone.

Laini grimaced, her lips pursed. "It's sort of beautiful, but also… unsettling," she said. "Only the heaviest of souls would find their way this deep into the ground."

The pool appeared to be at the bottom of a narrow canyon, and I studied the dull, blue-gray rock that nearly matched the color of the water. It was easy to guess why they called it the Gray Ravine.

"Lovely sliver of sky," Roxy reported next to me, her head tipped back to stare through the crack in the earth we were currently sheltered in. I looked up, seeing a wave of amber soul-lights for barely a second before they disappeared into the thickening mist. Everything in the Immortal Plane seemed crafted for misery.

A slight movement in my peripheral vision caught my attention, but before I could say anything to the others, the mist swirled and something pale and ghostly suddenly appeared above me at the edge of the pool. Roxy swore and kicked away from the rock ledge, splashing messily. I flinched, surprised by the speed of it, not entirely sure what the shape in front of me was.

"A little warning would have been nice," Kane said hotly to the wildlings, swimming to the edge beside me and hauling himself out of the water. "No one enjoys being surprised like that."

The wildlings ignored him.

"Hello, harvester," they all croaked in unison.

CHAPTER TWENTY-NINE

The harvester's human-shaped body was clear like a jellyfish, showing off a few pale pink organs and ghostly bones. When I tried to focus on their form, they blurred in my vision. Was this a he? Everything around him swung out of focus. In the center of his nearly transparent chest, a dim soul-light glowed and shadows flickered up and down his body—it was like watching blood running through a circulatory system.

The face looked half-formed. He had the most basic outline that suggested features, but there were no real details... like a staring theater mask completely void of any emotion.

"Welcome to my ferry," the harvester announced, his voice raspy and thin. He spread phantom arms, almost as though he were embracing the mist.

"Thank you for having us," Dorian said, his formal tone and manner almost amusing considering we were all bedraggled, bobbing in the water in front of a literal phantom.

I nodded, trying to keep my distance and be polite at the same time. "It's nice to meet you." I wondered if the harvester found mortals as strange as I found the creatures of the Immortal Plane.

Kane crossed his arms tightly over his chest. "These things always freak me out."

"He's funny." The harvester's whisper of a mouth turned up slightly. "There's no need to fear. Your secret is safe with me, vampire."

"I don't have secrets," Kane snapped back in a surprisingly sincere tone. "So, stop poking around in my aura." He waved an accusatory finger. "See, *this* is why nobody likes harvesters."

The harvester gently inclined his head up to the mist and whispered, "He didn't mean that, did he? People like me. I have friends."

I shared a wide-eyed look with Roxy, who seemed equally taken aback. She had swum to where Kane stood on the edge, and he lowered a hand. She ignored it, easily hauling herself from the water.

"Usually, I'd make fun of you for being creeped out by a sentient blob of aloe vera gel," she said quietly to Kane as the harvester continued murmuring to the mist, "but my kneejerk reaction is to flick holy water on this thing, so I'm going to let you have this one for free, okay?"

"So generous of you," Kane growled.

The harvester brought his vague suggestion of a face back to look at us.

Dorian—currently squeezed against the opposite side of the pool from me—cleared his throat. "Will you grant us passage on your ferry?" The hint of discomfort in his voice surprised me. He'd faced down far worse than this. Maybe he was worried about needing to be in close quarters for the next portion of the trip and how that would put us at risk of pain.

The harvester bobbed his head up and down. "He wants passage. Isn't that nice? Yes, of course. Let me help you." He extended a hand to me first, as I was closest, and after hesitating for a moment, I took it. It felt like falling through the ice of a frozen lake and being submerged in the bitterly cold water. Looking at him now, while holding his ice-cold hand, the form appeared more solid and the face gained detail. A gaping black oval of a mouth hung open, framed by lips as blue as a corpse's. The eyes, yellowed and blood-shot, held such a depth of pain that I wanted to weep, but he still managed to look at me with a kindness I couldn't fathom. I couldn't breathe, I couldn't speak, yet somehow my body clambered up out of the pool to stand, dripping, on the narrow path running down the canyon. As the harvester released my hand, I felt tears on my cheeks.

"You can never be too careful around these parts," he said, returning to his nearly invisible form. "The souls are so loud."

I swiped at my tears, nodding. The harvester was... interesting. After seeing his true form, I was less afraid than I had been before. Something about a creature containing that much suffering made it feel like less of a threat.

A boat awaited us. It was a long, narrow, flat-bottomed vessel with no benches or covering, barely large enough to fit our group and the dripping packs on our backs. It was a good thing we'd left the others behind at the Hive. We never would've fit.

It was odd to find a ferryman out here in the middle of nowhere —I couldn't imagine this path was well traveled. I eyed the harvester, thinking again of Bryce's comment about Kharon, the ferryman of the dead in Greek mythology, when we'd first seen the souls in the

Immortal Plane. The harvester whispered wordlessly to the mist above us as we all lined up to climb aboard. It was unnerving to realize that I couldn't tell exactly where he was looking.

I gripped the railing of the boat while I waited to board. The surface was as rough and porous as a pumice stone, and I winced as it scraped my hands, which were already sore from the wildling's scales.

"Thank you for your help," Laini called to the aquatic wildlings still floating in the pool. "We'll make our own way from here and will call you when we need to return."

The wildlings nodded and disappeared beneath the surface of the water, leaving no trace that they'd ever been there at all.

"How far is it to the city?" Roxy leaned in to whisper to me. Kane heard her.

"A night's journey," he said with a shrug. "Probably. I asked some of the scouts before we left, and they said the Gray Ravine goes almost right up to Itzarriol. The Immortals avoid the ravine, though, because it's *haunting*. Whatever that means. Those guys have probably lost their minds."

"Haunting?" I echoed doubtfully. The entire Immortal Plane was full of horrifying things. I didn't want to find out how the ravine could terrify even Immortals.

The harvester chuckled, the action made creepy by the way his organs bounced slightly. "Don't you worry. The crack only haunts the darkness in beings. Isn't life fun? I told my brother that once. Wait. Do I have a brother?"

Roxy and I stared at the harvester, then each other. A cryptic piece of advice from a seemingly mad creature who talked to mist failed to give us much confidence. I shifted my weight uneasily. I'd never cared much for horror movies, and this felt suspiciously like the start of one.

I waited until last to get on the boat. Dorian had gone first, and I hoped we would be far enough apart to keep the heartburn manageable. As I went to climb in, however, the harvester suddenly reached out to me.

He gently placed a ghostly hand on the front of my shirt. "Ooh, this is like me."

Dorian's stone warmed in its pouch around my neck. My stomach flipped nervously.

"Easy there, buddy. I know you don't get a lot of visitors down here, what with the *haunting* atmosphere and all, but she's taken," Kane muttered wryly. Roxy and Laini swatted him on each side.

I stared up at the harvester. "What do you mean?" I pulled back slightly, not afraid but still a little nervous. Although I wished his face were more expressive so I could tell what the hell he was thinking, I didn't want to touch him again and have the same icy, despondent experience.

The harvester smiled down at me. Even in this form his mouth had no teeth, only phantom gums. "I swallow things, and I give back different things," he said and gestured all around as if that would mean something to me. "You can get on the boat now."

I forced myself to move. I had no idea what had just happened. I gave Laini a questioning look, and she shrugged, eyes wide.

The harvester hummed happily as he wandered to the canyon wall. His movement was something between floating and gliding. "Funny how things find you," he muttered dreamily, reaching for a speck of amber embedded in the canyon wall, slightly brighter than the rest. He plucked the soul from the wall. The light flickered as the harvester pulled it closer.

I stared, horrified, as the harvester opened his gummy mouth impossibly wide like a snake unhinging its jaw. He dropped the soul into his mouth, swallowing it whole. Worse, we could *see* the soul through his ghostly body.

The amber squeezed down the harvester's throat. An incredible burst of light exploded, then an inky trail of darkness slithered away from the amber glow and spread throughout the harvester's form, for a moment making him more solid. Reaching back into his mouth, the harvester yanked the soul out, holding it almost tenderly in both hands before letting go. The soul drifted into the air.

"This is super gross and incredibly cool and I don't quite know what to feel," Roxy mumbled. The dark energy dissipated into the harvester, and he returned to near invisibility once more.

The soul floated for a bit, considerably brighter, before it sank back to the rock. The harvester nodded toward me. Even without facial features, his expression clearly said, *See?* but I didn't understand.

Kane shuddered a little, and Roxy elbowed him. "Dude, you rip open throats and drink dark energy through blood. I really don't think you have the high ground in terms of polite eating habits."

"At least I don't pull a blood clot out of my throat when I'm done eating," he muttered.

Laini coughed. "Harvesters process dark soul energy into magic, with which they imbue objects. I'd heard of it but never seen it before." She shivered. "A bit creepy but definitely interesting."

Okay, but what does that have to do with Dorian's stone? I stared at the harvester, hoping he might turn around and reveal his secrets. Preferably in clear, coherent language.

"You can't make magic," Roxy said to Kane, goading him in an obvious attempt to distract herself from her own discomfort. He didn't seem to mind, giving her a grin and flicking her on the ear.

"At least I'm not a *human*," he said, sneering.

The two of them bickered good-naturedly in the back of the boat, their voices not echoing despite the topography of the Gray Ravine. Instead, the sound seemed to sink into the stone like it was a sponge for noise. Dorian, for his part, maintained his composure where he sat at the prow. He didn't even look back to where Kane, Roxy, and I sat. I wondered if it was because he didn't want to risk increasing our pain, or if he was so preoccupied with his thoughts that he hadn't heard the childish exchange.

The harvester sang softly as he climbed into the boat. He seemed to be in another world—a happier one, I hoped. Settling in the back of the boat, he feigned the motion of a conductor pulling his horn, complete with an eerie approximation of the sound effect for someone who had never been to the Mortal Plane. The boat began to move.

"We're leaving," the harvester called up to the mist. "I hope we have fun."

CHAPTER THIRTY

The harvester stood at the stern with a long wooden oar, singing softly every so often. Some of the languages I recognized from the Mortal Plane, others I didn't. All the songs were sad.

On the floor beside my team, I watched the harvester's ghostlike arm move steadily as he paddled, guiding us away from jutting portions of the canyon wall. The same current that had carried us from the Hive to the Gray Ravine pushed the boat forward here. The warm air no longer smelled of blood, instead carrying a bitter, uncomfortably smoky tinge. If regret could be a scent, the Gray Ravine reeked of it.

Now that we were out of the warm water, I shivered in my wet clothes beside Roxy. We had swept water off our slick jackets as much as possible and squeezed water from our shirts and hair, but still we ended up sitting in swiftly cooling puddles. "Waterproof" was more of a dream than a reality, in my opinion. At least after being submerged for hours. The rivulets from each of us pooled in the bottom of the boat, swirling patches of gray and blue against the black wood.

"We should try to rest," I muttered, massaging the area over my heart. Even with Dorian as far away as possible, the boat was barely ten feet long, so the increase in pain was noticeable. The edges of my vision weren't quite beginning to fade, but it was hard to take a full breath and my ears were ringing.

Roxy nodded and rubbed her tired face, the water leaving her short hair in disgruntled spikes. Laini curled up next to us with Kane beside her. Dorian sat alone at the front. Roxy and I leaned against one another, hoping to at least doze fitfully. This situation held a hint of familiarity in this place where everything was unknown. We'd spent many hours together—maybe not this close to one another but still together—in choppers and trucks and camps in the wilderness, training, going on missions, surviving.

The boat rocked gently as the harvester pushed us. The vessel's edges almost touched the sides of the ravine as we went, the river was so narrow. It had to be night, or something like it. We had been up for more than twelve hours. I leaned my head back against the railing. Roxy already snored lightly, her ability to sleep literally anywhere once again making me envious. I tried to use my damp jacket as a pillow against the rough side of the boat.

Mark my words, I will sleep for a week when this business is finally over.

I fell into a daze that wasn't quite sleep and wasn't quite full consciousness as I tried to ignore my constant heartburn. Unfortunately, it was important to get used to the pain, since I could expect it for the rest of the journey. The gloom carried a weight here that hadn't been present even in the mountains or the redwood forest. A chill ran through me as I huddled closer to Roxy, and it had nothing to do with damp clothes. It felt as though the darkness drifted down onto our party, mingled with the water, rose up into the mist…

No, I couldn't let myself get wrapped up in it. Happy thoughts. I recounted a list of happy things, like running through the Highlands, puppies, Zach sneezing so hard while eating ramen that a noodle came out of his nose, and my days spent with Dorian back in the VAMPS camp. What would Zach say if he were here with me? He was always good at relieving tension, at looking on the bright side of things. There was a time when he practically did stand-up comedy for every family holiday dinner. I had a distinct memory of my parents, me, and Alan howling with laughter at his shenanigans.

I hadn't thought of Alan in a while. The Immortal Plane had become the only priority in my mind, but now the memory of him fell over me like a black sack over my head. My mind immediately leapt to one pivotal moment on the roof of Chicago HQ. How odd it had been to feel no love for him in that moment, only rage. Or perhaps what was odd was how long I had held onto my love for him when he was clearly unworthy of it. I shook my head, trying to dispel Alan's cold face from my mind.

He'd really thought he could convince me he was doing something good and right. Idiot. Scorching anger filled me, burning right alongside my heartburn. He'd tricked me, and so many others, for so long. He'd caused so much pain, so much damage, and had the ability to continue hurting us for as long as he lived. I could have beaten him, but even then he would have experienced only a fraction of the suffering he'd caused Arlonne. I wondered if she regretted her decision to let me take my uncle into custody. Part of me certainly did. I could have removed him as a threat right there on the roof. I'd had my gun. No one would have stopped me.

I should've killed him when I had the chance.

A gasp tore itself from my throat, yanking me from my thoughts. It was like stepping out of a trance. Mist hung around our boat, thicker than before, and it soaked up the sound of my distress like snow held onto blood. I looked down. My hands were shaking.

"Don't worry," the harvester whispered, but it was more to the mist than to me.

Next to me, Roxy had slumped sideways onto the floor of the boat. She twitched in her sleep, shaking and mumbling. Her hands flexed, then balled into fists. I nudged her gently, and she scrambled back to a sitting position. Her mouth twisted into a sneer as she brought her hands up, as though ready to fight. She glared at me and the surrounding mist.

"Oh," she said, suddenly registering my face in the haze. "I must've been dreaming."

"Are you okay?" I asked. The smell of burnt, lost things grew heavier in the temperate air.

She scowled, breathing hard. "I remembered when my middle sister ratted me out for stealing gum from a convenience store in seventh grade. Oh, I was *pissed.* I wanted to punch her stupid face in and break her teeth." She growled in frustration, all her muscles tight with rage.

I studied her. "Did you do that in real life? Hit her, I mean?" Roxy had a tough side, but I knew how she valued her family.

Her surprise pulled her out of her anger. "No... I didn't hit her at all. I yelled at her and got sent to my room. As punishment, my mom made me stay home from school for a week to babysit while she and my dad went on a cruise." She pulled a face. "The twins were still in diapers. And my mom didn't leave us a lot of money for food, so we just ate pasta for a week straight. I missed a few more days that year, and the counselor pulled me in to yell at me about truancy."

I kept my face neutral, knowing she would react badly if there was even a trace of pity in my eyes in response to her anecdote. Roxy very rarely mentioned her past or her parents, and if that was one of the stories that she was willing to share, who knew how many worse ones were hiding in her memories?

She stared at the mist and the dim souls peeking through the gray rocky sides of the ravine, shivering. "What the hell is this place?"

"Maybe this is what the Hive vampires meant by calling this place haunting," I guessed. "It seems to cause terrible daydreams."

The harvester chuckled behind us. The sound sent a shockwave through my nerves. "The darkness inside comes to the surface here," he said dreamily. "It floats here. Those with too much darkness go mad in the gray. They become overwhelmed by their own memories. It's exciting but rarely happens. Such a shame. It's interesting to watch." The harvester's tone was wistful at the end.

Laini stirred next to me, her eyes fluttering open. It didn't look like she'd slept at all.

"That explains why the vampires in the Hive use this route to the city," she mumbled, yawning. "The Immortals won't touch this place for fear of their own darkness consuming them."

That made sense. Even I wanted to leave the Gray Ravine behind as soon as possible, and according to the vampires I knew, my soul was pretty darn light. Yes, I had asked. Of course I had.

"This would have been good to know ahead of time," Roxy said with an angry huff. She wrapped her arms around herself. Laini gave a sympathetic nod.

"Yes. The darkness speaks loudly here," Laini muttered ominously. "It can be convincing."

I wondered what this misty place made her think of, but the pained grimace on her face killed that question before it formed.

"Any advice?" Roxy asked.

"Think happy thoughts," Kane sang out sarcastically.

I glanced toward Dorian at the front of the boat. If he was experiencing anything, it didn't show on his face, but I thought he might be holding himself more stiffly than usual. Though, honestly, that could be from the torture of bad thoughts and memories or the constant heartburn.

My Lyra. I had folded the letter carefully and placed it next to his stone in its little leather pouch. I hoped the Immortal Plane water hadn't ruined it. It needed to dry, but I wanted to bring it out and read it again so I could be filled with happier thoughts, as Kane so bluntly suggested. If I couldn't talk to him, at least I could linger over his words.

We'd had so many sweet, magical moments together, despite how frenetic our circumstances had been since we first met. I'd held him in that cold river as he raged against the police we'd seen kidnapping and selling the Amish boy, one of many who'd been sold to traffickers for their organs. I'd kissed him in a fit of rage and passion after we first betrayed the Bureau. We'd curled up together in the cold of our hideout in the mountains, sleeping through the night in a warm, intimate bundle.

I closed my eyes as a twinge burned through my chest. The ache rose and dipped like the motion of the rocking boat. I could visualize the pain on his face, see his eyes meet mine as though he stood right in front of me. My dream of not-Dorian rose up like a phantom in my mind. I'd watched him get destroyed in that terrible dream, not by magic, but my own touch…

I loathed this curse.

I hated what it did to Dorian. His insistence on starving himself to try to "fix" the pain. Going hungry didn't fix anything—it only put us all in danger.

A dark voice rose up inside me, bitter and hateful.

The curse isn't your real problem. It's just the excuse you keep blaming. You're just not right for him. Stop kidding yourself that you are.

My breath caught. The venomous words shook me. What if it was us? We were all push and no pull, two natural leaders constantly clashing over the right course of action. I didn't want to have to fight every day we were together. My stormy mood pressed down on all sides. I took a ragged breath, the humidity hot against my clammy cheeks, telling myself the words were just the worst version of reality being shoved to the forefront. We'd just made progress in our relationship, *good* progress. These were just my unfounded fears.

Suddenly, Laini jolted up in the boat. It rocked from side to side, water splashing up over the boards. She clawed at her face, screaming. My heart slammed against my ribs as she threw herself to the floor.

"Lanzon!" She curled up around her knees in the center of the boat, snarling and weeping. Every one of my nerves twisted as I leaned toward her. I froze. I didn't know what to do. I couldn't stop her from reliving the nightmare of her husband's death. The strength of her reaction was concerning yet not surprising. Laini was sweet and gentle, but she was still a vampire that fed on darkness. Was it just Lanzon that was haunting her?

Seeing Laini's heart-shaped face contorted in agony stirred everyone from their thoughts. Roxy hovered next to me, helpless to do anything. We had officially gone into abnormal territory, a place not meant for humans. Dorian watched from the front of the boat, unable to move any closer to help. My heartburn surged powerfully. His pained, grieving gaze met mine before he sat down once again, eyes not leaving Laini.

She called Lanzon's name a few more times, her voice filled with such sorrow and despair I found myself weeping in response. When her wails became animalistic cries of unbridled pain, I tried to crouch down to hold her, but she roared and lashed out.

Kane lifted a hand, indicating for me to wait. When Laini broke down into sobs, he gently took hold of her arm in a softer manner than I'd ever seen from him before. He propped her up, holding her against him before she could slump back to the ground.

"You're safe," he whispered gruffly. "Don't let the memories get hold of you."

I crouched down next to her, using the cuff of my shirt to dab at a scrape on her cheekbone that leaked shimmering blood. She kept her hands to herself this time. Roxy went to her other side, helping Kane prop her up.

Laini's bottom lip quivered, and she wiped her dull eyes roughly.

"Let it out. It's okay to be sad," Roxy said gently.

I had to marvel at Kane and Roxy. They wouldn't have been my first choice for emotional comfort, but they were proving themselves more than capable.

Laini let out a bitter laugh and shook her head. "I'm not sad," she snapped at Roxy, her fury thickening her voice. "I just… hate the hunters so much. I want to rip them apart until there is nothing left but their blood staining the ground." Her gaze turned inward, and she sat with the reverberations of her uncharacteristically vicious words, stiff and silent, in the circle of Kane's arms.

I had no idea what to say to her. Looking at her broke something inside me. Of all people, Laini usually appeared the most collected, the most forgiving, the most compassionate.

"I'd never fully realized how angry I am," she said, voice flat and hard. "How much hate for the Immortals is hidden inside me. I chose to come back to the Immortal Plane partially because I wanted to face and accept Lanzon's death. I thought I was ready for that. But I still have so far to go…" Silent tears fell as her anger melted into grief once again.

Kane smirked with dark amusement. "Don't worry. This is just what it feels like to be a normal vampire these days, Laini."

Laini let out a hollow chuckle. I squeezed her hand gently.

"You don't have to rush through grief, Laini, just because you feel you should." Dorian's voice drifted to us from the prow of the boat, dampened by the thick mist. "You loved him as fiercely and deeply as I did, and despite how long it's been, neither of us has had the chance to mourn."

The pain in his voice as he kept speaking wasn't from the heartburn.

"I know you look at me sometimes and see the ghost of him in my face for a moment, and I'm sorry for that." His breath hitched, and he paused. "I'm sorry I didn't save him."

The gloom and the mist turned him into a wraith at the other end of the boat. My heart broke for them both. It broke for all the vampires. Life had been about survival for the vampires since the moment Vanim fell. None of them had truly had the time to mourn their dead, their home, their lives.

"You saved me." Laini's voice was soft and distant. "And we're alive. That's all he could have wished for both of us. And if I get to see a hint of him in you sometimes, then I will not complain."

As she tipped her head back against Kane's shoulder, light from the souls soaked through a gap in the mist and illuminated her face slightly. Something about her profile struck me. She reminded me of the woman in my dream with Dorian. I studied her red-rimmed eyes as the heartburn in my chest ebbed.

In the dream, I'd known it wasn't truly Dorian, but now scraps of questions pulled together in my head.

I know you look at me sometimes and see the ghost of him in my face.

And if I get to see a hint of him in you sometimes, then I will not complain.

The dark hair, the different eyes, the similar build but not quite the same. Was I dreaming of Lanzon?

I couldn't be sure, since I had no real idea what he looked like. But if I was dreaming of him... *how?*

CHAPTER THIRTY-ONE

I t was impossible to tell how long the harvester had been rowing, but I had a vague sense that we'd been on the boat through the time that roughly constituted night here. None of us had slept. Instead, we slipped in and out of hazy nightmares. Worse, those nightmares were real in a way. They spoke of our greatest struggles and the cruelest thoughts we buried deep inside.

As we sat in the mist, I lost track of time, consumed by avoiding the horrors inside my own head and trying to piece together how I could possibly be dreaming of Dorian's brother, whom I had never met. There were questions I needed to form so I could ask Laini and Dorian. If I really was dreaming of Lanzon, I needed to figure out how and why.

I stared at Laini. She'd drifted back into her daze a few times but hadn't been as totally consumed as before. Even if I knew what to say, there was no kind way to ask her if it were possible that I was dreaming of her dead husband. While I didn't know what it meant or could mean, I knew there were more pressing matters to deal with first. Exhaling slowly through my nose, I counted my breaths. Maybe numbers could keep me grounded.

"Is it day yet?" I asked the harvester.

He seemed to absorb the mist, or maybe it was just possible to see the mist through his translucent form. In response to my question, I saw the suggestion of a nod.

"As close to day as we are wont to get," he said.

The light refused to brighten. I'd found that disorienting the whole time we'd been here in the Immortal Plane, but it was especially discomforting after a night with almost no sleep. Our mission was already difficult and dangerous. If none of us managed to rest properly, it would make our task nearly impossible.

I rubbed my chest, trying to soothe the lingering heartburn. Knowing I'd never have to wonder if he loved me was an ironic kind of comfort.

I drifted into my thoughts and tried to conjure up happy images. Kane sat nearby with Laini. Both had their eyes closed, finally peaceful. Kane hadn't had a single outburst during our trip, which surprised me. With his father's murder, I'd have thought he would be tortured by darkness. Roxy sat on my other side, occasionally letting her head rest on my shoulder. Once or twice, I heard her mutter empty threats to someone in her dreams.

I tried to get comfortable, but by now sleep had long ceased being a possibility for me. I leaned my head back to stare at the swirling mist when something in my peripheral vision caught my eye.

There was a glow to my left, growing brighter with each push of the harvester's paddle. A real glow, farther down the ravine. I sat up straighter and nudged Roxy. The light was dazzling, brilliant shades of every color in the rainbow and more. The colors shifted across the sky, burning away the mist.

"Ugh. What?" Roxy muttered sleepily. "You'd better have a good reason for waking me up. I just dreamed about punching that annoying girl who lived on my childhood street, and yes, she *did* deserve it."

"Do you see it?" I asked, shaking her slightly. She swatted my hands away with an annoyed huff. "I don't trust my eyes after all this time. Is the mist tricking me?"

Roxy opened her mouth to say something smart, but a shocked sound caught in her throat when she saw the unreal colors. "If it is, it's tricking me too," she breathed. "It's… beautiful." The word felt inadequate, and I could tell it didn't satisfy her from the twist of her mouth.

The water's current moved faster now as we traveled toward the kaleidoscope of color. The harvester hummed merrily as he paddled along. When we got closer, the rays of color peeked through a crack at the end of the ravine. The peculiar ray of light split somewhere inside the rock, producing a rainbow in a mystical spectrum in the misty air.

I leaned closer and strained to listen. Above the gentle splash of the harvester's oar, I heard the rising sound of a waterfall. White noise buzzed beyond that.

"It looks like our fun trip is almost at an end," the harvester announced sadly. "We are approaching the Immortal City. Everyone should wake up." He tapped his oar against the boat's edge, waking the rest of our party.

Stirring, Laini pressed her hand to her face, staring in awe at the strange colors before us. Kane rolled his eyes, unimpressed by the garish presentation.

In the front, Dorian leaned out over the prow as if to hurry us forward.

He glanced at me, and even across the distance, the heartburn roared to life as our gazes locked. I held on, despite the pain. He looked weary but fierce, the fire in his blue eyes scorching. *We're in this together, for better or worse,* his eyes seemed to say.

For better or worse, we're together, I replied with my eyes.

The boat creaked and wobbled as Dorian leapt to his feet. "That's it?"

"Your future awaits you," the harvester replied vaguely, the hint of a dreamy smile on his strange face.

We stared through the narrow gap in the jagged rock that signaled the end of the Gray Ravine. The river continued onward, cascading into a waterfall that I still couldn't make out clearly in the distance.

The soul-light in the Gray Ravine had produced only a murky glow. The dazzling rainbow of lights practically blinded me. I rubbed my eyes as the harvester stepped from the boat onto a little platform. He moored the boat and gestured for us to follow.

"Itzarriol. The City of Perpetual Light," the harvester said, gesturing to the gap in the rock. "Enjoy your visit."

Kane snarled. "Don't *ever* use that name for a place of such darkness and hatred."

The harvester said nothing, apparently unmoved by Kane's fury. Kane stormed off the boat, and Laini drifted behind him, some clarity returning to her tired face.

"Thank you," I muttered to the harvester as I left.

The transparent creature nodded. "Good luck to you. This is a place not meant for you. But the mist and I hope you do well in there."

I hoped so, too.

The group naturally gathered around Dorian on the little platform. He had slipped effortlessly back into leader mode. The tension around his eyes disappeared as his handsome face surveyed our team, but his gaze didn't stray to me.

"What's the plan?" Laini asked. Her violet eyes already looked less red around the edges, determined and ready.

"These next few days will be the most dangerous we have faced yet," Dorian announced, gesturing to the city light in the distance. The details were still obscured by mist. "While we have the safehouse provided by the Hive to use as a home base, we'll have to work mostly by improvising. We need to find ways to hide in plain sight, avoiding Immortal patrols in the sky and hunters in the street. They might not think we're crazy enough to come here, but I suspect they've upped their patrols to be safe."

Memories of teal magic shooting across the sky put a sour taste in my mouth. We'd escaped by the skin of our teeth before, and now we were walking into the monster's jaws.

"Each of you is here on this mission for a reason, and you are all *fully* capable of doing what you're here to do. We all know what we have to lose. The safety of vampires, humans, and the very existence of the Mortal and Immortal Planes are at stake." He purposefully continued to not look at me, but I sensed the emphasis in his pep talk. I'd expressed my doubts about my skill set to him. He wanted to assure me and everyone else that we had what it took to face the

Immortals. And maybe we did. We'd made it this far, despite the overwhelming odds.

Nevertheless, a tiny voice of doubt gnawed at me. We were an impressive team—I didn't question that. But the Immortals had powerful magic and more knowledge than any of us. I didn't know whether we could match them if it came to a showdown.

"Our first task is to get to the safehouse. We can shelter there and plan our next moves after that," Dorian said. "Stealth is extremely important for the next leg of our journey. We need to keep their safehouse a secret."

"So, we're charging in right now?" Kane raised an eyebrow. Although he leaned toward fighting for fun, even he was tired.

Dorian shook his head. "Not quite. None of us slept well on the boat. We'll walk to the end of the ravine, then take a long rest before we enter the city. Once we leave the ravine, there's no telling what we'll encounter."

This was our last bit of safety before the mission.

I looked back at the river. The harvester had left, vanishing into the mist. I'd barely noticed the funny creature go, propelling his boat through the water with his long paddle. What a strange being. I guessed swallowing souls for survival could have made him that way. After all, when the vampires fed, they saw memories from each dark soul. Perhaps the harvester experienced that, too. That would drive anybody a little mad over time.

Our group started walking, two by two, down the narrow path that clung to the ravine's wall, the surface slick from the occasional waves that rose up from the river as the water beside us flowed quickly to the waterfall. I fell behind, feeling isolated in my need to manage the pain. I hit the fifteen-foot limit, and the pain eased.

Somewhere inside the bright city ahead, a seedy darkness pulsed like a heartbeat. If the city was a monster, we needed to find the brain. That's where they made decisions and planned their diabolical strategies. It's where they would have planned their union with the Bureau, where they decided to begin the extermination of vampires. If the Immortal rulers continued to operate unchecked, the darkness in this plane would continue to grow and spread until it consumed the Mortal Plane, as well. I refused to stand for that. Our friends back home counted on us to do our best here. The future stood before us, perilous and fragile.

Roxy fell in step with me, breaking through my reverie, and flashed me a wicked smile.

"I'm tired of hanging with the vampire squad," she said in an exaggerated stage whisper, winking playfully. "And maybe I wanted to see if you were okay. Maybe."

I laughed, unable to help myself. Roxy and I had grown a lot through our experiences together. I used to think she was a loose cannon who had an issue with authority. Now, I would call her both a friend and a valued comrade. I shook my head. "Can you believe how much things have changed?"

"I was just thinking the same." Her eyes lifted with amusement. "Who knew I would ever find my annoying leader so pleasant?"

I snorted. "You were no angel yourself."

She waved her hand, buffeting my comeback away. "Nonsense. I've always been on my best behavior."

I scoffed good-naturedly, remembering all the instances when Roxy had decidedly *not* been on her best behavior. However, for every memory of disobedience, there was a new memory of her support, courage, and determination.

"Thanks for having my back," I said as we jumped over a small crack in the path, the water bright blue in the space.

She punched me in the shoulder as we drew level once more, trying to be gruff, but I saw the genuine smile in her eyes. "Maybe I should be thanking you for having *my* back."

I couldn't help my smile, hope momentarily drowning out my weariness. We had learned to support each other in ways I hadn't thought possible. Despite betrayals and the odds being stacked against us, we were still standing together, even stronger for the shared experiences.

Roxy shook her head, her eyes on the unreal colors of Itzarriol lighting the mist up ahead. "I wonder what my siblings would think about this if they could see what I'm seeing now." Her lips tilted into a small smile. "I hope they'd be proud."

The journey hadn't just changed me. It had changed everyone.

"I'm sure they would be," I said. "I'm proud of you. I'm proud of us."

She merely grunted in response, but I didn't miss the flash of delighted surprise in her face before she carefully covered her reaction.

I turned to face the future with her, feeling less alone as I mentally prepared for the days that lay ahead. I touched the cord of the pouch around my neck, feeling Dorian's stone there. Life consisted of two battles for me: one with our enemies and one within my own relationship. The fact was, I didn't know what to do about the curse. I hated lacking any solid ideas for a solution.

I had strong feelings for Dorian. Probably even loved him, though I wasn't quite ready to tell him yet. The curse had thrown a giant supernatural wrench into our plans once again, but I refused to give up. I gritted my teeth as a warm rush of determination flooded my body. It was the same high as adrenaline on the battlefield.

In the privacy of my own thoughts, I let myself consider the possibility that there might not be a good solution to the curse. Eventually, we might have to separate in order to function. Although part of me instinctively shrank away from the idea, I faced the possibility squarely and refused to let go just yet. Despite everything, Dorian and I had come so far.

Before long, we came to the gorge's end, where the mist cleared. The narrow ravine became a large, flat cliff that overlooked the city. Slipping through the crack, I pulled the scope of my disassembled rifle from my pack and stared out over the cascading water.

The next stage of our journey stretched out before us, menacingly beautiful, glittering with the light of a hundred thousand souls. The swirling colors of the city beckoned to be studied, but the first thing that caught my eye was a flash of red on the outskirts.

"Hunters," Dorian growled, squinting at the scene. Even with his excellent vision, the details were difficult at this distance.

Roxy pulled out her own scope, taking a quick look before passing it to Dorian. "Two of them, and they're chasing someone. Can't see who, though."

Tracking the flurry of motion, my throat tightened in panic as I saw two hunters mounted on huge velek shooting bolts of magical energy at a dodging figure just a few dozen feet ahead of them. The figure stumbled and fell, stilling for a moment, and I couldn't stop the small gasp of horror when their slick scout's cloak fell away.

"Kono," I whispered, recognizing the vampire by his onyx skin and his short, stocky form, which was unusual for a vampire.

"You know him?" Dorian asked, voice tense as he tried to follow the action through the scope.

Kono got to his feet again, taking off running through long lavender grass and around strange vine-covered shrubs, but the velek were gaining on him.

"Sike and I met him at the Hive," I said, rage and helplessness warring in my voice as I watched the hunters draw closer, knowing there was nothing I could do without blowing our cover before we'd even reached the city. "He helped us find Echen."

Roxy snatched the scope from Dorian. "They're going to catch him," she pronounced grimly. "He's exhausted and has nowhere to go."

"Can't one of you use your rifle? Take out the hunters?" Kane demanded, half focused on the pursuit and half on trying to find a path down the cliff below us.

Laini put a hand on his arm, tears and anger in her voice. "We can't go down there, Kane. I want to fight the hunters as much as you do, but we wouldn't get there in time. And they would call reinforcements from the city."

We all watched a white blast of energy rip open the ground a few feet from Kono.

"We'd just guarantee our own capture," Laini finished in a whisper.

"Guns won't work either," Roxy said tightly. "It's too far for accuracy. We're just as likely to hit him as the hunters. And it would give away our position."

I winced as one of the velek drew level with Kono, charging into him and knocking him off his feet with a blow from its monstrous horns. By the time he scrambled upright once more, the other hunter had leapt off his mount. He had hundreds of red-and-black braids that almost went down to his knees, and as I watched, a dozen of them shot toward Kono, the tips flashing metallic in the soul-light. There were hooks at the ends of the braids, I realized, hooks that sank deep into the vampire's arms, torso, and legs. Even from the cliff, we heard Kono's screams, all of us tensing with anger and despair. The other hunter, a tall female with white hair, white skin, and silver armor, wrestled a muscled arm around Kono's neck, the contrast of their skin stark even from this distance. She squeezed, and my stomach churned as I watched his legs flail. He fought for air, his body jerking against the hooks pulling at his flesh. It took several agonizing seconds for him to go limp. I wasn't sure whether he would be better off alive or dead.

The two hunters congratulated each other, raising a snarl of hatred from Kane. Cutting the braids from his head, the male hunter securely bound Kono, leaving the hooks inside him, before slinging the vampire's body onto the back of his velek.

As they headed back toward Itzarriol, I lowered my scope, unable to watch more. Looking at my team, we all wore similar masks of guilt and rage. But then an even more dreadful thought occurred to me.

"If they've caught Kono," I said slowly, "then either the hunters have already found the safehouse..."

"Or they're going to find a way to get that information from him," Dorian finished grimly. "Either way, our hideout will not be of use to us much longer."

"I say we camp here long enough to sleep and get our strength back, let the dust kicked up by that mess settle, and go see if the safehouse is still in one piece tomorrow," Kane murmured. "At the very least, we might be able to warn any other scouts still there that they need to get out. Send them back to the Hive so they know their safe-house isn't so safe anymore."

"So we're going in with no safehouse to use as a base?" Roxy asked. "No Hive allies. No intel about how to move through the city."

"We can't turn back now, or we'll have done all this for nothing," Laini said. "We'll just have to be incredibly careful. Keep to the shad-ows, find somewhere abandoned or out of sight to sleep, and always be on our guard."

I lifted my scope one last time, catching the last glimpse of Kono draped over the back of the velek as the hunters led their prize into the tangle of Itzarriol's streets.

Things had just become an awful lot more complicated, but Laini was right.

We couldn't turn back now.

READY FOR THE NEXT PART OF LYRA AND DORIAN'S JOURNEY?

Dear Reader,

Thank you for reading Darkworld.

Book 4: **Darkblood**, releases **January 11th, 2020.**

Visit www.bellaforrest.net for details.

I'm excited to continue this journey with you.

Love,

Bella x

P.S. Sign up to my VIP email list and I'll send you a heads up when my next book releases: **www.morebellaforrest.com**

(Your email will be kept 100% private and you can unsubscribe at any time.)

P.P.S. Follow me on:

Twitter @ashadeofvampire;

Facebook facebook.com/BellaForrestAuthor;

or **Instagram** @ashadeofvampire

DARKLIGHT

Darklight (Book 1)

Darkthirst (Book 2)

Darkworld (Book 3)

Darkblood (Book 4)

HARLEY MERLIN

Harley Merlin and the Secret Coven (Book 1)

Harley Merlin and the Mystery Twins (Book 2)

Harley Merlin and the Stolen Magicals (Book 3)

Harley Merlin and the First Ritual (Book 4)

Harley Merlin and the Broken Spell (Book 5)

Harley Merlin and the Cult of Eris (Book 6)

Harley Merlin and the Detector Fix (Book 7)

Harley Merlin and the Challenge of Chaos (Book 8)

Harley Merlin and the Mortal Pact (Book 9)

Finch Merlin and the Fount of Youth (Book 10)

Finch Merlin and the Lost Map (Book 11)

Finch Merlin and the Djinn's Curse (Book 12)

Finch Merlin and the Locked Gateway (Book 13)

Finch Merlin and the Forgotten Kingdom (Book 14)

THE GENDER GAME

(Action-adventure/romance. Completed series.)

The Gender Game (Book 1)

The Gender Secret (Book 2)

The Gender Lie (Book 3)

The Gender War (Book 4)

The Gender Fall (Book 5)

The Gender Plan (Book 6)

The Gender End (Book 7)

THE GIRL WHO DARED TO THINK

(Action-adventure/romance. Completed series.)

The Girl Who Dared to Think (Book 1)

The Girl Who Dared to Stand (Book 2)

The Girl Who Dared to Descend (Book 3)

The Girl Who Dared to Rise (Book 4)

The Girl Who Dared to Lead (Book 5)

The Girl Who Dared to Endure (Book 6)

The Girl Who Dared to Fight (Book 7)

THE CHILD THIEF

(Action-adventure/romance. Completed series.)

The Child Thief (Book 1)

Deep Shadows (Book 2)

Thin Lines (Book 3)

Little Lies (Book 4)

Ghost Towns (Book 5)

Zero Hour (Book 6)

HOTBLOODS

(Supernatural adventure/romance. Completed series.)

Hotbloods (Book 1)

Coldbloods (Book 2)

Renegades (Book 3)

Venturers (Book 4)

Traitors (Book 5)

Allies (Book 6)

Invaders (Book 7)

Stargazers (Book 8)

A SHADE OF VAMPIRE SERIES

(Supernatural romance/adventure)

Series 1: Derek & Sofia's story

A Shade of Vampire (Book 1)

A Shade of Blood (Book 2)

A Castle of Sand (Book 3)

A Shadow of Light (Book 4)

A Blaze of Sun (Book 5)

A Gate of Night (Book 6)

A Break of Day (Book 7)

Series 2: Rose & Caleb's story

A Shade of Novak (Book 8)

A Bond of Blood (Book 9)

A Spell of Time (Book 10)

A Chase of Prey (Book 11)

A Shade of Doubt (Book 12)

A Turn of Tides (Book 13)

A Dawn of Strength (Book 14)

A Fall of Secrets (Book 15)

An End of Night (Book 16)

Series 3: The Shade continues with a new hero...

A Wind of Change (Book 17)

A Trail of Echoes (Book 18)

A Soldier of Shadows (Book 19)

A Hero of Realms (Book 20)

A Vial of Life (Book 21)

A Fork of Paths (Book 22)

A Flight of Souls (Book 23)

A Bridge of Stars (Book 24)

Series 4: A Clan of Novaks

A Clan of Novaks (Book 25)

A World of New (Book 26)

A Web of Lies (Book 27)

A Touch of Truth (Book 28)

An Hour of Need (Book 29)

A Game of Risk (Book 30)

A Twist of Fates (Book 31)

A Day of Glory (Book 32)

Series 5: A Dawn of Guardians

A Dawn of Guardians (Book 33)

A Sword of Chance (Book 34)

A Race of Trials (Book 35)

A King of Shadow (Book 36)

An Empire of Stones (Book 37)

A Power of Old (Book 38)

A Rip of Realms (Book 39)

A Throne of Fire (Book 40)

A Tide of War (Book 41)

Series 6: A Gift of Three

A Gift of Three (Book 42)

A House of Mysteries (Book 43)

A Tangle of Hearts (Book 44)

A Meet of Tribes (Book 45)

A Ride of Peril (Book 46)

A Passage of Threats (Book 47)

A Tip of Balance (Book 48)

A Shield of Glass (Book 49)

A Clash of Storms (Book 50)

A Love that Endures

A Love that Endures 2

A Love that Endures 3

THE SECRET OF SPELLSHADOW MANOR

(Supernatural/Magic YA. Completed series)

The Secret of Spellshadow Manor (Book 1)

The Breaker (Book 2)

The Chain (Book 3)

The Keep (Book 4)

The Test (Book 5)

The Spell (Book 6)

BEAUTIFUL MONSTER DUOLOGY

(Supernatural romance)

Beautiful Monster 1

Beautiful Monster 2

DETECTIVE ERIN BOND

(Adult thriller/mystery)

Lights, Camera, GONE

Write, Edit, KILL

For an updated list of Bella's books, please visit her website: www.bellaforrest.net

Join Bella's VIP email list and you'll be the first to know when new books release. Visit to sign up: www.morebellaforrest.com

CPSIA information can be obtained
at www.ICGtesting.com
Printed in the USA
LVHW031634100320
649601LV00005B/588

9 789925 762170